The Divided Path

Karl Nilsson and Robert Nilsson were brothers—but each day they grew farther apart.

For Karl, America was a land to be cultivated with skill, patience, and endurance—a land to be made fruitful for himself, his wife, and his present and future children.

For Robert, America was a land filled with wealth for the taking by those men strong and ruthless enough.

One found his destiny in the farm he wrested from the wilderness. The other sought his fortune in the human tidal wave that crested in the gold fields of California.

Both played their parts in the most enthralling remaking of a land that history has ever witnessed. And here, a great novelist brings this great remaking to life.

Books by
VILHELM MOBERG

The Emigrants
Unto A Good Land
The Settlers
Last Letter Home
A Time on Earth

Available from
WARNER BOOKS

THE EMIGRANTS · III
VILHELM MOBERG
THE SETTLERS

Translated from the Swedish
by Gustaf Lannestock

WARNER BOOKS

A Warner Communications Company

The characters and situations in this work are wholly fictional;
they do not portray and are not intended to portray any actual persons.

WARNER BOOKS EDITION

This Warner Books Edition is published by arrangement with
Albert Bonniers Forlag.

Warner Books, Inc.,
666 Fifth Avenue,
New York, N.Y. 10103

Ⓦ A Warner Communications Company

Printed in the United States of America

First Warner Books Printing: September, 1983

10 9 8 7 6 5 4 3 2 1

Part One

FOUNDATION FOR GROWTH

The Land They Changed

A giant tree, uprooted by a storm, fell across a path that ran along the shore of Lake Ki-Chi-Saga in Chippewa Indian country. It remained where it had fallen, an obstacle to those who used the path. No Indian had ever thought to cut it in pieces and roll it out of the way. Instead a new path was formed which bypassed the tree; instead of removing it the Indians moved the path.

As the years passed the great tree lay there and moss covered its bole. A generation of forest life elapsed, and the fallen tree began to rot. The path round it was by now well tramped, and no one remembered any longer that once it had run straight in this place. Through the years, Indians wasted much time on the longer path, but to these people time was there to be wasted.

One day a man of another race came along the path. He carried an ax on his shoulder and walked heavily, shod in boots made on another continent. With his ax he split the rotten trunk in a few places and rolled it aside. The path was again straight and now ran its earlier, shorter course. And the man with the ax who could not waste his time on a longer road, asked himself: Why had this tree been allowed to obstruct the path for so long a time that it had begun to rot?

The tiller had come to the land of the nomad; the day the white man removed the tree from the Indian path at Lake Ki-Chi-Saga two different ways of life met head on.

The era of the nomad was coming to an end in this part of the world. The people who had time enough to wait a generation while an obstacle in their path rotted away were doomed. The hunter who moved his fire and his tent according to the season and the migration of the game could count his days. In his place came the farmer, the permanent inhabitant, who built his fireplace of stone and timbered his house: he had come to stay in this place where his hearth fire burned and his house was built.

Through a treaty which the Indians were forced to accept, the land was opened for settling and claimtaking. The hunter people were forced back before the power of the transgressors. Their hunting grounds, with the graves of their forefathers, were surrendered. Virgin soil, deep and fertile, could then be turned into fruitful fields with the tiller's tools. An immense country, until now lacking any order except nature's own, was divided, surveyed, registered, mapped, and separated into counties, townships, and sections. Millions of acres of wilderness were mapped on paper in square lots, each one intended as a homestead for a settler.

The newcomers were farmers without land who came to a country with land but no farmers. They came from the Old World where they had lived under governments they themselves had not elected and which they refused to accept. They had moved away from rulers and overlords, from poverty and suppression. They had left Germany because of revolution, Ireland because of potato blight, Sweden because of religious persecution. The immigrants were the disobedient sons and daughters of their homelands, who now settled down on a land that as yet had little or no government.

The disobedient folk of the Old World were young people: three quarters of the settlers in Minnesota Territory were under thirty. They had no useless oldsters to support. The immigrants were young people in a young country. The immigrants were not held back by the authority of an older generation. For them life began anew: they depended entirely on themselves and their own strength. They broke with many of the old customs, did their chores in their own ways, and obeyed no will except their own. Here they themselves must wield authority; in the wilderness they enjoyed in full measure the new freedom to disobey.

Here were no upper or lower classes, no one had inherited special privileges and rights, no one was by virtue of his birth superior or inferior. Each one was valued according to his ability, measured by his industry. Whether a man was better than another or inferior to him depended on what he could do. The virgin forests fostered self-assurance, developed free men.

The immigrant did not wait while an obstacle in his path rotted away; he did not have time to make a detour round a fallen tree. He had come to make a living for himself and his family, he must build a house and establish a home; he must build up a new society from its very foundation.

The first immigrants to take up claims were few and lived far apart. They could not talk to each other across their fences—their houses lay miles away from one another. But from 1850 on, the influx into the Territory increased. The settlers came in large groups, small groups, families and friends, or single individuals. and settled down along the shores of the heaven-blue waters that had given the territory its name: Minnesota.

Thus, the brown nomad gave way to the white farmer, the forest animals gave up their grazing meadows to domesticated animals, the deer pastures were turned into tended fields, the tall trees were felled and made into lumber for the settlers' houses. High and clear shone the sky above the wilderness where the immigrants founded their new domain. The far horizons in a land without limitations stimulated their minds and desire to create; all would be new here.

Great was the land and without measure, and the land broadened their dreams.

This is a continuation of a story of a group of people who left their homes in Ljuder, Sweden, and emigrated to North America.

Sweden was the land they left behind; the American republic received them; and the fertile valley near Lake Ki-Chi-Saga—between the Mississippi and the St. Croix rivers—was the land they changed.

I. New Axes Ringing in the Forest

1.

One day in May Karl Oskar Nilsson was out on his claim cutting fence posts. When the height of the sun signaled noon he stopped his work to go home for dinner.

He took off one of his wooden shoes and emptied out a few dried lumps of blue clay which had chafed his heel. On his shoe was a deep gash from his ax. What luck that he wore wooden shoes today; in the morning, while shaping the first linden post, his ax had slipped and fastened in the toe of his right shoe. Had he worn leather boots the ax would have split his foot. Not that he could choose. His high boots—of finest leather, made by the village cobbler before he had left his Swedish home parish—were long since worn out and thrown away. After all the many miles he had tramped in them, in all weathers and on all types of roads during his three years in North America, they were now entirely gone. He had tried his hand at the shoemaker's craft, as well as all other crafts, and he had mended and patched his Swedish boots, he had plugged and resoled and sewn as much as he could. But nearly all the footgear and clothing from Sweden was now useless, worn to shreds.

With his ax under his arm, he walked beside the lake on the path he had cleared, through groves of larch trees and elms, through thickets of mapel and hazel bushes. It was pleasant along the path today with the multitude of newly opened leaves and all the fresh greenery. Spring was early this year in the Territory. The wild apple trees were already in full bloom and shone luminously white in the lush greenery. A mild night rain had watered the earth so that a fragrance rose from grass and flowers. Between the tree trunks the whole length of Lake Ki-Chi-Saga's surface glittered blue.

For great stretches the lush green growth hung over the lake and no one could make out where the ground ended and the water began. Farther out the bay was full of birds—ducks, swans, and wild geese in such multitudes they might have been strewn from heaven by generous hands. From the shore could be seen a thick wall of tall elms. At first Karl Oskar had thought it was the opposite side of the lake but when he rowed out in his holed-out canoe along the shores he had discovered it was a wooded island, with still another great island beyond. He had discovered that Ki-Chi-Saga consisted of seven small lakes, connected by narrow channels so that the shores formed a confusing and ever straying coil. This was a lake landscape, a conglomeration of islets, peninsulas, points, inlets, bays, necks, headlands, isthmuses. Each islet, bay, or tongue of land had another islet, bay, or tongue of land behind it.

It took a long time for a settler to get to know this lake. Ki-Chi-Saga spread like an inundated deciduous forest where water had remained in the indentations as the ground had risen above the ancient flood. From a distance of a few miles it appeared the thickets of leaf trees on the out-jutting tongues of land grew far out in the lake.

High above the shore rose the imposing sandstone cliff resembling an Indian's head and thus called the Indian. The cliff's red-brown face with the deep, black eye holes was turned toward the lake, straining toward the east like a watchman over land and water.

The lake contained much that was unknown and undiscovered. The Chippewa name itself sounded strange; Ki-Chi-Saga—beautiful lake—sounded to a settler's ears as alien as all the foreignness he must familiarize himself with and make his own.

A wide flock of doves came flying over the bay, like a darkening cloud; their shadows reflected in the clear surface like quick-moving spots.

When the doves had passed, Karl Oskar stopped and

listened: the whizzing sound of bird wings was followed by another sound; he could hear the ring of an ax.

The May day was clear and calm and the sound carried far. Karl Oskar had two good ears, accustomed to discriminating between noises and sounds in the forest, and he was not mistaken. He could hear the echoing sound of a sharp ax in a tree trunk. The sounds came from the southeast and were fairly close: someone was felling a tree near the lake.

His eyebrows drew together. It could not be an Indian at work—the Indians did not fell trees with axes. It must be a white man; an intruder had come to his land.

But he had his papers as squatter for this ground; he had made two payments for his claim at the land office in Stillwater. His claim had been surveyed—it was number 35 of the section—and its borders were blazed. No one could now push him out, no one could deny him his rights. Here in his forest he had up till now heard only his own ax ringing; he would permit no other ax here.

Karl Oskar turned and retraced his steps to locate the intruder.

Last year, because of the danger of Indians, he had always carried his gun while working in the forest. It might also happen that he would come across an animal that would do for food. He often said that he did not feel fully clothed without his gun. Nowadays, however, he frequently left his weapon at home hanging on the wall, and this he had done today. Nor did he think he would need a firearm against the stranger; a man using the peaceful tool of the ax must be a peaceful man.

Karl Oskar strode toward the sound. The timberman was farther away than he had anticipated; sounds could be heard a great distance on a calm day like today. It appeared that the stranger with the ax was outside his border; no intruder was on his land.

Who could the woodsman be? He had no close neighbors; it could not be anyone he knew. He climbed a steep cliff, and now he could see that the sounds came from a pine grove near a narrow channel of the lake. A man was cutting at a straight, tall pine, his broad felling-ax glittering in the sun. The chips flew like white birds that might

13

have been nesting in the trunk and were frightened away by the blows.

Just as Karl Oskar approached, the tree fell with a thunderous crash, crushing the smaller trees near it. The undergrowth swayed from the force of the fall.

The tree cutter held his ax in his left hand while he dried perspiration from his forehead with his right. He was a powerful man, dressed in a plaid flannel shirt, yellow, worn skin breeches, and short-legged boots. Judging by his clothes he must be an American. And he used the same type of long-handled American felling-ax with a thin, broad blade that Karl Oskar recently had got for himself.

Suspicion of any stranger was still ingrained in the Swedish settler; apprehensively he stopped a few paces from the stump of the newly felled pine. The stranger heard him and turned around. His face was lean and weather-beaten, with high cheekbones and deep hollows. Tufts of sweaty, thin hair clung to his forehead; his chin was covered with a long brown beard.

The man eyed Karl Oskar from head to toe, his alert eyes those of a person accustomed to danger.

Before Karl Oskar had time to phrase a greeting in English, the stranger said, "You're Swedish, I guess?"

Karl Oskar stared back in astonished silence; deep in this wilderness he had encountered a stranger who spoke to him in his native tongue.

Leaning his ax against the stump, the man offered Karl Oskar his hand: "I'm Petrus Olausson, from Alfta parish in Helsingland. I'm a farmer."

Karl Oskar Nilsson gave his name in return, and added that he was a farmer from Ljuder parish in Småland.

"I knew you were a Swede!"

"How did you know?"

"By looking at your feet!" The Helsinge farmer smiled good-naturedly and pointed to Karl Oskar's footgear. "Your wooden shoes, man! Only Swedes wear wooden shoes!" He grinned, showing long, broad upper teeth.

Karl Oskar knew that the Americans called the Swedish settlers the wooden-shoe people.

Petrus Olausson took off his hat and uncovered a bald

spot on top of his head. He seemed to be about forty, ten years older than Karl Oskar. His clothes and his speech indicated he was no newcomer to America. He used the same mixed-up language as Anders Mansson of Taylors Falls, one of the first Swedes in the Territory.

"What kind of wood do you use for your wooden shoes, Mr. Nilsson?"

Karl Oskar replied that as alder trees did not grow in this valley he used basswood, the American linden tree. It was softer than Swedish linden wood and easy to work. But he had poor tools and was unable to make comfortable, light shoes.

He looked at the newcomer's ax next to the stump; it had an even broader and thinner blade than his own American felling-ax.

"You can work faster with American tools," said the owner of the ax. "The Yankees do everything easier. Better take after them."

He took Karl Oskar for a newcomer here and looked disapprovingly at the Swedish ax he was carrying, with its clumsy head and thick edge. Karl Oskar explained that it was an old split-ax he used for post-making, and added, "From Helsingland, eh? You look like an American to me."

He need not ask Petrus Olausson his errand here; no one felled trees for the fun of it. Olausson had come to stay.

The sound of timber axes in the forest had brought together two Swedish farmers. They had met as strangers but as soon as they had inspected each other's axes they felt they had known each other before and were now merely renewing acquaintance. They were both men of peaceful occupation, wielding the tools of peaceful labor. Karl Oskar Nilsson from Ljuder, Småland, and Petrus Olausson from Alfta, Helsingland, sat down on the stump and talked at ease, talked intimately as if for many years they had lived on neighboring homesteads in the same village.

Around the men rose the great, ageless pines, and as far as the eye could see not a human habitation was in sight. It was an unbroken, uninhabited land, these shores of Lake Ki-Chi-Saga.

"Good land," said the Helsinge farmer. "I aim to settle at this lake."

"You are welcome," said Karl Oskar, and he meant it. "Plenty of room, empty of people so far."

"Yeah, we needn't push for space."

Olausson pointed to a hut of branches between two fallen pines, about a gunshot's distance from where they sat; that was his shanty. He had begun felling timber for his cabin, and as soon as it was ready his wife and children would come. He had come to this country with his family, he told Karl Oskar, in the company of the prophet Erik Janson; that was seven years ago, in 1846. They had been living in Illinois but did not like it on the flat prairie; they wanted to live in wooded country, like their home province Helsingland. Another farmer from Alfta, Johannes Nordberg, had been up looking over Minnesota, and he had come back and told them the country up here was rich growing land and suitable for settling. It was on the advice of his neighbor that Olausson had come here. Nordberg himself would never return—he had died of cholera in Andover last summer.

Karl Oskar had heard that a farmer from Helsingland by the name of Nordberg was at this lake several years ago; he pointed to an island in line with a tongue of land. There were remnants there of a hut in which Nordberg had stayed. In summertime there were hordes of Indians here, and he had probably lived on the isle to be in peace. This first land seeker's name was linked to the place; it was still called Nordberg's Island.

"Johannes told the truth," said his onetime neighbor. "This is a land of plenty."

Petrus Olausson had picked a good place for himself, with fine timber forest and rich grass meadows. And he told Karl Oskar that several more countrymen were on their way to the St. Croix Valley, attracted by Nordberg's descriptions.

"Well, the country is getting to be known," said Karl Oskar. "How did you happen to stake your claim next to mine?"

16

"I went to the land office and picked it from the map," he said. "The east part of section 35, township 34, range 20."

The Helsinge farmer knew how to claim land; he had been in America twice as long as Karl Oskar, who, talking with him, felt like a newcomer beside an older and more experienced settler.

"I think my wife has something cooking—would you like to eat with us?" he asked.

"How far is it to go?"

"Less than a mile. I have the northeast claim."

"All right. Might as well see your place."

From the top of a young pine dangled a piece of venison he had intended to fry for his dinner, but it wasn't very warm today and the meat would keep till tomorrow.

The settlers got up from the stump. The younger man walked ahead and showed the way.

"When did you come and settle here, Nilsson?"

Karl Oskar told him that next Midsummer Eve it would be three years since he and his family had landed in New York, and they had arrived in the Territory the last day of July. In the same year, 1850, he had taken his claim here at the lake.

Without being conscious of it, Karl Oskar walked today in longer strides than usual. He was bringing home news that would gladden Kristina; after three long years of isolation they now had a neighbor.

2.

The two men stopped where the path left the shore and turned up the hill to the log cabin. Olausson looked about in all directions: pine forest to the west, oaks, maples, elms, and other leaf trees to the north and east, Lake Ki-Chi-Saga to the south. At their feet lay the broad meadow, partly broken, and a tended field.

"A likely place, I must say! First come gets the best choice!"

And Karl Oskar agreed—he had had good luck when

17

he found this place. He called his settlement Duvemala (dovecote) after his wife's home village in Sweden. A most suitable name, thought the Helsinge farmer; here too were so many doves that they obscured the sun.

The children playing outside the cabin had seen their father and came running toward him. They came in a row, according to age: Johan, the oldest, first; next Lill-Marta; after her, Harald; and behind them toddled little Dan, who had walked upright on this earth barely a year; his small, unstable legs still betrayed him so that he fell a couple of times, delaying his run behind his brothers and sister. But he was close to the ground and did not cry when he fell.

Karl Oskar picked up his youngest son and held him gently in his arms. It wasn't his oldest but rather his youngest child he wanted to show to his visitor; this little tyke was two and a half and the only one of his brats born in America, the only one of his family who was a citizen of this country, he told Olausson. His youngest son was an American, almost the only one among the Swedish settlers in this valley. He had been baptized with the name Danjel but had already lost half of it—they called him Dan, a more suitable name for an American.

The Helsinge farmer patted the little American on the head. The boy, in fright, glared at the stranger.

"I'm Uncle Petrus, and you are Mr. Dan Nilsson. Isn't that right, boy? You were born here and you can become President of the United States. Neither your father nor I can be President, we're only immigrants . . ."

Karl Oskar laughed, but his youngest son did not rejoice in the great future that opened before him. He began to bawl, loudly and fiercely, and clung to his father's neck with both arms.

"He's shy, hasn't seen any strangers," said Karl Oskar.

Johan felt neglected and pulled his father by the pant leg: "We saw a snake, Dad!"

"A great big'un!" added Lill-Marta, all out of breath.

"A green-striped adder, Dad!"

"He crawled under the house . . . !"

"Well, snake critters will crawl out with the spring heat," said the visitor "Better be careful, kids!"

18

Four-year-old Harald stood with his index finger in his mouth and stared at the strange man who had come home with Father. Harald ran about without pants; the only garment on his little body was an outgrown shirt, so short that it reached only to his navel. Below the shirt hem the boy was naked and his wart-like little limb pointed out naked and unprotected.

Petrus Olausson quickly took his eyes from the child as if uncomfortably affected.

"Lost your pants, did you, little Harald?" asked the father.

"Mother took them . . . she's patching . . ."

"He tore a big hole in his pants," volunteered Johan.

"Poor boy—has to show all he has . . ."

Karl Oskar was holding his youngest son on his right arm; he now picked up his pantless son on his left. Sitting there some of the little one's nakedness was covered. It seemed as if the sight of the child's male member had disturbed Petrus Olausson; he no longer looked like a mild "Uncle Petrus." Did he pay attention to what a four-year-old showed? The child could have gone entirely naked, as far as that was concerned.

"The kids grow awfully fast; they outgrow everything. Hard to keep their behinds covered up."

Olausson stroked his long beard and said nothing. Karl Oskar felt ashamed before the visitor that his children had to wear rags. They had hardly been able to get any new clothes at all. All four were dressed in outgrown, worn-out garments, patches on patches. After the long winter inside they had been let out in the open again, and now one could see how badly off they were. The bright spring sun revealed everything as threadbare, ragged, torn, shabby.

"I've seeded flax—last year, and this year too. The kids will soon have something to cover them."

"Well, at least they aren't cold while summer lasts," commented Olausson, as he threw a look at the father's own pants, patched over and over again.

Karl Oskar walked ahead to the door with two children in his arms and two at his heels. The door opened from

19

within and Kristina's head covered with a blue kerchief, appeared.

"You're late—I almost thought something had happened . . . ?"

"Yes, Kristina," said Karl Oskar solemnly. "Something has happened—we have a neighbor now . . ."

The Helsinge farmer stepped up and doffed his hat.

"Yes, here comes your neighbor . . ."

Perplexed, Kristina remained standing in the door opening. Then she dried her fingers quickly on her apron before she took the guest's hand. He told her his name and his home parish in Sweden.

"Svensk!!?"

"Still for the most part a Swede, I guess. We'll be next-door neighbors, Mrs. Nilsson!"

"What a surprise! What a great surprise!"

In her confusion she forgot to ask the visitor to come in. She remained standing on the threshold until Karl Oskar, laughing, wondered if she wanted to keep them out.

Once inside, Kristina welcomed the farmer from Alfta.

"A neighbor! What a welcome visitor!"

Petrus Olausson looked about the cabin with curious eyes, as if to evaluate their belongings.

"Have you made the furnishings yourself, Nilsson?"

"Yeah—a little clumsy . . ."

"No! You're learning from the Americans. Very good! They do things handily."

Petrus Olausson praised the beds that Karl Oskar had made of split scantlings, fastened to wall and floor; there was something authoritative in his speech and manner, one felt he was a man accustomed to giving advice and commands. There was also a hint of the forty-year-old man talking to the thirty-year-old, but more than their difference in age was the fact that he had been in America four years longer than Karl Oskar.

The Swedish settler had invited Olausson to dinner without knowing what Kristina had to put on the table. She apologized; she had nothing but plain fish soup— boiled catfish. And maple syrup, bread, and milk—not much to offer a guest. It was the time of year when food

20

was scarce: last year's crops were almost gone and this year's were still growing.

Karl Oskar remembered they had cooked the last of their potatoes only a few days ago.

"We have a bone of pork left," said Kristina. "I can make pea soup. But the peas take at least an hour to cook, they're tough . . ."

"Too long," said Karl Oskar. "We're hungry . . ." But it annoyed him that they had nothing better than fish soup to offer their new neighbor on his first visit.

"I can make mashed turnips for the pork," said Kristina, thinking over what supplies they had. "We have turnips out in the cellar, they cook quickly."

Karl Oskar picked up a basket and went to fetch the turnips, accompanied by his guest. He did not want to appear to Olausson as an inexperienced settler; rather, he wanted to show how well he had managed on his claim. He told him that more difficult than obtaining food was protecting it, against heat in summer and frost in winter. To build a cellar of stone as they did in Sweden required an enormous amount of work which he hadn't had time for yet; he had used another device to protect the vegetables from spoiling. He had dug a ditch for the turnips behind the cabin and covered it with straw and earth. Under such a roof, about ten inches thick, the roots were protected against the coldest winter.

Karl Oskar stopped before a mound and with a wooden fork cleared away the earth and the straw. When he had removed the covering he knelt and bent down over the ditch. The mound had not been opened for a few weeks, and an evil stink filled his nose. An uneasy apprehension came over him. He stuck down his hand and felt for a turnip. He got hold of something soft and slimy. When he lifted his hand into daylight he was holding a dark brown mess with a nasty smell.

"Damn it! The roots are rotten . . ."

The older settler stooped down and smelled; he nodded that the turnips were indeed spoiled.

Shamefacedly, Karl Oskar rose. The turnips they had intended to offer their guest for dinner need not be boiled;

down there in the ditch the roots were already mashed and prepared, a rotten mess.

"It's on account of the early heat," said the guest.

"I forgot to make an air hole," explained Karl Oskar.

"Your covering is too thick," said Petrus Olausson authoritatively. "Ten inches is too much—five inches would've been about right."

"Then the turnips would have frozen last winter."

"Not if you had covered the ditch right. You put on too much; you're wrong, Nilsson!"

Karl Oskar's cheeks flushed. He knew a ten-inch cover was required in order to keep the frost out. Only this spring heat had come on so suddenly he hadn't had time to open an air hole. That was why the turnips had rotted.

With a wad of straw he wiped the mess of rotted roots from his hand. Those damned turnips weren't worth a single dollar but he had wanted to show his senior countryman how well he preserved his food and kept it from spoiling.

And now, here he stood and received instruction from a master. It was not that he had done something wrong, he had forgotten to do the right thing. It was this that annoyed him.

They walked back to the cabin. Karl Oskar carried the empty basket, vexed and humiliated. Now what would they give their guest? He had seen in Kristina's eyes that she was anxious to offer the best they had to their first neighbor, but not even she could prepare a meal from nothing.

However, at the door a delicious cooking aroma met them. Kristina had put the frying pan over the fire.

"I won't bother with mashed turnips, I'll make pancakes instead, it won't take so long . . ."

She had flour, bacon grease, milk, and sugar, as well as some of the cranberries she had preserved last year. Now they would have cranberries and pancakes for dinner.

"Please sit down, you menfolk! I'll serve you as I make them."

The children might be a nuisance; if they smelled the pancakes she was preparing for their guest they wouldn't leave her any peace. She had given each of them a lump of sugar and told them to stay outside and play.

Karl Oskar's annoyance disappeared as he inhaled the smell of the frying pancakes.

"I believe you are a wizard, Kristina!"

She piled the pancakes in a bowl and even the Helsinge farmer looked pleased and appreciative.

"This is party fare, Mrs. Nilsson! Swedish food and Swedish cooking!"

Karl Oskar was pulling up his chair, ready to sit down at table, when Petrus Olausson, behind his chair, bent his head, folded his hands, and said grace in a loud voice:

> We do sit down in Jesu name,
> We eat and drink upon God's word,
> God to honor, us to aid,
> We eat our food in Jesu name.

Kristina, busy with her pancakes, repeated the prayer with him. She was deeply conscious of the fact that nowadays they almost always forgot to say grace. And, as parents, Karl Oskar and she ought to set a good and godly example for their children. But the settlers had begun to forget their old Swedish table prayers. Only Danjel Andreasson, her uncle, never missed saying grace. And she had told Karl Oskar that they acted like hogs rushing up to the trough to still their hunger. To forget, in this manner, the giver of all good things was un-Christian, beastly. The difference between animals and people was only this: the dumb beasts couldn't read.

But their new neighbor prayed over the food with a voice like a minister. He must be a religious man.

When she had finished at the stove, Kristina sat down at the table where the men were doing great honor to her pancakes. The guest told her that he intended to settle down in the neighborhood with his wife and three children.

"I never thought anyone would want to live this far away," she said.

"Well, this is rich earth, and the lake has plenty of fish."

Karl Oskar was eager to confirm that the earth was indeed rewarding. Last year he had planted four bushels of potatoes and had received forty-eight and a half bushels in yield—almost thirteen to one. And rye and barley gave good returns: the seeds were barely out of his hand before they began to swell and grow and shoot up blades in great abundance. One could spread sawdust on this earth and it would almost grow.

Kristina thought however fine the earth was, it could never take the place of people. However great its yield, it did not help against the loneliness out here.

"We are not only seeking our living in America," Petrus Olausson went on. "We are seeking freedom in spiritual things."

He explained that he and his wife had turned their backs on the false and dangerous Swedish Church and had followed the Bible's clear words and truths. After this they had been so persecuted and plagued by the clergy and the authorities of the home village that they had been forced to emigrate. They had followed Erik Janson of Biskopskulla and his group to Bishop Hill, Illinois, where they were to build the New Jerusalem on the prairie. But once in America, Janson had set himself even above God and had earned the contempt of all sensible men. After enduring Janson's tyranny for three years, Olausson had left the prophet of Bishop Hill, the year before this despot was murdered. He had gone to Andover and joined a free Lutheran church.

Petrus Olausson helped himself to a few more pancakes.

"Have you broken out of the Swedish State Church, Nilsson?"

Karl Oskar explained that he and his family had emigrated of their own free will; they had not been banished, nor had they fled as criminals. But an uncle of Kristina's and an unmarried woman in their group had been exiled by the court for heresy.

The rugged Helsinge farmer raised his bearded chin. In Sweden he had been fined two hundred daler silver because he had read a chapter from the Bible in his own house. In Helsingland and Dalecarlia many persons had been imprisoned for reading the Bible in groups. Holy Writ, the key to eternal salvation, was that dangerous for the wretched Swedish people. But here in America he could read the Bible from cover to cover, whenever and wherever he wanted, without punishment.

"Every evening in my prayer I thank the Lord God for my new homeland," he said emphatically. "Sweden has been ruined by her iniquitous authorities."

A scratching sound was heard at the window behind the guest's chair; Johan hung outside on the window sill and stared through the glass at the people eating inside. He had barely managed to climb that high and his eyes grew large at the sight of the pancakes; his mouth moved as if he too were chewing. Lill-Marta's flaxen curls could be glimpsed below the window—she was not tall enough to look through.

"Our young'uns smell the pancakes," said Karl Oskar.

"Only curious," said Kristina. "I just fed them . . ." The mother shook her hand windowward: how could they be so rude, looking at guests eating! The boy's face and the girl's curls disappeared immediately. Kristina looked uncomfortably at her guest; would he think her children didn't have enough to eat? But he must see by their bodies that they weren't starved. She herself never ate her fill until she knew they had sufficient. Well, perhaps a few pancakes would be left which she could give them afterward.

Petrus Olausson had returned to worldly matters and asked his host how they had managed to make a living and feed themselves on their claim for three years.

Karl Oskar replied that the first winter had been the hardest, as they had not harvested any crops that year. Then it had happened that they went hungry on occasion. But as soon as spring and warmth came, and the lake broke up and they could fish, it had become better. And during the summer they had picked wild berries and other fruit in the forest and then there was no need to starve. That fall they had harvested their first crops and got so much from the field they had had all the potatoes and bread they needed for the second winter. As they gradually broke more land their worries about food diminished.

25

During the second and third winter they had been bothered mostly by the cold; this cabin did not give sufficient protection. For the children's sake they had kept a fire going night and day through the coldest periods. The last winter had been so bad that the blizzards had almost turned the cabin over.

He had not figured on living in this log hut more than two or three winters; he had already laid out the framework for a more solid house. But he doubted the new house would be finished this summer. They would have to live in the cabin a fourth winter.

Kristina added that the weather was never moderate in this country, too hard one way or another. The summers were too warm, the winters too cold. It should have been spring or fall all year round, for springs and autumns were mild and good seasons. But all American weather was immoderate; the heat was hotter, the cold colder, the rain wetter, and the wind blew worse than in Sweden. And it was the same with the animals, big and little ones. Snakes were more poisonous, the rats more ferocious, the grasshoppers did more damage, the mosquitoes were bigger, and the ants angrier than at home. The wild animals in America seemed to have been created to plague humans.

"The Indians are more dangerous than the animals," said Olausson.

Kristina thought the brown people hereabouts had behaved very peacefully. During the winters Indians had come to warm themselves at their fire and she had given them food and treated them as friends. She tried to pretend she wasn't afraid of the wild ones, and they had never hurt her, but she was scared to death of them. They could have killed her a hundred times but she relied on God's protection. A few times they had heard rumors of Indian attacks, but nothing had happened here so far.

"The Chippewas are friendly," said their guest. "Some of the other tribes will steal and murder and rape the wives of the settlers."

Kristina had finished eating; she was looking thoughtfully in front of her.

"We have forgotten to mention the worst we have gone through," she said.

They had talked of weather and wild animals and Indians, but there remained something else: the loneliness at Lake Ki-Chi-Saga.

"I can't tell you how glad I am to get neighbors at last!"

The words had escaped from her full heart. Occasionally a hunter or someone from the lumbering company would come to their cabin. But what pleasure was there in guests she couldn't speak to? Months and months would pass before an outsider sat at this table and spoke her mother tongue. Now she must tell her countryman how it felt to live alone for three long years.

With no people living around, a person often felt empty and depressed, completely lost. And that hurt was worse than any physical pain; it plagued worse each lonely day that passed. And living here so long without seeing people might at last affect the mind. She knew how it was after these years; she was not telling a lie when she said that human beings could not live without other human beings.

While talking she had avoided Karl Oskar's eyes. Now he looked at her in surprise.

"I thought you had got used to living alone, Kristina."

"I don't think one ever gets used to it . . ."

She felt the tears in her eyes and turned her face away quickly.

Petrus Olausson had listened with great attention; now he turned to Karl Oskar.

"I'm sorry that Mrs. Nilsson feels so alone in America."

She asked him not to call her Mrs. Nilsson—she was no American lady, only a simple Swedish farm wife. "Please call me Kristina; and can't I call you Uncle Petrus?" Sitting here, talking Swedish with a Swede, she felt he was almost a relative.

"All right, call me Uncle! And now cheer up, Kristina! I'll be living next door!"

She rose suddenly. "I sit here and forget myself. I must put on the coffee!"

27

The Helsinge farmer too rose from the table and again said a prayer:

"All praise to you, O Lord, for food and drink!"

Kristina, standing at the fireplace, her hands folded around the coffee mill, repeated the prayer after him. To her, today seemed like a Sunday in the cabin.

3.

Karl Oskar was anxious to show Olausson around his claim, but Kristina wanted to keep him inside and talk to him. It was a long time since she had been so talkative, she was stimulated by the neighbor's call. Eagerly she re-filled his cup before he had emptied it.

The Helsinge farmer said that very soon more Swedes would be coming to settle here. Two families would be arriving this spring, one from Helsingland and one from Östergötland, and he knew them both. In letters to his friends in Sweden, he had described this valley and urged them to move to this land of plenty. He was sure many people would be coming over from Sweden; soon it wouldn't be lonely here any more.

This was wonderful news to Kristina, who had felt they would have to live alone forever beside the Indian lake. But she wasn't quite convinced; why would groups of peeple move from Sweden to this very region where only heathens worshiped their wooden images? She suspected their new neighbor was talking of arriving countrymen only to comfort her.

"How many Swedes might there be in this valley?" queried Petrus Olausson.

Karl Oskar counted silently. Their nearest neighbor toward Taylors Falls, he told Petrus, was Kristina's uncle, Danjel Andreasson, whose place was called New Kärragärde; he was a widower with three children. His neighbor was Jonas Petter Albrektsson, also a farmer from Ljuder, who had arrived with their group. Jonas Petter had a woman from Dalecarlia, called Swedish Anna, keeping house for him. In Taylors Falls an Ölander, Anders Mansson, lived with his old mother; also a trapper named Samuel Nöjd. At Hay Lake, near Stillwater, west of Marine, three young Swedes, who batched in their cabin, had moved in last spring; he had never met them and did not know their names. And they themselves were two grown people and four small children. If he had counted aright, there were eighteen Swedish people in the St. Croix Valley.

"And now we three families will settle here," said the Helsinge farmer. "That makes more than thirty Swedes. We must start a congregation."

"What kind of congregation?" wondered Karl Oskar.

"To build a God's house! In Andover we started a parish with only twenty-two members."

"A church parish . . . ?"

"Yes, we'll build a church!"

"A church!" exclaimed Kristina, breathlessly.

"Only a little log temple, a God's house of plain wood."

A silence fell in the cabin. Karl Oskar looked in surprise at his guest; the settlers out here had as yet not had time to build decent houses for themselves and their livestock. He had built himself a barn, but his stable wasn't ready yet, and this summer he intended to build a threshing barn. All the settlers still had houses to build for themselves and shelters for their cattle and their crops. How could they manage to build a church and pay for a minister?

"We mustn't strive so much for worldly things that we forget eternity! Need for stables is no excuse to delay building a house for God!" Petrus Olausson spoke in a severe preaching voice.

"Build a church . . . ?" murmured Kristina, as if talking in her sleep. "It sounds impossible . . ."

But Olausson went on: "America is full of false prophets swarming all over and snaring the settlers in dangerous heresies. I have seen, to my sorrow, some of my countrymen living in a pure heathenish and animal life, never listening to the Word. And some good, Christian men from my home village in Sweden got together a group and went off to the goldfields in California. They sought riches instead of the gospel truth, they looked for lumps of gold instead of the eternal life of the Holy Ghost. But they also perished within a short time because of their blindness; of twenty-eight gold seekers only four came back, and of these only one found enough gold for his future. Shouldn't this example dampen people from worshiping Mammon?"

"I had a younger brother with me when we came here," said Karl Oskar. "Two years ago he and a friend took off for California."

"Have you heard from these foolish youngsters?"

"Only twice so far."

From a box in the Swedish chest back in the corner Karl Oskar picked up a sheet of paper which he handed to Olausson: "The last letter from my brother. It came a few days ago; it was written early this year."

Petrus Olausson read the letter aloud:

"On the California Trail January 1853
"Dear Brother Karl Oskar Nilsson,
"How are you and Kristina and the children? I am well. Arvid and I are still on the California Trail. That road is long, you know, almost as long as the road back to Sweden. We have met many adventures. When I get back I will relate to you and Kristina everything I am now leaving out of my letter.

"We are getting along well but have had our troubles. We shall make out well in the gold land, be sure of that, Karl Oskar.

"I guess you are still poking in your fields. You like it. But I will play a lone hand, as you know. I am hunting for gold and will find it. Don't worry about me and feel no worry inside yourself. I will be back when I am a rich man. Before I will not come. Then I shall buy oxen for you and cows for Kristina.

"Arvid sends greetings to his old master and all Swedes in that part. I greet Kristina and the children.

"Your brother
Robert Nilsson."

Kristina pointed out, "Robert has not put down his address."

"He would have no permanent post office because he was on the trail," explained Olausson. "He says he is on his way. The gold diggers have to climb high mountains and cross wide deserts to reach California, and they need plenty of time for that road."

Karl Oskar looked toward the corner of the room where his brother's old bed still stood. With great concern he said, "My brother has been gone more than two years now."

"He said he wouldn't be back without gold," Kristina reminded him. "And he writes the same way."

"Who knows if he is alive at this moment," said Karl Oskar, thinking that of twenty-eight gold seekers only four had survived. And again he reproached himself. Couldn't he have prevented his brother from going on this dangerous journey?

"He says he'll give you a pair of oxen when he gets back," said Olausson, handing back the letter to Karl Oskar.

The latter expressed no opinion about that promise. But he asked the older settler:

"He writes something I don't understand—'play a lone hand'? What does he mean?"

"Your brother wants to go his own way."

"Well, he certainly did when he left for California . . ."

Karl Oskar put the letter back in the Swedish chest, and turned to Olausson. "Let's look at the livestock," he suggested.

While Kristina cleaned up after the meal, the men went out to look over the frontier farm. Karl Oskar wanted to show his neighbor what he had done during three years as squatter.

To the north side of the cabin he had started a stable, as yet only half finished. A cow and a heifer each stood in a stall. From the German Fisher in Taylors Falls they had three years ago bought a pregnant cow, and her calf had now grown into this heifer which had just taken the bull. With two cows they would have milk all year round. The

31

cow was called Lady—after a borrowed animal they had had the first winter—and the heifer was called Miss.

"When she calves we'll have to call her Missus," laughed Karl Oskar.

The stable, he pointed out, would have plenty of room for more stalls whenever they got more animals. The men looked at the sheep pen: two ewes with three lambs, already a little flock of five. Sheep were satisfying animals, easy to take care of, and their wool was always needed for socks and other clothing. Two pigs poked in the pigpen; of all the animals pigs were the easiest to buy, and they fed in the forest as long as the ground was bare. Pork was indeed the cheapest food. One corner of the stable was to be used for a chicken coop, but the roosting perch was still unoccupied; a laying hen cost five dollars.

In the empty coop Karl Oskar kept his new American tools. He showed with pride the cradle, its five wooden fingers attached to the scythe handle, so much more efficient than the old Swedish scythes. The cradle was heavy and difficult to handle but once he had learned to use it he couldn't get along without it. Then the grub hoe with an ax on one edge and a hoe on the other—a most ingenious device; while clearing ground and removing roots one need only turn this tool to switch from one kind of work to the other.

Olausson voiced his approval of Karl Oskar's imitating the Americans and using their clever inventions.

When they walked out to inspect the fields, Olausson eyed the furrows of the meadow:

"You've broken a sizable field."

"About ten acres. I plowed up most of it the first year."

By now he would have had three times as big a field if he had had a hundred dollars to buy a team of oxen. When he borrowed a team from the timber company he had to pay five dollars a day. He was short of cash and this was his greatest obstacle. Much of the field he had broken himself with his grub hoe.

Olausson's respect for Karl Oskar rose after seeing the tools and the field; this man was not a beginner working in the earth, he was not in need of an older farmer to tell him what to do.

Karl Oskar showed him his winter rye, almost ready to head, lush and healthy. The spring rye had just been sown, and next to it was the field where he intended to plant potatoes. Next fall he planned to sow wheat for the first time, that new kind of bread grain the Americans harvested in such quantities. Wheat had not been used much by the farmers in Småland, but it was said to be suitable for the fertile soil here. He thought it would be a fine thing to harvest his own wheat. In Sweden they had paid a great deal for the soft, white flour, and had only used it for holiday bread.

"I sure will like to taste my own wheat bread!"

Olausson advised him to raise Indian corn, which could be used as food for both people and livestock. The corn gave a fifty-fold return down in Illinois.

"You must plant the corn on high ground! It needs dry land," he added, and pointed up the hill.

Karl Oskar thought to himself that he knew best where his field was dry and where it was wet. But he put aside the thought and led Olausson a bit up the hill to a grove of tall leafy trees. Shaded by enormous sugar maples lay the foundation for his new house.

"Here's where I'll build our new home! I'll have a real house here!"

He pointed to the foundation. The house would be forty feet from gable to gable, eighteen feet wide, with two stories. They would have four or five times as much space as they now had in the cabin. And this time he wouldn't build with fresh logs as he had done earlier; the logs had dried out and left cracks that let in cold and wind in winter. But for his new house he had felled the timbers during the two winters past and had dressed the logs on all sides so that they had dried out well. He had intended to build the house this summer, but he must first raise a threshing shed so he needn't do his threshing down on the lake ice as he had done last winter. But next year his house would rise here under the shade of the maples. From the windows here on the south side he would be able to look out over his fields and the lake; they would be able to see all the way to those islets out there.

As he talked Karl Oskar became excited; he would not let the visitor interrupt. He talked about the house which didn't as yet exist, about roof and walls not yet raised, about the view from windows still imaginary. He touched the sills, the heavy timbers he alone had put in, he touched them as if caressing them: here would be the main room, here a bedroom on each gable, and just here—all this space for a large kitchen. And, pointing up toward the sky, up there would be a second floor with two large or four small rooms, as yet he hadn't decided which . . .

Petrus Olausson had paced off the foundation: "Too much of a house! Remember I told you so, Nilsson! You can't build that much!"

Kristina had told him the same thing, but a woman couldn't understand much about building, he had thought. Now, when his new neighbor raised the same objection, he became thoughtful. Perhaps he had laid out too big a house, perhaps it would be too much for him to build. Possibly he might have to shorten the foundation timbers . . .

But there was still something to show Olausson, something near the east gable. There, six or eight feet beyond the sill, Karl Oskar pointed downward with the look of one disclosing a great secret:

"Look here! See that thing growing there? It is from Sweden!"

In a little dug-up bed a small plant, six or seven inches tall and tied to a stake, poked its head up from the black soil. The plant had a few small dark-green leaves, and the bed around it was well tended.

"It came from home!"

Olausson bent down and pinched the leaves of the tender plant. "An apple seedling, eh?"

"A real fine tree! An Astrakhan apple tree!"

"From Sweden? Well, well . . ."

It was for his wife's sake he had planted the seedling, said Karl Oskar. She longed for home at times and it would be a pleasure and something to divert her thoughts
34

to have a growing plant from Sweden to tend and look after. He had written to her parents for seeds from an Astrakhan apple tree, and they had arrived a year ago last fall, glued to a sheet of paper and well preserved. And so he had planted them here at the east gable of their new home, at a depth five times their own thickness, as they used to do when planting trees at home. And this seedling had come up; it was growing slowly, but it was growing.

It was Kristina's apple tree, she took care of it. With this tiny plant, as yet so puny and tender, they had in a way moved something living from their old homeland.

"You might get some other kind of apples when you plant a seed," said Olausson.

"Yes—sometimes you get crab apples. We'll see!"

Karl Oskar had now shown his neighbor the fruit of all his work. Petrus Olausson could see that they had improved themselves during their first three years on the claim. If Petrus only listened to what Kristina had said about their loneliness out here, he might think all they did was walk about and sigh for company, doing nothing beyond getting their food from day to day.

The men went back to the cabin. Kristina wanted to warm up whatever coffee was left in the pot, but Uncle Petrus couldn't stay away any longer from his timber felling.

He had looked about closely, he said, and he had seen how much work they had done on their claim and what great improvements they had made. This was the beginning of a fine farm. But as a fellow Christian he wanted to add something before he left: work alone was not enough for a human being; daily prayers were also needed. As neighbors they ought to get together to help instruct each other in religious matters and share other useful thoughts.

"We'll see each other often, I hope! And my dear Swedish fellow Christians: don't dig yourself down in worldly matters so that you forget eternity!"

4.

When Karl Oskar and Kristina went to bed that evening they began to talk about this day which had become unlike all other days on their lonely claim.

"I think I like him," said Kristina.

"He seems a capable man with good ideas. He'll do here."

"He talked as godly as a minister."

"But he wants to have you do things his way. He wants to correct others. I don't like that."

"He meant well when he spoke that way . . ."

"I don't need a guardian—I'm old enough . . ."

"Yes, of course, but we must try to get along with them."

"They can take care of theirs and we'll look after ours. Then we'll get along as neighbors . . ."

"He must have thought we were heathens, not saying grace," said Kristina, after a pause.

Karl Oskar yawned loudly. He turned over on his side to go to sleep. In his deep fatigue after a long day's work he was glad to surrender to rest. But when he had walked a great deal, as today, he felt the old injury to his left leg, and it took longer for sleep to come. Tonight his leg ached persistently.

Kristina gathered her thoughts for her evening prayer. Petrus Olausson's exhorting words at his departure still rang in her ears. And as she thought about them, they sounded as a warning to her from God himself.

In this out-of-the-way place they neglected their spiritual needs. But someone coming from the outside and looking at them with a stranger's eyes could see how things were with them; they put religion aside. They neglected their souls and jeopardized their salvation. They were so busy gathering food for their table that they could not take even a moment to say grace. They hurried hither and yon from morning to night, and were so rushed one might think they feared they had not time to reach their graves. For in the grave they would end up at last. Here they labored, striving, and were so overloaded with daily chores that both their bodies and souls were submerged in worldly concerns. They lived the fleeting life of the moment and forgot that eternity awaited them.

Kristina sinned every day in many ways, gathering on her back an ever greater burden of sin. In Sweden, she had been relieved of this burden once a month through the sacrament, the Holy Communion. But now she had not been a guest at the Lord's table for three years. During this whole time she had not once cleansed herself in the Savior's blood.

From time to time she would talk of religious matters with her Uncle Danjel and confess her anxiety about her sin burden. But he considered himself so great a sinner that he was unable to help anyone else; each one must worry about his own soul. But Danjel did pray for her.

Karl Oskar at her side turned and tried to find a more comfortable position: "If those screech-hoppers out there ever could shut up!"

Outside, the crickets had started their unceasing noise. The penetrating sound screeched like an ungreased wagon wheel moving at a dizzying speed. The hoppers were never seen, but their noise was worse. These ungodly creatures had wings it was said, but unable to fly, they used them for their eternal complaint.

Kristina wondered what could make the poor critters wail like this all night through, as if they were suffering eternal torture. And she would lie and listen to that sound until it echoed within herself, the torture of her own anxiety responding to the crickets' wailing.

"Karl Oskar," she said, "you have a good remembering . . ."

"Yes?" he said sleepily. "What about?"

"Do you recall when we last had the sacrament?"

"The last Sunday before we left home."

"That was three years in April. Three years since we last received absolution."

He turned to her and sought her face in the dark but his eyes could not see her. He sounded surprised: "Are you lying there worrying about Communion?"

"I'm worrying about our sin burdens. They have gathered on our backs for a long time.

"We live in a wilderness, Kristina," he replied, "with no churches or temples; we can't get to a minister or to our own church. It can't be helped if we've had to be without the sacrament for three years. No one can take what he can't reach. God must know this and overlook it . . ."

"Perhaps he will forgive us . . . I don't know . . ."

No one could know if they were forgiven because they lived so far away from the church, she said. And Karl Oskar had not given much thought to this shriving. To tell the truth, he hadn't had time to miss the monthly Communion since he arrived here, and perhaps that wasn't so good of him.

"We've dug ourselves down in worldly doings," continued his wife. "We live only in the flesh. We forget our souls which will live through eternity. We forget death."

"I know I'll come to an end eventually. But one can't go around and worry about death all day long. If I did, I wouldn't get anything done."

If there was anything he could do about death, well, then it would be different, added Karl Oskar. If he himself could do anything to escape death, then he would do it, of course. But as it was, the hour of death was sure, he must come to an end sometime, death would take him without mercy. So it was no use to worry and fret about it. All one could do was lie down and give up one's breath when the time came, lie nicely on one's back and draw the last breath. So the old ones did: on their deathbeds they did not pay much attention to death, since it was inescapable. They usually thought more of their funerals. Death was one and the same for all, equally unmerciful to all, but the funerals could be different—different splendor for different people. And those who had received little praise or honor in life often wished to be honored as corpses.

"But there must be moments when you think of eternity, what comes afterward, Karl Oskar?"

What was the matter with Kristina and her religious question this evening? He didn't know what more to say.

But it was true, he did forget his prayers. A settler with endless concerns about keeping alive had little time to think of eternity.

Karl Oskar replied, with some hesitation, that he didn't really understand eternity. His head couldn't make out something that had neither beginning nor end. His mind could not grasp something that was to last forever. All he could wish was that God might have given him a better mind.

Kristina clung to this wish of his: Karl Oskar did seem humble tonight, at least more submissive than he usually was. She often felt that he lived arrogantly and trusted more in himself than in God.

Out there, on the other side of the window, the crickets screeched and wailed unceasingly. There was a host of them around the house tonight, their noise coming from the grass, from the boughs of the trees. But those peculiar bugs were hidden from human eyes. They were the night's whistle pipes, blowing away as if calling an alarm and warning against threatening dangers.

The long, drawn-out wailing of those invisible creatures turned Kristina's thoughts to eternity's torture.

"Karl Oskar—if you should come to an end this very night—do you believe all would be well with you?"

It was a minute before his reply came: "If I didn't believe so—what would you want me to do about it, Kristina?"

Now he was the questioner. And she had no reply.

"What do you want me to do for my soul? I can't get absolution for my sins. What else?" It was all he could say. They were in the same predicament. She had asked in order to be helped: he had no help to give. Their situation was the same. What could they do about it?

After this Kristina lay silent and did not ask any more questions.

"We must get some sleep," said Karl Oskar. "Tomorrow brings new chores—we will be useless if we don't get some sleep."

He was right, it wouldn't help to lie awake. They needed strength for the morrow. They must get up and labor through another day of their earthly life. It was man's

39

lot here on earth: to labor through each day in turn. And they must have rest so they could begin the new day with fresh confidence. The evening fatigue always depressed her spirits, but she would have them back again in the morning after sleep and rest.

Kristina could soon tell from her husband's deep breathing that he was asleep. But she continued to lie awake.

5.

A thousand days and more had passed since Kristina had heard the ringing of church bells.

That was in another world, the Old World. In her parental home, in another Duvemala, she had heard them from the distant church steeple. Every Saturday evening, with their clear tone, they rang in the Holy Day peace, every Sunday morning they vibrated over the village, calling the people together. And the villagers gathered on the church green and looked up and hearkened when the church bells began to peal: the men lifted their hats, the women curtsied. People heard the bells as a voice from above; they paid reverence to their Creator.

At home, each time something of importance happened, the church bells would ring: in war and pestilence, for forest fires or houses burning, at death and the crowning of kings, at marriage festivities and for funeral sorrow—man, made of earth, was brought back to earth with the pealing of church bells.

At all life's great happenings and holidays in the Old World, Kristina had heard the church bells ring. In them she had heard the Creator's voice, when he was in his holy temple, and their sound was the voice of the Holy Day. But for a thousand days now she had not heard that voice.

Here in the New World Sunday was like a weekday with all the sounds of a weekday. In North America, too, churches had been built, but she lived so far from them that the sound of their bells did not reach her. They rang from many steeples in this broad land but were never heard at Lake Ki-Chi-Saga. Nor could she listen to God's servant speaking in her language from a pulpit or altar, she could not hear the organ's pealing, the tones of the psalms, her fellowmen's voices in prayer and singing. For a thousand days she had heard nothing but the forest silence.

She had moved away from church bells, from altar and organ, to the land of the heathens where repulsive idols were worshiped.

But God had not forgotten her, had not lost track of her. He would find her whenever he wished. She was and remained a life, sprung from the Creator's hand, and he needed no church bells to reach her. And today she had heard his voice. She was convinced that he had called her with a message: she must not forget the immortal soul he had given her.

And so at last Kristina said her prayer to the Almighty, who was before the mountains, and would be after them. She prayed fervently for an answer to her question: what must they do—she and her husband—to save their poor souls? How should they manage so as not to lose their eternal salvation in this unchristian land where they had come to start life anew?

And she thanked God for the past day and the message he had brought her through a stranger—this day when Karl Oskar had heard a new ax ringing in the forest.

II. The Whore and the Thief

1.

It seemed to Kristina that their third winter might last forever. The cold was unmercifully severe. On the inner side of the door was a circle of rough nail heads which were constantly covered with hoarfrost. The nail heads, shining like a wreath of white roses on the door, were the winter's mark of sovereignty over the people who lived here; they were prisoners in their own home, locked in by the cold. The warming fire on the hearth did not have the strength to wilt the frost roses on their door.

The dark, shining, nail heads in the wood became the first visible sign of liberation; the cold had been forced to recede beyond the threshold. And what a joy to Kristina when she awakened one night and heard the sound of dripping water outside, melting snow dripping from the eaves. It ran and splashed the whole night through and she could hardly go to sleep again, so happy was she. Every drop from the roof was a joy to her heart; she thanked God for the spring that was near.

Since Ulrika of Västergöhl had married the Baptist minister Mr. Henry O. Jackson and moved to Stillwater, Kristina had no intimate friends in the neighborhood. Ulrika's visits were infrequent. Kristina herself was tied to her home by her own children and she hesitated to visit Ulrika because of the long and difficult road to Stillwater. In two years she had only once been to see Ulrika in her new home. That had been a winter day, and she had ridden with Uncle Danjel on his ox sled. It had been miserably cold, and in spite of all the clothing she had bundled around herself, she had felt as if she was sitting naked on the sled. They had brought along warm stones for their feet and had stopped several times on the way to rewarm them. Even so Kristina still had a frostbitten toe as a reminder of her visit to Stillwater on the slow ox sled.

During the last year, however, the lumber company had cut a new road all the way to Ki-Chi-Saga. Now the settlers could get a ride on the company's ox wagons, and when Kristina decided to journey to Stillwater this spring, she decided to use this transportation. Her errand was partly to visit Ulrika and partly to buy necessities. During the winter she had stopped suckling Dan. She now had no child at her breast, and as Karl Oskar could feed the little one, she could stay overnight with Mr. and Mrs. Jackson.

One pleasantly mild spring day she set out on the ox wagon to Stillwater. During this journey she had no need for warm stones, today she need not worry about getting her toes frostbitten as she sat on the wagon. The sun had warmed the forest, which seemed friendly and inviting along the newly cut road. And the company's ox wagon rolled steadily on its heavy, iron-bound wheels, quite different from the settlers' primitive jolting carts. Today Kristina traveled in comfort; the ride was a pleasure rather than an ordeal.

The Baptist congregation in Stillwater had built a new house for their pastor, next to the little white timbered structure that served as the church. Ulrika saw Kristina through the window and came out on the stoop to welcome her. On her arm Kristina carried the lidded shingle basket which she had brought from Sweden.

"I can see you're out on big business," said Ulrika. "But first you must have something in your belly!"

Pastor Jackson's house had one large and one smaller room, a good-sized kitchen with a storeroom, and an ample cellar under the house. The large room was used only during the day; Ulrika sometimes called it the sitting room and again the living room. The smaller room was a bedroom and in it stood the largest bed Kristina had ever seen; it was as broad as two ordinary beds put together On the wall above the couple's bed hung a framed picture with a maxim in gilded letters: The Lord Gives Us the Strength!

This house had one room for use all day long, and one for use at night, one room to sit in and one to lie down in! Since Ulrika of Västergöhl had become Mrs. Henry O. Jackson she lived like an upper-class woman.

Ulrika urged Kristina to sit down on the soft sofa in the living room. She wanted to show her something strange which she had acquired since Kristina's previous visit. On the wall hung a picture of Mr. and Mrs. Jackson as bride and groom, but it was not a painted picture of her and Henry, and that was the strange thing about it. She and Henry had been placed in the picture by an apparatus. It was like a miracle. Mr. Paul Hanley, a member of the Baptist congregation and now Elin's employer, had bought the apparatus; he was one of the directors of the lumber company and a rich man; he wanted to have a picture of them in their bridal outfit. To take a photograph, he had called it. It was a new invention. They had stood in front of the machine, quite still, for a few moments, while Mr. Hanley had gone to the other side of it with a cloth over his head and manipulated something. And so, quite by magic, they had got their likenesses printed on a thick paper, as nice as any painted picture. And their likenesses did not scale off or fade away but had remained there on the wall, exactly as they were now, for a whole year. They would stick to the paper for all eternity, Mr. Hanley had told them.

Next to the groom, who wore a knee-long coat and narrow pants, stood Ulrika in her white bridal gown of muslin and a wide-brimmed hat, her very first hat.

Below the picture of the bridal couple, a notice from the St. Paul *Pioneer* was cut out and glued to the wall. The paper had printed a piece about the Jackson wedding:

Baptist Church Is Scene of First Wedding

The first marriage in the history of the Stillwater Baptist Church took place Saturday, when Miss Ulrika of Vastergohl became the bride of the Reverend Henry O. Jackson, minister of the Baptist congregation. The bride belongs to the very old noble family of *Vastergohl* in Sweden.

The Reverend R. E. Arleigh who teaches at Bethel Seminary in St. Paul read the service.

Attendants were Cora Skalrud, bridesmaid; Betty Jean Prescott, maid of honor; Paul Hanley and Bob Orville, both best men.

A reception at the new home of Mr. and Mrs. Henry O. Jackson in Stillwater followed the ceremony.

Ulrika translated for Kristina, telling her that the man who had come to write about the wedding for the *Pioneer* had asked her if she belonged to a noble family in Sweden. The Swedes he had met previously in America had all been counts and barons. But she had felt that her ancestry was none of his business, an' 'o his rude question she had, of course, replied that she came from such an old noble family that it could be traced back to the time when Father Adam and Mother Eve walked about with their behinds bare in Paradise. Whether it was because of her English, which wasn't quite perfect yet, or because the writer had taken her seriously—whatever the reason—this writing man had printed in his paper that she had been born into an ancient noble family in Sweden.

And as she had been the first Swedish bride in the St. Croix Valley, it somehow seemed as if it were required of her to have a noble name. It was an honor to her homeland, perhaps. Anyway, it didn't hurt her to be taken for a noble Swedish lady. The aristocratic ladies in Sweden were of course quite uppity, but as far as she knew they did not have bad reputations. And she didn't feel their good names were besmirched when the paper raised her to noble status.

Ulrika prepared dinner for Kristina, sure that she was hungry after her long ride. She treated her to an omelet, warm from the oven, made of ten strictly fresh eggs which had been given to Henry for a sermon in Marine a few days ago.

"Henry is serving as priest in Franconia today," said Ulrika. "He won't be back until late. You must stay the night with us!"

"Come with me to the store and help me buy," pleaded Kristina. "I can't talk to the clerks."

"I'll be glad to be your interpreter, of course. But you must speak to Americans so you learn the language!"

Through her marriage to an American, Ulrika had become so familiar with English that she could understand it well and equally well make herself understood.

Kristina knew the meaning of a few English words but never tried to say anything in the foreign language. She was afraid of ridicule; the Americans laughed at the clumsy Swedes who attempted to use English. But Karl Oskar paid no attention, he just talked on.

"There's something in this tongue that stops me," she would say.

"Nothing except inexperience," he would reply.

But when she wanted to use the English words she had to twist and turn her lips and loosen her tongue, insisted Kristina. She felt as if she were playacting, making a fool of herself, when she used English. Her tongue was not made for this strange language. And if she listened to others speaking it, she got a headache; it did not suit her ears either.

"Let's go and get the shopping done with," said Ulrika.

Kristina rose and picked up her basket, while Ulrika went to the wall mirror in the living room to put on her hat. It was indeed beautiful and amply decorated; a tall plume swayed from the front of the hat—as elegant as the plume of a soldier on parade; the top and the brim were heaped with multi-colored feathers and flowers, and long, red, silken ribbons dangled down the back. She fastened the enormous hat under her chin with a broad, green band, which she tied in a large bow at her right ear.

"In Sweden I had no right to wear a hat," said Ulrika. "But in America I've become a free person."

She wore her fashionable American hat with her head held high on her straight neck, proud and unafraid. The way she stood there now she was not unlike some noble lady in Sweden; the hat was the final touch to a woman's transformation in North America.

Kristina tied on her old, worn, black silk kerchief which her parents had given her as a bridal gift and which she had worn now for eight years.

"Don't you think I should put on a hat too and lay aside my old kerchief?"

"No! You need no hat! You were honestly married when you came here—but unmaried Ulrika needed one!"

Ulrika added that liberty was not in the hat, exactly, but rather in the right to wear it. On her wedding day, two years ago on May 4, she had put on her hat for the first time. That was the day she had declared her independence. Now she celebrated the Fourth of May the way the Americans celebrated the Fourth of July.

And so they went on their way to do Kristina's shopping. Their route took them along the street which followed the river. During the spring months the St. Croix was covered with floating timbers, log beside log all the away to the bend of the river. Stillwater smelled of pitch and fresh lumber. In some places on the town's main street the two women waded through sawdust to their ankles. As they walked, they met men in flaming red woolen shirts tucked under broad leather belts, most of whom swung elegant canes. They appeared to be proud, cocky men; Ulrika called them lumberjacks. Almost every male inhabitant of Stillwater had something to do with lumber.

And almost every second man they met doffed his hat courteously to Ulrika; she was the minister's wife, she was well known in this town.

"Menfolk in America are so courteous and educated," said Kristina.

"Here they value womenfolk," replied Ulrika. "In that hellhole Sweden a man will use a woman as a hired hand in daytime and as a mattress at night. In between she isn't worth a shit!"

How had she herself been valued in the old country? Other women—married·and unmarried—had spat at her. But the married men had come to her for their pleasure. They had used sweet words, then. Then she was good enough. Good enough even for his honor the church warden of Akerby himself. But going to church on Sundays he did not recognize her. And he was one of those who had been against her participation in the sacraments. He was himself an adulterer, but men could whore as much as they wanted without being denied the holy sacraments. In Sweden the sixth commandment was in effect for women only; they must obey the catechism written· by that man Luther. But perhaps in that country the men· only followed the lead of the king himself, who whored with sluts from the theater, and the crown prince, who from his earliest years had been considered the foremost rake in the·kingdom.

At Harrington's General Store Kristina, with Ulrika as interpreter, bought so many articles and necessities that her old shingle basket almost overflowed. The two women carried it between them, each holding·her side of the handle. When they returned to the parsonage, Elin was waiting for them on the stoop; she had brought a message for Pastor Jackson from her employer, Mr. Hanley.

Kristina had not seen Ulrika's daughter for two years and was greatly impressed with the change in her. She was only nineeten but looked and acted like a grown woman. She had a well-shaped body and her fresh skin shone with health. But she did not resemble her mother; she had black hair and dark eyes. She must take after her father, whoever he was; that secret Ulrika had never divulged. Elin had a position as an ordinary maid in town, yet here she was, dressed in a starched, Sunday-fine dress with large flowers, and this in the middle of the week, during working hours. No one would now recognize the shy little girl who once had been with them on the emigrant wagon to Karlshamn. Then she had worn a discarded old skirt Inga-Lena, Danjel's wife, had given her, and carried a berry basket, and looked so forlorn. Today she looked like a young manor girl.

Kristina herself wore her best dress today, and it was worn and moth-eaten in places. At the sight of Ulrika's daughter she felt as if she were decked out in rags. She had put on her best finery, and Elin was in her working clothes, yet Kristina felt poor in comparison with the maid of the American rich people. Many things were topsy-turvy in the New World.

Elin spoke English to her mother, making Kristina feel awkward and pushed aside, excluded from their talk. And then, too, Elin at first acted as if they never had seen each other before. Although then she admitted that it was true, they had come together from Sweden. Had the girl really grown that uppity? It looked suspiciously so. Kristina might have asked her if she had outgrown the skirt Inga-Lena had given her to cover her body during the journey to America. But the girl, of course, didn't know any better.

After Elin left, Ulrika carried on at length with great pride about her daughter, who was, she said, capable and learned quickly. Mr. and Mrs. Hanley had increased her wages to twelve dollars a month, and they served fare that was better than holiday food in Sweden, where maids and hired hands had to be satisfied with herring all year round. But the girl caused her mother great concern because she was so beautiful; men were after her and played up to her, and Ulrika wasn't sure if they had marriage in mind. In Sweden a beautiful girl of poor parents was nothing more than prey for lustful menfolk, and even out here there was surely an occasional pant-clad animal out hunting. But this much she had made up her mind about: her innocent little girl would not be prey for such a human beast. Elin's maidenhead was not to be wasted in advance—like her own—without joy, but would be an honest man's reward in the bridal bed.

Ulrika set the coffee table in the living room. They sat down on the sofa again under the picture of Mr. and Mrs. Jackson which Kristina greatly admired. Pastor Jackson had been the first kind and helpful person she had met in America. When they had arrived on the steamboat, and were sitting down by the river in a cold rain, their brats whining, all of them wet through and through, hungry and homeless, without shelter or roof—then it was that Pastor Jackson had taken charge of their whole helpless group, had brought them to his home, prepared food, fed them, made up beds for them to rest on overnight, and helped them continue their journey the following morning. And to think that one of the women in their group had become his wife!

"You have been given a kind and good husband, Ulrika."

"Yes, Henry is gentle. He never uses a woman for a slave."

"But how could you and he understand each other in the beginning, before you learned English?"

"Well," said Ulrika, "a man and a woman always find a way if they like each other. We made signs and pointed and used our hands in the beginning."

She handed Kristina the plate with the buttercakes to be dunked in their coffee. American men were easy for an experienced woman to handle; they were so quick to offer marriage. Four men had proposed and offered her their name before Henry came along. Good, upright, American men.

"Ulrika," said Kristina reflectively, "before the marriage I guess you told your husband the truth about your life in Sweden, and he holds nothing against you, according to what you say?"

"No. And I hold nothing against him."

"Against him? Do you mean that he too—the pastor . . . ?"

"Yes, he led a wretched life; sinful like mine."

"That I wouldn't have thought," said Kristina, greatly surprised.

"I told you once, 'Henry is nothing but a great sinner forgiven by God. We're alike, he and I!' Don't you remember that?"

Kristina remembered. But she had understood this to mean that Pastor Jackson had been born in sin, like all people.

"Oh no! In his old body he lived in deep sin! One was no better than the other, Henry and I!" Ulrika held her cup firmly and looked steadily at Kristina. "Henry used to steal. The same as I whored. Those two actions even up."

Kristina opened her mouth quickly. She closed it again without speaking.

Ulrika continued: "Henry was in prison in England. For stealing."

He had had the same unhappy childhood in England as she had had in Sweden. She had lost her parents when four, he when three years of age. She was sold at auction to the lowest bidder, to be brought up, Henry had been put in a foundling home. Her foster father had raped her and taught her whoring, in the orphanage Henry had learned to steal. He stole food to satisfy his hunger. At the age of fourteen he had escaped from the home and continued to steal his food until he was caught and put in prison for three years. When he was released he had signed up on a ship to America. In New York he had lived among thieves and whores until he met a Baptist minister who converted him. He was baptized and given help to study for the ministry. For fifteen years now he had been a pastor.

Kristina listened, confused and embarrassed, and at first without taking much store in what she heard. But Ulrika couldn't have made up all these tales.

"Henry is an old thief—I'm an old whore. We're two of a kind and very happy together!"

Kristina thought Ulrika would feel hurt if she now tried to excuse her and her husband: "All that is now passed, all of it," she stammered.

"Yes, Henry and I have been immersed and live now in new bodies. We're forgiven by God. We're reborn. Our hearts are cleansed."

"I'll never forget your husband's kindness when we landed here. I couldn't believe he was a churchman. He was so kind and helpful."

Pastor Jackson of Stillwater was as different from the church officials at home as his rough-timbered church across the yard was different from Ljuder's stone church.

"Henry has suffered," said Ulrika. "People who have suffered are kind to other people."

Jackson was a nobler and stronger Christian than she, and she wanted to make that clear. He was a help to her when the temptation of her old body came upon her. She couldn't pretend to be better than she was. The old serpent tempted her; at times she could feel him tickle her weak flesh.

When she married Jackson, no man had been in bed with her for four long years. It was not easy for her to hold herself until after the wedding; she almost crept near Henry before that time. But she wanted so to wait until after the ceremony, to show him that she had conquered her old sinful flesh. And he had not tempted her—he was not that kind of raw and selfish man. And in this way he had helped her endure and preserve her new body innocent until the bridal ceremony was over.

When at last the time had come to pull on the bridal shift she had felt like a virgin. She couldn't quite explain it, but she almost felt like a girl going to woman for the first time when at last they got down to business. And in her new body, rebaptized and all, she really was a virgin, untouched by men. She was still in her best years, and it had felt so wonderful to be able to use her body for the purpose for which it had been created, now that God had joined them together.

Henry himself had had hardly any experience at all

51

when they married. He had slept a few times with ordinary waterfront whores in New York but that had been fifteen years ago. So she had had to instruct him and guide him. He had really had so little experience that he could be called a beginner at bed play.

"Jackson pushed in too fast in the beginning, that was the trouble . . ."

Before Kristina had time even to suspect what Mrs. Jackson was describing, with this last sentence, Ulrika had jumped up; she had just dunked a second butter cake in her coffee and had barely swallowed a bite of it when she suddenly groaned loudly and rushed to the kitchen, her hands on her stomach.

What was the matter with Ulrika? But before Kristina could ask, her friend had returned to the living room. She dried her mouth with the back of her hand, jolly and happy as ever:

"Excuse me for running out!"

"Did you get something in your windpipe?"

"No, it was only my 'priest.' He's on his way now."

Kristina looked out through the window but could see no one outside. "Is Mr. Jackson coming?" she asked.

"No, not Henry. I meant the priest I'm going to bring into the world. I went out to reek a little."

"Reek a little?"

Ulrika sat down again at the coffee table: "I'm in the family way, you see."

Ulrika used the English words and it was a few moments before Kristina understood. Ulrika went on to explain. She had decided long ago that her first son should be a minister, the same as his father. With a son in the pulpit she would be redeemed in the eyes of Dean Brusander at home, he who had excluded her from his congregation.

"I haven't had my regulars for two months and I puke like a she-cat. I'm pregnant."

In Sweden when a woman was pregnant she was said to be on the thick, and it sounded as if she were afflicted with a shameful disease, said Ulrika. That was why she used the English words for her condition, it sounded fine and elegant in some way. Furthermore, this was the first time she was married to the father of a child of hers, and it seemed strange to her, but not unpleasant.

"I wish you all luck!" said Kristina. "I'll carry your first-born to baptism as you carried my last-born."

"I'm sorry, but he won't be baptized until he is grown. We intend to immerse our brats in our own religion."

That was true, the Baptists did not christen their babies. Kristina was apt to overlook the fact that Ulrika had embraced a new religion.

"You're tardy with your pregnancy," said Kristina. "You've been married two years now."

"Yes, it's taken so long I was getting worried. I myself have borne four brats in my life but I was beginning to wonder if Henry was useless. Having born the others outside wedlock, I'm anxious to have a few real ones too."

Kristina sighed; the childbed Ulrika impatiently looked forward to she herself feared. Each month she trembled lest her period stop. And her apprehension had increased since Dan stopped suckling; she thought she had noticed that suckling was an obstacle.

Ulrika added that she had already bespoken a midwife, a Norwegian woman, Miss Skalrud, who had been maid of honor at her wedding. Miss Skalrud usually helped the women of their congregation at childbirth, and she had promised to help the little one through the portal into this world.

Toward evening Pastor Jackson returned from his journey to Franconia. He carried his bag with books and pamphlets and also a parcel which turned out to contain five pounds of wheat flour and three pounds of fresh butter, his wages for the sermon. In the doorway, he took his wife in his arms and patted her devotedly on the cheek with his big, hairy hand.

"Ollrika, my dear, forgive me! I'm late. My dearest Ollrika—and we have a dear guest . . . !"

The pastor welcomed his wife's good friend warmly. With blessing-like gestures he took Kristina's hands and smiled at her, the same good, kind smile she remembered.

Ulrika's husband had put on weight since Kristina had last seen him. His cheeks had filled out, his pants were tight around the waist, his stomach had begun to protrude. Ulrika had said, "I cook good food for Henry, don't forget it!"

The Jacksons spoke to each other in English, and Kristina again was left out. Once more she felt like a deaf-mute, excluded from the company. But Pastor Jackson was not one of those who would laugh at her, he talked to her through his wife. Was everything well with them on the claim, how were the children, had they enough food, was there anything he could help them with? And she replied through Ulrika that all was well at home, that several new neighbors were moving in this summer, beginning with a farmer from Sweden with his wife and three children.

But after a while it became rather tiresome to speak to another person through a third one. Nor was she sure her own words always were interpreted correctly. Kristina wished dearly that she could use the English language, if for no other reason than to be able to talk to Pastor Jackson directly; he was her true friend. Without understanding a single one of his words she felt the warmth from them in her heart.

2.

Ulrika made a bed on the living room sofa for Kristina. She would leave early next morning on the lumber company's ox wagon.

When the sun came up and Kristina had eaten breakfast, she thanked her friend for the hospitality and made ready to pick up her basket of groceries. Ulrika, to her surprise, brought her another basket, new and made of willow. A cloth was spread over it.

"A small present from the two of us, Kristina!"

Behind Ulrika stood Pastor Jackson, nodding eagerly as if he understood the Swedish words.

Mysterious cackling and chirpings could be heard from the basket. Kristina lifted a corner of the cloth and peeked. In the bottom of the basket sat a live brown-and-white speckled hen. But hers was not the only life in the basket: tiny chicks poked their heads through the wings of the mother, the little beaks shining like pink flower buds.

Kristina cried out joyfully, "Chickens! A hen!"

"We hope you like them! She's hatched twelve, a whole dozen!"

Pastor Jackson smiled his kind smile: "Twelve young chickens!"

Ulrika said, "Henry is as proud of the chicks as if he himself had hatched them. The hen was given to him by a young couple in Taylors Falls as payment for a marriage service."

Kristina choked, weeping with joy. If there was anything she had missed on the claim it was chickens. Now her throat was so full she couldn't say thank you the way she would have wished; she could only mumble.

Ulrika gave her a small bag of rice for chicken feed: "Be careful with the basket! The little lives are delicate."

Pastor Jackson picked up the grocery basket and Ulrika the basket with the hen and chicks, and the two of them accompanied Kristina to the lumber office at the end of the street. It was almost an hour before the wagon was loaded, but her friends remained with her until the driver was ready to start. When the wheels had already begun to roll, Ulrika called to her once more: she must be careful with the newly hatched feather-lives there on the driver's seat.

Each time Ulrika had come to visit Kristina in her home she had brought gifts to her and the children. Once Kristina had complained of rats and rodents in their cabin that gnawed at the food and spoiled much of it for them, and next time Ulrika had brought a cat. The cat was a good mouser, but after a time they had found him in a bush near the house, bitten to death; some wild animal had torn out his throat.

And now she was driving home with Mr. and Mrs. Jackson's most welcome gift. During the whole journey she sat with the basket on her knee and held on to it with both her hands, listening in quiet joy to the hen's cackling and the peeps and chirps of the chicks. When the wheels rolled over stumps, or down into holes in the forest road,

55

and her seat fell and rose, she clutched the basket more firmly.

In trees and bushes, along the whole stretch of the road, Kristina heard the spring birds of the forest, but she was unaware of them; their song was drowned by the determined chirping from the domestic birds on her knee. A hen, chickens, eggs! An egg each Sunday, eggs for cooking during the week! Egg bouillon, egg milk, egg pancakes! This was what the chirp from the chickens meant. Boiled eggs, fried eggs, eggs in omelets, eggs in the pan, eggs, eggs, eggs!

If she now had decent luck so that at least half of the twelve chicks were pullets! A rooster was good for only one meal, devoured at one sitting, but hens' eggs would be food year in, year out.

Kristina's thoughts turned gratefully to Ulrika and her husband. Her friends in the Stillwater parsonage had proved themselves her friends in every need. The Jacksons were the kindest people she knew in the world, despite the fact that both had led such wretched lives in their homelands. Here they had turned into new beings, they had become transformed in America. She had herself seen how Ulrika had blossomed in this country.

The same thing had happened to a great number of the immigrants. When they no longer had masters over them but could live their own lives as they wished, they became different people. When they could make their own decisions and need not obey others, they became new beings.

Kristina recognized that she herself had changed some out here; she valued people differently. In Sweden she had gone along with the common opinion and valued those whom others valued, looking down on those whom others looked down on. And at home there were those of a higher class whose opinions one should heed, for their ideas and actions were considered the right ones. But here she knew of no particular persons who were held up as examples; in this country, it seemed, people did not care what anyone thought or said about others.

And since no one out here was considered better than anyone else, each one must form his own opinions. She herself must stick to what she felt for others and knew of their deeds. She must make judgments that she considered right. Thus it came about that she now valued people differently. In this way she explained to herself the feelings she had about her friends in Stillwater.

Kristina had visited in a home where the husband had been a thief and the wife a whore. But this couple were her honest, devoted, indispensable friends. Outside her family, her best friends in America were the former thief and the former whore.

III. Planning and Planting

1.

As soon as Petrus Olausson had raised his log house, his wife and children arrived. His wife's name was Judit. She was a tall, rather lean, woman with small, quick, sharp eyes, a strong nose, and a severely compressed mouth which seemed distorted—the right corner was pulled up higher than the left. The couple had a girl fourteen years old and twin boys barely twelve.

Kristina felt a little shy with her neighbor the first time she came to call; her tongue was slow to converse with her. Judit Olausson, in her black, tight-fitting dress with a white starched lace collar which came all the way up to her chin, did not seem like an ordinary settler's wife but rather like a matron on a well-to-do farmstead. There was something austere and commanding about her, whether it came from her penetrating look or the wry mouth; Kristina did not feel on equal footing with her neighbor. Olausson's wife was also fifteen years older than she.

Later in the spring two families from Småland settled at Fish Lake on the east side of the valley. It was a great distance from this lake to Ki-Chi-Saga and the names of the newcomers were not known, nor which parish they came from.

But with the Olaussons' arrival Karl Oskar and Kristina at last had close neighbors. The settlers gave each other a hand when need be; Karl Oskar lent Olausson a few tools, although the newcomer had brought along more implements than Karl Oskar had owned when he staked his claim. And it seemed the Helsinge farmer also was fairly well supplied with cash.

Petrus Olausson immediately suggested that the families hereabouts meet every Sunday at each house in turn to enjoy the comfort of religion and help each other with matters.

At these Sunday meetings, Olausson read from the Bible and gave a brief explanation of the passage he had read. Each time he mentioned the punishment he would have suffered in Sweden had he there attempted to explain the Bible.

He told them about the persecution he had experienced at the time he and his wife were Erik Janson's apostles. The prophet had one day come to their home at Alfta to sell wheat flour—he was called Wheat-flour Jesus. At that time Janson was of a world-renouncing mind and adhered strictly to the Bible, considering all other religious books to be false. Because of this, the clergy had asked for his imprisonment and sent the sheriff after him. For several weeks they had hidden him under their barn floor. Three or four times a day they had carried food to him and later they had followed him to North America. The prophet from Biskopskulla had founded Bishop Hill, Illinois, where he intended to build the New Jerusalem. And Erik Janson had seemed to his followers as humanity's great light, sent by God to restore Christianity. Here in America he would found a new and cleansed Lutheran Church.

His teachings had been honest and humble in the beginning, but he soon became puffed up with self-righteousness and destroyed himself thereby. No longer was' he God's representative on earth, he set himself above God. On the Illinois prairie he treated his people worse than the Americans treated their slaves; he ruled them as if they were his personal possessions. When a married man wanted to sleep with his wife he must first report his desire to Janson. And when the prophet gracefully had condescended to the bedding, then it must take place in full view of the whole congregation. Such was the shameless man's pleasure. When people grew sick or old or useless for work, he simply commanded them to lie down and die. If the sick did not obey him and failed to die the same day, they were excluded from the colony.

The overbearing man brought on his own evil end: a murderer's bullet.

And Petrus Olausson spoke of the Lutheran Church and the Reformed Church, of Baptism and Methodism, and explained the differences in the religions which decided where a human was to spend eternity—in Heaven or in Hell. To Kristina the whole seemed confusing and difficult to understand. But she understood how easily a person could become ensnared in a false religion which would lead to eternal damnation. God himself had not given clear instructions about the right road, and an ignorant, simple sinner like herself could not find it without guidance. That was why ministers were essential.

Man did not obey God when obeying authority, said Olausson, and that too sounded strange and confusing to her. As a child she had been taught that no authority existed except that which derived its power from God. But her previous instruction, it now seemed, was a falsification of the Swedish clergy, according to the Helsinge farmer. The sheriff who had chased Erik Janson under the barn floor and put Bible-reading persons in prison on bread and water had not received his office from God but from the Crown. The provincial governor was a successor to Pilate, who had sentenced Christ to crucifixion. And nowhere in the Bible did it say that God had ordained sheriffs to plague Christian people who read the Bible in their homes. The sheriffs in Sweden were successors to the Roman soldiers who crucified Jesus at the order of civil authorities.

In her catechism, however, Kristina had learned that she ought to respect and obey authority for the Lord's sake, and she often felt that her neighbor was mistaken.

Petrus Olausson urged the Swedish settlers in the valley to get together and build a church without delay. Karl Oskar pointed out that they also needed a schoolhouse;

their children were growing up and they needed Christian schooling unless the parents wanted them to become heathens. Johan was already of school age and Lill-Marta only a year younger. He and Kristina had tried to teach the brats as best they could, but they had no Swedish spelling book and no catechism. Karl Oskar had taught Johan the letters of the alphabet from the Swedish almanac, but it was not very good for spelling since it had so few words in it. The boy learned too slowly in this way, and Karl Oskar was not much of a teacher. And both Johan and Lill-Marta would soon need to learn the contents of other books as well; it would be useful for both the boy and the girl to be able to read and write.

Karl Oskar had often discussed the building of a schoolhouse with Danjel Andreasson. There were three children in New Kärragärde, older than their own, whom their father had instructed so far.

The Olaussons too, had instructed their children, first and foremost in the true Lutheran religion, in order to instill in them from tender years the pure faith. Olausson thought they could use the church they intended to build as a schoolhouse, but Karl Oskar thought they should not wait—building a church might take several years—and they could not get along without a schoolhouse for so long, or their children would have become too old to go to school.

There were many matters for the settlers to attend to. They must build and build again—temples for God, houses for people, schoolhouses for children, shelters for the cattle, barns for the crops, storehouses, implement sheds. Karl Oskar had laid the foundation for a new living house which he hoped to have roofed by next year, and that was only a poor beginning. As he thought of the coming years he could see himself constantly occupied with eternal carpentry, eternal sill-laying for new buildings.

2.

In order to please Kristina, Karl Oskar had named his new home Duvemala, and had written to his wife's home for apple seeds, and had planted an Astrakhan apple tree for her; this was his remedy for her homesickness. He wanted to know if it had helped and asked her if she still suffered as much as before. She replied that she thought perhaps her longing for home had died down a little.

Now Kristina could say: I live again at Duvemala, this is my home, I hold it dear, here I will stay as long as I live. And she was pleased with the little seedling that had grown from the apple seeds. She looked after it constantly and tended the small plant as if it were a delicate living being.

Thus far all was well. But neither the name, Duvemala, nor the seedling could divert her thoughts from her old home. On the contrary, they now turned more often to her native country.

Even during the night she would return in her dreams, in which she moved back to her homeland, with husband and children. Happily there, she wondered over her foolishness ever to have undertaken the long journey out into the world. What business had she had far away in America? She had a good home here. Well, anyway, everything had turned out all right, all of them were unharmed, back in their old village. She might even dream that the whole emigration had been an evil nightmare.

But in the morning she always awakened in America.

Kristina tried persistently to suppress this longing, this desire for and loss of something she would never have again. She wanted to conquer her weakness and be as strong as Karl Oskar. She had made her home here forever, she must learn to feel at home, become part of the foreign country. But in this, her will would not obey her; something in her soul refused to obey.

And spring in Minnesota, with its dark evenings, was her difficult season; then she yearned for the land with evenings of another hue. She longed for Sweden as much as ever, but she kept this from her husband. She must carry this incurable soul-ache in secret, hide it like a shameful disease, as people hid scabby and scurvy sores on their bodies.

How many times hadn't Kristina wished that she could write a letter to her parents! But Swedish women were not taught to write. Perhaps if she herself had insisted, when she was little, she might have learned to write. But how could she have known what was in store for her? As a little girl she could not have imagined that her life would be spent on another continent. Nor had anyone else at home imagined that a woman of their village would move so far away from her relatives that she needed to write letters to her parents. Her fate had not been anticipated by the village school laws.

Now she was separated from her dear ones; not a word from her could reach them except through another person. After Robert had left for California, Karl Oskar had written a few short letters for her to her parents. Robert had helped her to express her thoughts, but Karl Oskar had difficulty in forming the sentences and capturing her feeling in writing. The letters became the same, almost word for word: she was well, all was well with them, her father and mother must not worry about their daughter, her daily thoughts were with them in her dear old Duvemala. These last were the truest words in the letters.

It was always her father who answered, as her mother too, being a woman, could not write, and he wrote equally short letters, using direct biblical words: their daughter must put her trust in the Lord in North America, she must bring up her children in the Lord's ways and with strict discipline, as she herself had been brought up in her home, she must obey the Ten Commandments and live irreproachably so that they might meet in Heaven.

His final words confirmed her belief that she never again would see her parents and brothers and sisters on this earth. And she asked dejectedly: Why must the world be so immensely large? Why must the roads across it be so dreadfully long?

Kristina suffered because the world was so large that she never again would meet her relatives from the homeland in life.

3.

When the tall drifts round the cabin melted away in the spring, the landscape seemed empty and bare. Without their winter covering the log walls appeared in all their wretchedness. Now their home looked like a simple outhouse, a hay barn or a shed. There was nothing to indicate that this was a human habitation. A flower garden was what was needed.

Flowers cheered one up and were a decoration outside a home, and company for one when alone. When she was first married, Kristina had planted a flower bed against the wall of their house in Korpamoen—resedas, asters, sunflowers, larkspur, lavender, daisies, and other flowers.

This spring she would prepare a flower bed in front of her new home. She hoed a patch under the south window, and decided to try to get the same kind of flowers she had planted at home, if they were obtainable here.

Mr. Abbott, the Scottish storekeeper in Taylors Falls, had all kinds of seeds for sale. And shortly before Whitsuntide she had an opportunity to ride to Taylors Falls with Jonas Petter and Swedish Anna. Like her they were going to the Scotsman for their holiday purchases.

All three had finished their shopping and were sitting on the wagon, ready to return home, when Kristina remembered that she had forgotten the flower seeds. She jumped off and walked back to the store alone.

Mr. Abbott, behind the counter, greeted her with a lift of his white cap and adjusted the pencil behind his right ear; he was much more courteous to women than to men. The tall Scot was one of Ulrika's rejected suitors. But a couple of years ago he had married the daughter of the German Fisher, and his wife had borne him a daughter who already managed to crawl about on the floor, both behind the counter and in front of it.

Kristina had become acquainted with him and was able to buy from him, even though they did not understand each other's language, since he usually guessed what she wanted and would point to the shelves where his wares were displayed. But she did not know where he kept his seeds, nor did she know what they were called in English. Perhaps flowers had the same names in both languages. She tried the foreign tongue for the first time:

"I wanta planta blooms . . . *blommer* . . ."

The storekeeper listened without changing expression. He did not understand her and answered in words she in turn did not understand. In vain she looked around the shelves for seed bags. He must keep them in a drawer—but which one?

She grew embarrassed and annoyed at herself; was she unable to buy a few seeds for her own patch? She would take any kind, whatever he had, for it would be futile to stand here and ask for aster, lion-hearts, and other Swedish flowers she wanted. The question now was, could she get any seeds at all?

Then she saw a paper hanging from a shelf with a red flower painted on it. Relieved, she pointed to the paper and exclaimed:

"I wanta this! *Blommer!*"

Mr. Abbott's face lighted up:

"Ah—you want seed, Mrs. Nelson?"

But she knew the meaning of the word "seed." Karl Oskar had bought seed for their field, she did not want rye or barley.

"No! No! Not seed! I wanta *blommer!*"

Mr. Abbott brought out a heap of small bags and spread them on the counter; he opened one of them to show her that it was seed. Well, perhaps it was the right kind; she could see the seeds with her own eyes, but the English printed on the bags she could not read; she must buy blindly.

Kristina fingered the small bags and chose five. As far as she could see, there was different printing on each one, so at least she would have five kinds of flowers.

She told Karl Oskar when she came home that she had blindly bought five kinds of flower seed for her patch under the window. She thought it would be amusing to see what she had picked; she hoped some of them would be the same varieties she had grown in Korpamoen.

Her new flower bed lay against the long front side of the house, on the south facing the sun; they would surely grow here. And she cleaned the earth well, picking away roots and weeds before she put the seed in the ground. She pushed it down in rows, one kind to each row, filled the holes with earth, evened out the bed, flattened it with a piece of board, so that it looked neat and orderly.

Flowers would grow near the house, they would be at the entrance, the place of honor. Flower beds belonged to a home. No one planted flowers in front of a barn, a stable, or a pigpen; a flower bed distinguished a home from an animal shed.

Here her flowers would grow right under the window so they would catch her eye as soon as she looked out. And people would see from a distance that human beings lived in this cabin of rough timbers.

When Kristina finished her planting and had her flower bed in order she felt she had moved a little patch of ground from her homeland to the settlement at Ki-Chi-Saga.

4.

Minnesota's hot season was approaching. Each day the sun felt warmer. The earth dried out, and Kristina watered her flower bed every evening. Flowers responded to the care given them, they grew better if they were watched and cared for, they appreciated water and attention. And flowers changed from one day to another; in the morning sun they proudly raised their heads, in fog and rain their heads were bent, sad and depressed; as with people, their appearance often changed.

Karl Oskar kept busy hoeing turf on the new-broken field; with a team he could have plowed and enlarged his field faster. Here lay the whole meadow with wild grass which was good only for hay. How much more wouldn't it give him if it were cultivated! It had been lying here in fallow ever since the day of creation. Now the tiller had arrived, and the time for the earth to give bread to people.

At the house wall Kristina had planted her own little field. The flower bed would amuse her, and perhaps lessen her thoughts of longing. She needed something different to occupy her here, something to shatter her homesickness.

Each morning as Kristina rose she looked out at her flower bed: had they come up yet? The days went by but nothing was seen aboveground. It took time . . . but she asked Karl Oskar what he thought; was it possible that Mr. Abbott had sold her old seeds that wouldn't grow? He assured her that he had bought seed grain and seeds for rutabagas and carrots and parsnips and all had come up.

Then Karl Oskar too began to look at the flower bed. Each day he seemed more thoughtful. And one morning he said to his wife:

"Come and have a look at your claim, Kristina!"

In a headlong jump she was out of bed: small, awl-sharp blades were shooting up from the earth. In the early sun they glittered like grain shoots. These were not tender flower stems; what she saw were shoots of grass.

"That's what I thought!" she exclaimed, annoyed. "He gave me old seeds—only weeds are coming up!"

"Weeds do not grow in rows," said Karl Oskar calmly.

"In rows?" A new thought struck her. "You don't mean I've planted . . . ?"

She bent down and looked closely. He was right: the grass grew in row after row—in five long rows.

"Exactly where I planted the seeds! Good Lord, what's this . . . ?"

Karl Oskar pointed and explained: "Here at the edge grows timothy, the next row is clover . . ."

"My Lord, how I've been fooled!"

Kristina had planted fodder grass instead of flowers in her garden bed. And when Karl Oskar mentioned clover she realized what had happened: when she asked for seeds in Mr. Abbott's store she had pointed to a paper with a red flower—a clover blossom!

Neither asters nor resedas came up outside her window, neither daisies, nor sunflowers, neither larkspur nor lavender. Clover plants grew there, stands of timothy, and other grasses, rough, reddish, American fodder grass, unknown to her. But these plants she need not cultivate—they grew wild in abundance around the house, they stood yard-high everywhere, there were such quantities of them they could not save half.

"Laugh at me, Karl Oskar! Poke fun at me! I'm a fool . . ."

Why had she been so dumb as to try to speak English when she knew she couldn't? Why hadn't she asked Jonas Petter or Swedish Anna to help her buy the flower seeds? And where had her senses been when she was planting—she knew the difference between flower seeds and grass seed. She had thought the flower seeds looked unusual, but then, everything in America was different . . .

It was a little annoying, said Karl Oskar, but nothing to take seriously. He too in the beginning had made mistakes when he bought things. The English language was so confusing, it was hazardous to speak it, some words were so mixed up in that tongue. He had had great trouble when he bought seed rye: as long as the rye grew in the field it was called crop but as soon as it was harvested and threshed it was called grain, even though it was rye all the time. She was not the only one to make a mistake.

But Kristina was a perfectionist. Therefore, it was of no comfort to her that Karl Oskar could make similar mistakes. It did not worry her so much that she made a fool of herself to others, but she felt a fool in her own eyes, dejected, and that was worse.

"Someone like me ought to stay home. I ought not to poke my nose beyond the claim. I am so stupid in English I ought not to mix with other people."

"But this mistake is easily remedied!" exclaimed Karl Oskar.

She could plant the bed with new seeds; he would buy the right ones for her next time he had an errand in Taylors Falls or Stillwater.

But after all her worry and concern for the plants she had thought would become flowers, she did not wish to start all over again this summer.

She pulled up the grass plants, each and every one, hoed the bed, and planted cabbage instead.

She should have learned this much by now: it was, and remained forever, difficult to transplant the homeland in foreign soil. A person could not change countries and make a *foreign place* into *home* overnight. Perhaps she would not even live long enough to do that.

One thing was sure—it would be some time before she again tried to speak English.

IV. Guests in Their Own House

1.

Spring brought potent growing weather; it was dry during seeding and planting time, then when the fields were prepared a generous rain fell for several days without letup; it poured down in sheets from low-hanging, pregnant clouds. The cabin's sod roof began to leak and the Nilssons brought out all available vessels to catch the drip. The roof had never leaked before, but this was the most persistent downpour they had experienced in Minnesota.

During one of the rainy nights Karl Oskar was awakened by his wife touching his elbow: "Someone is knocking on the door!"

He sat up in bed and listened. Out there in the black night the rain was pouring down, beating against the window. It dripped from the ceiling and splashed in the vessels on the floor. But above the sounds of the rain came a heavy banging against the door.

"There's someone out there—it woke me," said Kristina.

Karl Oskar pulled on his pants and lit a candle on the table. Who would come at this hour of the night? Someone must have lost his way and was seeking shelter from the rain.

Kristina too slipped out of bed and pulled on her petticoat. She whispered, "Ask who it is before you open!"

It might be one of the new neighbors in need of help. But they could expect unfriendly callers day or night and must not be taken unawares; their door was always well bolted at night.

Before Karl Oskar had time to ask, a man's voice was heard through the door: "I'm a lone wanderer. Please give me shelter, good people!"

These pleading words were in Swedish and that was enough for Karl Oskar; he pushed back the heavy bolts.

A man in a long, black coat and a black, broad-brimmed hat stumbled across the threshold, his legs unsteady. His coat was covered with mud and soaked through with rain; it hung on him limply. Water splashed in his boots with every step. He sank down on a chair, collapsing like an empty sack, and breathed heavily, "Much obliged. Thank you, my good Swedes."

Utterly confused, Karl Oskar and Kristina eyed their unexpected night caller, a thin young man with a pale, narrow face and large blue eyes. He carried a handbag of shining black leather, and his muddy clothes were of fine quality. He had white, well-cared-for hands, like those of a scrivener or a nobleman. The stranger looked like a gentleman, not a trapper or a settler. Why was he wandering about in the wilderness in this ungodly weather?

The man removed his hat, and the water ran in runnels from the brim; his hair, too, was thoroughly wet and clung to his skull. From his coat and pants water ran onto the floor and formed puddles round his chair.

Kristina pulled on her night jacket. "You're out in evil weather," she said.

"Where do you come from?" asked Karl Oskar.

"I've walked from St. Paul." He panted for breath, exhausted from fatigue. "I'm worn out . . ."

It was evident to both of them that he was in a sorry condition.

"Make a fire so he can dry himself!" said Kristina.

Karl Oskar pushed aside the kettles and bowls, earthen crocks and caldron lids, which stood on the floor half-filled with water, and made a passage to the fireplace. He found some dry kindling behind the chimney and soon a great fire blazed on the hearth. It lit up the room so that he could see the stranger more clearly. What he saw shocked him: on the man's forehead and on his neck were horrible, bleeding spots.

"You're bleeding! Has someone stabbed you?"

"I was attacked by many enemies . . ."

"Enemies! Where? In the forest?"

"I was asleep . . . they came over me . . . a whole swarm . . . they pierced me with their arrows . . ."

"The redskins? Are they on the warpath?"

A few weeks earlier a message had come from Fort Snelling that the Sioux had been active in Carver County along the Minnesota River. Some of the settlers had fled to St. Paul. But a few days later they had heard that the rumor was false. They were, however, still uneasy; before the second message had arrived they had been prepared to hide in the forest.

Kristina listened intently, turned her eyes quickly to the sleeping children. "The Indians! Are they coming this way . . . ?"

"No . . . , it wasn't the Indians. I was attacked by . . . mosquitoes . . ."

The stranger pushed his chair to the fire and began to pull off his boots; the water splashed round his feet; on one boot the leather had burst at his big toe, which stuck out through the hole.

"A swarm of thousands of mosquitoes attacked me in the forest," he explained. "They made these wounds with their sharp stingers . . ."

Kristina breathed more easily; she was familiar with those torture bugs. She preferred them to Indians on the warpath, their faces smeared with red paint.

The guest took off his dripping coat as well. His pants were torn, his shirt stuck out through a hole in the back.

The poor man must be hungry, thought Kristina, and she took some of the barley porridge left from their own

70

supper and put the kettle over the fire. She poured fresh milk into a bowl, and put out bread and syrup.

Their guest's appearance and way of talking indicated he was an upper-class man, and Karl Oskar did not use the familiar "du" in talking to him. Not wanting to seem curious, he told the man his own name and the place in Sweden he came from, hoping the stranger would do as much. His suspicion of strangers would not leave him.

"My name is Erland Törner," the man said. "I was born in Östergötland."

"Are you here to claim land?"

"No. I am a minister in the Swedish Church."

"What's that . . . ?"

"A minister!"

The exclamation came from Kristina. She almost dropped the jar of maple syrup. "A minister from Sweden? Did I hear aright?"

"Yes, I am sent by the Church at home."

Karl Oskar stared at the man whose feet in worn-out socks rested on the hearth. This country was a gathering place for all sorts of people; a great many crooks and swindlers found their way here, as well as lazy, useless people who wanted to live off others. He was not one to believe an unknown person's words right off. Here, in the middle of the night, had come to his house a stranger, a man who wandered about in the wilderness without errand; he had arrived muddy, his clothing torn, covered with blood, the toes sticking out of his boots, a hole in his behind, telling them he was a man of the Church from Sweden, consecrated by the bishop to preach. A real minister, not one of those American ministers who apparently were a breed of their own. How could this man expect to be believed right off?

But Kristina had no doubts. She had wondered about his long black coat and his black leather bag and his way of talking. She should have understood at once that he was a churchman. And now she spoke to him as to an entirely different person, respect and reverence in her voice. "When did you leave home, Mr. Pastor?"

"Half a year ago."

And it seemed he had guessed Karl Oskar's suspicion—he searched in his bag and found a thick paper. "I'm entirely unknown to you, my dear countrymen. Here are my papers to prove what I said."

He handed the paper to Karl Oskar, who learned from it that their guest was Pastor Lars Paul Erland Törner, born at Västerstad, Östergötland, in the Kingdom of Sweden, May 16, 1825. The pastor was two years younger than himself.

"We did not doubt you, Mr. Pastor!" Karl Oskar assured him quickly.

"Mr. Pastor, you must change your wet clothes!" said Kristina.

The young minister had begun to revive; he smiled at her. "Don't call me Mister, Mrs. Nilsson! Pastor is enough."

"And don't call me Mrs. My name is Kristina. I'm not of the upper class!"

"But here in America all married women are called Mrs."

This she must know, he added, there was no difference here between nobles and ordinary people; all were equal. And that was why he liked it so much in this country. God had never created different classes, only people.

"Here, Pastor, are some dry clothes," said Karl Oskar.

He had found the wadmal suit the village tailor had made for him at the time of his emigration. He had now worn it for three years, on weekdays and Sundays, for he no longer had any special Sunday clothing. Most of the settlers wore equally poor clothes.

"If you can wear them, they're the best I have . . ."

"Thank you, Mr. Nilsson. Any dry clothing is blessed clothing."

The young minister changed in front of the fire and his host hung up the drenched garments to dry.

Karl Oskar had a full, strong body, while Pastor Törner was lean and spindly; he did not nearly fill the clothes he put on. Around the minister's thin legs the settler's pants almost stood by themselves, stiff and unbending, and his hands disappeared entirely in the long coat sleeves. The roomy garments enveloped the thin body and hung on it as if it were a post.

To Kristina, their guest looked like a scarecrow in Karl Oskar's coat and pants. It was almost a dishonor to the Church to clothe a minister this way; it was a degradation for one anointed for the Holy Church. She was tempted to laugh; she could not help but visualize the decked-out figure in a pulpit! But she must control herself; it meant nothing how Christ's servant was dressed. Christ himself had no real clothes, only a poor mantle. He did not even own boots, no shoes or footgear of any kind, but walked barefoot like a beggar. And his disciples were dressed even more poorly than the settlers of this valley.

She filled the washbowl and handed it to the minister so that he might wash off the blood on his neck and forehead. And now that she knew who he was she began to worry that the food she offered him was too poor; could one really treat a minister to warmed-up porridge?

She curtsied: would the pastor partake of their simple supper?

"Mrs. Nilsson, you could not offer food to a more grateful being than myself!"

Pastor Törner sat down at the table and turned up the right coat sleeve so that his hand was free to use the spoon. Then he filled his plate to the brim with barley porridge.

His hosts sat down a few paces from the table; they wanted to be courteous. Kristina could not quite believe what was taking place in her home this night. A man of the Church, who had stood in the pulpit and before the altar in Sweden, who had officiated at baptisms, weddings, funerals, and Holy Communion, had come to their house in the wilderness, and was sitting at their table, wearing Karl Oskar's clothes, and eating the remnants of their supper. It seemed like a miracle.

"I got wet to the skin as I was crossing a creek," said the young minister.

"The streams are overflowing with all this rain," said Karl Oskar.

"I lost my way, then I happened onto a field and realized I must be near a settlement. God has led me to this hospitable home."

With his last words Kristina suddenly held her breath. She was working up to a question.

Karl Oskar sat in amazement. Three kinds of people emigrated from Sweden: the poor and landless ones, those who preached religious opinions differing from the state Church, and those who had committed crimes. A minister was never poor, he had a home and a salary, he was well off. And he preached the right religion. So the question was, had he done something wrong? Why otherwise would a minister emigrate?

He dared a direct question: "Why did you come to America?"

"Because of the emigrants."

"Because of us . . . ?"

"Yes. I wish to help look after the souls of my countrymen. That's why I left my homeland and resigned my position there."

Pastor Törner had eaten with ravenous appetite and having scraped up the last spoonfuls of porridge from his plate, he began to talk. In his parish at home he had preached against the so-called Church Resolution, which decreed heavy punishment for those poor souls who, through negligence of the clergy, became ensnared in heresy. Fines, prison sentences on bread and water, exile—these measures, he said, did not bring any strayed souls back to the fold of the Church. You could not force people onto the right road by severe civil laws, but only through Christ's mild gospel. For sermons of this kind he had been rebuked by bishop and chapter. By the Church's grace he had been permitted to resign, and when some farm families from his parish emigrated to America, he had joined them as their pastor. He had not wished to have them or their fellow emigrants become prey to the many false teachings that were sweeping North America. In this country he aimed to give spiritual aid to his landsmen wherever he found them.

And he added, with a look at the sleeping children, "I am sent to prevent your children from growing up heathens in this foreign land."

He rose from the table. Kristina's eyes were fixed on him. This thin, pale young man, with little strength to endure physical tribulations, had traveled the same long, hazardous road and had sought them out in their new settlement to help them in their spiritual vexations.

He had come to the right place; he had himself said that God had shown him the way through the wilderness to their home.

And now she realized fully the miracle that had taken place tonight.

2.

Karl Oskar and Kristina got little sleep that night; they sat up talking to the young minister.

"I was told in St. Paul that Swedes were living near this lake," he said.

"There are only a few of us as yet," said Karl Oskar.

"I'll look up all of them."

"You say you resigned your position at home—who is paying you now?"

"No one. Kind people feed and shelter me, as you're now doing in this home."

Karl Oskar said that he thought that as a minister had spent much money on expensive schooling he ought to receive definite pay for pastoral duties.

"There's nothing stated about that in the gospels. Paid positions for pastors are human inventions."

God had nowhere ordained wages for ministers, continued Pastor Törner. The Bible said nothing about it. And Jesus promised no pay to his apostles when he sent them out to preach among all the people of the world. The apostles lived in great poverty. Christ had not designated parishes or bishoprics for them. He appointed no chapters, set forth no ecclesiastical domains. The establishment of positions for gospel preachers came about long after his life here on earth, when those in worldly power had taken over and falsified his teachings. In the present age, the official positions (the state offices) were the greatest hindrance to spreading the gospel among the people. But within a hundred years these positions would undoubtedly be discarded throughout the world, even in backward Sweden. In that country, religious persecutions had become so intense that protests had been raised by other, more enlightened, countries.*

Karl Oskar and Kristina thought their guest was a most unusual minister.

"Have people in these settlements forgotten the Ten Commandments? Have they God's Word with them here to read?" he asked.

From their Swedish chest Kristina fetched the two books which, together with the almanac, had accompanied them from their home village: Karl Oskar's confirmation Bible and her confirmation psalmbook.

"I see that all is well in this house!"

Pastor Törner had visited several Swedish settlements where God's Word was missing. In one settlement of nine families on the Illinois prairie he had been unable to find more than two Bibles; all the settlers had been physically healthy and thriving, but although he had been pleased with their worldly success he had felt depressed by their spiritual poverty; he had encountered grown men and women who remembered no more than two or three of the Commandments but he had aided them to the best of his ability. One poor old man, tottering on the edge of his grave, knew not one of the Commandments. And many were filled with hatred against Sweden and the Lutheran religion and lived happily in their conviction that the devil had ordained the authorities in that country in order to assure for himself all the souls there, without interference.

Pastor Törner had encountered no slackness in morals among his countrymen out here, he was glad to relate. He had already baptized many newborn children in the Swedish settlements, but only two had been born out of wedlock, and they had been begotten on board ship during the crossing, so those sins had not been committed here in America.

* "The situation had become so serious that the United States and several European countries sent protests to Sweden concerning the persecutions . . ." George M. Stephenson: *The Religious Aspect of Swedish Immigration*, p. 143.

Kristina had long been sitting with a question on her lips, the anxious question, so important to her:

"Could you, Mr. Pastor . . . would you be kind enough to prepare us for the Holy Communion . . . ?"

"With greatest pleasure, Mrs. Nilsson! I carry the Lord's token with me in my bag. I distribute these means of grace to all who ask for them."

"We have not enjoyed it for more than three years."

"Couldn't I hold communion for all the Swedes in this neighborhood at the same time?" wondered the young minister. "It would strengthen their spiritual solidarity."

"We live so far apart here," said Karl Oskar.

"And we have no church," said Kristina.

Pastor Törner smiled kindly and waved his hands in Karl Oskar's long sleeves, brushing away their objections with the greatest of ease. He had held communion in dense forests, on the open prairie, in log cabins and kitchens, in sheds and stables and cellars, on ox wagons, on riverboats—and a few times even in a church! What need had he, a poor God's servant, of a gilded pulpit, an expensively decorated altar, when the founder of Christianity himself had preached from a naked mount, and his disciples from dim dungeons! Should he consider himself above Jesus?

He looked about in the room: "Could I be permitted to use this home for a communion?"

Karl Oskar and Kristina looked worriedly at each other, then they answered, both at the same time: "Our home can be used, of course . . . if our simple log cabin is good enough . . . of course we will . ."

"Thank you! Then we will invite the people and set the Lord's table here in this house!"

And the minister waved his long sleeves with increased liveliness; it was already decided, then!

But it was late, their guest was tired and needed rest. Kristina said she would make a bed for Johan and Harald on the floor and let the minister sleep in their bed.

"Don't awaken the boys for my sake, Mrs. Nilsson!" he insisted. "Last night I slept under a pine tree. I'll sleep on the floor, as long as I'm under a roof."

Kristina then offered her own and Karl Oskar's bed

77

and suggested they sleep on the floor. She had an old mattress cover they could fill with hay. Karl Oskar took the cover and went out to the barn where there was hay from last year. Outside, the rain still fell in streams. In the barn, he filled the mattress with the dusty old hay and carried it inside and prepared a bed on the floor against the hearth.

"An excellent bed for me!" said the young pastor.

But Kristina would not give in: they could not allow a man of the Church to sleep on the floor, in the fireplace corner, as beggars and hoboes did at home. They could not remain in their own bed and send God's anointed to the shame-corner. It would be degrading to the Church; they would commit a grave sin. No, their best bed, their own, must be given to the guest. And she spread a clean sheet on it.

Their guest explained that he really was not a churchman, since he no longer held a position in the Church, but as their bed was offered him with a good heart he would accept.

And Pastor Törner undressed and lay down in the settler couple's bed, where he fell into a deep sleep within a few minutes.

"Poor man," said Kristina. "He was completely worn out."

And so they themselves again went to bed. This time they lay on the hay mattress, in the chimney corner, while the minister from Sweden snored heavily in their bed. Karl Oskar still wondered about him; he had given up a good position in the homeland and was wandering here through the wilderness, without food or shelter. Otherwise, his talk and general behavior seemed to indicate that he had his senses intact.

Kristina felt a blessed assurance in her heart; a stranger had come to them in the night and promised her the Lord's Supper. One night in early spring she had in her anxiety directed a question to the Almighty: What should they do about their sins here in their isolation? What must they do to save their souls?

Tonight she had been given an answer.

3.

Before Pastor Törner awakened the following morning, Kristina had found thread and a needle and mended the torn places in his coat and the hole in the seat of his pants. To have a minister walk about with pants that had a hole in the behind was a disgrace to the Church which she must at once erase. Then she brushed and cleaned his muddy clothes.

When the pastor awoke and put on his suit he hardly recognized it. He praised Kristina: "Give a woman a needle and thread and as much cloth as she needs and she can turn herself into a queen and her home into a palace!"

Kristina smiled. She was walking about in such old rags it would be a long time before she looked like a queen. But it would be a shame if a woman with a needle and thread couldn't baste together a few holes in a garment.

After breakfast Pastor Törner made ready to continue on his way. He opened his black leather bag, which contained a flask of communion wine, a small sack of communion bread, a couple of white, newly starched minister's collars, and a dozen small jars of a remedy for fever and chills. This was quinine and the price for each jar was seventy-five cents. In his bag the pastor carried remedies for both soul and body.

Another minister from Sweden, Pastor Hasselquist in Galesburg, Illinois, had come across the medicine and sent it along by Pastor Törner for those Swedish settlements where fevers and chills constantly plagued the people. Pastor Hasselquist had also hoped his colleague might earn a little by selling the medicine. But the settlers had little cash, and most of the time he had to leave the jars without payment. Many of them needed quinine for their bodies as much as they needed communion wine for their souls. He presented Kristina with a jar of the remedy as a small reward for bed and board.

He promised to return within a short time and set the date for the communion in their house. But first he wanted to call on the other Swedish settlers in the St. Croix Valley.

Karl Oskar walked a bit on the road with Pastor Törner to show him the way to their nearest neighbor, Petrus Olausson from Helsingland.

Gradually it stopped raining, and in the late morning the sun came out. Kristina picked up the mattress she and Karl Oskar had slept on; the cover seemed moist to her, perhaps it had got wet when Karl Oskar went to fetch the hay, and she wanted to dry it. She carried the mattress to the barn and emptied it near the door. She had barely finished when she let out a piercing scream. Something that looked like a dry tree branch had come out of the mattress with the hay, but she had paid scant attention to it; now she saw that it was a wriggling, living thing she had shaken out.

Karl Oskar, who was just returning, was near the stoop when he heard his wife's cries from the barn. He ran to her as fast as he could.

"A snake! Karl Oskar, a snake!"

Kristina shrieked as if someone had stuck a knife into her. She stood with the empty mattress cover in her hands, staring at the hay wads inside the door.

"What happened? Have you hurt yourself?"

She pointed in front of her: "That thing . . . it was in the mattress . . . in the hay . . . !"

Karl Oskar, standing beside her, saw in the hay a snake, extended to its full length. It was light gray with brown stripes and thick rings on its tail. A rattler!

The sight of the reptile had frightened Kristina so, she was unable to move from the spot. Karl Oskar grabbed her by the arm and pulled her away. "Get out of his reach! He might strike!"

He pushed her still farther away, while he looked for something to kill it with. "Be careful! The snake might throw himself at you!"

As yet he had never killed a rattler. He had seen such snakes, curled up in low places, but none had attacked him and he had not disturbed them. They were not so easy to dispatch as the snakes in Sweden which only
80

crawled on the ground. Rattlers were more dangerous—they could raise themselves on their tails and throw themselves at a person as fast as an arrow from a bow. But this evil thing must not escape; if it crawled under the barn they would live in eternal fear of it.

Under the oak at the side of the barn was a pile of fence posts. He grabbed one, and took down the scythe which hung in the tree. He held the scythe in front of him in his left hand and the post in his right. Thus armed he stole slowly, with bent back, toward the reptile at the barn door.

The rattler was still lying quite still in the hay; it seemed drowsy in the sun.

"Karl Oskar! Don't go so close! Be careful!"

It was Kristina's turn to urge caution. She had found a rake which she held in front of her; couldn't she help him kill the nasty creature?

Karl Oskar was a few steps from the snake when the animal raised its head. Its tongue, red and shining like a flower pistil, shot out of its jaws—the reptile was showing its stingers where death lurked. And now the rattling sound was heard from the tail rings—the warning signal; the rattler had begun to coil to throw itself against its enemy.

Karl Oskar jumped at the same time as the reptile; he threw himself forward at the very last second. With the scythe he met the snake halfway, pressed the back of the scythe against the snake, and pushed it to the ground. But the wriggling monster fought wildly and furiously, twisting and turning itself under the pressure, throwing its head back and forth until the scythe steel tinkled. The tongue's red pistil shot forth, it hissed and sizzled like a boiling kettle. Against the soft hay the flexible snake body with its sinuous motions struggled to get away from the scythe-hold.

Now the monstrous creature raised its head against the barn sill, and this gave Karl Oskar an opportunity to use his second implement: with a few heavy blows of the post he crushed the rattler's head against the sill.

"The Lord is protecting you, Karl Oskar! You risked your life!"

Kristina stood behind him, the rake in her hand, her lips blue-white, every limb trembling.

"Don't be afraid! I've killed him now!"

Karl Oskar lifted the rattler with the point of the scythe; the crushed head hung limp. Then he stretched out the snake on the ground to its full length. The first rattler he had killed was also the biggest one he had seen. It was over five feet long and had seven rattles. He had heard that this kind of snake got its first rattle at the age of three and from then on one each year; this one must be an old devil.

"That sting-eel was a little dazed and sluggish; if he had been quicker he could have killed me!"

Karl Oskar's hair was plastered to his forehead with sweat. Kristina felt her legs give way; she sank down on her knees in the hay, timidly eyeing the dead snake. The critter's upturned stomach was greenish and glittered prettily in the sun. The wild animals in North America were dangerous and beautiful.

"He purred like a spinning wheel," she said.

"That was the rattles. They're two inches thick!"

Karl Oskar pushed the scythe end into the jaws of the snake: "He has teeth like a dog! Sharp as awls! Wonder if he was blind—they say rattlers are so full of poison they go quite blind during the summer."

And Kristina knew that if a rattler bit a person in a blood vessel that ran directly to the heart, that person would die on the spot.

Her voice almost failed her as she tried to say:

"The snake was in the mattress I was emptying . . ."

Karl Oskar looked at the cover she had thrown on the ground, he looked at the rattler he had carried into their house with the hay last night. When he had filled the mattress, in the dark barn—if his hands had happened to . . .

They were both silent for several minutes.

What was there to say about what had happened during the night? They had shared their bed with the most poisonous snake in North America. They had slept their sweet sleep with death underneath them in the bed.

82

". . . to think . . . that we're all right . . ." he said in a low voice.

"Perhaps we're saved because we gave shelter to a man of the Church," said she.

With the scythe Karl Oskar cut off the tail with the seven rattles, which he wanted to keep as a souvenir. But Kristina could not understand how he could want to keep anything of the evil creature. Even though it lay dead in front of her, it still inspired fear in her.

Nevertheless, she could hardly take her eyes away from the glittering, color-changing snake body. Something so obnoxious, so slimy and repulsive, one ought not to look at willingly. But she couldn't help it. There was something strangely fascinating about the old serpent. The tempter, the devil himself, had assumed this animal's shape. It was the Evil One who had sneaked into their house last night—the Evil One had crept all the way into their bed.

Never had Kristina so surely and manifestly experienced God's protecting hand over them.

4.

Pastor Törner returned two weeks later. It was then decided that he would come back to the settlement of Duvemala the following Sunday and hold the first communion for the Swedish settlers in the St. Croix Valley.

Kristina at once began preparations. A great honor would be bestowed upon them; their home would be used as a temple. Their table, which Karl Oskar had made of a rough oak log, would be raised to the dignity of an altar. Their simple log cabin would be turned into a holy room. In their own home Karl Oskar and she would be the Lord's table guests.

She read in the Bible about the first Lord's Supper, the first day of the feast of unleavened bread, when the disciples asked Jesus where he would go to prepare to eat the Passover: he sent two of them into Jerusalem where they were to follow a man who carried a pitcher: "Follow him into the house where he entereth in. And ye shall say unto the goodman of the house, The Master saith unto thee, Where is the guestchamber, where I shall eat the Passover with my disciples? And he shall show you a large upper room furnished: there make ready."

Where is the guestchamber? When Jesus wanted to institute the Holy Supper, he, too, had looked for a place in Jerusalem where they could meet, as Pastor Törner had looked for a house among the settlers where he could give the sacrament for the first time. And in their cabin, at the Indian lake, Ki-Chi-Saga, the miracle would take place. They could not offer a great upper room, ready and furnished, as those in Jerusalem had at the first communion. They had only the single room in which they lived, in which they ate and slept and sheltered their children. But for the holy act she must put her home in order, clean it to the best of her ability.

Kristina scrubbed the floor more carefully than ever before, she washed the furniture and polished her utensils. Against the ceiling beams, and above the fireplace, she laid maple and elm boughs; the rich, fresh leaves made the room look festive. She pasted gray wrapping paper over the roughest and ugliest parts of the log walls. She picked the most beautiful wild flowers she could find but she had no vase to put them in. Her eyes fell on the spittoon at the door; she emptied it, washed it, filled it with flowers, and put it on the shelf above their table. No guest would recognize their old spit-cup elevated thus, filled with flowers and decorated with greenery.

On Saturday evening she inspected the room carefully: it was as fresh and green as a summer pavilion. Everything was in order. But what to do with the children, if it should rain and they couldn't be outside? With all the guests, there would be no room for them inside, and they might disturb the service. They could not leave them in the barn, now that they knew rattlesnakes might be there. But if it rained they must be under a roof. They would have to shut them in the cowshed during the Holy Communion. In their worn rags they were not much to show to the guests anyway.

But the weather turned out to be blessed: Sunday dawned with clear skies. Now the children could stay outside, and no one would bother to inspect their clothes too closely. She saw to it that Karl Oskar was Sunday-clean; she handed him a newly washed and ironed shirt, a wooden spoon filled with soft soap, and a bowl of luke-warm water, and then he went outside in the yard and cleaned up. Of suitable communion clothes he had none, he must wear the same clothing he had long worn to work in. Kristina herself had her black dress of which she had been so careful that it still looked nice.

On Sunday morning Pastor Törner arrived at the log cabin on foot, carrying his black leather bag with the sacred bread and the wine, and a parcel with his minister's surplice. This had become wrinkled, as he had bundled it up, and Kristina warmed her iron to press it.

As she reverently handled the ministerial garment, a thought came to her. She had not been churched after her last childbed, and Dan was more than two and a half years old. The boy was so big that she no longer could give him the breast, even though she had wanted to do so in order to delay a new pregnancy. Should she ask the young pastor to church her? But perhaps by now so much time had elapsed that it was too late. A wife ought to be churched before she knew her husband carnally, and in that respect it was more than two years too late in her case. Should she now ask the pastor if it was too late for her?

She felt ashamed to ask him. Perhaps he would be greatly upset that she delayed two and a half years after the childbed. She remembered her mother saying that it would have the same effect as churching if a woman shook a minister's hand. And she had shaken hands with this young pastor each time he had come to their house. Could this be sufficient? Why couldn't it be counted the same as churching? She did not know. But as long as Pastor Törner remained in the neighborhood, she would continue to shake his hand whenever she had the opportunity.

The communion guests had begun to arrive, and as they entered the cabin, Pastor Törner wrote down their names in turn. He recorded that Danjel Andreasson of New Kärragärde was present, accompanied by his two sons, Sven and Olof, who were of confirmation age and today for the first time would go to the Lord's table. Jonas Petter and his housekeeper, Swedish Anna, had also arrived on Danjel's ox cart. From Taylors Falls came Mother Fina-Kajsa and her son, Anders Mansson. The old woman was perky and talkative but looked unkempt, her gray, matted hair in tufts. Anders Mansson was shaved and combed, but his eyes were bloodshot, and he seemed shy and depressed; he seldom showed himself among people. Petrus Olausson and his wife, Judit, had brought along their daughter, who, like Danjel's boys, was to participate in her first communion.

With Karl Oskar and Kristina, there were twelve communicants in all. All the Swedes in the valley who had received an invitation had come, except one: Samuel Nöjd, the trapper in Taylors Falls. He had said to Swedish Anna, who had brought him the message, that he did not wish to participate in any of the foolery or spectacles of the priests. He had hoped, out here, to be left in peace by those black-capped sorcerers who in Sweden had plagued him with their catechism and religious examinations. Swedish Anna had replied that Jesus had also redeemed his soul with his dear blood, but this Samuel Nöjd had denied: his soul was not to be redeemed by anybody, whatever the price, for he was a free, thinking human being.

The sturdy, red-hued Swedish Anna was greatly disturbed over the blasphemer Nöjd and his way of living: recently, he had taken in an Indian woman to live with him, and what he did to her, each and every one could imagine. He was known to be heathenish, and now he was also carnally mixing with the heathens.

Swedish Anna was considered a deeply religious woman and she was looked up to by her countrymen for her irreproachable morals. Kristina had a deep respect for this woman from Dalecarlia. Swedish Anna was a kindhearted women, but kept so strictly to the true religion that she had difficulty in enduring Ulrika after she had turned Baptist, but Kristina defended Ulrika when Swedish Anna called her a hypocrite and a slovenly woman.

Danjel Andreasson praised his niece for having decorated the cabin so nicely: it was attractive and made up to look like a real church, he said.

The table stood in the middle of the room, and Karl Oskar had put planks on sawhorses for the people to sit on. When all were seated there was no place for him, so he went to the woodshed and brought in the chopping block for a chair. The fresh planks smelled pungently of pine and pitch. On the foodboard Kristina had spread her only tablecloth of whole linen, ironed and shining white. There stood the pitcher with the communion wine, and one of Karl Oskar's huge *brännvin* glasses which was to be used as a communion cup. On a small plate lay the communion bread, thin, flat, dry breads, not unlike cookies.

Pastor Törner took his place at the end of the table where the family Bible lay open. His cheeks were newly shaven and shiny, and his thick, light hair was combed straight back. As he stood there in his newly ironed surplice and white collar, Karl Oskar and Kristina could not imagine that this was the same man who on that rainy night had sought shelter in their cabin, dripping like a wet dog, his clothes torn, muddy, his face bloody with mosquito bites.

Today the sun shone through the windows and through the open door into the settlers' home, and in there the Lord's table stood prepared. The immigrants were to partake of their first communion in the new country.

The young minister pointed out that there had been twelve communicants when Jesus gathered his apostles for the first Lord's Supper in Jerusalem, there were twelve here today when he would now distribute Christ's flesh and blood to his countrymen in the wilderness. In his wine flask here on the table he had only very little left of the dear sacrament, which therefore must be divided with great economy to make it last for all. There would hardly be more than a sip, a small teaspoon for each one. Bread, however he had in sufficiency.

They were ready to begin and the pastor gave the number of the opening psalm. Just then Dan, the baby, came rushing in from outside, yelling at the top of his voice. The boy stopped in the doorway and howled. Kristina jumped up and took him in her arms. The child had done both his needs in his pants. She turned to the minister, greatly vexed: this was most embarrassing—would he forgive her but she must first look after . . .

She took the boy outside and cleaned him and dried his behind. Then she let him run without pants—it was warm enough. Dan was a troublesome child; he still whined and complained because he no longer could have her breast; but while she was still suckling him he had grown several sharp teeth, and when he was hungry and impatient he would bite into her nipples until she yelled with pain. Now she put a small piece of maple sugar into his mouth to make him keep quiet and be on his way.

Pastor Törner had been waiting patiently while she attended to the boy; he only smiled at the little one as he cried and carried on. She very much liked this minister who never showed any severity. He seemed to realize that a small, innocent child, only lately a suckling, could not wait to do his business until the service was over.

Now the pastor took up the psalm: "For thy wounds, O Jesus dear, for thy anguish and thy suffering . . ." He himself sang with a powerful, vibrant voice, but his communicants in the cabin had trouble with their singing. They had only a few psalmbooks—three or four people jostled for each one—and it was a long time since they had attempted psalm singing.

The minister read the text:

". . . And hath made of one blood all nations of men for to dwell on the face of the earth, and hath determined the times before appointed, and the bounds of their habitation; that they should seek the Lord, if haply they might feel after him, and find him, though he be not far from every one of us . . ."

At the sound of the holy words the participants sat stone still as if bound to their seats. These settlers, who at home had attended services almost every Sunday, had not listened to a sermon in years. And now they heard God's Word again, in their native tongue, spoken by a minister, spoken well and beautifully. They listened, tense and still.

"I speak to settlers," continued the minister, "to people who have left their homes in the Old World to build new homes in a new continent; that is why I have chosen the text from the seventeenth chapter of the Acts. More than eighteen hundred years ago these words were uttered by St. Paul to the Greeks in the judicial place in the town of Athens, but they have a meaning to the immigrant Swedes of Minnesota today: wherever human beings live on the earth, they are of the same blood, the same race, and the Lord lives near them. He is not far from us at this moment, in this settler home."

Twelve immigrant Swedes listened, packed together in the small log cabin. Twelve pairs of eyes were riveted upon the young minister at the head of the table. The twelve listened, and their lips parted, their mouths opened, as if their ears were unable alone to catch the speaker's words.

"God has decided to what distances on the earth people shall travel and move their habitations!" The minister made a sweeping gesture with his hands, as if wanting to measure the journey's length. "I speak to men and women who have traveled over one third of the earth's circumference, who have moved from one continent to another, in order to found new homes in these wild forests. You, my countrymen gathered here, have participated in an emigration covering a greater distance than ever before in human history!"

And his countrymen listened. It was a sermon all of them understood well: it was about themselves. They had forsaken that part of the earth where their forebears had lived for thousands of years, to wander to another part of the globe where they still were aliens. This sermon explained the fate which the Creator in his inscrutable wisdom had prepared for them—the fate of emigrants.

Karl Oskar recalled his parting from Dean Brusander, who had depicted North America as a sky-high Babylon of sin and who had told him that, through his emigration, he broke the Ten Commandments. It was a comfort now to learn from another minister that their emigration was not contrary to God's will; rather, it sounded as if God had planned and arranged for their move.

Kristina thought that the pastor there at the end of the table was himself a proof that the Lord had not forsaken them in a foreign country. She knew who had sent him to their distant dwelling; the Almighty knew the roads even in the unbroken Territory.

She listened to the minister intently, but also with half an ear to the yard outside; if the kids only didn't start yelling or coming in to disturb them! They had been told to keep as quiet as mice. But through the open door she could hear the brood-hen cackling, persistently. What an awkward sound, coming like that between the words of a sermon! It was a fine hen, this present from Ulrika; already she had deserted her chicks and started to lay. Now she must have laid an egg in some bush behind the cabin; she could hear it in the tone of the hen's cackling: she wanted to announce that she had just laid an egg. Why couldn't she have waited to lay that egg until a little later in the day, after the sermon . . .

"The Lord has decided where people shall live. To you emigrating Swedes he has indicated Minnesota. The brown-skinned sons of the wilderness have ruled this land for centuries. But the Almighty sweeps away one race from the surface of the earth and plants another. You are the new race to build the land. But it is your duty, my dear countrymen who are born in a Christian land and know the Ten Commandments, to treat these heathens as brethren. Indians, too, are our neighbors; they are not of the same color as we, but they have the same Creator. Be kind and patient with the vanishing race . . ."

The hen outside cackled ever more lustily. Kristina turned in her seat; it sounded as if the obnoxious creature had made up her mind to drown the minister's voice! Had ever a pastor endured such a hen cackle during a sermon? Kristina was grateful for the new egg, but if she could have imagined that the critter would have made so much noise for the sake of an egg, she would have locked the hen in the barn before they began. What must the minister think? He was so kind, he wouldn't reprimand her for not keeping her feathered livestock under control.

He continued his sermon, without appearing in the least disturbed by the critter, and none of the other listeners paid any attention to the hen. But now the cackling was right outside the door. The hen was accustomed to come here for food when the door was open. And the door was open now . . . If the hen should come tripping into the room . . . Once she had flown up on the table—suppose the beast repeated that maneuver! What would they do? It would reflect on them. Oh, if that shameless creature would only stay outside . . . !

The service continued, and the hen did not come in, God be praised. And it seemed no one except Kristina had heard its cackling. Soon she too was able to close her ears to the bird's chatter and entirely immerse herself in the minister's words.

In the cabin it was as still as if everyone had stopped breathing; no noise or sound in the whole world could disturb this, the settlers' service, in Karl Oskar's and Kristina's home. And soon the communion would begin, and they would sit down at their own table and receive Christ's flesh and blood, which would lift the three-years burden of their sins. Today they were guests in their own house.

5.

"Kneel and read after me the confession of your sins!"

Twelve people knelt around the table. Twelve had gathered around Jesus at the first supper, and Pastor Törner had seen a deep significance in the fact that the number of guests here was the same as it had been at the institution of the Sacrament: Christ's Church would be rebuilt here in the wilderness.

The minister read the confession. The kneeling men, women, and children each read after him in his or her own way, some loudly and openly, some in low and mumbling voices. Child voices repeated the words clearly, vibrantly; thick male voices halted and stammered:

". . . and I have in all my days—from my childhood, even until this moment—many and bitter sins committed . . ."

The communion guests knelt on the floor, their hands folded over their breasts, their heads bowed. Married couples knelt side by side, and children next to their parents. It was crowded for the twelve around the table, but no one pushed for space; they pressed their arms close to their bodies, kneeling in a circle around the table. It was intensely warm outside, and with the crowding it began to grow hot inside. Drops of perspiration appeared on foreheads and cheeks. A breath of wind from the door felt blissfully cool. From the outside no more sounds were heard from two-legged or four-legged livestock. But in the midst of the confession, suddenly lusty child laughter reached them from the yard.

". . . thine holy words I have often neglected and avoided . . ."

Some were behind in their reading, and the young minister repeated the words slowly, so that the stragglers would catch up.

One of the participants needed no one to read the words for him—Danjel Andreasson. He knew the confession word for word, and he knelt there on the floor as if reading to himself, as if he were alone in the cabin. Thousands of times he had repeated these confessional words, both aloud for others and silently for himself, and each syllable was familiar to his tongue.

At a sound from the door, Danjel turned his head. But it was only the wind stirring. Did he expect some other caller? At his last communion, in the old country, he himself had distributed the holy sacrament, and it had taken place in the night, in his own home, because he had been denied the sacrament by the clergy. And while he had been thus occupied, a noise had been heard at the door. He had gone to open it, and in had come the dean and the sheriff, who forcefully had scattered the guests at the Lord's table. All had been fined or imprisoned, he himself exiled. When he confessed his sins in Sweden he violated law and authority.

Danjel Andreasson was exiled from his homeland, but not from the Kingdom of God.

And now he was here in the new land which the Lord had promised him. He need not now fear any disturbers of the peace. Here no worldly authority would interfere with their gathering. What he heard from the door was

92

only the cool summer wind which blew over the grass and the trees. It was not the noise of a sheriff, not the hard, commanding voice of authority, silencing the voice of conscience in the name of the law, writing ordinances for people's souls. It was the Lord's own voice Danjel Andreasson heard in the sounds from outside—it was God's free wind, blowing hither and yon over the earth of his new homeland.

Kristina was kneeling to the left of her uncle Danjel and to the right of her husband. Karl Oskar got mixed up in his confession, he read haltingly and fell behind. And Kristina herself found that in a few places she had forgotten the words. She caught herself making mistakes.

". . . I have had lust to evil: I have been vain; I have sought the wicked and sinful world . . . I have been greedy, covetous, short in compassion, gluttonous . . ."

With tense breath and trembling lips she enumerated all the sins and transgressions she had committed. While repeating the words after the minister, she was overwhelmed by the multitude of her wrongdoings. Contrition overtook her, repentance burned in her breast. But only through repentance could she become worthy of participation in this sacrament. And while she repeated the confession, and her lips moved, she prayed a wordless prayer within her: "O Lord, give me repentance . . . ! Help me repent enough . . . !"

Karl Oskar's bowed head was close to hers. His face was quite unlike itself today; it was hard and solemn, severe and closed. Had he repented enough, did he repent deeply enough now, was he worthy? She would have liked to whisper to him: You must not confess your sins with your lips only! You must not enumerate them the way you reel off the chores you've performed, at the end of each day! You must confess from your heart! You must feel *forced* to do it! Unable to refuse! You must feel your sin burden as so heavy that you're unable to struggle another step without forgiveness! You must be consumed with hunger for the bread, thirst for the wine, yearning for forgiveness!

"Whosoever eateth of this bread and drinketh from this cup, he receiveth the Lord's body and blood . . ."

You must repent, Karl Oskar, repent, repent, repent! You who receiveth . . . but I myself . . . ? Do I repent sufficiently . . . ?

"My grievous and many sins press me hard and are like unto a burden too heavy . . ."

Kristina's limbs began to tremble. Her knees began to shake as she held them bent against the floorboards. For a moment she was on the verge of falling forward. Perhaps her heart's repentance was not complete. Perhaps it was not sufficient to kneel at the Lord's altar. Perhaps she should bend still lower, feel greater humiliation, throw her face against the ground, lay herself at the Lord's feet, become dust and ashes under the Creator's tread . . .

The confession was over. The floorboards began to sway under her.

"Show thy Grace to me, wretched sinner that I am, and receive thy dear son Jesus Christ's innocent suffering and death as a full payment for all my sins!"

The minister asked, "Do you ask with a repentant heart the forgiveness of your sins?"

Kristina's reply was a faint whisper only, barely audible to herself, but it was a whisper that shook her whole being: "Yes . . . yes . . . you know it, Lord . . . I've prayed to you for this moment. For long, long, I've wished it. I've waited and wished and prayed. You know how I've wished forgiveness through the sacrament. And you have heard my prayer . . . you came to me here in my home—during the night . . . Now I am ready—I am prepared to approach thy table, to be thy guest . . . I come . . ."

She leaned her forehead against the edge of the table so as not to fall. Her surroundings began to blur, she felt so dizzy. She could hear the minister's voice, but not what he said. She heard psalm-singing, but not the words of the psalm. Human bodies were close to her, but she recognized them no longer. For now she was alone. She was alone in the world with her Savior, who on the cross had paid her sin debt with the blood which flowed from his spike wounds:

Behold, behold, all ye present . . .
How sorely Jesus suffers . . .

The words of the psalm completed the contrition. They cut through her breast, opened it wide, and exposed her repentant heart. Trembling and dizziness were upon her. Now she must submit, become dust; she had a sensation of fainting . . . fainting away . . .

So as Jesu' suffering was,
No one's suffering ever was . . .

Then came the sobs which shook her, the first tears, trickling. People around her cried, loudly, steadily; to the right and to the left of her they sobbed and wept. But she did not hear them, she was absorbed in her own tears, surrendered to her own weeping, blissfully unresistible. So overpowering a weeping had not come on her since she was a little child.

And so it took place, while dissolved in tears, kneeling there as if separated from all other people, liberated from all earthly things, as if she were the only human being in the whole creation—thus Kristina, for the first time since her emigration, partook of the Lord's Holy Supper.

Afterward she felt dazed and exhausted. Her limbs still trembled but it felt good in both body and soul to tremble this way. And on her face, her tears now dried by themselves—now the Savior dried them all from her cheeks. Her breast was still full and tense, her breathing still hot—but it was now only with joy that her heart overflowed.

Kristina had been a guest in her own house. And afterward she felt lighter of heart, more satisfied, than she had ever been since arriving in North America.

V. Man and Woman in the Territory

1.

About midsummer the little Swedish colony at Ki-Chi-Saga was increased by two new families; Lars Sjölin and his wife Ellida, a childless couple from Hassela, Helsingland, took land at the lakeside below Petrus Olausson's claim, across from Nordberg's Island. They were both in their forties. From Kettilstad in Östergötland came Algot Svensson and his wife Manda, who settled on a piece of land to the west of Duvemala. They were about the same age as Karl Oskar and Kristina and had five small children. It was further known that several families had come from Småland and were squatting along the southern shores of the lake, and that still more Smålanders were on their way.

Immigrants from three Swedish provinces had found new homes around the big Indian lake. Karl Oskar and Kristina had Helsingland neighbors to the southeast and Östergötland neighbors to the west. Now they speculated where people would come from to claim the still unoccupied piece of land to the north of them.

They became acquainted with their new neighbors from Östergötland at once. Algot Svensson was a kind, small man, rather taciturn, the kind of settler who made little noise. His wife, Manda, on the contrary, was sociable, jolly, ever ready to talk. She related that she came from an old, well-to-do farmer family and that her parents had rejected her for marrying the hired hand on the farm. Manda Svensson had brought with her from Sweden two loom reeds, one of which she now presented to Kristina, who did not own one. The winter before, Karl Oskar had made with great difficulty a primitive loom, but he had been unable to make the reed, and there was no reed-maker among the settlers. Kristina almost jumped with joy at the gift from her neighbor. Through Ulrika's efforts she had last year obtained a spinning wheel from Stillwater; it had been made for her by the Norwegian, Thomassen, who was both shoemaker and spinning-wheel maker. She had already spun last year's flax, and with the blessed reed she could weave new clothing for them next winter; no one in the family had any longer an unpatched garment to put on.

Hard winter work awaited Kristina, while Karl Oskar labored most intensely during the warmer seasons. He was working on his threshing barn, which he hoped to have ready when the crops were ripe so that he could flail them under shelter. In years before, the ice had been his threshing floor, and the crops had lain unthreshed until the lake was ready to put down its floor; meanwhile, the pestiferous rats, mice, and other rodents had taken a sizable toll from his rye and barley. By putting up a threshing barn he would save many loaves for his family.

Now he split shakes for the barn roof, cut and worked the timbers for his new main house, dug on the foundation for his cellar, put up fences, mowed and dried grass and put the hay in stacks. All these chores must be done before the crops were ripe, when harvesting would take all his time.

When he was preparing the ground for the winter wheat field his southeast neighbor came and filled his ears with praise of the Indian corn. A word of advice from Petrus Olausson seemed like a command: let the field lie over winter and plant corn next spring!

Olausson had already planted this wonderful grain on his claim, he had begun banking the plants when they were an inch tall, and now they grew an inch a day in this heat. Corn would give up seventy bushels an acre. But he must choose the right kind of seed, the big kind, which gave ten ears to each plant, and three or four hundred kernels to each ear! Several thousand grains from one seed, many thousandfold! Because of sinful man, God had cursed the ground, but over one of the grains he had let flow his blessing—over the Indian corn! And corn was the healthiest and tastiest of foods for people and animals;

97

bread was baked of corn, porridge and soup was cooked from it, pancakes made, a potent drink brewed, sugar distilled; livestock and hogs were fattened on it. Corn bread was the healthiest ever, it had in it some purgative power which gave the body its blessed opening; bread from Indian corn was the best remedy against hard bowels.

It was called lazy-man's grain because the Indians cultivated it in their small patches, letting their poor women tend it alone. Karl Oskar wondered why God had so richly blessed the heathens' corn above the grains of Christian people.

Petrus Olausson said that the name lazy-man's grain did not suit the corn since it did not grow by itself, like hair on a head or nails on toes and fingers; it needed constant attention—weeding, hoeing, banking. But a well-cared-for field of corn at the peak of its growth was the most beautiful sight God had created on this earth.

Until Olausson raised corn none of the Swedes in the valley had tried this grain. They stuck to their old crops and were suspicious of new kinds. For what good could be expected from the Indians' wretched farming? It was like dealing with the Evil One directly.

But after Karl Oskar had seen his neighbor's cornfield he decided to plant some himself next year. He was never afraid of new ventures. And why shouldn't a Christian Swede follow the heathens' example, if it was good and useful? Why shouldn't he grow the wild ones' grain?

If the hot Minnesota summers made the corn grow an inch a day, the humid heat sucked one's strength. In the evenings Karl Oskar fell asleep, completely worn out. A settler was said to get used to the heat after a few years, but to him it was the same ordeal summer after summer. The heat squeezed and sucked the sweat from his body until he felt completely dried out. The nights were the worst; the heat interfered with breathing and prevented sleep; hot, humid air penetrated his nose and mouth and made breathing heavy and cumbersome. It was as if wet wool wads had been put into his mouth. His lungs worked slowly and laboriously and his heart felt like a heavy invisible lump in his breast.

The cabin became unbearably sultry during the nights,

so when Karl Oskar was unable to sleep, he walked outside and lay down on the ground behind the house. Here
he had no bedding other than the cool grass, no cover except the dark night sky with the tiny star lights. Stretched
out on this grass mattress he would at last go to sleep although only to dream tortuous dreams of choking.

2.

The shakes were ready to be put on the new threshing
barn and Karl Oskar had asked Jonas Petter and Anders
Mansson to help him. He himself placed the shakes in
straight rows, Jonas Petter nailed them down, and Mansson acted as handyman, fetching and carrying up and
down the ladder. On the roof, the sun burned like a brand-
ing iron; up there it was too hot even to fry bacon, said
Jonas Petter; the sun would burn it to cinders.

The men had to quench their thirst every quarter of an
hour; they drank gallons of cold buttermilk to which had
been added fresh, cool spring water. Once every hour
they rested in the shade of the maples, stretched out
dazed and indifferent. Even Jonas Petter held his tongue
for long periods, obviously not himself.

The Ölander, Mansson, was stingy with words in any
company. His eyelids were swollen and there was also a
swelling over his cheekbones; he did not look well. Time
and again he went on a binge and ended "flat on his
back," his mother said. He neglected his claim because he
was busy emptying whiskey kegs, and this spring he had
had to sell a cow to pay his debts.

Jonas Petter had said to him, "Take a wife! Then you'll
have so much to do at night that you'll have neither time
nor strength to drink in the daytime! But if you must
drink—do it in the morning when you're sober!"

Anders Mansson had proposed to Ulrika but she had
married another man. And how many women remained to
propose to?

The Ölander said, "In this country a man is forced to
live single."

"A hell of a shame that a young buck like you must remain a bachelor!"

But Jonas Petter knew how things were—what could a man do here in the Territory, with one woman to twenty men? Nineteen of the twenty had to lie alone, sighing, lusting, suffering. Here men slept in their lonely beds night after night, year in, year out, until white moss grew on their tool.

Those who couldn't stand it forever, continued Jonas Petter, must do as Samuel Nöjd did, he had taken an Indian girl to live with him. She was skinny as a bird and had a dirty face but had a pretty good shape. Jonas Petter himself had seen several Indian wenches a white man could get hopped up about. Their black eyes burned with something that roused a fire in one's loins. But it was forbidden on the Tablets of Stone for a Christian Lutheran to spill his seed in the chambers of heathendom's daughters. But perhaps the Tablets of Stone were not in force in a wild land with a scarcity of women. When God made Eve he told Adam he was giving him the help a man needed. According to the Bible, then, every man had a right to have a woman in his bed. And the Bible said nothing about a man and a woman having the same color skin in order to lie in bed together.

Karl Oskar said that as far as he was concerned he couldn't have bed play with an Indian woman however long he might have to go without.

"If you had to, you would do it!" insisted Jonas Petter.

Anders Mansson said, "I know white men who have made children in brown women."

"They're all right in the hole, although too tight," said Jonas Petter. "Yet, they drop their brats like rabbits; perhaps their children come on the thin, narrow side."

Jonas Petter had figured out a remedy for the lack of women in the Territory: they ought to write to the authorities in Sweden and ask for a shipload of women. All men who lived alone must sign a petition, and then they would send it to Dean Brusander of Ljuder Parish. He could announce from the pulpit that unmarried girls were in demand as wives for the settlers of this women-empty country. He would have no trouble getting a shipful of fine women. Only honest, upright, chaste, capable women must volunteer, of course; no slut in the load.

And the women must have definite promises of marriage; each man who signed the petition would guarantee to marry a girl the moment she arrived in Minnesota Territory. No need to wait. The men must promise in writing to relieve the girls of their maidenheads on the day of arrival, or at least not later than the following night; they must promise this honestly and conscientiously as decent men and citizens. If any one of the women had her maidenhead intact the following morning at sunup, she would have a right to claim a thousand-dollar indemnity.

Anders Mansson laughed. Karl Oskar only smiled a little; ever since leaving their home village he had heard Jonas Petter's continuous stories of women and bed play and it was beginning to bore him. Such talk might be excused in younger men who were familiar with the words but not the act; between grown men there were more important things to talk about. He had his own strong desires and he suffered greatly when pregnancies and childbeds prevented him from knowing his wife, but at other times they enjoyed each other and were well pleased. To him, this act belonged to secrecy and night and became unclean and profaned when men spoke of it in daylight openly and directly.

But Anders Mansson loved Jonas Petter's tales. When the roofers took their next rest in the shade of the maples, Anders turned to him and said, "Tell us a good story!"

Jonas Petter dried his forehead slowly with a handkerchief stiff as bark from many days' sweat. Today the weather was not suitable for storytelling; in this heat Jonas Petter's head stood still. But he remembered a true happening that had taken place recently concerning a man and a woman here in North America. It was a serious story which anyone might learn from and find useful, for it was a story of loneliness.

This is what had happened:

A middle-aged man and a woman of the same age emigrated from the same land in the Old World and settled down in the same neighborhood in the New World. They

101

met, and the woman was employed to run the man's house.

In the old country the man still had a wife, whom he had left because they couldn't get along; he was so tired of his life with her that, to be on the safe side, he had managed to put the Atlantic Ocean between himself and his marital bed. In the New World he sought peace. The woman who ran his house said that she had emigrated for the same reason. She had a good mind, a fine body, healthy and unused. Among her countrymen she was held in great esteem for her honesty, chastity, and religious devotion.

The man treated her well and they got along fine. She looked after his house, cooked his food, mended his clothes, prepared his breakfast in the morning and his bed in the evening. They never used evil or angry words between them. During the day they shared the work hours and the moments of rest and enjoyed each other's company. Not until bedtime did they part; then they slept in different beds, in different rooms. Then the man became the master of the house, the woman, the housekeeper in his employ.

The man had already lived a whole year without a woman. But that which his body had been accustomed to for twenty-five years could not be denied without loss and suffering. He was not meant for a hermit's bed. He was a sociable man and he valued highly the company of women, even outside the bed. In their presence he felt an increased well-being. And here he had a woman under his roof, within reach all day long. And so when evening came, bedtime, it seemed only natural to him to extend their companionship to include the night and the bed.

A person will suffer a loss more keenly if what he has lost is within view yet beyond reach. Thus it happened with this man; in the lonely night he lay awake, he pined and yearned. Only a wall separated the man and the woman. She was so close here in his house—so close and so unreachable. A few steps would take him to the woman's bed, but those steps were longer than the distance between Sweden and North America. The man had emigrated to the New World to find peace. But when the woman came to his house, restlessness and distraction had moved in with her.

He was tempted to go in to her and confess his great suffering and plead with her to have compassion on him and satisfy his will. But each evening through the wall, he could hear her read her evening prayer and the confession in such a forceful and compelling voice that his courage failed him. How could a man go in to a woman who had just confessed her sins and try to tempt her to a new sin?

At length, however, the thought struck him that he could at least confess to the woman the sinful lust he felt for her. This confidence she could hardly take ill; it was only right for a Christian to lay bare his honest heart and his lustful thoughts and desires. At the same time he could use the opportunity to ask her forgiveness.

Thus one evening, shortly after she had retired, he went in and sat down on a chair beside her bed, timid and embarrassed; he had something important to tell her. And he confessed honestly that he looked upon her with desire.

She was not insulted, not even surprised. She replied that she had already guessed he was exposed to this great suffering. And she had read God's Word as loud as she had just so he might hear it and gain strength from it against his temptation.

He said he would have liked to ask her to become his wife, but he already had a wife in the old country, and bigamy was a great sin with which he did not wish to burden his conscience. And anyway, here in the wilderness, he was unable to obtain the papers necessary to commit this sin.

The woman then told him something which stunned him: she too was married. She too had a mate alive in Sweden. They were equally bad off. She had married a miserable man who drank and caroused and lay about instead of earning a living for his wife and children. She had supported that good-for-nothing louse for many years, but when he rewarded her by whoring with other women, she had tired of stuffing his gullet; she had taken their two children and had emigrated. During the crossing both children had died of the ship sickness. She had arrived in the New World alone and without relatives, and she had decided to live alone ever after without menfolk.

He was a good employer, she told him, and she liked living in his house. But if she moved into his bed, or he to hers, then they would commit double bigamy, since both of them were married. And if an accident, or some other sudden death, should overtake her, and she had to depart unforgiven, she would be condemned to eternal fire in Hell for this grave sin against the sixth commandment. Therefore, everything must remain between them as it was.

To this the man replied that the sixth commandment was written many thousands of years ago on the Stone Tablets for a Jewish country with as many women as men, or perhaps more women than men. God could not have intended this law for settlers in Minnesota Territory, where women and men were so unequally proportioned as one to twenty. God could not have written laws for America many thousand years before that country had been discovered. He didn't do things that far in advance. Therefore, the sixth commandment could not have been meant for Minnesota, at least not in all its severity. Here life began anew, as in Genesis, where God made a woman for the man. And the Creator's intent was that even out here every man should be allowed to live with a woman for comfort and enjoyment. Why, then, must they be condemned by a many-thousand-years-old law on a stone tablet? Furthermore, Moses might have misunderstood the sixth commandment; he had grown rather old and his eyes and hearing were poor by that time.

And they got along well during the day, persisted the man. It could not be held against them as a great sin if they also had their bed in common.

The woman replied that in her marriage she had greatly enjoyed the bed play with her husband and that during her years of loneliness she had often missed it. But it was not indispensable to her and the pleasure was not of so great a duration that its price was worth eternal torture. Whoever was willing to pay such an outrageous price must be a big fool.

But she appreciated deeply his confession and she

wanted to help him further to fight his desires—if it would aid him any she would read the confession still more loudly each evening.

The man had to leave the woman's bedside, his purpose thwarted, and everything between them remained as before.

As time passed they grew more and more intimate. And at bedtime it seemed more and more difficult for him to part from her and repair to his own lonely bed. His conviction grew stronger for each day that the Stone Tablets from Mount Sinai were not meant for Minnesota.

A year passed, then one evening the woman came in to him after he had gone to bed. She in turn had a confession to make: they had lived so long under the same roof that she had become a victim of the same temptations as he.

A woman's body too was made of flesh and blood, and it was not easy for her to live so close to a man for years, with only a wall between them. Many times a day she prayed to God for help against her temptation, unable to overcome it by herself, fragile human being that she was. But to her great consternation God had not answered her prayers. What could he mean by this? She had been at a loss for an answer. And the Lord's ways were said to be inscrutable. Here she had been left to fight her temptation all alone. And she had long withstood it—it had begun to assail her many months ago—she had repelled it; again and again, she had been the victor. Scores of evenings she had been visited so grievously by her desire that she had been on the verge of leaving her bed to seek him out. But she had summoned all her strength to conquer her desire. At last her strength had given out, she was no longer able to conquer her desire. What should she do now, when her prayers hadn't been heard? At last she could do nothing else but commit this weakness—sin—here she stood in all her weakness, beside his bed in nothing but her shift; she wished to comply with his desire. Why hadn't God given her strength to fight off her temptation?

This the man could explain: a person's prayers were heard only when asking for something good and useful. And it was good for neither her nor his that they slept in

105

different beds. Why should they lie apart and suffer in two separate beds when they could enjoy themselves together in one bed? So now they could both see what God's finger was pointing at: two miserable creatures in an empty wilderness; she missed a man, he a woman, and their Creator had taken pity on them and had brought them together for comfort and joy.

So the woman stayed with the man, and in his bed nothing was left undone during the night.

Next evening he in turn went to her, only to meet a horrible disappointment. She would no longer give herself to him. She was deeply repentant and had decided never to repeat what had taken place the night before. And now she wanted, she insisted, yes, she demanded, that he should help her carry out her decision. She wanted him to join her in prayer for strength for both of them—first and foremost for her—to withstand in future their unclean thoughts and desires.

The man was greatly disturbed at this demand. He realized what great danger they might be in—the danger of their prayer being heard. Perhaps not so much when it came to strength for himself; he didn't anticipate any change there. But he knew what could happen to a woman's strength. Women were always on and off, back and forth, in between.

He made excuses: people must not pray for things that weren't good for them. And it wasn't good for them with separate beds. And too persistent and stubborn prayers were against the Almighty's will.

But the woman refused to budge. He was a fellow criminal in a sin she had committed last night, it was his duty to help her stand fast. If he refused she would no longer remain in his house.

Thus he was forced to comply. He prayed with her, although without great fervor. The words came from his lips rather than from his heart, which was secretly sad over them.

Time passed; they lived apart as before. Neither one of them referred to that single good night when they had shared one bed. As far as the woman was concerned she seemed to have stricken it from her memory, and the man sensed it would not be wise to remind her of it.

Then one evening after he had gone to bed his door opened—the woman had come to him again. All her prayers had been in vain, her great weakness was upon her again, she could not resist it.

The man offered her all the comfort he was capable of. And that night too they left nothing undone on his couch.

Again the woman regretted her act and her weakness and insisted it would not be repeated. And he said nothing, only waited in patience. Now he knew she would be back in his bed again, as indeed she was after the expected delay.

By and by a regular order was established in their lives, with two bed communions a week. This satisfied the man. And to the woman the in-between-time of repentance was indispensable. She admitted that repentance to her was a bliss she could not do without. For the peace of her soul she needed the assurance that her sin was forgiven each time.

Luckily, she had passed a woman's fertile years so they need not fear a pregnancy. Their bed play need never be known. People would have censored them severely if they were discovered. But only their Creator knew how things were between them, and they relied on his silence.

Thus everything turned out well with the man and the woman. They had both found the peace they sought in the New World, and the woman could besides enjoy the sweet repentance she felt after each new fall.

Thus this man and this woman lived happily together, and if they weren't dead yet, they were probably still alive, concluded Jonas Petter.

Karl Oskar looked askance at the storyteller after he had finished his tale. He remembered a Sunday morning last winter when he had happened to have an errand at Jonas Petter's house. He had knocked on the door but no one had opened it. Perhaps they had already gone out. To make sure he had looked in through the window and had seen Jonas Petter and Swedish Anna sound asleep in the bed under the window.

Karl Oskar had turned away and walked over to Dan-

107

jel's to visit for an hour. When he returned Jonas Petter was outside the house, inspecting the window.

So Jonas Petter had told this story to make it clear that he relied on the silence of the man who had seen him with Swedish Anna. Only Karl Oskar and the Creator were in the know.

Anders Mansson, however, had listened with the expression of one hearing a wonderful fairy tale. Jonas Petter's stories struck him as being completely unreal, but he always listened intently and asked for more.

"That's a good story, Jonas Petter! How can you make up such yarns?"

It was time for the men to resume their work on the roof in the humid heat of the Minnesota summer. As they began to nail down the shakes again, Mansson said, "There's a small part of truth in that story—that part about the menfolks' loneliness out here. It's like a hot iron right through the heart, this terrifying loneliness in Minnesota Territory."

The storyteller kept his silence. And the third roofer thought that never to a living being, not even to his wife, would he betray what he knew of the man and the woman who had been brought to share their bed through loneliness in the St. Croix Valley.

VI. Starkodder the Ox

1.

To plant and to seed, to harvest and to thresh, that was the order of the chores from spring to fall, the cycle of labor, year in, year out. Karl Oskar Nilsson had cut, harvested, and threshed his third crop from the clearing. His old Swedish almanac contained blank pages between the months, intended for a farmer's notations; on these he had written down his harvests in Americ

> Anno 1851 I harvested 18 bussels
> Rye, 11 bussels Barley and 32 bus-
> sels potatoes, all ample measure;
> Ditto 1852 harvested 24 bussels Rye,
> 16 and a half bussels Barley and 48
> bussels potatoes, ditto measure.

Now he continued on the same page—between the harvest month of August and the autumn month of September:

> Ditto 1853 I harvested 38 bussels
> Rye, 26 bussels Barley and 69 bus-
> sels potatoes, ditto measure;

He was getting along on his claim; his third crop was more than double his first.

What he missed more than anything was a team of his own. For three whole years he and Kristina had been their own beasts of burden. How much hadn't they carried and dragged during that time! They had carried home all their necessities, trudged long roads with heavy loads. From Taylors Falls to Ki-Chi-Saga, they had carried their burdens in their hands, in their arms, on their shoulders, on their backs. They had trudged and shuffled along, and lugged and carried and pulled, until their backs were bent and their arms stretched beyond their normal length. Out here they had indeed undertaken labor which in Sweden was relegated to animals.

There were two kinds of immigrants in the Territory— two-legged and four-legged. The people were few, the animals fewer, but the latter were indispensable to the former. Animals were therefore imported; cattle were driven in herds, or freighted on the rivers, from Illinois. Many of the animals died during the long and difficult transportation, and those that survived were so expensive on arrival in Minnesota that a squatter could not afford them. "Oxen for Sale! Cheap for Cash!" Karl Oskar had seen these signs in Stillwater and St. Paul. But the cheap cash price for a team was still eighty, ninety, or a hundred dollars, and that much money he had not as yet held in his hand at one time since they settled here. What cash he received for surplus hay or other crops was needed for groceries, tools, and implements. He must himself raise his cattle. Meanwhile he must continué to lug his own burdens, while Lady's and Miss's bull calves grew into oxen.

But one day, on an errand to the lumber company in Taylors Falls, Karl Oskar learned that one of the company's oxen had broken both of his front legs and that they had been forced to slaughter the animal; now its mate was for sale. Karl Oskar looked over the beast and made an offer: he had come to collect twenty dollars for hay which he had sold the company—he would write a receipt for that money and pay ten dollars more for the single ox if he might owe them this sum until next summer, when he would sell them more hay.

Thirty dollars was cheap for a thirteen-hand ox but the company manager accepted the offer even though the whole sum was not in cash.

"I trust you, Mr. Nilsson!" he said.

This was the first time in America that Karl Oskar had received credit. Before, when he asked for a few nails or a spool of thread, cash had been required. In his dealings with people, no one had trusted him until today. He felt as if he had been singled out for an honor, even though the sum was only ten dollars. As a squatter he had managed to remain on his claim for three years—perhaps the Americans at last realized that he intended to stay.

So Karl Oskar returned to Duvemala the owner of a sturdy old ox. The beast had an enormous belly, his horns were thick and nicely curved, his coat black with a white spot in the middle of his forehead like a shining star. A stone-hard enlargement on the neck, with the fur entirely worn off, told of the many heavy loads this ox had pulled; this yoke mark, the bald lump, was the beast's letter of recommendation.

"That's a lordly ox!" exclaimed Kristina as Karl Oskar came up, leading the animal. It had a lumbering walk, moving slowly, one foot after the other, but it held its horn-crowned head proudly in the air. It was indeed a lord among oxen.

From a thick oak log Karl Oskar sawed off four trundles—the wheels of a settler's wagon; he also made a single yoke for the ox's neck. Now he had his own wagon and his own beast to pull it.

Up to now he had shared the lot of cotters and other poor people back in Sweden, who walked and carried their burdens on their backs, while the farmers loaded theirs on their wagons riding and snapping their whips confidently. After only three years on his claim he could now ride his own ox wagon and feel like a farmer who owned something in America.

Petrus Olausson came to inspect his neighbor's new beast: "I too will buy an ox! Then we can team up and break land together."

A few days later Olausson came home with a thirteen-hand ox, entirely white, that he had bought in Stillwater.

Karl Oskar measured the animal and said, "Our team is the strongest in the whole valley!"

The two men yoked the black and the white oxen together and helped each other break new fields during the fall, plowing the same number of days on each claim. They used Olausson's plow, which had an iron bill and cut deeper than Karl Oskar's wooden plow; but however deep they plowed, the team managed.

Before the frost came and stopped their work, Karl Oskar had added five more acres to his field. Already he had more acres to seed than he had had in Sweden.

The black ox became their most valued and beloved animal. He was strong, good-natured, untiring. Standing there, sated with rich grass, chewing his cud which dripped down the tuft of his chin, he was a picture of true contentment. His enormous belly was round as a barrel, he was heavy and immobile as a huge boulder, encompassed in a superior calm which nothing in the world could disturb. The black ox radiated his security to his owners.

Karl Oskar named the beast Starkodder. It was a name he had taken from the saga of a brave Viking; Starkodder had been a hero strong as three men and endowed by the god Odin with a life span of three ordinary humans. It was the hero's strength Karl Oskar had in mind when he named his ox. The saga warrior had also been headstrong, unruly, evil-tempered; when at last he fell in combat, his decapitated head had bitten into the turf and chewed the earth angrily.

Thus the temperament of the Viking did not fit the ox Starkodder, who was calm and tractable in all his activities. He became the Nilssons' devoted helper, breaking their land, pulling home their supplies, and relieving them of much drudgery. They lifted their burdens off their shoulders and backs and laid them all onto his neck; everything was loaded on his bald, thick neck-swelling. And the old beast received it all patiently.

Starkodder was a sacrificial animal: he sacrificed himself for them.

2.

Pastor Erland Törner had stayed with the Swedes in the St. Croix Valley and had conducted services throughout the summer and fall. Now he was recalled to the Swedish settlement in Moline, Illinois, where newly arrived immigrants had brought cholera with them. It had raged among the settlers, who urged his return, for there were no ministers to conduct funeral rites. The timber and boards purchased for the new church in Moline were now being used for coffins for the cholera victims. Decent death couches and resting ground must be found for the dead ones before a house of prayer could be built for the living. The Illinois settlers found no time for their autumn plowing, for they spent their days digging graves in death's field. Instead of sowing their winter wheat they now put friends and neighbors into the earth. A minister would have much to do in Moline and Galesburg and neighboring villages, and Pastor Törner intended to remain through the winter. His mission to the St. Croix Valley had been to give spiritual comfort to the settlers and lay the foundation for a Lutheran congregation. Now as he was about to leave the Swedes, they wished to pay him for his sermons. They collected twenty dollars for the young pastor, a dollar or two from each homestead.

When Kristina learned that Pastor Törner was to move away she made a decision: she would ask him to church her before he left. She regretted she had not asked him to perform this ritual the first day he came to their house; she ought not to have received Holy Communion without first being cleansed from her childhood. But now at last it would take place.

She made her decision a little too late; the following day she discovered she was pregnant.

No minister would church a woman who was again carrying a life. And here she was, pregnant without being cleansed and blessed from her earlier birth, so indifferent and negligent had she become in religious matters. How would God view her neglect? Would he make a special dispensation for a settler wife who had both participated in the Lord's Supper and become pregnant again without churching?

Almost three years had passed since the birth of her youngest child and she had hoped it was her last. Her fervent wish was to remain barren for the rest of her life. She had already borne six children, four of whom were living, and she would be twenty-eight next St. Michael's Mass. The strain of so many pregnancies and the heavy work over the years had begun to leave their marks on her. The bloom of youth was gone, her rounded girl-cheeks thinner, her face lined with wrinkles. Recently she had lost her front tooth, and as she showed it, lying in her palm, to Karl Oskar she said, "This is the first sign of old age."

He replied that they had gone through so much, as emigrants, that they were in reality older in body and soul than those of the same age who had remained at home.

This would be her seventh child. Her concern for her children would now have to be shared by one more, and she felt depressed not only for her own sake, but for the children's sake. The more of them there were, the less each could expect.

If she and her husband stayed apart, she would not become pregnant again, but the holy bonds of matrimony intended that they should know each other bodily and beget children. God wanted them to enjoy each other in that

113

way. And the physical attraction was so powerful between Karl Oskar and herself that they couldn't stay away from each other for long. What took place between them was according to the Almighty's will; through them He created new people. And now He had again created a life in her. What could she do about it? It would be sinful to attempt to avoid pregnancies by such devices as long breast-feeding. No one could expect to fool God with such tricks.

A pregnancy reminded a woman that God trusted her—it was a sign of his confidence in her, a blessing. Barrenness was a curse, a punishment, which, when it struck biblical women, caused them to lament.

Thus Kristina, again blessed, dared not offer the prayer in her mind. How could she ask to escape a blessing and pray for a curse? But couldn't she ask the young minister if it would be sinful to pray that this pregnancy might be her last?

But when Pastor Törner came to say goodby she was embarrassed to ask him the question; her tongue refused to speak the words. He was too young. If he only had been an old minister, one she could have looked upon as a father, then it would have been different. With a man so near her own age, she felt too much a woman. And the pastor, himself unmarried, could hardly be expected to know much about these matters. She might embarrass him with her question.

Pastor Törner promised to return in the spring and help them establish a Lutheran parish in the St. Croix Valley. He had become deeply attached to his countrymen here. Now he counseled them not to become confused by the arguments between the many religious groups in America. After all, a fight for souls was better than spiritual indifference.

Kristina watched the young pastor from the door as he departed. She had not told him that on his return next spring there would be one more in the log cabin. Her seventh child so she calculated, would come into the world next May.

3.

The shores of Lake Ki-Chi-Saga were most beautiful in fall when the color of the deciduous trees mingled with the pines. There stood a green aspen next to a brown oak, here a golden elm beside a red maple. The maples had the largest leaves and the thickest foliage—the scarlet flame of the autumn forest. When the sun shone it seemed the stands along the shore were on fire, burning with clear flames, so intensely did the leaves glitter. In Ki-Chi-Saga's sky-blue water this leaf fire was stirred into billows. In the depths of the lake the shores's maple forest burned with a strange, unquenchable fire.

In mid-October the leaves came loose from the trees and fell into the lake, swimming about on the surface, forming into large, multi-colored floats. The oak still held its leaves, but leaf-floats from maples, aspens, ash, elm, and hazel separated from the shore and started on long voyages. Inlets and sounds were covered with the summer's withered verdure. The shore forest undressed with approaching winter and its garments floated away, while the trees stretched their naked branches over the water. Reeds and shore-grass rustled and crackled in the wind, and Ki-Chi-Saga's water darkened earlier each day. The hood of dusk fell over land and water and thickened quickly into the dark autumn night.

In the evenings enormous flocks of wild geese, flying southward, stretched over the lake. Kristina heard their calls and honks as they followed their lofty course—the birds up there knew what to expect and moved in good time; winter was near.

Their fourth winter lurked around the corner, ready to pounce on them any day now. For the next five months Kristina would have to live imprisoned by the snow, chained by darkness and cold. She would have to bend before the sharp sickle of the winter wind, trudge through the snow in her icy, slippery wooden shoes, blow into her stiff, blue-frozen hands to try to warm them with her breath. And the frost-roses would bloom around the door inside her home, bloom the cycle of their season.

In the sky whizzing wings carried away the migrants; down here on the ground she stood and listened. She was chained here, she had her home here—here she would remain forever.

Then at times she caught herself thinking she was still on her emigration-journey; this was only a resting-place; one day she would continue her journey.

4.

November came and no more calls were heard from the sky. The oaks lost their leaves. The weather was still mild, the ground bare.

Karl Oskar was readying himself to drive to Bolle's mill at Taylors Falls before the first snowfall. He loaded the wagon the evening before: two sacks of rye, two of barley; with two bushels to each sack it made a good load for his trundle cart, as heavy a load as the ox could manage on the bumpy forest road.

He arose before daylight and yoked Starkodder to the cart; he wanted to start at the break of dawn to be back before dark. Johan, always awake early, wanted to ride with his father, who once had promised to take him along to Taylors Falls. But today his load was heavy and Kristina felt the boy should stay at home; he would only get cold riding on the load such a long distance. It wasn't freezing yet, replied Karl Oskar, and as the boy kept on pleading he relented. It would be good for the boy to get out a little; he would soon be eight and children ought to get around a little at that age.

Children should be hardened was an old saying, but Kristina wound her big woolen shawl around Johan to keep him warm on the journey. She lingered in the door and looked after them as they rolled away into the forest; Karl Oskar walked beside the cart, the reins in one hand, while he steadied the wagon with the other. Johan sat on top of the sacks and waved proudly to his mother; the

116

gray shawl, covering everything but his face, made him look like a wizened old woman.

The ox cart rocked and bumped in the deep ruts—how easily it could turn over on the bumpy road.

"Drive carefully, Karl Oskar! The boy might fall off!" Kristina called after them.

Her husband and son disappeared from Kristina's view, enveloped by the gray mist of dawn. She sat down in front of the fire with her wool cards; she ought to card wool days on end, all of them needed new stockings before the winter cold set in, and besides the work made the hours fly. But she could not get the cart out of her mind; so many things could happen to Karl Oskar and Johan. Suppose they had to wait at the mill for their grind—then they wouldn't be home until after dark and could easily lose their way in the forest. The cart might turn over and pin Karl Oskar under the load, badly hurt and unable to move. The cart might break down on the wretched road, preventing them moving from the spot, or Johan might fall off and break an arm or a leg. Busy with her carding, she still could not help thinking there was no end to all the things that might happen to an ox cart.

In the late afternoon she began to listen for the sound of the wagon; wasn't it time for her to hear the heavy tramp of the ox and the rolling trundles? But she heard nothing. At last she put the wool cards aside and walked out to the edge of the clearing. Once outside she understood that there was still something else that might have happened to Karl Oskar, something she had not imagined—the very thing that must have happened.

Indeed, they had been forewarned. She should have remembered the previous evening—the sun had set fiery red as a peony.

5.

The forest had much to offer a child's eyes and the road to Taylors Falls was all too short for Johan. From his high seat on the load he had a good view of all the

117

creatures of the forest. The flying squirrels, so much shyer than ordinary squirrels, fluttered among the distant branches like enormous bats. The woodpecker hammered his arrow-sharp beak into a dry tree trunk until the noise echoed through the forest. At the approach of the noisy wagon, large flocks of blackbirds lifted from the thickets, and the long ears of curious rabbits poked up from the grass in meadows and glades, their white tails bobbing up and down as they took off, their hind legs stretching out behind them. But the skunk, that evil-smelling animal, was not so easily scared—he sat down among the bushes and examined the wagon; better avoid that critter or it would piss on you.

Of all the animals, Johan was most familiar with the gophers, which were always visible near the house. Now he saw them wherever the ground was free of trees and bushes. The gophers had gray-brown coats with two black streaks along the back, and were bigger than rats but smaller than squirrels. They sat upright on their tails, blinking curiously at you, but if you tried to catch them they dove quickly into their holes. Gophers were not dangerous, Johan had been told, they neither clawed nor bit you. But the gray wildcat with its short legs and bobbed tail, which sometimes sneaked all the way into their house—he could both claw and bite, and if he was very hungry he might tear little children to pieces and eat them. Johan had been warned about that cat.

With a lumbering gait the black ox pulled the cart, the oak trundles turning slowly over stumps, into and out of ruts. The axles were well greased with bacon rind to prevent them from squeaking; Karl Oskar's cart was no screech-wagon announcing a coming settler miles away. It was the first time in America he had driven a load with his own vehicle and his own beast, and the first time he was accompanied by his oldest son.

Johan had a mind ahead of his years, always quick to notice things around him. He had begun to help his father, looking after the cows and the pigs when they were let out, carrying in water and wood. He was a willing helper as far as his strength went. In time the boy would be a great aid to Karl Oskar.

"If you're cold, come down and run beside the cart!"

No, Johan wasn't cold; he wanted to ride on the load. The weather was mild and he was warmed by the excitement of his new experience, by all he saw and heard. He was only afraid the road might come to an end, and only too soon he spied the river; they had arrived.

Stephen Bolle, the Irishman, had built his little mill near the rushing stream above Taylors Falls. The mill house had been raised without a single nail; the walls were held together by pegs. The millstones were only eighteen inches in diameter; the small stones could grind only a rough flour. It was really a dwarf mill, a little makeshift contraption, but it was the closest one. Marine and Stillwater could boast of steam mills to grind the settlers' crops.

The miller looked out through the door of his dwarf house, frightening Johan. Bolle was a thick-set, fat man with heavy white hair hanging down to his shoulders like a horse's mane. His face was black-gray with white spots, like hardened, cracked clay, and in the cracks, dirt and flour had gathered; Bolle never washed his face. In the center of this black-gray, flour-white field, his mouth opened like a hole with one long, black tooth. To the boy the miller looked like an old troll.

One of his daughters, a widow, took care of the miller's household, and a little granddaughter with fiery red hair ran around his legs, peeking curiously at the newcomers.

Stephen Bolle was a laconic man who grunted like an Indian; Karl Oskar could not understand half of what he said. But the Irishman understood the purpose of a man with grain sacks, and Karl Oskar knew the cost of grinding per bushel; further conversation was unnecessary.

There was one load before them; Karl Oskar would have to wait an hour until the other settler's grind was finished, then his own sacks would be poured between the grindstones. Meanwhile, Karl Oskar and Johan opened their lunch basket: bread, potato pancakes, fried pork, milk from a bottle Kristina had tied in a woolen sock to keep warm. As they ate Bolle's granddaughter, the little girl with the flaming hair, eagerly watched them. She tried to talk to Johan but he couldn't begin to understand what

119

she was saying. Her forehead above her snub nose was covered with freckles; she was the troll child and her grandfather the old troll; Johan disliked them both.

He asked his father about the miller and the girl and Karl Oskar told him that the Irish were a special race of people, unlike the Swedes except for the color of their skin. They were ill-tempered, always fighting among themselves or with other people. They quarreled willingly and worked unwillingly. But English happened to be their mother tongue and so they got along well in America, in spite of their bad behavior. That was the strange thing about this country—you might meet all kinds of people. So Johan mustn't be surprised at the way people looked or acted.

The Irishman's ramshackle mill ground slowly and it was one o'clock before Karl Oskar's grain had been turned into flour. While they were waiting, the weather had unexpectedly changed. The sun was no longer visible, the whole sky had clouded over, and suddenly the air felt much colder.

The old miller dumped the last sack onto the cart, squinted heavenward, and grunted, "Goin' to get snow—pahaps—uh . . ."

The Swedish settler nodded goodbye to the Irishman and hurried to turn homeward. His ox cart would need four hours on the road and the day was far gone; he had no time to lose if he wanted to be home before dark. Of course he was familiar with the road and could follow his own tracks so he was sure to reach Duvemala even if he had to travel the last stretch in darkness. Nevertheless . . . he urged Starkodder: "Git goin'! Hurry up!" But the black ox had once and for all set his own pace, and moved his heavy body with the familiar slow speed, shuffling his hooves in the same rhythm; this steady beast was not to be ruffled by whip or urgings.

Johan had again settled himself on top of the sacks but after a couple of miles he complained of being cold. Karl Oskar helped the boy down and had him walk beside the cart to keep warm. Karl Oskar buttoned up his own heavy coat. It had indeed turned cold, and there was a peculiar thickness in the air, indicating a change in the weather, the

120

kind that took place so suddenly in the Territory. Men said the temperature could fall from twenty above to twenty below within a few hours. And the Irish miller had croaked something about snow. Well, it was time, of course . . .

But there was another word in connection with snow, and that word Karl Oskar did not even wish to voice. But it was surely too early for that kind of weather, now, at the beginning of November. Yet, anything could happen weather-wise in this country—if they were unlucky. He began to feel apprehensive as he peered at the clouds; they were thickening and darkening above the tree tops. And the trees, which had been still when they drove past them a few hours ago, had begun to sway—slowly, to be sure—yet it was not a good sign; it boded ill.

But a storm couldn't come on so suddenly; he had time to get home. Well, to be on the safe side, perhaps they had better take the road by Danjel's and Jonas Petter's claims, on Lake Gennesaret. This was a little farther, a mile or two, but in New Kärragärde they would find shelter should the threatening storm break. They would have to turn off at the creek, a few hundred yards farther on. He hesitated, scanning the fir tops every couple of minutes—it couldn't come that quick . . .

Johan was unable to keep warm even though he ran behind the cart and kept in constant motion.

"I'm cold, Father! It burns . . ."

He wound the woolen shawl tighter around Johan's head and shoulders and showed him how to flail his arms against his body to keep warm. He had no mittens but Karl Oskar dug his own out of his pocket and put them on the boy's ice-cold hands. As the cold became more intense, the boy became a problem, for he was sensitive to it in a way a grown person was not. If Karl Oskar had suspected the weather would change he would have driven alone to Taylors Falls. But in the morning it had looked promising . . .

For his son's sake he now decided to take the longer road through Danjel's claim and, if need be, seek shelter. At the creek Karl Oskar left his old tracks and turned off toward New Kärragärde. This stretch should take only half an hour, certainly not much more, if he just could get his ox to move a little faster.

He cut a juniper branch and struck Starkodder a few blows across the hindquarters. "Git goin'!" The black ox stepped up his pace a little, and sniffed the air as if he could smell an approaching calamity.

A raw fog was enveloping the wagon from all quarters. A sharp wind, which penetrated their clothing and cut the skin like a knife edge, had come up behind them from the northeast. In the air, high above the trees, a heavy roar could be heard; it sounded like breaking waves on a distant shore. The trees bent back and forth, swaying like masts of a ship. This was a sure sign: a northeaster was breaking. But it might not last long . . .

Karl Oskar looked skyward and discovered that he no longer could see the tree tops through the fog. Snow was all right, but that other word . . . No, he liked no part of it; it was a terrifying word in the Territory—*blizzard*. One's life was always in danger in a blizzard if one happened to be more than five minutes from a house.

They were still only half way home but they might reach Danjel's cottage. Another half hour—if it didn't get too bad in the next half hour. It couldn't come that quickly. They would make it. He urged the ox on, he yelled and hit and slapped the reins. The cart was moving forward; each time the wheels turned he took a few steps, three long steps. They had to reach shelter.

The noise from above was closer, the tree tops were bending lower, the motion of the trunks had increased. The blizzard was hitting the forest at a terrifying speed, rolling across the valley in darkening clouds, bursting furiously over hundreds of miles while the cart trudged only a quarter of a mile. It had come upon them so unbelievably fast that they could feel its impact already; the first snow-hail was whipping Karl Oskar's cheeks.

Like a hawk after its prey, the blizzard dove down upon the cart and its people.

Within a few moments it was upon them. It began with whirling hail, biting like gravel into the skin; then after this first smarting blow, it hurled snow masses with mighty force. All at once the world around them was en-

122

veloped in snow, hurling, whirling, whipping, piercing, smarting snow. Only snow could be seen. The northeaster drove the blinding mass through the forest, swept the valley with its blizzard-broom. Without warning, they had fallen into the ambush of a great blizzard.

If the onslaught had come from the opposite direction they would have been unable to drive on. Against such a force the ox would have been unable to move; the cart would have stopped in its tracks. Now they were driven forward by the storm.

Shivering and trembling, Johan clung to his father: "Dad! Please! Help me please, Dad!"

The boy cried pitifully. Karl Oskar took the blanket which covered the sacks and wrapped it around him and put him back on top of the load. He reined in the ox for a moment—the boy had lost his wooden shoes in the snow and Karl Oskar must find them. It took some moments, for the dense snow stung his eyelids, blinding him.

The thick, snow-filled air darkened the forest; a premature dusk fell about them. Karl Oskar felt as if he were naked, so penetrating was the fierce wind. The northeaster's icy scraper tore at his face. Johan, despite being well bundled, whimpered and cried with the painful cold. Only Starkodder, in his thick hide, had adequate protection against the blizzard.

The ox plodded along between the shafts, pulling the cart and following the clearing among the trees. The wheels turned, the cart moved, but had they not been somewhat sheltered by the forest it would surely have turned over.

On, on! They must reach Danjel's, they must find shelter. It could not be far now—if the boy was able to stand it . . . Karl Oskar walked beside the wagon and held onto it as if he were afraid of losing it. Now and again he felt for Johan to make sure he was still there; at the same time he watched his beast ahead of him. Starkodder tramped steadily through the blizzard, pushing his big-bellied body through the whirling snow masses like a slowly rolling boulder. The ox no longer seemed black—his coat was covered with snow and between the shafts he looked like a moving snowdrift with a pair of horns sticking out.

123

The snow lumped itself under Karl Oskar's clogs, hung like a freezing cover over his back, stuck to the trundle wheels in big clumps. The cart rolled more slowly as the snow grew deeper, but they did move forward. God be praised for this ox; he was tough, he could get through.

And the blizzard broom-swept furiously and hurled the snow-masses over the St. Croix Valley. Karl Oskar had not seen the like of this storm in November. But a blizzard that came on so quickly usually did not last very long. It might be over in an hour, perhaps sooner. An hour, though, was too much for them; even a half hour or a quarter might be too much. So much could happen in a quarter of an hour in weather like this; indeed, a few minutes could mean life or death. They must find shelter quickly; their lives were now in danger.

The roar of the blizzard rose and fell. Sharp, crackling sounds were heard above the din: broken tree trunks that crashed in the forest. Here trees were felled without an ax, and the storm thundered and rumbled and swallowed all other sounds with its own tumult. The cart trundles, however, were still turning, the black ox still pulled his wagon, even though the snow had changed his color to shining white.

The driver's cheeks were stiff, frostbitten; he rubbed them with snow. How long would his time of grace last? How long could the boy endure? No protection helped a body against this cold, however well bundled up. He called cheeringly to his son, who lay on the sacks like a bundle of clothes. A weak complaint was his only reply. Johan's life was in danger, his resistance was not great . . .

The storm-broom swept with its mighty strokes; the forest crackled, to right and left they could hear trees falling. Karl Oskar yelled with all his might at his beast, urging him, hitting him, but his voice was drowned in the blizzard's hissing caldron.

Suddenly he stopped; his clog had struck against wood. He took another step, yes, he was standing on wood. He recognized the place. They were crossing the wooden bridge which Danjel and Jonas Petter had built over the brook Kidron. They were now in the little valley which the biblically inclined Danjel had called Kidron's Valley.

If he remembered rightly he now had only about half a mile left to Danjel's cabin. If the ox didn't slow down they could make it in a quarter of an hour, surely in twenty minutes. On a clear day they could have seen the lake from here, and the house, they were that close. Within fifteen minutes they would be out of danger, sitting in the warmth of Danjel's cottage. He called to the boy that they were almost at his uncle's.

But the trundles turned more heavily in the drifted snow, the cart moved ever more grudgingly. Karl Oskar tied the reins around his waist and pushed the cart from behind with all his strength. This would also warm him. And the trundles kept turning, still rolling, and each turn brought them a few steps closer to the house down there at the lakeside, a few steps closer to safety.

If he hadn't been forced to wait at the mill they would have escaped the blizzard, he thought, and would now be sitting in front of the fire at home. They were in bad luck today.

Just then, the greatest of bad luck overtook them. A heavy crashing sound cut through the roar of the blizzard somewhere close ahead of them and the cart stopped with a jerk. Karl Oskar hit the ox with the reins, urging him on. But Starkodder stood still. Karl Oskar walked up alongside the ox, feeling his flanks. Why had the beast come to a stop? He walked forward to Starkodder's head, which the ox was shaking in annoyance; a branch hit Karl Oskar smartly across his face; he brushed the snow from his eyes and now he could see that a giant fir had fallen across the road, its roots poking heavenward. The tree had fallen close to the ox, who now stood in a thicket of branches; the beast was shaking his head, twisting and pulling it to free his horns, which had become ensnared in the fir's branches.

Further progress was cut off. With only a short distance left the blizzard had felled a tree and caught them. Now they could move neither back nor forward.

Karl Oskar pulled out his ax from under the sacks, cut a few branches from the fallen tree, and liberated the ox; he unyoked the beast and secured him with the reins to the cart. Johan made a faint sound. Karl Oskar climbed up and felt the bundled-up child body.

"Awfully cold, little one?"

He took the boy in his arms, stuck his hand into the bundle, and felt the tiny limbs. Terror struck him.

"You're cold as an icicle!"

A faint whimper from Johan: "Are we home, Dad?"

The father began to rub the stiff limbs so violently that the boy cried out: "Stop it, Dad! It hurts! Please!"

Feeling still remained in the little body, no part of it was as yet frozen through. But Johan was terribly sleepy and wanted to be left alone. He knew the cart had stopped moving and thought they were home—". . . home with Mother."

Karl Oskar shook and rubbed the tiny limbs. The boy cried out in pain. The cold bit and burned, cutting his skin like a knife. Johan could not understand: they were home, he had called Mother but she didn't answer him. Why? With no reply from Mother he clung to Father, closer, shivering.

"I'm cold, Dad, worse, awfully bad . . ."

Karl Oskar Nilsson held his oldest son in his arms and tried to find protection from the blizzard behind the cart. He sat down in the snow, squatting against the sharp sweep of the storm. The cold snow whirled around him. He crept under the cart with the child; it did not help noticeably. Where could he find protection for Johan against the merciless cold? He himself shook with cold and his limbs stiffened as soon as he stopped moving them; he had no warmth left for his son. What must he do to keep life in the little body?

Should he try to cut the tree and clear the road? It was only a short distance to Danjel's. But he wouldn't have time; before he could cut half through the giant fir, his son would be frozen to death.

No, there was nothing he could do, nothing that would help him. All he could do was pray to God for his poor soul. And sit under the cart and wait for the child in his arms to stiffen to a corpse.

At home Kristina was waiting with three more children and one unborn life, while he sat under an ox cart, prepar-

126

ing himself for eternity. A tree had fallen, and parted them forever; he had driven off to the mill, never to return. The blizzard had parted them forever. Was this the way his life would end?

Hadn't the storm gone down a little? Or was the blizzard just catching its breath? No, it couldn't be over so soon. There was no hope of that. And so all would be over. Over? No! He mustn't give up! He had never given up! A person must use his sense and his strength as long as a drop of blood was left in his body. He mustn't be tempted to think that nothing would help. He must try and try and try again. He still had some fight left in him. And it wasn't the first time that a life close to him had been in danger. He had never given up before—why should he now? Hadn't he any guts left?

A third life was with them—the ox, Starkodder, who bellowed now and then between the gusts. The black ox had seldom before made any sound, but now he bellowed in fright. Even a dumb animal could sense danger to life. Yet the beast would probably endure the longest of them, the ox would survive its owner and the owner's son, the animal would survive the humans. Yes, how long could an old, tough ox withstand the blizzard? He did have a thick fur coat.

Now that the branches of the fallen tree had swept the snow from Starkodder's back he was black again; only the white star on his forehead shone through the mist, the animal's big belly had been washed clean by the snow and shone wet.

They were so close to human habitation. He could try to get through alone, the piece that was left. But Johan, what should he meanwhile do with the child?

Karl Oskar rose with the boy in his arms and walked toward his trusted beast of burden, who bellowed helplessly against the roaring blizzard; the man was approaching his beast for help, for a thought had come to him. There was still a chance—he must make a last effort.

Johan clung to his neck, his arms stiffening with the cold. The boy was small, the ox large. The little one could find shelter with the big one, a human being with an animal. Starkodder was his good, reliable beast, but he was only an animal, and a new animal could be found in his place. But no one could replace his son if he froze to death.

Karl Oskar had the necessary tools with him, the ax and the knife. He could to it quickly, it was still light enough for him to see. But he must hurry, it must be done within minutes. And it wouldn't take long.

Karl Oskar had never moved as quickly as he did in the following few minutes. He bundled up Johan in the shawl and the blanket and laid him in the snow under the cart. Then he led the ox a few paces away, to the side of the road. Starkodder followed him trustingly, stopping when the man stopped. They walked with the wind, yet were almost blown over by its force. In the lee of a great tree trunk Karl Oskar halted, gathered the reins, and tied the right foreleg of the ox to his left hind leg, down low, near the hoove. The ox stood still, patient, accommodating. Karl Oskar picked up his ax and stationed himself near the head of the beast.

Starkodder stumbled toward his owner, sniffing his master's coat as if seeking fodder hidden under it. Karl Oskar raised his arm with the ax but let it drop again; the ox's mouth touched his sleeve, his tongue licked it, as if expressing his devotion. The animal's behavior caused the master to stay his arm momentarily, but he hesitated only a few seconds. He remembered the life he was trying to save; there was no time to lose.

Grasping the handle firmly with both hands, he raised the ax above his head, aimed at the little white star between the ox's horns, and let the ax hammer fall with a murderous blow on the beast's forehead.

With a piercing bellow, the ox staggered to his knees, his head against the ground. The butcher hit again in the same spot. Now the ox was down; from his throat came a bellow of agony which for a few moments drowned the blizzard's roar. With the third blow the bellowing died to a faint sound. The ox's head was in the snow but his body still rested on his hind legs; Karl Oskar jerked the reins with which he had fastened the animal's legs and the beast toppled over. The heavy body rolled on its right side, but the legs still kicked in the air.

128

Karl Oskar alone had never butchered an animal so big, but with a firm hand, he pushed the knife into the neck all the way to the handle. As he pulled it out, he saw that he had hit the right spot; blood pumped out in a heavy stream as if he had pulled the plug from the bung hole of a barrel. The snow around the ox's head was stained dark red, fumes rose from the spurting liquid, and Karl Oskar warmed his frozen hands in the steaming blood from the ox. He stood bent over the animal as long as the red stream flowed; soon it trickled in drops. The black ox still kicked, but these motions soon weakened into feeble jerks.

Its blood drained, its life gone, the butchered animal lay still. Karl Oskar picked up the reins again and managed, with some difficulty, to turn the heavy carcass over on its back, to facilitate removing the entrails. With the ax he quickly severed the ribs, put the ax handle into the hole and widened it enough to get his hands through. Then, with his knife, he opened the carcass from the chest to the tail and cut loose the entrails—heart, lungs, kidneys, spleen, liver, bladder. A fetid odor rose in his face. His fingers moved cautiously around the ox's big stomach, lest he puncture it with the knife. Below it he groped for the intestines, entwined like a coil of snakes, the pale light from the snow shining into their nest.

The butcher wiped the icicles from his eyes; the blood from his hands smeared his face. All entrails must be removed from the carcass to make sufficient room. He cut out organ after organ and threw them in the snow. Most difficult to handle was the large stomach sac, which flowed in all directions like an immense lump of dough, steam issuing from it as if it were a boiling caldron. At least the carcass was clean, and round about it lay the entrails strewn in the snow.

Karl Oskar had prepared a warm, safe room for his son.

He pulled the bundled-up Johan from under the cart, carried him to the ox, and placed him inside the carcass. There was plenty of room in there for the child, and the animal's warmth would start the blood circulating in the boy's frozen limbs.

Then the father folded the edge of the hide over the child, who already was reviving; he felt the thick fur with his hand: "At home, Dad?"

"Yes, go to sleep again, boy . . ."

With the ox hide over him Johan thought he was at home in bed under their thick comforter; he fell asleep again, contentedly. The father wrapped the shawl around him as best he could. Then with the reins he tied the carcass together, leaving a small air hole above the child's mouth. He stood for a moment, listening to his son's breathing. But Johan was already sound asleep, as comfortable inside the carcass as if he had been sleeping in his own bed.

Karl Oskar's arms and legs were still shaking, no longer from the cold, but from suspense and the effort of butchering. His hands and clothing were covered with blood and entrail slime, but it was done and he had succeeded; his last effort to fight on. He had found shelter for Johan in the ox's cavity. He would last a good while there. And now with the boy safe, Karl Oskar could seek shelter and aid.

He didn't feel the cold now; the butchering had warmed him. And perhaps the storm was going down a little. The black clouds seemed a little lighter and higher above the tree tops. Heavy gusts of wind still shook the trees, but not so persistently. Perhaps the blizzard would die down as suddenly as it had come on. Trees were still falling, however, and it was hard to walk upright.

It was barely half a mile to Danjel's—could he make it? Of course he could, even if he had to crawl on his hands and knees. Even though it was almost dark, he remembered the trees they had blazed for the road, and the wind would be at his back.

Karl Oskar picked up his ax and began to cut his way through the huge fir which had blocked their progress. He hacked at it furiously, grateful that he still had strength for one more effort against the elements. He would find his way through the blizzard, his bloody hands would knock on Danjel's door . . .

6.

Yesterday, when she had seen the sun's blood-red globe, she knew it boded a storm. Why hadn't she remembered that Karl Oskar left? Why hadn't she warned him?

Kristina asked herself these questions when the blizzard broke in the late afternoon, imprisoning her and the children in the cabin.

The day was followed by the longest, most wakeful night of her life. She clung to a single *if*: *if* her husband had been warned about the impending blizzard, then he and Johan might have remained at Taylors Falls. Otherwise they now lay frozen to death somewhere in the forest.

Life could be snuffed out quickly in a blizzard. Last winter a settler's wife in Marine had gone out to feed her chickens in a blizzard; she had never come back. After the storm was over she had been found, twenty paces from her door. An ox cart, overtaken by such a storm, could stall in a drift. The snow would cover ox, cart, and driver, who would remain hidden until the first thaw of spring. The cold would have preserved their bodies: there would sit the driver, still upright on his load, the reins in his hands, his mouth open as if he were urging on the ox to greater speed. And the ox in the shafts, the yoke on his neck, his horns in the air, would have his knees bent for the next step. So the cart and its occupants would remain immobile under the snow mantle all winter long, as if they had been driving through the entire winter. In March the death cart would be unveiled by the sun.

All night long, Kristina could see Karl Oskar, with Johan on the load behind him, driving in the same spot, driving the road to eternity.

In the evening, the blizzard had died down. After a night of agony, which denied her merciful sleep for a single moment, dawn finally came. And in the morning she beheld through the window a strange procession approaching their house: Uncle Danjel came, driving his ox

131

team, and their own black ox, which yesterday had been yoked to the cart when Karl Oskar had left for the mill, now lay on Danjel's wagon. The animal's limbs dangled lifeless, his large head with the beautiful horns hung over the side of the wagon. Danjel walked beside it, Karl Oskar came behind, carrying a shapeless bundle.

Kristina stepped back, fumbling for something to hold onto. She recognized the shawl she had tucked around Johan yesterday morning. Her lips were tightly pressed together to hold back her instinctive cry. With trembling knees she walked to the door and opened it.

Karl Oskar stepped over the threshold, and walked slowly into the room. Silently he laid his burden on the bed nearest the door.

Kristina glimpsed the little head in the shawl. Her voice failed her, and she could barely whisper: "Is he dead?"

Relieved of his burden, Karl Oskar straightened up.

"The boy is all right."

"But how . . . ? The blizzard . . . ?"

"It let up. But we decided to stay over with Danjel."

"Yesterday afternoon . . . when it began . . . last night . . . I thought . . . I . . ."

Again her voice failed her; she could not go on.

Karl Oskar had carefully washed away every sign of blood from his face, hands, and clothing, so that his wife wouldn't be frightened, but now, as he unbundled the shawl, he discovered a large, liver-red spot on Johan's neck, clinging like a fat leech.

Kristina cried out.

Quickly he said, "Don't be afraid! It's only ox blood!"

". . . the ox . . . ?"

"Had to kill him to save the boy . . ."

It was not easy to explain why he had butchered his fine ox. Now that the storm was over and all was still again, he couldn't quite understand it himself.

"I put the boy in the ox's stomach while I went to Danjel's. When the storm died down, we went back and found him still asleep. It saved his life."

And so Karl Oskar was again without a beast of burden.

He kept the hide of the black ox to use for shoe
132

leather, but sold the meat to German Fischer's Inn at Taylors Falls for ten dollars, the sum he still owed for the animal. Kristina thought they should have kept some of the meat, but Karl Oskar said he would be unable to swallow a single bite of it. After having had to kill Starkodder, he felt the animal had assumed a sacrificial significance: not only had the ox given them his strength in life, he had given his life to save their oldest son.

VII. Ulrika in Her Glory

1.

One Saturday afternoon, having fired the bake-oven and raked out the embers, Kristina was just ready to put in the bread when she heard someone stamp off the snow outside the door; Ulrika, warmly dressed, stepped across the threshold.

Sledding was good now along the timber roads, and Ulrika had ridden in a sleigh most of the way from Stillwater in the company of her husband, who had been called to preach in St. Paul on Sunday.

"I took the opportunity to visit you!"

Kristina had been standing in front of the hot oven, the rake and the ash broom in her hands; she forgot to dust the soot from the hand she offered to the caller, so glad was she to see Ulrika. She enjoyed no visitor more. Although Kristina had neighbors and had met the settlers' wives, it was difficult for her to feel intimate with them. Perhaps it was the long isolation that had made her feel shy and awkward in company, but she never quite knew how to act with new people; she was afraid she might appear backward and foolish to them. In order to become friends with the neighbors, great efforts were demanded of her, and she rarely felt up to such efforts.

But when Ulrika came to visit her, however inconveniently, all guards were down and all concerns forgotten, even today—besides the baking, Lill-Marta was in bed with a cold and a throat irritation. Kristina quickly put a coffeepot over the fire. But the rising bread must be put in while the oven was hot, so as soon as Ulrika had removed her coat and shawl she took the bread ladle from Kristina's hands to help her. She stood directly in front of the oven opening even though Kristina warned her she might get soot on her fine clothing.

Ulrika was in the last month of her pregnancy, and had grown ample around the waist and become clumsy in her motions. But she handled the ladle firmly and within a short time she had all the bread in the oven.

It had been an unlucky day for the children, Kristina said. Dan had crept too near the fire and burned himself on the forehead and she had had to melt sheep fat and put it on the burn. Barely had she attended to the little one when Harald, playing with a piece of firewood, had got a splinter under his fingernail and cried like a stuck pig before she could get it out. And the girl in bed was forever complaining of her sore throat and needed attention. All these things had more or less upset her household this morning.

But despite her problems, Kristina soon had the coffee on the table and could sit down with her visitor for a rest.

"You're overloaded with work," said Ulrika sympathetically. "American women have it much easier. The men scrub the floors and wash the dishes for their wives."

Kristina said, "When Karl Oskar comes in from work in the evening he's so tired out that I wouldn't dream of asking him to wash up after supper."

"If he were an American man he would offer to do it," insisted Ulrika. "He is still too Swedish!"

Swedish men were ashamed to do women's chores, she continued. Think of how it was back home. After eating, the menfolk just lolled about, resting and breaking wind, while the wives cleaned up and waited on those lazybodies. Weekdays and Sundays alike. And many women in Sweden had to do the men's chores as well—carry in water and wood, thresh, plow, load dung. They were hardly better off than the animals. If they only knew how much

134

easier their lives would be as wives to American men, the whole Kingdom of Sweden would be empty of women in a few weeks.

Kristina noticed how big Ulrika had grown since their last meeting. "You too will soon have more to do, I can see!"

"Sure enough!" Ulrika felt her enormous belly. "My priest was made in March. I'll bear him before Christmas, I guess."

She had had such horrible vomitings during this pregnancy, she was sure it would be a boy. A woman puked more when she carried a male child than she would carrying one of her own sex. This was only natural.

Kristina confided to her guest that she, too, was pregnant again.

Ulrika looked at her compassionately. "I thought you looked kind of pale-faced. But you have such a big household and so much to care for; you should really go barren and empty for a few years."

It was a nuisance to protect and look after babies out here during the winter, said Kristina. She would never forget all the trouble she had with Dan the first winter. But this time she would bear in May, just the right time for a birth; the little one would come into the world in summer and warmth.

Ulrika looked about the cabin. "It won't be easy for you with five brats in this little log hut. With five kids to care for you need space to turn around."

"This is our last winter in the cabin. Karl Oskar has promised to have the new house ready by next fall."

Kristina only worried, she told her friend, because his plans called for so large a house she was afraid he wouldn't be able to raise it. It was to be two stories, with rooms both upstairs and downstairs. Everything he undertook was on such a large scale. She could never persuade him to be moderate.

"But he is an extra fine man!" said Ulrika with conviction. "He can use his hands and do everything for himself."

She added that she had heard how he had managed in the blizzard and saved both Johan's and his own life by

135

killing the ox while the storm was at its height. The Swedes in the valley were talking about nothing else, and Karl Oskar was said to be both able and ingenious. Ulrika herself knew from earlier experience that he was neither a weakling nor at a loss as to what to do.

"I'm only afraid it's going to his head," said Kristina.

Karl Oskar was fearless and undismayed, and never gave up; he insisted it always paid to fight back however hopeless things looked. But he was getting so that he thought he could depend entirely on himself. And to tell the truth, however well he had managed during the blizzard, the saving of the boy was God's miracle. He himself had frostbitten ears and cheeks, but Johan had not a frozen spot on him, and this was a miracle. What would Karl Oskar have done if the blizzard had continued to rage? Then he couldn't have got to the boy in time and Johan would have frozen to death inside the ox belly. And that was just what Kristina had told Karl Oskar.

He had insisted that a person in danger had no time to spend on prayers but must try all the tricks he could think of to help himself. Waiting for someone else to do it would bring no result. And Kristina feared that his saving of Johan in the blizzard had had a bad influence on him; he called it his own doing, and this was arrogance. He was getting so big-headed that he relied more on himself than on God.

"Well, it seems at times the Lord wants people to help him a little when he performs his miracles," said Ulrika.

Karl Oskar was after all one hell of a good man, no one could deny that, she insisted. And he made children one after another; for this he needed no one's help, either. But this was one activity he ought to curtail. If he rested occasionally from his male duties it would be good for Kristina. But she guessed a man couldn't hold back what he didn't hold in his hand.

Someone else was stamping off snow outside, this time the heavy stampings of a man. Petrus Olausson entered the cabin. In his hand he held an enormous auger. He shook hands with Kristina, and looked questioningly at Ulrika. Kristina introduced them. "This is Ulrika from Stillwater, who has come for a visit."

136

She was about to explain to Petrus a little further who this woman was, but Ulrika stood up and took the words out of her mouth: "I'm Mrs. Henry Jackson, a good friend of Mrs. Nilsson. I gather you're one of the new neighbors?"

"That's right, Mrs. Jackson."

Petrus Olausson glanced at Ulrika sharply; tall, ample around the waist, she stood there displaying her big belly. The farmer's eyes roamed over her body; the sight of the pregnant woman seemed to affect him uncomfortably.

He turned to Kristina. Tomorrow, on the Lord's Day, he had invited a few friends among the Swedes for spiritual conversations in his house; he hoped Kristina and her husband would come for the edification of their souls: "We will have a speak-meeting."

Kristina wanted to go to Olausson's, but she hesitated. Ulrika intended to stay over Sunday and she felt she could not leave her.

She put a third cup on the table. "Sit down, Petrus! Have a cup of coffee with us."

Olausson sat down, and as Kristina filled the plate again, he began to talk to Ulrika. The Swedes out here needed to gather for spiritual communion, he told her. Last fall he had built a big barn, which had plenty of room now that his crops had been threshed. He thought they could use this barn for services until they built themselves a church.

"Barns are fine for sermons, agreed Ulrika." "But you can't use them in winter."

Petrus Olausson said that as the Swedes in the valley still had no church, they could hardly be looked upon as devoted users of God's Holy Word. A formal service every Sunday and at least two sermons during the week were the least a good Lutheran Christian needed; daily prayers, morning, noon, and evening he took for granted, health permitting.

But Ulrika shook her head. "It's unreasonable to have services that often! God doesn't expect it!"

Petrus Olausson looked at her, startled.

Ulrika continued. Yes, she was sure God expected moderation in their devotion. A person should never be-

137

come excessive in spiritual matters. Her husband preached about ten sermons a week, at different places, and it was all he had the strength to do. His journeys over the bad roads wore him out. And neither God nor his flock had any joy from a tired-out priest who came home so bedraggled that he was unable to say his evening prayers or perform his manly duty to his wife.

Olausson's mouth had dropped open while Ulrika spoke; now he said, "Are you married to a man of the Church, Mrs. Jackson?"

"Yes, that I am."

"Well, this is a surprise . . ."

"It's the truth—my husband is a priest."

"Where does he preach?"

"My husband is serving as priest in the American Baptist Church in Stillwater."

Petrus Olausson's eyelids twitched violently as if suddenly he had got something in his eye. His lips moved eagerly; he seemed to have words at the tip of his tongue, but only a grunt came out.

He rose like a jack-in-the-box.

Kristina turned from the fire, the coffeepot in her hand. "Sit down, Petrus. I've just warmed the coffee . . ."

"Thanks! I care not for coffee today!"

"Please, Petrus!"

"I'll find Nilsson outside—I just wanted to return his auger . . ."

He nodded stiffly to Kristina, picked up his hat, and without another look at Ulrika he stomped out of the cabin.

Greatly disturbed, Kristina looked through the window after her neighbor. "What got into him?"

"The man jumped up as if someone stuck an awl in his ass!" laughed Ulrika.

"But he usually acts so friendly. Did he think my coffee was poisoned?"

"Perhaps it was the looks of me he didn't like."

"Why?"

"Because I'm thick. But I told him I was married. I have both Christian and legal right to be thick."

"Nonsense! He didn't run away because of that."

138

"I've known pious Lutheran men who detest a woman who dares show herself while pregnant. They hold her unclean—especially when she's as big as I am."

Such an explanation Kristina could not accept; their neighbor was indeed pious and hard in his judgments, but he couldn't detest a woman because she was pregnant. So she worried to herself about Olausson's strange behavior.

Ulrika, however, brushed it aside.

"Now I want to tell you *my* errand," she said. "I've come to ask you and Karl Oskar to a party during the Christmas holidays."

Kristina clapped her hands in joyful surprise. "I don't believe it! Are you going to give a party?"

Ever since Ulrika's marriage she had wanted to give a big party for all the Swedes who had emigrated with her from her old parish. It would be a great pleasure to invite her old countrymen to a feast. In Sweden she had never entertained; she was considered too low at home—who would have come? And one couldn't have a party without guests. But here in America those she invited would come, here she would have guests. And this Christmas feast would be the first party she had ever given.

"But you aren't going to have a party before the child comes, are you?" asked Kristina.

"Lord no! It will be a christening at the same time; I want to show off my little priest!" And Ulrika caressed her protruding belly: for her childbed she had bespoken Cora Skalrud whom she greatly trusted. All Norwegians she knew in Stillwater and Marine she valued highly. The Norwegians did not play up to upper-class people the way the Swedes did. They had never had any nobility in their country, Miss Skalrud used to say, but were, all of them, born with nobility: no Norwegian would ever give up his inborn right to haughtiness. So the Norwegians walked with straight backs, even in their homeland. But in Sweden, the ceilings were so low that people had to travel all the way to Minnesota to straighten out their backs.

Kristina understood Ulrika perfectly. For years she must have been thinking of this party, of showing her American home to her countrymen, showing them how well things were with her. It would be the crowning event of her rehabilitation. Kristina promised her dear friend that she and Karl Oskar would be most happy to come to Ulrika's first party.

2.

During a dark night in December, eight days before Christmas, the birth took place. Pastor Jackson had to leave his bed in the middle of the night to fetch Miss Cora Skalrud to help his wife. It was over before dawn. The Norwegian woman had been a midwife for twenty-five years and approached her duties with experienced hands. Ulrika was successfully delivered, without other assistance.

The mother lay quietly in her bed regaining her strength, while Miss Skalrud, a strong, resolute woman, fussed with the newborn child, washed and cared for it. Pastor Jackson waited in the living room, into which he had been pushed unceremoniously by Miss Skalrud, not yet aware that all was over.

The midwife was surprised that the mother had not immediately asked the sex of the child. Now she volunteered to Mrs. Jackson that she had borne a girl.

Ulrika raised herself quickly on her elbow. "What are you saying, woman? Did I hear you right?"

"I said, you've borne a little girl . . ."

"Do you mean to insist that I . . . ?"

The mother fell back on her pillow. She lay in silent thought for a minute. It had not crossed her mind—she had known in advance the child would be a male. Then she spoke. "Look again!"

The midwife stared at her; was this woman out of her head? Or why didn't she believe her words concerning the child's sex? She replied gruffly; perhaps she hadn't spoken clearly enough? It was a girl she held in her arms.

But Ulrika knew that Miss Skalrud's eyesight was poor. She had of course held the child too far away from her eyes. Besides, it was still quite dark outside, and their
140

only light was the pale flame of a tallow candle; the midwife was obviously wrong.

"Take the candle and peek closer!"

This was an insult to Cora Skalrud's professional pride. She replied that in her life she had helped more than a thousand children through the portals of this world—who would know the difference between male and female better than she?

Ulrika sat up in bed. "But you are shortsighted, Skalrud! And you are a stubborn woman because you are Norwegian. Give me the brat and the stump of tallow and let me look for myself!"

Without reply the midwife held the newborn child close to the mother's face and let the candle shine on the wriggling little body. Ulrika looked herself.

"Well, what do you say now?"

Ulrika said nothing. She had sunk down into her bed again.

This child could not become a minister. No woman could be consecrated for pastoral duties.

The midwife remained at the bedside, the child in her arms, reproaching Ulrika. She should be proud to have given life to such an unusually well-shaped girl. Why did she act as if she were disappointed and annoyed? Miss Skalrud had assisted at the births of creatures born blind as kittens, ill-shaped, hare-lipped, one-handed, one-legged, noseless, or crippled changelings. In such cases she could understand if the mother were unhappy and complained. If she had put any such monster in Ulrika's arms there would have been cause for wailing!

The words rang true to the mother and she asked for the girl. Miss Skalrud was right—she was a beautiful child, a wonderful little bundle. The baby was amazingly well made, perfect in every way.

"Yet a thief for a father!"

"What's that?"

"And a whore for a mother!"

"Have you lost your mind, woman?"

The midwife was greatly disturbed. She went in to Pastor Jackson to tell him that his wife was successfully delivered, but she added: "Your wife is out of her head. I'm afraid she has childbed fever."

Pastor Jackson became greatly upset. He immediately sent for Dr. Christoffer Caldwell, a contractor, carpenter, and blacksmith in the town, but first and foremost a capable doctor. He examined Ulrika and pronounced her a woman with the strength of a horse; never had he seen a woman so fully recuperated one hour after a birth.

Ulrika had no childbed fever. After a few days she was up, attending to her usual chores. And when one evening the Baptist congregation offered a prayer of thanks for Mr. and Mrs. Jackson's newborn child, the pastor expressed his gratitude to the Lord.

But now, at the big Christmas party which Ulrika intended to give, there would be something amiss. She had planned to step forward with a boy-child on her arm and say to her guests: Look at this little one! He will be a man of the Church! He will stand in his surplice before the altar! He will climb the pulpit in full regalia! He shall be as important a man as Dean Brusander back in Ljuder, Sweden. And she who has carried this Lord's servant in her womb for nine months is Ulrika of Västergöhl, the old parish whore from Ljuder, who at home was denied the holy sacrament and forbidden the Lord's house. She is the one who stands before you now in her glory—the mother of a priest!

So she had intended to speak. But now she could not. And Ulrika searched her soul, realizing she had not yet managed to shed her old sinful body, and that God looked upon her as unworthy of mothering a minister.

But that day would come if she continued to improve. At the age of forty she had not many years to lose—she must make sure she became pregnant again as soon as possible.

3.

On the "fourth day of Christmas" Mrs. Henry O. Jackson gave the first party of her life, in the Baptist minister's home at Stillwater. Her Swedish guests, grown-ups and children, came from Taylors Falls, from New Kärragärde, and from Duvemala. Two Norwegian immirants from Stillwater, Miss Skalrud and shoemaker Thomassen, were also invited. Karl Oskar and Kristina came with their four children; they would stay the night with the Jacksons. Only Swedish Anna did not come. Jonas Petter told them his housekeeper had awakened during the night with chills and running bowels and dared not travel the long road in this winter cold. The chills, that horrible disease, was prevalent among the settlers this winter, he explained. But they all knew that Swedish Anna refused to have anything to do with Ulrika after she became a Baptist.

Jonas Petter offered the excuse innocently, at face value, and Ulrika replied that she realized chills and loose bowels were the most annoying of ailments since they reduced a human body to a shadow within a short time, making it useless for both one thing and another. But a human soul could, in spite of this, remain honest and truthful. Then she whispered to Kristina, "I bet Swedish Anna prayed the Lord for this diarrhea!"

The only American among the guests was Pastor Jackson himself, and in his own home today he was not the host; it was his wife's party and he also was an invited guest. The language barrier separated him from most of the others but some of them spoke English passably, so he wasn't entirely deaf and dumb. He tried to make himself understood with motions of his hands, nods, pointings, and winks, and when he himself failed to understand what was said to him, he smiled his radiant smile, filled with friendship and warmth, making everyone feel happy.

Ulrika offered her guests old-fashioned Swedish Christmas dishes: boiled pig's head, preserved and rolled pork,

143

stewed pork, meatballs, chopped calf liver. She had made sausage of lamb and veal, prepared sweet cheese and cheesecake. This was not ordinary food, it was holiday abundance, not meager, everyday fare but sumptuous Christmas dishes—the Christmas delicacies of Sweden served to the Swedes in the St. Croix Valley.

The guests helped themselves from the smörgåsbord and found places to sit down with their overflowing plates. They ate in silence. The fat rolled pork melted in their mouths, their tongues savored the aftertaste, the jellied pork from the pig's head trembled on their plates, the smell from the sweet cheese penetrated their nostrils. It was a revelation: they had forgotten this taste. They had forgotten how wonderful all these dishes were. But after a few bites memory returned and they ate in silence and reverence; it was the taste of Christmas in Sweden!

Only a few times had they eaten these dishes since they left their homeland. After having been away for so long this feast became to them a return home, as it were. They saw, they tasted, they smelled Christmas in the homeland. It penetrated their eyes, mouths, and noses. The Christmas fare they devoured affected them more than physically—it penetrated the souls of the immigrants.

Memories from that land where they had eaten these dishes every Christmas filled the minds of the guests. A vision of that land suddenly appeared before them with Christmas tables and festivities, with close relatives, intimate neighbors, forgotten friends. In their vision, they sat down with people they would never again see; they were sitting in a company who no longer belonged to the living. They remembered *that* year, and *that* Christmas, and *that* party—what festivity and hilarity! But she? She was at that party, and she is dead now. And he? I'll never see him again.

To the Swedish settlers in Minnesota Territory Ulrika's party became a party of memories; their old-country past caught up with them in the new, dwelt with them in this room. Ulrika's table brought back their homeland in concrete reality. They had left that country, but the country was still with them.

Here they sat at memory's table, in the company of the living and the dead. And they talked of the country they never again would see.

4.

Kristina felt liberated, at home, in this company where the language did not separate her from the others. She could listen and understand, talk and reply. It was as if she had been given back an essential faculty that she had lost in North America and missed sorely. She felt lighthearted and happy as she said to Karl Oskar, "This is exactly like a Christmas party back home."

Home—it still lay across the sea. And she was still out here.

Kristina began to watch Anders Mansson. He ate very slowly from his well-filled plate, staring in front of him, staring with a fixed expression at the wall where there was nothing to see. But perhaps Anders Mansson did see something, perhaps it was Öland, his home province, which he envisioned. He had once said that he had only one wish left: to eat Öland dumplings once more before he died. And Kristina had promised to prepare them for him but had not yet had the opportunity.

Anders suffered from the same ailment as she did: he longed for the homeland. When that disease attacked him at its worst, he drank *brännvin* until he became insensible and lay flat on his back. She would have liked to talk with him about that ache and anguish, of their common loss. But he was a close man, and morose, and shied away from confidences. Perhaps he would not have taken to drinking in his misery if he had found a woman to share his life on his claim.

Kristina sat on the sofa beside Thomassen, the Stillwater Norwegian who had made her spinning wheel. Samuel Nöjd, the trapper, came over with his plate and sat down on the other side of her, grinning: "I keep to the ladies!"

Kristina had a feeling that a stink of slaughter and ran-

145

cid hides always rose from Nöjd, and his evil language offended her. When he had been invited to Communion last spring he had sent a blasphemous refusal. This old man, so near to meeting his Creator, was an unbeliever. He was a disgusting man, who lived with an Indian woman, a persistent sinner. He had lived so long among the heathens out here that he had lost all his Christian conceptions. In spite of this Ulrika had invited him today; she would not overlook any of her countrymen, and she felt that the heathen Nöjd, more than others, needed to meet people who lived like Christians.

Nöjd pushed a large chunk of preserved pork into his mouth; the juice ran from the corners onto his chin, and he swallowed ravenously.

"Can she cook, that Ulrika! Oj, oj, oj! What a cook! I'm sorry she wouldn't marry me!"

"But you have a woman, I've heard," said Kristina.

"That Indian wench cooks regular pigs' slops for me. All she does is stir up some wild rice and corn now and then."

"Why do you keep her, then?"

"Oh, she's useful for other things. She's good to sleep on."

And Samuel Nöjd chuckled and winked at Kristina with his small green eyes. "She's somewhat narrow in the right place, Indian girls always are . . ."

Shoemaker Thomassen pricked up his ears when the hunter described his Indian woman. He leaned so far forward that his yellow hair fell over his forehead.

"It's not nice of you to use the poor woman in that way!" exclaimed Kristina.

"I'm only helping her," chuckled Nöjd. "She came to my cabin one night last winter. She was almost starved to death, and frozen stiff. She nearly died. I let her stay. I've taken care of the girl."

Ulrika was walking about among her guests, urging them to refill their plates. She stopped near Nöjd and listened as he continued:

"She has nobody who is interested in her. Her tribe doesn't live hereabouts. I've been kind and human to her."

"But you get paid for your kindness," interrupted Ulrika. "Every night you exact payment from the poor girl!"

"My Indian girl sleeps with me of her free will!"

"She has no choice!"

"No! That's a lie!" insisted the fur trader, insulted. "The French trappers forced the squaws on their backs, but I've never used force with any woman, not even with one of the savages."

Ulrika wanted to be kind to Nöjd and said, "Well, you're not one of the worst of the white men in the Territory. There are men who go after the poor animals. You, at least, keep to the human race."

"Must men be so horrible and need it so much!" exclaimed Kristina, her voice half choked with repulsion.

The yellow-haired Norwegian at her other side nodded to her as if agreeing with her.

"What do you expect of men?" said Ulrika and looked from the Swede to the Norwegian. "They're created that way!"

"You mean we can't help ourselves," grinned Nöjd.

But Ulrika explained how matters were: first God created man, and he did it on the afternoon of the same day in which he had made the animals, each according to its nature. He was a beginner with people, he had as yet no experience. When he attempted man he only knew how to make animals. And the man turned out the way he did because of this. Much later God created the woman. Then he had had experience, then he knew what a human should be like.

"But I'm no wild animal!" said Samuel Nöjd, annoyed. "The Indian girl isn't faring ill with me, she would be much worse off among her own people."

He cleaned his plate and walked up to the table for more. The Norwegian moved closer to Kristina. His lustful eyes had been on her all the time. She remembered that look from the day when they arrived in Stillwater and he had shown them the way to Taylors Falls.

"The women here in the Territory are unjustly divided," said the Norwegian settler, thickly. "So many of us men have to go without them."

"But new women are coming in right along," said Ulrika.

Thomassen, however, complained that no woman had been left over for him.

Ulrika turned to him with deep understanding. Both men and women suffered with great desires and had to fight against them, she told him. It was only natural that the men in the Territory had hot pants, spending their days and nights alone. But partly they had themselves to blame; they needn't, for example, drink so much of that egg beer they all bought at Pierre's Tavern down at the river. She knew lumberjacks and other men who practically lived on that stuff; it contained four eggs to each quart of beer. It was of course a healthy and strength-giving drink. But a more sexy drink was not to be had in the world. And the men complained they couldn't hold themselves back, after first having stirred up their lusts. She had heard that Thomassen used to go to Pierre's Tavern; her Christian kindness compelled her to advise him: if his flesh cried out for women, by all means stay away from the egg beer!

Ulrika walked away to talk to other guests. The blond Norwegian had not taken his eyes off Kristina. When Ulrika left them he put his hand on her shoulder.

Kristina could feel the strong yearning emanating from the man. His eyes were so strangely penetrating; she felt they were seeking her sex. His lust lay so open today she became uncomfortable. She pulled back her shoulder, shivering and began to praise the spinning wheel he had made for her: it was so easy to handle, the pedals moved lightly. She didn't tire from spinning all day at a stretch. Spinning and weaving were her winter occupations.

The Norwegian touched the hand in which she held her plate:

"Come and visit me sometime!"

He was talking in a very low voice—what did he mean? He had said that the women were unjustly divided among the men hereabouts—did he mean that several men should share one woman? Would he himself wish to share her, perhaps?

"Please, come in and see me—I live all alone."

148

Yes, that was what he meant: he wanted to have his share of her. He wanted to lure her to his lonely house.

She looked for Karl Oskar—he was sitting at the other end of the room, talking in his halting English with Pastor Jackson. What would Karl Oskar have said if he had heard Thomassen's invitation? Something unpleasant would have happened to the shoemaker, of that she was sure. She also was sure that there was one threshold in Stillwater she would never cross.

Little by little she moved away from the man, until he was forced to take his hand from her shoulder.

He smiled, awkwardly: "You aren't afraid of me?"

"No, I had not thought of you as being dangerous."

"I am a very peaceful man."

There was something of a child's helplessness in the little shoemaker's voice. And something childlike came over his face when he smiled. Her fear and repulsion were overcome by compassion: perhaps he hadn't meant anything by his invitation. Perhaps he had asked her out of pure kindness and only wanted her to come and visit him—he must suffer from lack of company. If he wanted a woman, could she reproach him for that? She could understand a lone man's predicament in this frontier country. She could imagine what it would be for her were she forced to live alone, without husband and children. She could not have endured it, absolutely not. Yet most of the men out here must endure such a life, year in, year out. Perhaps they were not to be judged too severely if they were tempted to adultery with other men's wives, and God must overlook it even if they mixed with heathen women and had unnatural relations with animals.

Samuel Nöjd had gone to sit alone in a corner with another heaped-up plate in front of him, oblivious to everything except the food. Her judgment on him and his treatment of the Indian girl may have been too thoughtless. Perhaps he had told her the truth, that he was so kind and good to the girl that she gave in to him willingly. Samuel Nöjd had been born in a Christian land and had once known what sin was, but had forgotten. The heathen girl should not be judged, she did not know God's Ten Commandments.

Again she heard the low voice of the Norwegian: "I am a kind man and would not harm a woman."

Kristina turned to him. To live alone was too much for a human being. She had gone through so much, she knew. She herself would not wish to live without a man, and she thanked her Creator that she had one. She wanted to tell Thomassen how sorry she was that he must live alone. God had made men and women for each other and he wanted them to enjoy each other. She told him that she hoped so many women would move into the Territory that every man who wanted a wife could have one; that he too would find the companionship he longed for, so he would no longer have to suffer the cruel lot of the lonely ones.

The little yellow-haired man listened intently. Then he touched her hand and said in a controlled voice: "You are a good woman."

Kristina felt perhaps she had been able to comfort another human being.

5.

At the height of the party Ulrika had an announcement: when she had planned the party she had hoped to have one more dear guest present, a little man-child. But as far as she could see it would be another year or so before he could be welcomed. In his place had been sent another guest, a little girl, whom they now would see for the first time.

Cora Skalrud came in carrying the tender child, the little newborn girl, bundled up in her swaddling clothes, and showed her to the guests. Miss Skalrud was as proud of the little one as if she herself had borne her. She predicted that the daughter would one day be as beautiful as her mother. Ulrika replied that in America a girl could make good use of a fair face. But such a girl born in Sweden to poor people would only have to suffer because of it, as she would be considered permissible prey for the men.

150

"Well, now I have introduced the wench," she said happily, and Miss Skalrud carried the baby back to bed.

In the meantime, Jonas Petter had been telling a ribald story to a few of the male guests who sat in a circle around him. It was about a rich farmer at home in Ljuder who was unable to become a father and wanted to hire the village soldier to make him an heir, after his wife had agreed to do her part of the work. The farmer offered the soldier ten sacks of rye for his trouble if a male heir were the result, and five sacks if a female was born, all ample measure. That was how great a difference in value of the two sexes there was in Sweden. The soldier at first pretended hesitation, hoping the farmer would raise the offer. But it had been a year of bad crops and grain was high priced and at last he accepted the pay—it would give bread to his own large flock of children. Next time when the farmer had an errand to town and had to stay away for a couple of nights, the soldier was called in for duty in the couple's marital bed.

He broke it off, however, when Ulrika displayed her newborn child, and when the little girl had been carried to her room he refused to go on. He realized suddenly that it was not a suitable story for a party in a minister's home—he would tell the rest of it some other time in a less pious place.

Jonas Petter understood more English than any of the other men who had come to America with him; during the winter evenings he had studied language books and this last year he had been reading *The Pioneer*, the American paper for settlers, printed in St. Paul. And tonight Pastor Jackson had discovered Jonas's ability in English; they had talked in the pastor's tongue and understood each other easily.

The pastor now approached Jonas Petter, took him by the arm, and led him to a corner. He was speaking in a whisper—it seemed he had a secret to confide. And Jonas Petter's ears were wide open:

Pastor Jackson had thought of a surprise for his wife at her party tonight: he intended to give a speech in her own language: "I want to pay tribute to my wife in Swedish, you see!"

151

From his Swedish friends he had picked up a few suitable sentences and had practiced their pronunciation in secret. But Swedish was a very difficult language and therefore his speech would be short, only seven or eight brief sentences. He practiced this speech for a long time. He wanted to honor and thank his beloved wife in her own language, but in his address of respect he wished also to include all the other women who had come from her country. He valued and thought highly of them all.

The little speech he had prepared with so much effort was written down on a piece of paper. Now he wanted to show it to Jonas Petter and get his opinion as to whether it was good enough. He was anxious to know if he had made any mistakes in the language—would Jonas Petter be kind enough to look through it?

Pastor Jackson handed him the paper. Jonas Petter walked over to the nearest wall candle and read by the light from the tallow:

"Dear my beloved Ollrika! I wish you a bit of speech on your party-feast today. I wish to say unto you thank you my dear. I am joyful and filled with happiness that you became a wife of mine. You are the best of wives in this world. I want you this to know. I would like to make speech and honor all Swedish womenkind today. I enjoy them and find happiness in them all. *Svenska flickor knulla bra.*"

Twice Jonas Petter read through what Pastor Jackson had written. He read slowly and carefully and his face assumed a thoughtful mien.

The pastor stood behind his back and explained. It was the chastity and virtue of the Swedish women he wanted to praise in these words. Of all the people who had moved into Minnesota, the Swedish women appeared to him the model of pious morality.

The pastor was still talking in whispers. Jonas Petter whispered back: there was one sentence he wanted to ask about—where had the pastor picked up the very last sentence of the speech?

Jackson replied he had it from a Swedish timberman he had met in Franconia; he had asked this man to write down in his own language a few words of praise for

152

Swedish women, indeed, the best praise he could give with a clear conscience. And the Swede had written it on paper he had copied, so Pastor Jackson did not think there could be any mistake in the language; he remembered that sentence very well—it was the last one, and he had copied it correctly.

Jonas Petter also spoke in a whisper when he answered that this was an elegant and worthy speech. It was well suited for the occasion here tonight. All that was written down on this paper was clear, unadulterated truth; from the first word to the last it was the whole truth. And he was sure the women present would like it; they would be well pleased with the praise they received. Nor were there any mistakes in Swedish grammar; all was well put together.

But he would advise the pastor to shorten the speech with one sentence, only one little sentence. If, for example, the last sentence were cut out, the very last one. It was more or less superfluous anyway. What it conveyed had already been repeated so often that everyone knew it. It was indeed correct and right and true, that line also, perhaps the truest of them all. Jonas Petter himself could from practical experience verify its truth, for that matter. It contained great honor and much praise for the Swedish women, and they would indeed feel honored when they heard it. But a speaker ought not to repeat what everyone knew. So the last sentence was entirely superfluous. The fine speech would have its best effect if it were removed.

Pastor Jackson nodded eagerly and thanked Jonas Petter warmly for the advice; of course he would follow it. Jonas Petter pulled out his red carpenter's pencil, which he always carried in his hip pocket, and drew a line through the last four words on the paper, a thick, forceful line which almost obliterated them.

The speech Pastor Jackson gave in honor of his wife came as her crown of honor. The surprise was almost too much for her—now old Ulrika of Västergöhl was indeed rehabilitated; she had invited these guests to her new home, they had willingly accepted her invitation, yes, they had felt honored by it. And they were happy and sated with food and good cheer—with one voice they had

153

praised her ability as housekeeper and cook. There was no end to their praise of her "Swedish table" with its delicious dishes. And she had been proud to show them a well-shaped daughter, born in wedlock, in a Christian marriage. Even as a mother she had received honor and praise. And then at last, entirely unexpected, utterly surprising, came this further honor, respect and praise to her—this speech in her own language which her dear, beloved Henry gave for her.

Her fellow immigrants. the people from her own home parish, could hear in their own language, clearly and loudly, how grateful her husband was to her, how highly he esteemed and respected and honored her. It was a mark of honor surpassing all others—it raised her so high she felt dizziness overtake her. Ulrika of Västergöhl had come into her glory. What more could she wish in life?

Ulrika rushed over to her husband, who opened his arms to her for everyone to see, resting on his breast she could no longer contain her emotions. She burst into tears of happiness.

And Jonas Petter returned to his seat and helped himself to more of the hostess's delicious cheesecake. He had undoubtedly done a good deed today; he had prevented a great scandal at this party. He had done so because it was Ulrika's first party. But now he sat there wondering about himself and the way he had acted. He wondered if he hadn't in some way begun to change—if Pastor Jackson had asked his advice in this matter a few years ago, then he would surely have urged him to give his speech without shortening it Why had he this evening refused such a malicious pleasure?

Like Ulrika of Västergöhl, he must have become a better person in America.

VIII. "That Baptist Ilk"

1.

Karl Oskar and Kristina were celebrating their fourth Christmas in the new country. They had made things as Yule-like as possible, both inside and outside. At threshing time Karl Oskar had put aside a dozen sheaves which he now set up for the birds in front of the window; there the yellow barley straw broke warmly against the tall white drifts. Just finished for Christmas was a little sled he had made for the children on which they could slide down the drifts as soon as the snow packed. The weather was mild this Christmas, their last in the log cabin.

Karl Oskar was in the habit of writing to his parents twice a year, at Christmas and at Midsummer. Now he sat with pen and paper for several evenings during the holidays and wrote his letter to Sweden. Last summer his letter had been very brief; he wanted to make his winter letter a little longer. But when, at the very beginning, he had noted down that all of them enjoyed the precious gift of health, he seemed to have said almost all there was to say, and he had to work laboriously to compose further sentences.

On the last day of the old year Karl Oskar received a letter from his sister Lydia, who had written in their father's place. Father's hands shook so, she wrote, that Nils Jakobsson was afraid his letters from now on would be so poorly written that his son in America would be unable to read them. But both he and Mother were well and active, even though they no longer made any use of themselves in this life. His sister wrote that she, during the past year, had joined in wedlock a farmer at Akerby, so that her name from now on would be Lydia Karlsson. Since her marriage she had borne a son who at the moment of her

155

writing was six weeks old. She mentioned the names of a few parishioners, recently dead, whom Karl Oskar had known, and she wrote that many farmers from Ljuder and the neighboring villages of Linneryd and Elmeboda had emigrated to North America during the year, but she did not know where they had settled. Finally, she wondered what had happened to their brother Robert, whom they had not heard from for almost two years.

Karl Oskar could not allay her apprehensions concerning Robert, only share them. Almost a year had passed since he had received the last letter from his brother. And next spring three years would have passed since Robert and Arvid started out on their journey to the California goldfields.

Neither of the young men was made for long, dangerous journeys, nor were they in shape to endure hardships. One could only hope Providence had protected them on the road to the goldfields. And what could Karl Oskar have done to stop their venture? He could not have denied his brother the right to make his own decisions. He could not put his brother in a cage. Moreover, Robert would have escaped had he done so. Even as a small child he would run away, and his parents had had to put a cowbell around his neck to find the straying boy. The day he was to begin his first service as a hired hand he had tried to run away and leave the home village, and later he had escaped from his master. Robert was the eternal escapist. If he only reached Heaven he would try to escape from it too, thought Karl Oskar. But why didn't he write more often? He could write well.

"Robert won't come back until he has found gold," Kristina said.

"And just because of this I'm afraid he'll never come back."

Karl Oskar was beginning to think that his younger brother was no longer alive.

2.

Another new year began—1854—and again they were without a new almanac. Notations about crops, purchases, sales, dates when the cows took the bull, and other important days were still recorded in the old almanac.

With the new year came severe cold. Night and day they kept the fire burning. The fireplace—it was the cabin's heart and center, the capitol of the home kingdom. The hearth was the home's altar, and on that altar were sacrificed all the cords of firewood that had been cut during the summer and stacked against the cabin wall to dry. The fireplace—it was the most essential part of the home, the source of blessed warmth. The fire must not go out. In the light of the fire they performed their chores, round the altar of flames they gathered to warm their cold limbs. The fireplace gave the people in the cabin light and warmth, it was the defender of life.

Each morning the wreath of white frost roses bloomed anew on the nail heads. On the walls of round logs the cold found ever new holes and cracks. But next winter it might penetrate here as much as it pleased; no living soul would then be in this place, and no fire would burn on the hearth. Next winter they would be protected in a real house. The child Kristina was expecting would have its delicate body sheltered by well-chinked timber walls. The child—that is, if it now turned out to be only one . . . The thought had begun to hover in Kristina's mind, that perhaps a twin birth was in the offing. The new life felt so heavy in her body—hadn't it felt the same way once before? She had had twins earlier, but only Lill-Marta had survived. If again she gave life to two, would they both live? It was futile to worry about it but she couldn't help it; she was made that way.

Early one Sunday morning, shortly after New Year's, the Olaussons came to call unexpectedly. Karl Oskar had been out in the woods looking for a pig which had broken out of its sty, and he had just returned. Neither he nor

157

Kristina had had time to think of their Sunday rest, and they had not yet cleaned up. They were surprised at this early call from their neighbors; when Bible discussions and spiritual gatherings were held, the families did not get together until the afternoon of the Sabbath.

Kristina pulled forth chairs for the callers, who were dressed in their Sunday best. Petrus Olausson had put on a tie and trimmed his beard, and his thin tufts of hair were combed and orderly. Judit wore her best white-frilled black dress which buttoned all the way to her chin. Her black hair was pulled back severely and parted in the middle, displaying a line of skin like a straight white ribbon from her forehead to the top of her skull. On the back of her head she wore a black cap with white embroidery. Her powerful nose stuck out sharply, a spy for her prying eyes. Her mouth as always was tightly closed, the right corner slightly higher than the left.

The couple's expressions were set in their customary Sabbath severity which Karl Oskar and Kristina recognized from earlier Sundays, but their faces also displayed something serious and ominous. What could they want so early on a Sunday morning?

The Olaussons sat stiffly and ceremoniously and twisted awkwardly on their chairs; they had not come just to amuse themselves, that much was clear.

Karl Oskar began telling them about the pig he had been hunting for over an hour. What luck the weather was so mild this morning—it was an important pig, a sow he intended to send to the boar for mating when her time came again.

Petrus Olausson listened absentmindedly. Then he said, "We have come to call on a matter of great spiritual importance."

He raised his chin with its newly trimmed beard and spoke as if he were reading aloud from the Bible. "We have come to open your eyes and to warn you, our beloved neighbors and fellow Christians."

"To open your eyes, indeed!" interrupted the wife, adjusting her cap, which had slid down over her left ear.

"It is the duty of a person who sees to warn the one

158

who is blind," continued the husband. "It is our duty as Christians to safeguard our neighbors' souls."

"Exactly so," echoed the wife. "We are here to fulfill our duty."

"It concerns your souls, our dear neighbors . . ."

Karl Oskar and Kristina listened with increasing confusion. Their neighbors spoke as if the Almighty himself had sent them here with the message that the Day of Doom would come on the morrow.

Petrus Olausson went on. "We have for a long time thought about this. We have hesitated, delayed. As Christians we can now no longer be responsible."

"What's this all about?" exclaimed Kristina. "What in the world is going on?"

"I will tell you." He rose and moved closer to her. "Some time ago I met in this house an unknown woman. A Swedish woman. You must recall our meeting . . . ? The woman had . . ."

"You said she made a fright of herself in a hat!" interrupted Judit.

"That is correct—she wore a hat on her head. A very large piece of headgear, full of vanity and most outlandish."

Judit Olausson had her opinion. "A Swedish woman gone plumb crazy of vanity! Putting on a hat when she gets to America!" Her voice was brittle with disgust.

"I have now learned who this woman is," said Petrus Olausson slowly, as if announcing a great discovery.

"You must mean Ulrika, I gather," said Kristina.

"That's her name, that scarecrow," confirmed Judit, pulling up the right corner of her mouth still further.

"But Ulrika didn't put on a hat from vanity—she is as good as any upper-class woman," said Kristina. "We're intimate friends."

"Friends?" interrupted the neighbor. "My poor woman—this 'friend' of yours is married to the Baptist minister in Stillwater!"

"She has gone over to her husband's religion and she has been rebaptized!" echoed Judit.

"I know all that; it concerns no one but herself."

Olausson straightened up to give greater weight to his

words: "You also know this: we must have no connection with lost souls! We must keep clear of sectarians. And that is why you must have nothing to do with this woman who is the wife of the Stillwater priest."

Karl Oskar and Kristina stared at each other. At last they began to grasp their neighbors' purpose.

"Look out for this Mrs. Jackson. Don't let that woman into your house. Don't ever open your door to her again."

Karl Oskar snorted loudly. Petrus Olausson's advice seemed to him so outrageous that he wanted to laugh. But he held his tongue.

"With this Mrs. Jackson you admit the Evil One into your home," continued Olausson. "I heard that woman's raw and unbecoming speech. She carries the devil's own tongue in her sweet mouth. Without you being aware of it, she pours irreligion's poison into your ears. Only because of Christian love do we wish to warn you. It concerns your soul!"

"We do our duty as Christians!" added Judit.

"We only wish your best, dear neighbor. Listen to your friends' advice; have nothing more to do with that woman!"

Olausson turned toward Kristina, whose face had stiffened as she listened. Words stuck in her throat as she tried to answer.

"Uncle Petrus . . . do . . . do you know . . . you're talking about my best friend in America . . ."

"Yes, I know. And because of this friendship the danger is so much greater for you."

"You're blind!" insisted the neighbor wife. "Friendship blinds people."

"Mrs. Jackson offers you her hand and you do not perceive the claw hidden in the paw."

"Because you are blind!"

Kristina's face had turned flaming red. What was this her neighbor asked of her? She needed time to collect herself in order to understand. They asked that she sacrifice her friendship for Ulrika and close her door to her! This friendship . . . She remembered so well what Ulrika had once said to her: I sold my body at times for a loaf of bread, but my friendship costs more than any man or woman can pay. I don't throw it away on just anyone. But you have it, Kristina. You have it for all time. Of that you can be sure. You got it that time when you shared your bread with me on the journey. You have received the most valuable possession I have to give to any human being. That was what Ulrika had said, that was how valuable was her friendship. And she, Kristina, had it; Ulrika had by her actions proven it to her. And here came these people, demanding that she repay good with evil and deny her friendship for Ulrika, that she behave treacherously, that she betray her best friend . . . !

Kristina had her own ideas about right and wrong toward other people, and never had anyone been able to sway her. Nor would Petrus Olausson and his wife be able to do so, not to the smallest degree. They asked her to betray a friendship, they asked her to wrong a person, they demanded that she commit this gravest of sins.

And there stood Uncle Petrus and continued to talk to her in the patient voice of an admonishing father. He knew from experience the dangers of heresy, he himself had for a time followed a false prophet. But one day his eyes had been opened to the true light, and now he wanted—along with true Swedish Lutherans—to found an Evangelical Lutheran Church in America, which would be free from interference by worldly authorities and unblemished by heresy. And among those true Christians who must build this Church were Kristina and her husband. He must therefore protect them against false prophets who called themselves Baptists. They were sent by the devil to spread dissension among the Swedes. They were sunderers, this Baptist ilk, they wanted to create dissension and dissolve the true faith.

He took Kristina by the arm, pleadingly, admonishingly, mildly rebuking her as if she were his beloved, disobedient, self-willed child.

"Dearly beloved Kristina! These sunderers and false prophets deck themselves out like friends. You do not recognize them for what they are. You do not know the Fiend in the soul of this Mrs. Jackson! But as long as she continues to come here, your home is besmirched. Therefore, beloved Kristina, do not ever let her cross your threshold again. Will you give me this promise?"

"No!" she screamed out. "No! No! No! Never!"

And Kristina violently pulled herself away from him, as if he were unclean and had besmirched her. Her explosion was so sudden that Olausson took a few steps backward. His wife jumped up from her chair.

"This is enough!" cried Kristina. "Listen to me, you, once and for all. You come to me and talk ill of Ulrika— what do you mean? Do you think I'm a fool? I'll tell you something, both of you! Pretending to be my friends, ah?"

"Poor child! How you talk!" said Judit Olausson and turned her head so quickly that her cap slid down over her right ear.

"Dear Kristina, calm down!" pleaded Olausson.

"Wretched woman! The devil speaks through her mouth," added Judit.

With Kristina's sudden explosion, Olausson lost his composure. He turned to Karl Oskar. "You must correct your foolish wife, Nilsson! She acts as if she had already been led astray. Help us bring her back to her senses."

Karl Oskar rose from his seat and straightened up to his full height. "This is crazier than hell!"

"Yes, yes, here we come as friends and fellow Christians and your wife treats us as if we were . . ."

"You have given order in my house, Olausson. But you have done it for the last time."

"What's that, Nilsson? Are you too against us? Are you as blind as your wife?"

Karl Oskar looked steadily at his neighbor and raised his voice until Olausson drew back. "You leave Kristina alone! She can open her door to whoever she wants! And this I had intended to tell you before: I don't need a guardian! Nor does my wife! Now you know!"

"But Nilsson—my dear neighbor—you must understand us! All we want is to warn you against the sectarians . . . you know—those Baptists! We must be careful—every moment of our lives we must watch out against . . ."

162

"That's enough! You force me to tell you right out: take care of yourself and shit on others!"

Kristina had stepped between the two men, her eyes aflame. "Let me have a word in this matter! I want to be open with you, Petrus—you come here and try to separate old friends. You insist I kick out the best friend I have. And you speak of sundering and dissension! Who is the sunderer? Who is trying to spread ill will and dissension? No one but you!"

In her excitement she no longer called her neighbor Uncle Petrus. He tried to get a word in in reply, but she wouldn't let him. "You shut up—it's my turn to talk now! You try to part Ulrika and me! You yourself are the sunderer, you spread discord, you slander Ulrika and accuse her of evil deeds! You belie your fellow men! You've forgotten the eighth commandment, Christian that you call yourself! You bear false witness against your neighbor! You run about and spread evil rumors—you, a grown man! You ought to be ashamed! Or haven't you any shame in your old body? Haven't you any decency, you evil old man!"

Petrus Olausson remained frozen, listening. His eyes were riveted on Kristina; his look was one of sorrow rather than anger. It was as if he looked upon his neighbor's wife as a father might look at a difficult and straying child.

"You ought to feel ashamed of yourself, Petrus Olausson!"

"Dear neighbors—I'm amazed and saddened. It is with sorrow and pain that I hear . . ."

"Come, Petrus!" said Judit Olausson, adjusting again her black cap. She took her husband by the arm. "That woman is possessed! Insulting us like that! Let's go!"

"But our duty as fellow Christians . . ."

"You can see we're too late," said his wife.

"Dear Judit, it's never too late to lead a straying soul back to the true . . ."

"But can't you hear—the sectarians already have snared her in their nets. Let's go home. Come, Petrus!"

Judit walked toward the door. Petrus Olausson cleared his throat and turned once more to Kristina, lecturing her kindly. "Our Christian love for our neighbors brought us here today. We so want to warn you, and you reward us with insults. But I forgive you, Kristina. I overlook your words. For it is an evil spirit that speaks through your mouth."

"Shut up about your evil spirits! No one has led me astray! I intend to remain a Christian Lutheran as long as I live! But I won't betray my friends! Now you know! And so shut up!"

"You are a foolish woman. We must pray God to protect you against snares. We will pray for your mind to change so that you never again will admit that Baptist ilk into your home. As Christian people we must avoid this unclean house until it has been cleansed."

"Out with you!" shouted Kristina, trembling. "Out of my house, both of you! Not clean in here! That I'll never forget as long as I live!"

At this her voice failed her.

3.

The Olaussons left. Karl Oskar and Kristina sat down to rest, exhausted as if by some heavy chore.

"Well, I guess our neighbor-peace has come to an end," said he.

Kristina thought of the spring day last year—it had seemed to her then like a Sunday—when Karl Oskar for the first time had heard their new neighbor's ax ringing in the forest.

"I lost my temper—but I don't regret it," she said.

Her voice still trembled: what did they take her for, this Olausson and his woman? Who did they think she was? A nodding doll, without a mind of her own? A stupid woman they could lead wherever they wished, one whom they must lead by the hand? A silly sheep, in utter simplicity letting herself be devoured by those ugly Baptist wolves, Ulrika and her husband?

But the neighbor's remark about her unclean house had hurt her the most.

164

"Well, now they know how we feel," said Karl Oskar. "Let them get mad if they wish. How stupid that we must quarrel with our neighbors because Ulrika jumped into the river and got herself baptized. It doesn't make sense."

Ulrika was not as close to him as she was to Kristina. The former parish whore still had many characteristics he found difficult to accept. But over the years he had learned to value her more and more. And regardless of who the person was, no outsider could come to him and dictate whom he could admit to his house and whom he must exclude. They would open their door for whomever they wished.

"No neighbor shall make decisions for us!"

After Kristina had calmed down a little, she began to think she must not be unjust toward her neighbors; surely only the best of intentions had caused them to call today. Uncle Petrus was perfectly honest in his concern for them: his talk to her had been sincere and fatherly.

But Karl Oskar replied, why must people eternally worry about other people's souls? Why not be satisfied with the care of their own? Olausson was a thrifty and capable settler, and his advice and examples were often worth following. A man like him was needed among the immigrants: he was interested in communal matters and got things started. The only trouble was that he tried to manage people without being asked, and against their will.

"Like Uncle Danjel, he has been punished at home for his Bible explanations," reminded Kristina.

"Exactly—in Sweden Olausson himself was a sectarian, yet here in America he can't stand them!"

"It's very strange; how can he be so intolerant out here?"

Karl Oskar volunteered that Petrus Olausson had become so warmly attached to religious freedom that he no longer allowed it to anyone but himself.

Well, the pleasant neighborliness with the Helsinge family seemed to be over. The Olaussons had been shown the door and were not likely to return. But new neighbors had arrived, and more would come, by and by. The first settlers at Ki-Chi-Saga need no longer live as hermits.

However, said Karl Oskar, he would rather live without neighbors than have to fight with them.

For a long time Kristina continued to think about Uncle Petrus, this strange man. In Sweden he had suffered punishment and persecution for his belief, in America he himself persecuted people who believed differently. Could anyone understand this kind of person?

How could people who had sprung from the same Creator and belonged to the same race be so intolerant of each other? It was a shame. Here in these great wild forests a small group of people had settled; they came from the same country and spoke the same language; all of them had to begin life anew, in a new land; they were poor, dependent on themselves, and needed each other's company; they lived so far apart that the distance between their houses in itself kept them apart. Must they now also close their doors against each other because different churches and different faiths existed in this country? Must they separate even more—and because of religion? Because of Christ's gospel, which preached that all people were brethren?

Was it impossible to live in unity and enjoy each other because of one's faith?

If any people in this world needed to live harmoniously it was the small group of Swedish settlers in the St. Croix Valley. It must be God's intention that they be friends.

IX. *Hemlandet* Comes to the Immigrants

1.

Early one morning in the first week of May the anticipated increase in the Duvemala family took place. Kristina escaped the dreaded twin birth; she was delivered of a girl. The evening before, she had sent a message to Ulrika, who had dispatched Miss Skalrud to aid her. The

Norwegian midwife arrived at the cabin a couple of hours too late, but remained for a few days while Kristina stayed in bed. Never before had she felt so weak and worn out after a birth.

Shortly before her delivery Pastor Erland Törner had returned from Illinois, and he had now resumed his pastoral duties in the St. Croix Valley, where he traveled from place to place among his countrymen, as he had done the year before. He came one Sunday to Duvemala and christened Karl Oskar's and Kristina's newborn baby; with a minister available they had no excuse for delaying the baptism.

This time the mother alone had chosen the name for the child. The little girl was named Anna Evelina Ulrika, the first two names after Kristina's own mother—Anna Evelina Andersdotter. But the girl was to be called Ulrika.

By giving her daughter Ulrika's name Kristina had in her own way cleansed her home, which the Olaussons considered unclean and degraded by Mrs. Henry O. Jackson of Stillwater.

The neighbors had said: do not open your door to this woman! She had replied, and let them know where she stood: she welcomed an Ulrika who would be a permanent part of the household.

2.

Great things were happening at Ki-Chi-Saga this year. During the spring and summer of 1854 the first great wave of Swedish immigrants washed over the St. Croix Valley. They came in large groups, by the hundreds, and the population of the valley was doubled many times over.

The settlers began to arrive as soon as the ice had melted and the steamboats could ply the river. Already in March and April the first arrivals found their way to the big lake. They had emigrated from Småland, Helsingland, and Östergötland. Larger groups came later in the summer, mostly Smålanders. One group of fourteen families claimed lands along the shores. But a great many of these immigrants settled in the eastern part of the valley, where there were passable roads and more easily accessible claims.

All the claims suitable for farming around Ki-Chi-Saga—the fertile meadows along the lake slopes—were now taken. The newcomers put up their log cabins along bays and sounds, on jutting points and tongues of land. On the surveyor's map, obtained from the land office, the Chippewa word Ki-Chi-Saga had been changed to Chisago Lake. The metamorphosis of the lake had even reached its name. And the thirty-six squares, or sections, around the lake which had been surveyed for settling were now referred to as Chisago Township on maps and deeds. This in turn was part of a larger square, comprising thirty-six square miles. Each section was divided into four claims; thus the whole district contained 144 homesteads. There was still room for more settlers in Chisago Township.

The newcomers told of an immense emigration from Sweden to come next year. Thousands of people were planning to leave, and it was expected that this horde would head for Minnesota to settle among their countrymen.

So the Indian lake Ki-Chi-Saga was renamed. The heathen water was christened by the white tillers and divided into squares and the name written down on deeds and entered on records. The nomad people were pushed farther and farther away from the forests where they had hunted and the waters where they had fished. Their fires had gone out, their camping sites lay unoccupied.

But on the western shore, high above Ki-Chi-Saga's surface, the Indian still stood watch, the red-brown sandstone cliff with its image of a savage, still rose like a heaven-high, unconquerable bastion. The Indian's immense head was turned to the east; with empty, black, cliff-cave eyes he watched day and night over his old hunting grounds and fishing waters. Each spring his crown of thickets turned green, but with each spring he saw more trespassers arrive. And his eyes remained fixed, as if mir-

168

roring an inconsolable sorrow in the dark depth of the cliff. From the east they came, this race of intruders, and the high watchman spied forever in that direction from where the land's new inhabitants approached in ever increasing numbers.

One race wandered into the land, and the other wandered away. But the Indian at Ki-Chi-Saga remained at his watch, looking in the direction of the rising sun.

3.

The only unclaimed quarter of Karl Oskar Nilsson's section—the northeast corner—was taken in the spring by an immigrant from Småland. Their neighbor to the north was Johan Kron from Algutsboda, Kristina's home parish. Kron was the village soldier but had retired from the service and emigrated with his large family, his wife and eight children. The family had brought along two cradles, one for each of the smallest children, who were twins. So the last homestead suddenly had ten inhabitants.

Section 35 of Chisago Township, the new name for Ki-Chi-Saga, where Karl Oskar had been the first settler, was now entirely claimed and occupied.

Axes ringing in the forest—no longer were these unfamiliar sounds. This spring when Karl Oskar walked over his land he could hear echoes from all directions. Here Swedish axes went after the trees, here trunks fell all around, here logs were piled on logs for new homes. Who could have imagined that so many would have followed him from Sweden? Farmers from his own parish were felling trees for log houses, farmers from Algutsboda, Linneryd, Elmeboda, and Hovmantorp, all neighbor parishes of Ljuder. As yet he had not run into anyone he knew from home but he expected to do so any day.

The ring of the axes was a joyous sound to Kristina's ears; it brought her the message of new neighbors building their houses; it told her of new people who would live close to her. It rang out the end of the great loneliness. Living here would no longer be so drab. Already enough

169

people had arrived to make up a good-sized village, even though the houses weren't as close together as in the old country. If the emigration continued, perhaps eventually there would be enough people to make up a large parish. And with each family's arrival she felt the same wonder: why had they come so far to settle in a corner of the world so remote?

Karl Oskar said that it looked as though all the people in the old country were following their example and moving to the Territory. And there was plenty of space out here—there was room for the whole Kingdom of Sweden. But the upper classes would probably remain where they were; those useless creatures lived well and in comfort in Sweden.

Yes, it seemed as if the homeland was coming to America. And in a way it did come to the immigrants that spring—in the form of a newspaper.

It came about through Pastor Törner; Pastor Hasselquist in Galesburg, Illinois, had begun to print a paper in Swedish, *Hemlandet, det Gamla och det Nya* (*The Homeland, the Old and the New*), and he asked his colleague to spread the word in the Swedish settlements. As Pastor Törner traveled about he wrote down the names of those who wanted to subscribe. The paper would describe the most important happenings in both Sweden and America and would appear fortnightly. The price was only a dollar a year, but the publisher appealed to the better-off among his countrymen for an extra fifty cents in order to purchase Swedish type. His press did not have all of the Swedish letters, and since they were difficult to obtain in America, he must order them from Sweden.

Karl Oskar felt it would be worth a dollar (plus fifty cents for the Swedish type) to obtain news from Sweden twice a month; he subscribed to *Hemlandet, det Gamla och det Nya,* and from then on, picked up his paper every second week in Mr. Abbott's store in Taylors Falls. Algot Svensson, his neighbor to the west, was also a subscriber, and they decided to pick up the paper in turn so they need not go to the post office more than once a month.

And *Hemlandet* was received in the settler's home as a dear and welcome guest. They held the paper with cau-

170

tious hands as if afraid it might fall to pieces in the handling.

The news sheet had four pages, and five columns to each page, all printed in Swedish. Karl Oskar and Kristina read and discussed almost every word in *Hemlandet*. After supper he would read to her while she finished her chores. On Sunday afternoons, when she was free for a few hours, they would sit down at the table, with the paper spread before them, and go through paragraph after paragraph systematically.

Through *Hemlandet* they learned that a great war had broken out in Europe a few months earlier: on March 28 war had been declared between Russia on one side and England and France on the other. Besides, the Russians and the Turks had been fighting since last fall, because the Russians were not allowed to protect the Turkish subjects of Christian belief. It was assumed that Sweden would join in the war against Russia to retrieve Finland. But Kristina felt Sweden shouldn't bother with this; she had two brothers of military age and she did not like to think of them participating in human slaughter. Only people who wanted to should take part in wars. Karl Oskar had no close relatives who need go—only his sister, Lydia, was left in Sweden of his generation—but he too hoped the old country would remain at peace. War was an amusement for lords and kings but no plaything for farmers, who had more important things to do. All this warring would probably in the end destroy the Old World.

Another amazing piece of news was that the Swedes were thinking of building railroads here and there in the country, beginning with the provinces of Värmland and Skåne. It was not easy to imagine that perhaps one day a steam wagon might come rolling through Ljuder parish. As yet, Karl Oskar thought, they and the other emigrants were the only Swedes who had traveled in that way.

Telegraphy was the newest contraption. Messages were sent along steel wire with the speed of lightning. This invention too had reached Sweden: a wire had recently been strung all the distance between Stockholm and Goth-

171

enburg. ."A Simple Explanation of Telegraphy" was the title of the article in *Hemlandet*:

> A Telegraph is the name of an instrument through which people can make signs to each other over great distances. It carries tidings from one end of the Union to the other, speedier than a wink of the eye. It has been agreed that certain signs represent certain letters in the alphabet and in this way a conversation can be carried on. It is unimportant if the two communicants are a mile or a thousand miles apart; the conversation goes on with equal speed and what is said with signs arrives on the moment.

In almost every issue of the paper there was a description of some new, amazing invention which the clever Americans had made. There was Pitt's threshing machine, which threshed a bushel of wheat in a minute; the reaper, which was constructed in such a way that it cut the crop with steel arms; the sewing machine, which could baste and sew when tramped by a human foot. From now on one could sew garments with one's feet instead of one's hands. Kristina had just finished her first weaving of last year's flax, and she could have used this tramping apparatus now that she was ready to make clothes for all of them.

They read about the broad city streets with railroads in the middle, about illumination from a vapor called gas, about the iron pipes which led water under the ground and at any moment squirted a stream if one needed water. But the strangest discovery was a new, secret power called electricity. It gave heat and light, it could be used to pull vehicles, it could heal sickness, like lameness, fever, epilepsy. Electricity returned hearing to deaf people, taught the mute to use their tongues. *Hemlandet* had a clarifying article about electricity:

> The cause of lightning is a peculiar power called Electricity. Ligntning emanates from

clouds up in the sky which have become electric. How the clouds have become such is not known. But if a lightning-cloud comes close to an object on earth, an electric spark passes with lightning and thunder from the cloud to the object, and then we say that lightning strikes. It is entirely unfounded, as some people say, that a wedge hits the earth when lightning strikes.

Lightning had once struck and burned a hay-filled barn belonging to Karl Oskar and he therefore felt great respect for electricity. When it was loosed it was much more dangerous than fire: in a single second it could shake a person to death. The paper related that a farmer in Indiana had brought suit against his wife for attempted murder with the new discovery: she had put electricity in her husband's underwear so that it had shot into his body and almost killed him.

In the paper's editorial on electricity, the question was raised as to whether or not Benjamin Franklin had broken God's ordinances by inventing the lightningrod whereby man neutralized the bolts. It seemed self-evident that God must cause hurricanes, floods, and other natural-catastrophes to kill those people he originally had intended to kill by lightning. Mr. Franklin had thus with his rod interfered in the business of the Almighty and caused him unnecessary trouble.

Pastor Hasselquist's paper fought for the true Evangelical Lutheran religion, the world's only right religion, and condemned sectarianism. He lauded highly the new law passed by the Swedish Riksdag, which condemned the Baptist and prescribed high fines for any layman distributing the sacrament. Of the sects in America, the Mormons were described as the most horrible; they preached the rawest gospel of the flesh since Mohammed descended to Hell. Utah, their place of habitation in the Union, had grown like a festering boil on the American nation. The Mormons had recently made a great conquest in Sweden: one hundred and fifty foolish young women had gone to Utah and had been divided ten to each man; in the new land, they now satisfied men's carnal lusts.

The paper printed a list of Brigham Young's wives, thirty-nine in number at that moment. The wives were numbered from one to twenty-seven and a few also had a name, but after twenty-seven they had neither name nor number. Number one was called Lucy Decker, and she would be raised to queen at the resurrection. Those wives who had been given only a number Brigham Young had married for this life only, but those named he had joined for eternity as well. When he held his Sabbath he retired to some lonely place for peace and quiet, taking with him six or seven deeply beloved wives with low numbers.

The *Hemlander*'s editor warned his countrymen not only against spiritual dangers but also against worldly snares and perils, especially those connected with the confusing money matters of North America. Every issue had a column headed *Bank Swindles*, enumerating the banks especially started to cheat people. It was useful for Swedes in the wilderness to know which bills were phony, or worth only half of their face value. And it was emphasized to the readers that neither in the Old World nor in the New did a single bank exist which gave its depositors full security. But there was one Bank, with no human directors, and no earthly safe—the Bank of Grace—which, because of its inexhaustible capital resources—Christ's Blood and the Forgiveness of Sins—always and everywhere was in a position to redeem its bills at their full value: the promise of eternal joy in the Heavenly Chambers. Readers were advised to make their deposits in that bank.

4.

And so *Hemlandet* came to Karl Oskar and Kristina with news of the world outside the Territory. They had little knowledge of the broad, changing country which had become their home; now they read many amazing things about it. And with the aid of this paper in their native tongue they were also able to educate their children; they used the paper in place of the missing ABC book. In the

Hemlandet Johan and Lill-Marta learned to recognize Swedish letters, both small and capital letters, and by and by the children began to form syllables and words from them.

Inquiries was the headline of one column in *Hemlandet;* where readers made inquiries about relatives living at unknown places in America. Parents were looking for their children, brother for sister, and sister for brother, engaged couples who had lost touch sought to find one another, friends asked the addresses of friends. Here inquiries were made for relatives who had lost their way on the journey and had not arrived at their destination. Many Swedes apparently were wandering about in North America, vainly looking for family connections.

Inquiries was the narrative of people's hopeless quest for each other. Kristina felt great compassion for these unhappy beings who couldn't find their dear ones. Somewhere, hands were stretched out to them, but they didn't know where; they fumbled in a great darkness in the broad land. Kristina had seen this land, she knew how broad it was. The world was entirely too vast for a poor lost person.

Now she wanted Karl Oskar to write an inquiry to *Hemlandet* and ask about Robert. They hadn't heard from him in a year and a half, and Karl Oskar was almost sure his brother was dead. Moreover, he felt an inquiry in the little Swedish paper would be useless, since he doubted it reached as far away as California. But to please Kristina he sat down one evening and wrote an inquiry and sent it in. With some changes in the spelling, the piece was printed in *Hemlandet*:

Brother Sought.
Axel Robert Nilsson from Ljuder parish, Sweden, who left for California in the spring of 1851, in the company of Arvid Pettersson from same parish, has not been heard from since Janary, 1853. He is 21 years of age and tall. If anyone knows where Nilsson is, or has seen him, please notify his brother, Karl Oskar Nils-

son, at the address of Taylors Falls Post Office, Minnesota Territory.

They waited a long time, but no answer came. Theirs was a message lost in the wilderness.

5.

"Timberrim, timberram, timberrammaram . . ."

On Ki-Chi-Saga's shores the timberman's song was heard again. Karl Oskar Nilsson was building his third American house this summer.

His first house had been a simple shed, or shanty, of boards nailed together; his second house had been built of logs; but this third house would be one of hewn timbers—a true, sturdy main house on a farmer's land. A main house. Until now Karl Oskar had lived as a squatter, but when he moved into a main house he would feel he had become a farmer on his own land. Then he could stand erect; the well-timbered building would be the sign of his independence.

The board hut, the log cabin, the timbered main house to these are the three chapters in the story of a settler's progress.

But Karl Oskar had been forced to shorten his foundation by one third in order to get the new house roofed this year. He would eventually build a larger house than this one, but as yet he didn't have the necessary cash. He had to give in to those who had warned him and said that he was attempting too big a house. It irked him sorely that he had to cut down on its size. A man makes an estimate and figures out what he would like to do—he puts in the foundation of a new house—and then his strength is not sufficient to raise it. This had happened to him before with other projects, now it happened again. He felt as if he would never have the time to accomplish what he intended. He managed a part, a good part, but when would he be able to accomplish the whole?

And in the evenings his fatigue was greater than before,

176

lasting even till morning and the new day of labor. At times Karl Oskar felt his strength was beginning to wane. Yet, he was only in his thirty-first year, maturity was still between him and old age. He could build once more, he could raise a fourth house, this time the one he had in mind, the great big house he had promised his wife their first year out here. And he said to Kristina: "Next time! Wait till I build next time!"

They had lived in the wretched shanty for two months, for four years they had had their home in the log cabin; how long would the timbered main house be their home?

The roof must be up before the new crop was ripe. They were three timbermen, as Danjel and Jonas Petter were helping him. The walls grew a little bit each day, while Jonas Petter sang the timberman's song. They were building higher than they had before—this main house would have two stories.

And the three ax hammers fell heavily against the solid timbers, in rhythm to the song:

What's your daughter doing tonight?
What's your daughter doing tonight?
What's your timberman's daughter doing tonight?

Four years had passed since the building song last was heard on this homestead. In the log cabin they had timbered them, two new human lives had been lit. Karl Oskar's hands had changed the contours of the ground; many things had happened to them. For those who began life anew in Minnesota Territory, a span of four years equaled more than eight had they stayed in the old, quiet, unchanging home village.

It was the log cabin's last summer as a home. One period was coming to an end in the lives of the immigrant family; their log-cabin days were ending.

X. Surveying the Forest

1.

On the twenty-fourth day of May that year, the immigrants from Sweden met in Petrus Olausson's barn and formed the first Lutheran parish in the St. Croix Valley.

Fifty-eight grown persons were registered as members of the congregation, and forty children. Pastor Erland Törner was chosen as minister, and Petrus Olausson as warden. It was agreed eventually to construct a church, but until it could be built, a smaller building was to be erected and used for a school, parish meeting hall, and church.

In the sermon which Pastor Törner preached in the barn on the day of the founding of the parish, he said that the immigrants of the Territory were in the same situation as the first Christians were after the Master's ascension: the disciples had also been without a temple in which to worship their God and had therefore met under the open skies, or in caves, or in shepherds' huts. Here the immigrant Swedes were holding their meeting in a barn, which had been built for the storage of crops from the fields. But when Christ's Church was founded today, ninety-eight sheaves of that nobler crop of human souls had been gathered.

The founder of Christianity was born in a stable. It was utterly fitting that the first Christian congregation in the wilderness be founded in a barn.

2.

May 24, 1854, was a great day for the Swedes in the St. Croix Valley; in joining together in this first congregation, they laid the foundation for a new community.

During the first years their most urgent needs had been for food and shelter for themselves and their animals. Not until these needs had been met could they make preparations to fill their spiritual needs. This order had been in effect for Man since the beginning of time.

These people came from the same land and they were already united in a common language, and by similar customs and usages. But the life of the Swedish village had provided an anchorage which they missed here; the church and the church green had been the community center, intimately involved with life's great happenings. In their new land they were parishioners without parish or church. And so they now strove for a new center to replace the one they had lost when they emigrated.

In the home village the church and the church green had been the gathering place where both spiritual and worldly needs had been satisfied. From the pulpit they had heard both the Holy Word and important announcements concerning animals for studs, auctions, farms for sale. From the pulpit prayers were read for parishioners seriously sick, or lately deceased; the banns of matrimony were proclaimed. Everything of importance that had happened in the parish from Sunday to Sunday was announced from the pulpit. On the church green they met every Sunday relatives and friends and were made aware that they belonged to a group greater than the family.

The immigrants would now build a church and a church green and found a new parish for themselves.

They would have to begin—as with everything here—from the very beginning. They must find a teacher and a house for their children's schooling; they must elect a governing board for their parish and school; they must establish a mediation board where disagreements could be settled in their own language; they must organize a district and elect representatives who could speak for them in the territorial government.

In the homeland they had been subjects of the Crown and its authority; here they were their own temporal and church authority. There were no laws laid down by authorities they had not helped to elect. Their new parish was a free parish; no bishops or deans had power over them; they themselves were the church power.

In their new situation, however, demands were made on them unknown in the homeland. There was no oppressive authority but by the same token they were without aid from any authority. They alone were responsible for their parish and could expect no help from others. Whether a church would be built where they could enjoy God's Word, whether a schoolhouse were to be erected, if a parish hall were to be constructed for social gatherings depended on them entirely. They alone must decide and order, but they alone must also carry out their decisions and be responsible for them.

When immigrants established a new community, a price for their liberty was exacted of them. From the irresponsible, responsibility was demanded; from the selfish, a will to unified effort; from the arbitrary, willingness to listen to the opinions of others. From each of the settlers was required his ability to use his newfound liberty: in North America they were all faced with the tests of free citizens.

Because of the new country's demands on the immigrants, capabilities would be developed for which they had had no use in the homeland. They changed America—and America changed them.

3.

Four of the Swedish-born settlers met early one June morning and walked together through the wilderness. They had set out to choose a place where their commuity could bury its dead; these four men had accepted the responsibility of selecting the cemetery site for the new congregation.

Once before they had walked in company through the forest. Then they had been seekers of land. They had gone out to choose the ground where they would settle down and live out the rest of their lives. Today they were selecting the ground where they were to be buried.

It was a calm and bright morning; the St. Croix Valley spread out under a clear sky. A heavy dew had nourished the earth during the night—grass, herbs, and leaves were still moist and exuded a fragrance as after rain. To the west the Indian cliff had doffed its night shawl of fog and vapor and turned its brown-gleaming brow toward the eastern morn. The fertile ground was beginning to warm itself in the sun's fire. The oppressive summer heat had not yet begun but the earth was already in the cycle of fertility: growth had begun, fresh-green and potent, and the thickets were full and lush. The fields displayed their promise of crops in shoots and stalks, in buds and boughs, in blades and blooms, in grass and growth—in all the clear, shining verdure of the earth.

The four men walked southeast, through a deep valley with thick stands of leaf trees. They passed through groves of red oak and black oak, black and white walnut, elm, and linden trees. They penetrated thickets of rasp-berries and wild roses, blackberries and sloe-berries—huge, thorny bushes. Here wild plum trees stood in full bloom, here grew black cherries, the biggest of all the cherry trees, their smooth, thick trunks much taller than a man. Round and about the men was all the summer's wild splendor, soon to bring forth berries and fruit. Today the valley displayed to them its greenery and glitter of blossoming light as if it would bud and bloom and gleam forever.

The men had gone out to select a resting place for the dead, but this June day the earth seemed a paradigm of life eternal.

As they walked silently, facing today's errand, along paths that had been cleared, they were more than ever reminded of the irrevocability of their emigration. In this country they would not only live out their lives, here they

181

would also rest forever. At the time of their emigration they had not thought through to its conclusion: that their graves would be dug far from those of their forefathers. Now as they walked, surveying the ground, they meditated on this final discovery—that their emigration had been not only for this life, but for all eternity.

The forest thickened, the tree crowns rose taller and taller. The men had reached the dense forest. They followed the Indian path which meandered round sand cliffs and over ravines. They crossed streams with water cascading from the rocks. Then they reached an open spot with a few mounds, overgrown with tall grass. The mounds were shaped like overturned bowls, rising in the glade like green-furred, shaggy, evil animals.

These were Indian mounds; under the tangle of weeds the former rulers of this land decayed. The settlers had come upon one of the old burying places of the nomads.

The tillers stopped to inspect the hillocks. At times they had happened to plow too close to a similar mound, and skulls, human bones, and food bowls had been brought to the surface. Then they had hurried to rebury the human remnants and refill the hole. The Indians supplied their dead with food and drink—the ungodly beliefs of the savages penetrated even the earth. White people, born in Christian lands, avoided the graves of the heathens. No Christian settler would wish to lie after his death in earth besmirched by heathendom and idolatry. The cemetery of the new parish must not be placed in the vicinity of these mounds which memorialized a heathen race; bones of Christians and heathens could not rest side by side.

The searchers continued their walk until they reached Ki-Chi-Saga. They followed the shores of the lake in a wide arc round a bay which cut deep into a grove of maple, oak, elm, and walnut trees of lush beauty. Now and then they stopped, exchanged a few words, deliberated. Wasn't this a suitable piece of ground? The cemetery site must be in beautiful surroundings where survivors would be able to see objects that would minimize their sorrow and invoke comforting thoughts. It would be fine if roses and lilies grew on such ground. It was a consolation when flowers grew on a grave, even before it was dug. The resting place of the dead should also lie on high ground, on a knoll or gentle slope; it must have elevation so that it could be seen. And the rising ground would, as it were, point out the road to Heaven—the road the dead ones had taken before the survivors.

The four men wandered about for hours; they hesitated in a number of places; they discussed the location, examined the soil, speculated on roads to the place, compared one spot with another, deliberated, weighed arguments. But they continued their walk, continued to seek. As yet they had not gone far from the shores of the great lake.

They reached a promontory which cut into Lake Ki-Chi-Saga, and stopped again. The point comprised about five acres. On the lakeside it ended in steep sandstone cliffs to the water. It was heavily wooded with deciduous trees, silver maples predominating. The sugar maple provided the settlers with sugar and syrup and it was a harder wood than the other maples, but the silver maple was more beautiful, friendlier. It was in some way a sociable tree: the settlers preferred the silver maple above all other leaf trees. On this promontory hazel, hawthorn, and walnut also grew in profusion. A level place in the center was overgrown with sumac, cheerful with its red blossoms. The opening with its sumac was like a furnished room in the forest's house. And the steep cliffs formed nature's own protection, fencing in the point with a wall of stone.

The four stayed a long time examining the point. Their conviction grew stronger and stronger. They need seek no farther. They had arrived. This was truly a resting place for human beings.

They sat down in the shade of a wide-spreading silver maple, leaning their backs against the trunk of the tree. It was comfortingly calm in this elevated grove, isolated by the lake on three sides. They looked at the blossoming ground, they squinted toward the sky, out over the water. No heathen graves lay within sight. This was the home of quietude. The June day's perfection and the absence of wind increased the great stillness of the place. The leaves of the silver maples glistened in the sun, the gentle surf

183

was a faint, peaceful purl against the boulders below the stone wall. This point had already been fenced to the north, south, and west by the lake, fenced by the Creator himself when on the third day he separated land and water.

The four men listened to the soft wind and to the purling water; here sitting under the silver maples people could enjoy a momentary rest, and later that longer repose which at last would succeed this earthly life. This was a resting place for both the living and the dead.

The men held a short deliberation, after which they agreed that they would advise the new parish to have the ground on this beautiful point near Ki-Chi-Saga consecrated as a burying place for their dead.

Once the men had chosen their last resting place they sat for a long while, preoccupied. Within themselves each posed a question. It was a question that could not be answered by what they could hear or see, it could not be answered by any human being—it arose and made itself felt of its own volition who would be the first to lie in his grave here on this point? Who would be first to rest under the silver maples?

Would it be a man or a woman, a child or an adult, young or old? The shareholders in this, the burial plot they had selected, were mostly people in their youth or blooming prime, but none among them had any promise of the morrow. Life in this country offered so little security and so may dangers that only a few could hope to die in bed, full of years.

Perhaps one of them, one of the four who today rested in the future parish cemetery, might be the first to lie under the silver maples.

Four human beings sat at the site of their last destination in life's journey. Wherever their steps led them in this world, here their wandering would finally cease. However much they strove, whatever they undertook—they would eventually be carried to this plot of ground on the lakeshore. During their wandering today they had been reminded anew of the old truth, the truth they had learned from those who had gone before them, the truth they felt

184

shudderingly, deep in their souls: they were of the earth and inexorably chained to the earth. The four men resting in the shade of the silver maples belonged to the turf under their feet. And today they had searched out their own turf of death.

And now having finished their search in the forest and having taken their rest, the seekers rose and returned to the life which still remained to them.

XI. The Letter to Sweden

New Duvemala at Taylors Falls Post Office in Minnesota, North America, Christmas Day, 1954.

Dearly Beloved Parents,
Hope you are Well is my Daily Wish.

I want to write to let you know that various things are well with us. We have health and since I last wrote nothing of weight has happened to us.

Last October we moved into our new Main House which has two storys. It is built of timbers which I have rough hewn by hand on both sides. In this building we have plenty of room, it is warm also and lacks nothing.

Concerning my situation in North America it is improving right along. I have this fall paid for my whole land at the landoffis, 200 hundred dollar for 160 acres. I have broken new land three times as large as Korpamoen and fensed in about 300 yards, one yard equals 3 Swedish feet. I have four cows in the stable and 3 young livestock in pens. I have cut a pair of Bull Calfs which I raise for oxes. In America no one reaches Comfort in one day but we are satisfied with our improvement.

We have now built up a school house in our Parish. Johan and Marta go to school and learn various subjects from Books, English also. We pay for a pastor in our Parish with 65 dollar a year and free fire wood. Sometimes he travels to other Settlements and Preaches. Here is much disagreement in Religion. But the Pastor can not exclude anyone from the Parish or from the Sacrament, but two thirds of the parishioners can fire the pastor from his job.

We shall this winter select a Swedish justice of the Peace among us. But there is not much Authority here and I like that well. Here in America the Officials are appointed as servants to attend to their duties. When they do not attend to their job other Officials are put in their place. It is not like in Sweden. They have a perverted Government at home. Sweden has too many lazy dogs to feed who do not wish to work.

I think it is sad for you to sit alone. Is it cold in your room in winter? Have you enough wood for fires—I wish I could send you some of the wood we have here in abundance.

I got apple seeds from Duvemala which I planted and a sapling has grown up but it will take time I reckon before the tree has fruit. Around the new house Kristina made a flower bed and I have planted 5 Cherrys and 12 Goosberrys and wine berries and some places for strawberries which will bear next summer.

It is Christmas Day today and I have taken the whole day off to write to Sweden. I remember the Christmas games at home, but the joyful and happy mind of a youth is no longer mine; It is hard to claim wild land and I feel it in the Body although not yet Old. I do not hop about on my feet as lightly as in my youth.

It would be a Joy to come home to you once more in Life and sit down at the old table and cut slices of the Christmas Pig, like in my childhood days.

Many days have now passed since I offered you my hand in farewell and left a dear Childhood home. I apologize if I have been slow in writing and write so seldom. I am thinking every day I must write but always delay.

Immeasurable Seas separate us but Daily I have my dear Parents in my thoughts, and my letters to Sweden shall not cease.

You are greeted heartily from your relations in a far-off land. Greetings also to my dear sister Lydia and ask her to write to her brother in North America, if Father's Hands do tremble.

Your devoted Son
Karl Oskar Nilsson.

Part Two

GOLD AND WATER

XII. The March of the Hundred Thousand

> If it be romance, if it be contrast,
> if it be heroism that we require,
> what was Troy town to this?
>
> Robert Louis Stevenson,
> *Across the Plains*

About the middle of the nineteenth century, an immense river of human beings pushed its way across North America, from the east toward the west. It was formed in the springtime, from smaller streams and rivulets, at the frontier outposts in Missouri and Kansas and from there streamed over wild and unknown country, across great deserts and salt marshes, over the prairies' grass and the Rocky Mountains' snow, over flat land and high mesas, uphill, downhill. Its path—two thousand miles long—was called the California Trail—but the name was all that existed; it had been given to a trail that was yet to be defined and mapped.

Over a path that was everywhere and nowhere, the March of the Hundred Thousand pushed on, from spring to autumn. Its goal was the furthermost western country, washed by an ocean greater than the one crossed by the millions of immigrants.

This train was made up of the strangest conglomeration of people that had ever traveled two thousand unknown, uncleared miles together. It was a caravan never before seen, and never to be seen again.

Men and women, married and unmarried; babes in cradles strung inside the covered ox wagons; old people with trembling limbs. There were proud, honorable

191

women in homespun wadmal, harlots in silk and frills. There were religious people, and atheists. Pious and upright men and women, noble and high-minded people, murderers and robbers, degraded criminals of both sexes. Puritans and libertines, celibates and rapists, the young girl with her virginity intact and the whore who opened her arms to a thousand men. There were thieves and card sharks, counterfeiters and practitioners of every vice known to the world. There were farmhands and maids who had fled from service, soldiers from their regiments, prisoners from their jails, seamen from their ships, mental patients from their asylums, men who had run away from their wives and wives from their husbands, children from their parents, and officials from their posts and positions. There were truthful people and liars, bright people and simpletons, people with normal minds and people a little off. The healthy people and the sick, giants and dwarfs, well-shaped and deformed; one-legged, one-armed, one-eyed, limping ones, seeing and half-blind; all these God-created creatures could be found in this train, in the train of the hundred thousand.

They came from every land on earth, and spoke all the dialects and languages of the earth. This caravan was humanity's parade in white, black, brown, and yellow; whites and Negroes, Hindus and Chinese, fullbloods, halfbloods, quadroons, the bluest noble blood and the rawest plebeian dregs.

Workers in all trades took off and joined this strange caravan: the carpenter threw away his plane, the timberman his ax, the smith his sledge hammer, the cobbler his last, the baker his spatula, the cook his spoon, the scrivener his pen. They streamed in from all nations: there rode in his ox wagon the English merchant, the Irish lawyer, there rode on his mule the American preacher and surgeon; the Jewish peddler kept whipping his ox. In the train were the Spanish captain, the Italian monk, the Norwegian forester, the German craftsman, and the Swedish farm hand.

In the caravan traveled, side by side the nobleman and the servant, the high officer and the low soldier, the editor and the actor, the singer and the player, the magician and the circus-performer, the ventriloquist and the snake charmer, the fire eater and the tight-rope dancer, the master marksman with the revolver and the man who had never touched a fire arm. In their rucksacks, in their wagons or saddlebags, they hid what they held dearest in this world, objects they least wished to part with: the most diversified objects a human heart can cling to: Bibles and decks of cards, holy pictures and dirty pictures, canary birds in cages, whelps in baskets, gifts from parents and dear ones, knives, sewing baskets, crochet hooks, swingletrees, psalmbooks, songbooks, musical instruments, belts, clocks, rings, and amulets.

And an immense animal caravan accompanied the train intended as sacrifice for the people: in the train of the hundred thousand were 60,000 oxen, pulling 15,000 wagons, 25,000 horses and 10,000 mules who carried people on their backs. Fourlegged creatures in the train supplied the two-legged with food and drink: 10,000 cows gave them milk twice a day, and a herd of 5,000 sheep gave them mutton and chops which sizzled with delicious odor over the evening campfires.

The train over the plains and deserts was accompanied by song and music—the musical instruments for religious services as well as those for idle play were brought along. Solemn tunes were heard from mouthorgans and psalmodikons, and dance tunes vibrated from fiddles and banjos. Hallowed psalms were sung to the guitar, and lewd songs to the harmonica, strings were strummed for prayer and reverence, while sin was lauded and debauchery acclaimed. Ministers and blasphemers held their services, and their voices and words rose to the same heaven, that lofty, indifferent heaven above the California Trail.

But these hundred thousand people of all nationalities and colors, speaking all languages, confessing all faiths, practicing all means of livelihood, indulging in all vices, consisting of all types, with all character traits, had one thing in common: *the Goal.* It was the goal that united the members in this folkwandering, the strangest migration ever to take place on the earth. It had forced them to leave their homes in widely separated countries and continents and had brought them together in civilization's outposts in North America from where the caravan started. It drove them across prairies and deserts, over mountains and plains, over rivers and marshes, and made them endure the desert-heat and the mountain-cold. Any one unable to move forward on this road was also unable to turn back; there remained only to stay in the place and await the final end. The cowards, the cringers, had remained at home, and the weakest had been weeded out before horses' or mules' hoofs had taken a single step toward the west.

So the train pushed on, along the unblazed trail that was only a name, enduring the heat of the fiery sun, resting under the vaulted, starry night sky, through the days and months, from spring to fall. Only a dream could unite this human horde, and before the train of the hundred thousand there moved as guidance, day and night, a mirage, a pillar of fire: *gold!* It was their common goal: *GOLD!* It was the end of the road that united them: *The Land of Gold!*

And broad was the land and unmeasured, long was the road, and without end, greatminded and daring the participants, and immeasurable their dreams.

The Gold Caravan traveled every year, from spring to fall, over the California Trail, but it happened that two out of three who followed its pillar of fire never reached their goal.

XIII. A Youth Who Is Not Young

1.

One June evening as Karl Oskar Nilsson made his way through his field, hoeing his corn, he saw a stranger approaching along the lakeshore. A tall, stooped man with a rucksack on his back came toward him, jerking along and swinging his arms as he climbed the road up to the old log cabin. He veered off toward the maple grove, walking as if he had no command over his tall, loose body. Then he stopped and looked at the new main house under the great sugar maples.

Karl Oskar rested against the hoe, staring at the man. During their first years on the claim they had barely had one visitor a month, now someone came almost every day. But this man was not one of their neighbors. And the stranger looked from one building to the other as if he had lost his way. When he saw Karl Oskar in the cornfield, he turned and walked in that direction.

He was a gaunt young man, and judging from his clothing he must be a fur trapper. He wore a broad hat, a long black-and-white-checked coat, and a hunting shirt of flaming red flannel. His pants were made of deerskin, held up by a broad yellow leather belt; his snug leggings fit into high boots. He was a skinny man; his clothes seemed too big for him, hanging on his body as they did.

To Karl Oskar the stranger's walk reminded him of his brother Robert. But he was taller than Robert, and as he came closer Karl Oskar could not discern any likeness to his brother.

It must be someone who had lost his way and wanted to inquire about directions.

"Hello, Karl Oskar!"

The farmer stood openmouthed with the hoe in his hand: a stranger, in strange clothing, with a strange face, in a hoarse voice he had never heard before, called him by name.

"Don't you recognize your brother, Karl Oskar?"

Could it be possible that someone was trying to pretend to be the brother who had left for California four years before?

"I'm back from the California Trail!"

The evening was still light; Karl Oskar peered more closely at the newcomer, looked him in the eye, and began to recognize him, feeling rather than seeing who it was. His younger brother, Robert, was standing in front of him.

Slowly, almost hesitantly, Karl Oskar put down his hoe and offered his hand: "Back at last! Welcome, Robert!"

"Thanks, Karl Oskar. Didn't you recognize . . . ?"

"Well, you've grown taller. And changed!"

It was the height that had confused him; Robert had grown several inches—that was only natural, he had been gone four years. But the clothes; he had left in his old Swedish wadmal, and now he returned dressed like an American trapper. The greatest change, however, was in his face. When Karl Oskar had last seen his brother's face it had been round and full with only the first down of a beard and still with a childish softness in its contours. Now his cheeks were cavernous, bones protruding under the scabby, pale-yellow skin which looked as if worms had gnawed it. Deep, dark gray furrows underlined his eyes. It was a ravished youth-face he now saw. And when Robert smiled, black holes from missing front teeth appeared.

Robert had been eighteen when he set out. Now he was twenty-two. He was still young but he looked old.

"We thought you were dead . . ."

"But I wrote—many times . . ."

"Only two letters have come."

"Well, some were lost, I guess. They often rob the mail out west."

Karl Oskar took hold of Robert by the shoulder, holding him as if wishing to convince himself that this was really his brother: Robert's body was wasted to bones and sinews.

"Nice clothes you have!"

"Did you think I would return looking like a ragbag, Karl Oskar?"

And Robert again smiled his black, toothless smile.

"I came up the river with the steamboat—to St. Paul. Then I got a ride with an ox team. The last part I walked. You have roads through the forest now . . ."

He interrupted himself with a racking, hollow cough, accompanied by a growling noise from inside his chest. "I caught a cold on the steamboat."

He turned and looked up at the new main house. "You've raised some house, Karl Oskar!"

"It isn't as big as I planned but it'll do."

"Two stories!"

196

Karl Oskar replied that he had not yet had time to finish the inside of the upper story, but downstairs they had one large room for daily use, a bedroom for the children, and a good-sized kitchen. He had built sturdy fireplaces so they would be warm in winter.

Robert had only praise for the new house, so pleasant on the slope under the maples, which gave shade in summer and protection in winter. And the maples were full and handsome. When he compared the new house with the old log cabin, he realized that things had improved for his brother while he had been away.

"Let's go home!" said Karl Oskar, and picked up the hoe from among the furrows.

"I see you've started to plant Indian corn."

"This is the second year—it's well worth it. And I've sown wheat for three years now. Wheat and corn go best in Minnesota."

Yes, Robert knew that wheat was king of the grains in America, and Indian corn the queen. And he thought that much had indeed changed since he left.

In a burst of brotherly affection Karl Oskar put his arm on Robert's shoulder as they walked up to the house. He had been almost sure that his brother was dead. Now joy at his return and bafflement at the changes in him mingled within Karl Oskar: Robert's emaciated body, his jaundiced, unhealthy complexion, the hollowness of his voice, his stiff motions—something of life itself was missing in Robert. He stooped as he walked—the halting gait of an old man. Perhaps he had grown too tall to carry his body erect, perhaps he was forced to stoop a little. His brother was ten years younger than he, yet he didn't seem young any more. What was the matter with him? Was he sick?

"I don't think Kristina will recognize you either, Robert."

They entered the new house through the kitchen door at the back. Kristina stood at the hearth tending the pot containing the pea soup for their supper.

After a momentary look of surprise and hesitation she gave a cry of recognition: "Robert! Robert! Are you back . . . ?"

Her voice was filled with joy; she threw her arms

197

around her brother-in-law. Her throat choked with tears, so moved was she. It was with difficulty that she found words to express her feeling.

"You recognized me sooner than Karl Oskar!"

"I've missed you terribly!" she said. "But I've always been sure you would come back!"

Robert unshouldered his rucksack and dropped it on the floor.

"You come dressed like an American gentleman," continued Kristina. "And you have grown terribly tall—but so skinny . . . ?"

The children came running into the kitchen but they were shy with the newcomer when he approached them. Robert had been away so long they had had time to forget him. Only Johan remembered: "You are the uncle who lived with us in the old house!"

"You've grown a lot, Johan. How old are you now?"

"Nine!"

Robert picked up Dan and lifted him high in the air: "You lay in swaddling clothes when I left!"

"We have one more little one now," said Kristina. "A girl we call Ulrika—she's thirteen months."

Robert picked up the girl too and lifted her into the air; but her uncle's intimacy did not please Ulrika—she began to yell at the top of her voice and he had to put her down. Then Robert felt in his pocket and pulled out a bag of sweets which he divided among the five children. After this they were no longer shy of the stranger but jostled about him.

Karl Oskar sniffed the aroma from the pot on the fire; pea soup with boiled pork was to him a delicious dish and he knew his brother liked it. What luck Kristina had such fine fare today; Robert looked as if he needed nourishing food.

"You've walked a long way—you must be hungry."

"I am thirsty, rather," said Robert. "Would you have some drinking water, Kristina?"

She handed him a quart measure which she had filled from the wooden bucket on the floor against the chimney wall. He drank it down, with noticeable enjoyment. "Wonderful water! Did you find a spring?"

Karl Oskar told him that he had dug a well in the slope during the first year but it gave brown water with a brackish taste to it and in a long drought the well went dry. Then last summer he had found a spring in the oak stand behind the old cabin. It gave this clear, fresh water—the best drinking water one could wish. It was about a ten-minute walk to the spring but the water was well worth it.

Robert said, "Good water is worth any walk!"

"Where's Arvid?" asked Kristina. "Did he come back with you?"

"No, Arvid didn't come back with me."

"But you were together . . . ?"

"Yes, we were together. But then we parted."

"Where is Arvid now?"

"He is out there. He stayed."

"Stayed . . . ?"

"You mean Arvid remained in the gold fields?" interrupted Karl Oskar in surprise.

"Yes, he remained. He is still there."

"Oh?" said Kristina and looked questioningly at her brother-in-law.

"Yes, Arvid stayed behind."

Robert's replies to their questions were short and indifferent, as if they did not concern him.

Karl Oskar tried again. "I guess neither you nor Arvid had much luck? Or do you carry your gold with you in that sack?"

He pointed to his brother's rucksack—it was made of thick, excellent skin and looked new.

"Do you think I could carry the gold with me? I can tell you've never been on the Trail!"

Robert smiled his broad, toothless smile; so Karl Oskar thought a gold digger could carry his gold with him? That he would come with a sack of gold on his back when he returned? Gold was heavy, almost the heaviest thing that existed. No one was able to carry gold very far. And one could easily be attacked and robbed along the way. Oh no! One put the gold in safekeeping as soon as one found it. One didn't carry it in one's pocket, not a single nugget could one risk. Every grain was of value and was well

199

taken care of. He had learned how to handle and keep gold: one put it in a bank for safekeeping.

Karl Oskar eyed Kristina as he listened to his brother. He winked knowingly. She was irresolute as to how to interpret it.

"Isn't supper ready?" wondered Karl Oskar.

The peas had not yet boiled enough, replied Kristina. But she could see that Robert was worn out from his journey; he could go into the gable room and lie down while she got supper ready. Anyway he would have to stay in there with the children, she thought. Only she and Karl Oskar and the baby slept in the big room, the living room, as they called it.

Karl Oskar showed his brother to the bedroom. He would have time to inspect their house later, he told him—not that there was much to show; as yet they had only a few pieces of furniture but he kept making more whenever time permitted. Wouldn't Robert lie down? He looked as if his legs were a little shaky after the long walk.

Karl Oskar went back to the kitchen. "My brother isn't like himself," he said to Kristina. "His face is yellow . . ."

"He has had a hard time, you can see that."

"I believe something is wrong with him."

"He might have some ailment, his hands feel hot."

"He said he caught a cold on the steamboat."

Kristina was taking plates from the open shelf, setting the table. "But he sounds as though he had luck in the gold fields. Wasn't that what he said?"

"Yes, I heard it."

"He talked as if he had put his gold in the bank. He may be rich, perhaps."

"It sounds that way."

"You don't believe it?"

"Not a single word of it!"

"He makes it all up, you think?"

"I know Robert by now! You remember his lies on the ship? Remember the dead Indian in the treetop?"

Karl Oskar had a good memory. When they had landed in New York, Robert had spread a rumor that their cap-

200

tain was a slave trader and intended to sell them to the infidel Turk. It had caused great trouble. And during their first winter here it had been the incident at the Indian cliff. Robert had found a dead Indian, hanging from a treetop, and he had sworn that the Indian had shot arrows at him!

"He has lied before, that's true," admitted Kristina. "It's a failing with him."

"He is not going to fool me any more!" declared Karl Oskar with finality.

Kristina caught the sharp determination in his words. "Why would Robert come and lie to us again?" she asked.

"Perhaps he is ashamed to return empty-handed."

"But he has bought new clothes and a new rucksack."

"He must have worked for someone and earned a little."

But Kristina felt that Karl Oskar was too eager to suspect the brother who had barely crossed their threshold. Why couldn't they believe he had found gold? In California even a child might happen on the right place. And Robert had been gone four years—plenty of time to roam far and wide.

Karl Oskar said that he did not intend to ask Robert if he had found any gold; not even here in America did such miracles happen. To him it was enough that his brother had returned alive. A merciful Providence must have looked after him. One couldn't also ask of Providence that Robert return with riches.

"I feel sorry for Robert," he added. "He must be ailing. But until he shows me his gold I won't believe a word of it! This time he won't make a fool of me!"

Robert's unexpected return caused great excitement in the settler home; Kristina fell behind with her chores and supper was delayed. But at last the family gathered around the table in the kitchen, Robert between his brother and his sister-in-law. The children gaped at him and little Ulrika clung to his knee begging for more sweets.

Kristina looked closely at Robert. "You must have had a hard time of it?"

"Hunting gold is hard on one's health."

"Have you ailed in any particular way?"

"Everyone on the Trail suffers from the gold-sickness."

But Robert did not further describe it. He looked around the new kitchen with its painted walls. In four years a person changed, and on the Trail one changed very fast. If he were to tell them all he had experienced they would have to sit at table here from now till Christmas, and still he wouldn't get through more than half.

"We won't ask you anything tonight," said Kristina. "You must be tired."

She filled his plate brimful with pea soup: he must eat and then get some sleep. She would put Harald's and Johan's bed in order for him; the two big boys could sleep on the floor for the time being.

"You are very kind, Kristina. You remember the food you prepared when I left—it lasted a long way on the journey. You've been kind to me in many ways."

"You're using a lot of English in your talk, Robert."

Yes, he said, during these years he had really learned to speak English and it was a great help in traveling through this country. But with his own people he would of course always use his mother tongue, except when he forgot himself.

Before Robert had time to empty his soup plate, Kristina refilled it. "Put on some weight now! You're only skin and bones!"

But two plates was all Robert could manage. When they left the table he picked up the quart measure from the hearth shelf, filled it with spring water from the bucket, and drank. "Good water is wonderful! Better than anything else!"

After supper Kristina sat down to give the breast to Ulrika. Then she put the girl in the cradle. Karl Oskar had recently put rockers under it and was mighty proud of his handiwork. Robert looked it over carefully. If only he had had such a cradle with him in the gold fields, he said. Gold had to be treated exactly like babies—put in cradles and rocked until all sand and refuse and dirt was winnowed away and at last it lay pure-clean and glittering in the bottom.

Kristina forgot what she had just promised and asked, "Where do they find gold?"

"All over. In the most unusual places."

Gold could be found not only in the earth and the river sand and the rocks, explained Robert, but sometimes . . . well, as an example he would like to tell them about something that happened the first year he was in California. Among his gang washing gold in a stream was a Negro. One evening when the gang had finished for the day and were on their way home, the Negro suddenly became very ill. He got such an intense stomachache that all he could do was to lie on the ground and yell to high heaven. Nobody could understand what was the matter with him and there was nothing to do for the sick man. He was unable to walk to the tent, so they left the yelling and whining Negro where he lay. Next morning when they started out for the stream the Negro still lay on his stomach where they had left him. But now he was quiet and yelled no more—he was dead.

Then one of the men guessed what had caused the man's peculiar stomachache. He took his knife and cut open the cadaver. When he opened the stomach the glitter of gold was revealed; the insides of the Negro were gilded, filled with nuggets and gold sand.

The Negro had been a gold thief. He had stolen the gold from the others, a pinch now and then, and had hidden the gold in a safe place. He had put it in his mouth and swallowed it. He had of course expected the gold to come out intact when he went to the privy. But that was where he figured wrong; the nuggets caused a stoppage that killed the poor fool.

Now the thief's comrades took back the gold he had stolen from them, cleaned out and washed each of his intestines. When they exchanged it for cash to divide it among themselves, it turned out to be worth four thousand dollars.

There were eight men in the gang, and each one got five hundred dollars, concluded Robert. Well, that was how one could find gold: he himself had been one of those digging for gold in a man's stomach.

Kristina listened in horror to her brother-in-law. "How could they! That was terrible!"

Because of the heat the kitchen door stood open, and Karl Oskar sat on the threshold where he could still see in the lingering dusk, filing his wood saw.

"You have had horrible experiences, Robert!" said Kristina, looking at him with ever-widening eyes. He turned his head as she spoke to him, so that his right ear was turned toward her; his hearing must still be bad in his left.

"Did you hear that, Karl Oskar?"

Karl Oskar had heard every word but he acted as if he hadn't been listening. He filed away at his saw, filed and kept silent. Once his eyes sought Kristina's, as much as to say: you understand, don't you?

Kristina was so stirred by Robert's story that she could not hold back any longer—she must know. "Robert . . . is it true . . . have you really found gold in California?"

"I am satisfied."

"Is it true? I mean . . ."

She did not wish to hurt his feelings by sounding incredulous, she was searching for suitable words.

"You know why I left, Kristina," he replied. "And I wrote in my letters I would not come back until I was a rich man."

"And now you are rich?"

"I have done my last day's work and had my last master. I have plenty. There'll be enough for all three of us!"

Robert was standing close to the cradle, as if addressing himself to the child. He had said, almost casually, that he was so rich he had enough for himself, his brother, and his brother's wife!

Kristina's foot, rocking the cradle, came to a standstill when she heard that she was to share in his riches.

"I have plenty, Kristina! Of that you can be sure!"

But she sat in speechless confusion. Should she answer him: I don't believe you! You are not rich! It's a lie! But he spoke so calmly, so irrefutably. His words were as confident as if he were reading from Holy Writ.

From the doorway only the rasping of the file against the saw teeth could be heard. Karl Oskar must have

204

heard his brother: I am rich. I have enough for all three of us! but he was unmoved. He remained silent and continued to file.

Karl Oskar had heard Robert, but he only felt that his brother had not learned anything from the times he had been found out and proven to be a liar. At his return he seemed more impudent and cheeky with his lies than ever before.

Was it right to pretend to believe him? Was it good for Robert himself? Wouldn't it be kinder to speak out now and end his tall stories? Once and for all put an end to his lying?

The rasping and grating from the saw stopped; file in hand, Karl Oskar walked over to his younger brother. "Please, Robert, brother of mine. Stop lying to us! I can't bear it any longer—it annoys me!"

Robert slowly turned his right ear toward him in order to hear better.

"I can't stand a brother lying like that! Stop it!"

"You don't believe me, Karl Oskar?" Robert asked in a dry tone.

Kristina looked in apprehension from one brother to the other.

"You know you've brought no gold with you. But no one holds it against you. We are glad you're back, glad you are alive!"

"You think I haven't anything . . . ? You think I lie . . . ?" Robert sounded deeply hurt. "All right! All right!"

He turned quickly on his heel and walked through the door into the bedroom.

"You will only drive him away!" said Kristina, reproaching Karl Oskar. "You could have waited, at least this first evening."

"I can't bear this nonsense! And I had to talk honestly with my only brother."

But Robert returned in a moment with his new rucksack in his hand. His brother and sister-in-law looked puzzled as he put it down on the kitchen floor and unlatched the thick leather thongs that secured it. From the sack he pulled out a small leather bag which looked as if

205

it had been badly worn. He opened it and pulled out a paper bundle. Without a word he handed it to Karl Oskar. Again he stuck his hand into the bag and pulled out a second bundle of rustling paper which he laid on Kristina's knees.

"These notes are for you. I don't have any gold in my sack. But these have the same value as gold."

Karl Oskar stared at the bundle of bills in his hand. Kristina looked down at her apron; on it lay a bundle of paper money.

"I drew out a little cash for pocket money."

Robert put the leather bag back into the rucksack and leaned over the cradle holding the fretful baby; the little girl was restless and wouldn't go to sleep.

Robert smiled at the child as he spoke casually to her parents: "It's your money. Take it and enjoy it."

He had taken out some of the contents of his leather bag and given to his brother and sister-in-law. After this they became silent, dumbfounded. Now it was only Robert who talked, to the little girl in the cradle, pretending she answered.

Then he turned to Karl Oskar, as if he too had been a little child in need of instruction and advice. In order to make use of gold it had to be turned into money. A bank in Bloomfield, Indiana, had changed the gold into notes. The bank had taken one seventh of the gold value for its trouble; American banks were awfully greedy. But at least he had his possessions in safekeeping and he could draw money whenever he needed cash.

"These few bucks are for you, Karl Oskar and Kristina."

Karl Oskar looked embarrassed, as if his brother had tricked him in some shameful way, as if his brother had cheated him with this gift.

The evening darkness was beginning to fill the kitchen; Karl Oskar lit a taper in the wooden candlestick on the mantel; then he took a note from his bundle and inspected it in the light. He turned it: it was green on one side and black on the other, the colors he had always seen on American notes. And on both sides, in all four corners, was imprinted: *100*. In eight places it was clearly indicated the note was worth one hundred dollars.

And in the center of the green side Karl Oskar could read in big black letters: INDIANA STATE BANK, BLOOMFIELD, INDIANA.

At last he spoke again, mumbling as if dazed. "If someone hasn't hexed my eyes this must be a hundred-dollar bill."

And he began to look through the bundle which Robert had tossed to him like waste paper: all the bills were identical. They were wrinkled and spotty, soiled by dirty fingers, but the value of each was the same—one hundred dollars.

Karl Oskar counted them slowly; there were twenty in the bundle. He counted them again, he wet his fingers and counted them a third time; they still amounted to twenty.

"You gave me five dollars when I left," said Robert. "I am paying you back with interest."

Kristina had not yet touched the bundle in her lap; she only sat and stared at it as if it were a bird that suddenly had flown into the kitchen and perched on her knee. Now she handed the bills to Karl Oskar.

He counted his wife's money also; the bills were exactly like the ones in his own bundle, and there were also twenty of them.

"Four thousand dollars in cash . . ." He spoke as in a deep trance. "Four thousand in cash . . . !"

And Robert called this pocket money.

"I promised to share with you when I came back from California."

Karl Osar Nilsson looked askance at his younger brother. He was deeply embarrassed, feeling that he had been wrong, but he could not force himself to admit it.

His sight *must* be failing; he must try to see aright again. He held a couple of the bills against the candle flame, turned them, rubbed them between his thumb and forefinger, let the light shine on them again, thumbed them again: were they real money? Wasn't the whole thing some swindle?

Robert smiled. "You can see the money comes from the Indiana State Bank. If you think I lie . . ."

He added that he had delivered four sacks full of nuggets to the bank in Bloomfield. He had asked for smaller bills—fifty and twenty dollars—but the bank didn't have enough on hand to let him have all he wanted; they were printing new notes as fast as they could. A great many gold diggers had returned from California and turned in their sacks at the same bank. It would probably take a couple of months before all he owned could be exchanged for ready cash.

"You mean you have more . . . ?" Karl Oskar's voice was thick.

"Of course! Much more!"

Robert had given his brother and sister-in-law four thousand dollars in cash. And as yet they had not said one word of thanks. Karl Oskar and Kristina could not thank him, they could say nothing at all, because they were overwhelmed by such a gift.

This was something they must think through, it took time, they must get their bearings.

"Now go out and buy what you need, Kristina!"

She grabbed Robert's hand with both her own, tears gushing. "You told the truth . . . You have had luck . . . You give us all this . . . God bless you, Robert . . . !"

"Now don't let's talk of gold any more." He yawned and grinned broadly, seeming thoroughly tired of the subject. "I can't tell you how sick of it I am—I've got too much of the damn stuff!"

Kristina leaped up. "I must make your bed! You must be dead tired . . ."

She had noticed him moving his hand to his left ear time and again; he had had an ache in that ear ever since his master, Aron of Nybacken, had boxed it so hard that something sensitive inside it had broken.

"Does your ear still bother you?" she asked compassionately.

"Yes, it carries on something awful in there."

And in a lower voice, as if wishing to share a confidence with Kristina, he said something strange she was to remember afterward: "My ear can talk! Do you understand . . . ? You should only hear what it tells me during the nights!"

208

2.

Robert went to bed, but Karl Oskar and Kristina sat up late on this strange, confusing evening.

Karl Oskar spread the forty hundred-dollar bills before him—they covered most of the table. He sat and stared at this new tablecloth of green and black.

Four thousand American dollars were worth the same as fifteen thousand Swedish riksdaler. Before he emigrated he had sold his farm, Korpamoen, for fifteen hundred riksdaler. Ten times that sum was now spread before him. On the table in his kitchen this evening lay the value of ten farms. A fortune!

The money spread under his eyes could change their whole life.

If only there wasn't something wrong with his sight. If these green-black papers on the table were what they were supposed to be. For he couldn't entirely believe . . . he wasn't quite convinced . . . It had happened too suddenly. Would this evening, with the turn of a hand, bring to an end his five years' struggle for cash?

"I felt right away that Robert wasn't lying this time," said Kristina.

"We mustn't lose our heads," insisted Karl Oskar. "We can't be sure."

"Do you still doubt him?"

"The bills might be worthless."

"Do you think your brother is a counterfeiter?"

No, he didn't mean his brother had printed the bills himself. But there was so much confusion about money in America. Some states were flooded with bills entirely without value, printed by banks that had opened only to swindle people. Robert's bills were well printed and consequently suspicious. They must be cautious.

Kristina felt a hundred-dollar bill. "They're creased and crumpled—they look like good ones."

When she found time she would iron out the big bills and remove the grease spots and dirt. Such big bills ought to be clean and smooth. Then she was sure they would pass for their full value.

"I had better go to the bank in Stillwater and ask them," said Karl Oskar. "But I can't get away before Saturday. Then we'll know what Robert's money is worth."

Today was Monday; he had promised to go with Algot Svensson to the land office in Stillwater on Saturday to witness his neighbor's right to his claim. He would take the bills with him to the bank and ask their value and if the bank was willing to accept them. Before the end of the week he would know. And before that time they must not mention to a single soul the four thousand dollars which had found its way into his home so unexpectedly.

Kristina said that this was riches. First of all they must now find a good place for safekeeping. Everything else they would think about by and by . . . Forty bills, each one worth a hundred dollars! If they had had a single one of these bills when they had arrived five years ago then it would have saved them many troubles and privations. And if they had had this sum in Sweden they would never have needed to emigrate . . . It was strange to think of that.

"Dare we keep the money in the house?"

Karl Oskar thought there would be no danger; no one would search for riches here. Robbers and thieves knew that whatever else they might find in a settler's house, it would not be cash.

With loving hands Kristina gathered the bills together into one big bundle, wrapped them in her silken kerchief, and put them down in the bottom of her Swedish chest. It was the safest place she could think of. And yet it would be difficult for her to sleep tonight—what a worry to have fifteen thousand riksdaler in cash in the house! They must be careful with the fire tonight.

Karl Oskar went out to the stable to look after a sick calf; he should have done it earlier but this evening he had forgotten both people and animals. He gave the calf some milk in a bucket and looked to see that his livestock was all right; one never knew: some animal might get tangled up in its chain and choke itself to death. Never

210

would he go to bed of an evening without first checking that all was well with the animals in his stable.

When he returned Kristina had already gone to bed. In this new house they each had a bed on opposite walls of the big room. He started to undress although it would be a long time before he could go to sleep tonight. His head buzzed with questions: What about this money? Was it real or not? And how had Robert got his hands on it? He couldn't have earned that much through work; had he actually found gold? Kristina had said that a little child could have such luck . . . Well, that could be true. And in California one might dig gold in the earth as easily as potatoes here in Minnesota. If one had luck. Luck! While he had slaved here on his claim every working day for four years and not been able to save a cent of cash, Robert had dug up a few lumps of gold which in one turn had made him rich—so rich that he never need do another day's work in his whole life. At least that was what he said. Could it be the truth? It didn't seem right, if it had happened that way. He had never believed in success except through honest work; luck and good fortune could aid for a while, but the only permanent reward came from honest work. If Robert had told the truth, then he—Karl Oskar—had been wrong in his thinking.

He always tried to keep a clear head. And he must do the same this time. He must not be fooled. In America one heard so many tales of swindles. During the last year so many good-for-nothings had arrived in the Territory; they didn't want to break the land, only speculate in it. They wanted to be rich without working, just like Robert. They were parasites, vermin, trying to live off the settlers, like bloodsucking lice lived on the human body. It always irritated him to hear of these lazy speculators who had descended on them and who wouldn't leave. As yet there was no real order in the Territory; the land was too vast, the farmers too few, and the speculators and the swindlers too many.

He said goodnight to his wife, who still lay awake in her bed. He had barely put his head against the pillow before a thought came to him which made him quickly sit up again. The paper! *Hemlandet!* He could find out right now!

Why hadn't he thought of that at once? Every week the Swedish paper had a column—Bank Swindles—which enumerated the banks that printed and issued valueless or below-par money. Recently he had counted twelve banks in the column. Wasn't one of them an Indiana bank? Wasn't the Indiana State Bank of Bloomfield listed in the paper?

He could find out this very moment about Robert's riches in hundred-dollar bills. He had saved every copy of *Hemlandet*. He had put them away on a shelf in the cupboard within arm's reach of his bed.

He almost called out to Kristina: We needn't wait till I go to Stillwater on Saturday! We can find out right away if we have become rich tonight! Or—if we are as poor as before.

But from his wife's even breathing he could hear she had already gone to sleep. He mustn't disturb her. If she were to learn the truth, the truth as he suspected it to be, she would take the disappointment so hard that she wouldn't go to sleep again. Let her rest, let her be rich for one night. Tomorrow would be soon enough for her to learn, if it were so. But he himself must know the truth this evening.

Cautiously, silently, Karl Oskar rose from his bed. He lit a candle and stood in his nightshirt before the cupboard. From the shelf he took the accumulated copies of *Hemlandet,* every one of them, put them on the table, pulled up a chair, and began to read.

The latest paper had come on Friday. He found the headline: Bank Swindles. In that column the Indiana State Bank was not listed. But in the adjoining column his eyes fell on a notice about counterfeit twenty dollar gold pieces that the public was warned about: they were easy to recognize, the world *sold* above the head of the figure representing Liberty was missing on the false coin. But this did not concern him; it was not a question of stamped coins, it was bills . . .

Danjel Andreasson had once last year been cheated with a five dollar coin that a hog buyer from St. Paul had fooled him with. This coin had even been stamped IN GOD WE TRUST and that was why he had accepted it. Afterwards Danjel had been greatly disturbed that counterfeiters announced on their coins that they had faith in God. He had never thought that in America—the Lord's Promised Land—such dishonest people existed who would invoke God's name in their own counterfeiting.

Karl Oskar picked up the next copy. He went through issue after issue of the paper and read all the lists of banks which cheated people with valueless bills. He found the names of only two banks in Indiana. But the one which had printed Robert's bills—the Indiana State Bank of Bloomfield—he did not see. That bank was not listed.

With a deep sigh he blew out the candle: the bills must be real then. Robert had probably told the truth.

When he crept into his bed for the second time this evening and pulled the blanket over him, Kristina awoke.

"Karl Oskar—are you asleep?"

She had been dreaming that she was washing and ironing hundred-dollar bills. She had moved the ironing board out into the barn and there she had pressed the long green bills, so large they had hung over the sides of the board! Karl Oskar too had been in her dream: he had the big shovel and shoveled so fast that the bills flew all over the place and up against the roof of the barn. She dreamed that they had harvested a whole crop of hundred-dollar bills and now were about to thresh them—she ironed and ironed while perspiration ran off her body.

"I was so glad when I awoke. For after all, I had dreamed the truth!"

For it was still this Monday evening when the goldseeker had returned; when he stepped across their threshold and had brought riches into their house.

XIV. But the Returned Goldseeker
Does Not Sleep

What does Robert's injured ear tell him during the night?

His left ear buzzes and rings and keeps him awake. As soon as he puts his head on the pillow in the evening the ear begins to roar and thunder, it sings and rings and tinkles, songs are heard, bells toll, shots are fired. The buzz and the roar can be of such intensity that it sounds like a storm at sea in there. In bed at night his heart moves up and throbs in his ear. Each beat feels like a wasp's sting, like a knife point. It is difficult to sleep when one feels the heart-sting in one's ear with each beat.

It cracks and crackles, it peeps and weeps and wails. It is too crowded with a heart in there—it swells and pushes, it boils and seethes and aches. He has one heart inside his chest and another in his ear, and the ear-heart stings him many times a minute as he counts its beats.

The goldseeker lies awake and counts the beats. They are his own sounds, those he keeps hidden in there. No one can hear them except he himself; they belong to him only; what his left ear tells him at night is his secret.

It has been aching since that day when he lay on his back under the open sky, whistling and singing, although he had been told to dig a ditch. His master had come upon him and lifted the biggest hand he had ever seen on a human being. The enormous, heavy fist had hit him smack on his left ear.

He had emigrated to get away from masters, but his ear accompanied him with its buzzing and turmoil. He had run away from service, he had crossed the ocean, but the sound in his ear remained with him. He had fled the Old World for the New, but the aching ear accompanied him.

It followed him on the road to California, and now it had come back with him. He had traveled over lakes and rivers, he had walked across plains and deserts, he had journeyed thousands of miles over land and water, but the ear still pursued him. He had not been able to escape from it—wherever he fled it followed him, clung to him. The echo of a box on the ear in the Old World still reverberated; his persecution by his left ear was the punishment he must suffer because he did not want to dig ditches.

And now he has come back to his brother's house, and the ear is with him in the bed where he rests. And his heart moves into his ear again, where it pushes and roars and fills his head. He feels the sensation of stinging pain in sensitive tissue each time his heart beats. He turns his head on the pillow to the left, he turns it to the right, he raises it, puts it down, but the ear is the same. He rests on his right cheek, he changes over and lies on his left cheek, he rests on his forehead, but the knife-cuts remain inside the Ear.

He had fled from his service, he had fled from his homeland, he had fled from his masters, but wherever in the world he flees, he has a guardian he cannot escape, a pursuer he cannot get rid of, a master he cannot flee from: *the ear*.

And so he has been forced to get along with his eternal companion, who keeps him awake during the night hours. He lies still and does not try to escape any more, for he knows he can't succeed. The pursuer forces his company on him; the ear forces him to listen to all its sounds. It tells him, relates to him in detail, all it has recorded: human voices and animal cries, laughter and weeping, sounds of joy and of pain and of sorrow, his own words and those of others, the voice of his friend Arvid, shouts, the swearing of men whose names are foreign to him. He hears the creaking wagon wheels in the desert sand, neighing horses, bellowing oxen, lowing cows, braying mules. The whipping, wind-driven sand, the pelting rain, the noisy great rivers, the sweeping storm over the prairie buffalo grass. It is the echo of shots and barking dogs, of muleteers hollering, fighting voices, drunken men's slob-

215

berings, voices in delirium, calls, danger warnings, nature's forces at play—every audible sound and noise.

The ear remembers much he himself has forgotten, or has tried to forget—the ear digs up the forgotten past and makes it vivid and present. So did it happen! Exactly so! And he lies awake and listens as it brings back to him every one of the four years of days and nights on the California Trail.

What does the injured ear say to Robert during the nights?

XV. The First Night—Robert's Ear Speaks

(There you lie—and here I am! You'll never be rid of me! We share our secrets. But don't worry: no one except you can hear me! My voice belongs to you only. All I say remains between us! It stays right here, with. If another ear tried to listen in—how silly! It wouldn't hear the slightest little buzz, not the smallest whisper! So don't worry! Not a peep from me!

Listen closely to me now! How was it? Do you remember how it happened—that first summer—that time when Arvid wanted to—well, you remember what he had in mind . . . ?)

1.

It was April when they started on their journey.

On the paddle steamer from Stillwater they got jobs as dishwashers in exchange for free transportation to St. Louis. Together they had twenty-five dollars, well hidden in a skin pouch.

The last time they had traveled on the Mississippi they had gone upstream on the *Red Wing*; now they traveled downstream on the *New Orleans*.

On his first journey up the Mississippi—the world's greatest moving water—Robert had heard a song about liberty and freedom: I will be free, as the wind of the earth and the waves on the sea . . . Ever after he had been lured by that song and had trusted its promise. But then he had been a passenger; now he was a dishwasher below deck. He and Arvid sat in a dark, narrow, dirty galley and peeled potatoes for the cook. Whole barrelfuls of potatoes were rolled up to them, and as soon as they saw the bottom of one, another appeared. During the whole long, light spring day, as the *New Orleans* glided by the verdant river shores, Robert and Arvid sat in the galley, the peelings wriggling like snakes about their feet. By afternoon the heap of peelings reached their knees, by evening it was up against their thighs.

"A helluva lot of potaters they grow in America," said Arvid.

"America is the homeland of the potato," said Robert. "The Indians invented this root."

"Then the heathens must be quite brainy," said Arvid, who liked potatoes.

Late in the evening, when the piles of peelings had reached all the way to their groins, the youths were liberated and could go onto a lower deck. They were forbidden, however, to go onto the upper deck, where the paying passengers promenaded and viewed the wonders of the shores along the world's broadest river.

As they steamed south, the days grew warmer and it became oppressive in the narrow galley. Any grown person can with equanimity peel potatoes for a few hours, perhaps a whole day, and a patient individual can perhaps peel for a few days, even a whole week, without despairing. But from morning to night, day after day, week after week, penned up in a dark corner on a ship during beautiful spring days, would be enough to make the stoutest heart fail. Arvid sat half buried in a nest of peelings sad and depressed. But Robert comforted him; they must

217

keep this in mind: admitted, they were on a boat peeling potatoes—but they were on their way to California: they were peeling their way to the Land of Gold! Once there they would sit buried in gold sand up to their thighs! And when they returned from the gold fields it would be as passengers on the upper deck, where they would promenade, smoking cigars and viewing the scenery! They would wear broad gold watch chains across their vests and heavy gold rings on each finger, every pocket of their clothing would be filled with large, rustling bills!

Spring advanced as the *New Orleans* floated farther souh on the river, and an ever hotter sun shone down on her deck. The Mississippi widened, the shores grew more lush and the vegetation richer. And the heat increased in the galley under the deck where two Swedish farmhands sat and peeled their way to California.

The crew members who did the loading, fired the engines, filled the bunkers, served the food on the *New Orleans* were nearly all white men, although the officers on the steamboat preferred a black crew. This time, however, there hadn't been enough Negroes; there were only about half a dozen. The command preferred Negroes because they were pleasanter to the passengers, happier and jollier; they entertained the passengers. The blacks could also stand the heat better than the whites; and they endured the beatings they got, while such rough treatment was not allowed with a white crew.

One evening Arvid and Robert watched as a uniformed officer beat up a disobedient Negro. Arvid wondered; were they allowed to do that to people in this country, as they did at home? Robert explained that only black-skinned people were allowed to be beaten in America, for it was written in the laws of the American Republic that all white people were equal. What luck, said Arvid, that time when God decided what color their skins should be.

In the evenings the crew—firemen, loaders, kitchen helpers, waiters—gathered on their own deck and lit torches. The flickering torches reflected in the dark river water on either side of the boat while the crew sang their songs, strange songs whose words had little meaning:

218

Corn and pudding and tapioca pie,
Hi ho, hi ho!
The geese play cards and the chicks drink wine,
Hi ho, hi ho!
In the crowd, on the shore,
In New Orleans,
There stands my girl on the shore!
She is young and she weeps and she is mine,
The girl on the shore in New Orleans!
Corn and pudding and tapioca pie,
Hi ho, hi ho!
When the geese play cards and the chicks drink
wine,
While floating down the river to the sea!

Robert and Arvid thought that tapioca pie must taste good, and they were disappointed never to sample it.

They counted their days on the river, and the barrels of potatoes they peeled through but which never came to an end. They felt that through their work they were paying too much for their transportation on the *New Orleans*. But they must save their cash.

At last one day when the bell rang they heard the words they had been listening for each time the boat docked: *St. Louis!* They were free! The two boys threw their peeling knives onto the deck with shouts of joy, picked up their rucksacks, and ran down the gangplank. They had traveled the first stretch of the road and it hadn't cost them a penny.

They had come to a place with crowds of people and jostling animals and vehicles on the streets. Stillwater was a river town on the St. Croix, but St. Louis was a larger town on a larger river. It was the biggest town they had ever seen, except for New York. It seemed to be fenced in by the river. But it wasn't yet completed, and outside of New York they hadn't seen a town in America that was completed: all were a-building, all were like a shell of a house, ready to be finished up. In St. Louis timbers and boards were strewn over the streets, hammering and digging went on everywhere. People sat eating bread and fruit outside shacks that were so primitive the boys wondered if they were lived in or in the process of being built. A great many Negroes mingled in the crowds, half-naked, woolly-haired, and Arvid remarked that there was much black hide to be beaten in this town. The blacks were slaves, they knew, slavery being permitted here in the South, but they didn't see a single one in chains or shackles.

In St. Louis the two boys got along better than they had in New York the previous year. I am a stranger here, Robert had told the people then, but he had not been able to make anyone understand. Now he could say almost anything he wanted in English—although a little haltingly and not always according to his language book—and he understood most of what people said to him. It was harder for Arvid; he did not know many of the English words as yet, even though he usually pretended to understand everything. Robert did not let on that he knew Arvid pretended; Arvid had never learned to read or write his own mother tongue—how could he learn English?

From the pier the boys followed a broad street, perhaps the town's Broadway, although it wasn't half as wide as the street of that name in New York. But here, too, wonderful fruits were sold, many kinds whose names they did not know. At one stand they bought oranges, and sat down on some boxes against the tin wall of a nearby shed to eat them.

The sun felt good on their faces as they sat eating the juicy fruit; this was a fine place, and summer had already arrived.

Robert and Arvil had traveled over water to St. Louis. Now they would continue over land to California. Robert had figured out they would walk as far as possible on that road; their own legs would have to pay for the journey which their money couldn't afford. But all who traveled over land, and on ground in general, needed a road. If they rode horses, or wagons, a road was required. Even those who used their legs must have a road bed to walk on.

Now, where was the road to the gold fields of California?

In Stillwater Robert had bought a map of the United

States. These grew in number and size for every year; they expanded so fast that nearly every year a new map had to be printed of the Northamerican Republic. This was a country that grew night and day, throughout the week, the whole year round. Robert had therefore asked for the latest map which the president in Washington had issued as the official map for this country this year, 1851, a map with no state left off, however small, empty, and insignificant it might be. It had cost him one dollar and fifty cents for the latest edition, completely revised, but he would get back that sum with the first little grain of gold he saw on the California ground.

Arvid knew that if one had a map and a watch one could find any road in the world, however crookedly it ran and however bad its condition. Robert had the map, he himself had the watch. He pulled it from his vest pocket, the nickel watch his father, Petter of Krakesjö, had given him as a parting gift. It was his paternal inheritance from Sweden, and Arvid had chained it to his vest buttonhole. His father's labor had earned it for him; much sweat had gone into that watch, many long days' toil, many evenings with a sore back. It was not an old-fashioned spindle watch with unreliable works, it had cylinder works. A cylinder watch had a more precise mechanism and kept better time—this watch kept time to the second.

And now they would have great use of this cylinder watch. If Robert's map showed the road they must take, then this watch would show the time it would take to walk it.

Now where was the road they were to take to California and how long was it? How much farther to the gold land?

Robert spread his map of the United States across the empty boxes beside them. He had not had access to a table on the boat and had been unable to inspect it earlier. Now he looked at it carefully, and the longer he looked, the wider his eyes opened; could it be right? Was this map correct?

California, the newest state of the Union, was the long, narrow strip of land near the Pacific Ocean. If they walked overland from St. Louis straight west, they would

221

reach the Pacific Ocean, and the sun setting in the west would point the way for them. But how long was the road?

"Let me see . . ."

Robert used a six-inch pencil to measure as he figured the size of the United States. From the east coast to St. Louis the distance was exactly the length of the pencil. But then it took two whole lengths of the pencil and still another half to reach the Pacific Ocean!

He measured several times, but he couldn't make the distance across the broad continent an inch shorter; they did not yet have one third of the way to the Pacific behind them. And the distance before them was two and a half times longer! Last year they had traveled one month through the country to Minnesota, this year from Minnesota to Missouri, and they were not yet halfway through America! Not even a third!

At this discovery Robert grew very serious. With a pencil and a map on an empty box he had obtained his first general view of the New World. It made him dizzy. He felt as if he had been kicked in his behind and flung back a couple of thousand miles. Arvid would be scared to death if he were to know how great a distance they had left to go; he had better keep the discovery to himself.

He folded the map quickly and said truthfully, "We have a goodly part left—America is broad!"

But where was the road to California? They must ask someone.

Robert and Arvid resumed their wandering through the town. Whom should they ask? Robert chose with great deliberation among the people they met on the street. Here came men riding sleek horses, dressed from head to foot in soft deerskin, with ten-inch-wide belts from which dangled revolvers and knives. But these riders sat so loftily on the horses—how could a walker dare stop them? Instead Robert turned to the crowd on foot, more simply dressed people; he asked those who had neither revolvers nor knives in their belts, feeling in some way on equal footing with them.

The road to California . . . ? Some replied at length, others in few words, but all replied willingly and kindly.

Some smiled, thinking perhaps the question was a joke, some looked serious or surprised.

"To get to California is more complicated than you think."

This was the general reply; some said about the same thing in different words: to travel to the gold fields was not an easy undertaking. And concerning the road there was no definite information; on this all agreed. When Robert had asked half a dozen people and added together their replies, he came to the conclusion that *no road had been built—nay, not even staked out—to California!*

The goldseekers found their way, as best they could, along different routes which had a name in common: the California Trail. People traveled in large parties, a thousand persons or more; the distance was over two thousand miles, and the crossing took four months—a whole summer.

But there was no specific road to the gold fields.

"No road . . . ?"

Disappointed, Robert repeated the words to himself: that was the silliest thing he had ever heard! In the Old Country, roads ran to the smallest hamlets where only potatoes and grain grew in the fields, but here a road was not even surveyed to the fields which produced gold! Nothing in the world could be more important than to build a wide, even road on which people could travel in comfort to the gold land!

"They could be lying to us," suggested Arvid. "They might like to get there before us and take the gold?"

"No road!" repeated Robert without listening to his companion. "Of course there must be a road to the gold fields!"

Arvid thought for a few minutes, more intensely than was his custom; then he said: "If there is no road to California we might have trouble finding the place, or what do you think, Robert?"

They must stay in this town for a while and think over their situation. It was late in the afternoon and they began to look for a cheap boardinghouse. On the outskirts of town they found a place where they could sleep for twenty-five cents apiece. They could hardly expect to find cheaper lodgings in a big town like St. Louis. Their host was a fat Irishman who showed them their bunks in the Jameson Lodging House: mattresses filled with rotten straw, spread on the floor and for cover, torn horse blankets. Four men had to sleep on one mattress. Their sleeping companions had already gone to bed, two bearded horse grooms who slept with their boots on, even though a notice on the wall pleaded with gentlemen guests to please remove their boots before going to bed. The place smelled of manure, whether from the bedding or the sleepers.

Robert and Arvid reluctantly unstrapped their rucksacks. This was a poor lodging, but to them it smelled in some way of home since it exuded such a strong odor of stable; once they had lodged together in the stable room at Nybacken.

Their host was talkative and when he heard that the Swedish boys were on their way to California he was ready with good advice; he himself had a brother who had set out on the Trail last spring, so he could tell them all they needed to know.

There *was* a road to the gold land, in fact, three different roads—the Overland Trail, the Santa Fe Trail, and one trail between these two, following sometimes one and sometimes the other. Most travelers used the Overland Trail, which started at Independence, Missouri.

"You must go to Independence and join the golden army!"

Robert had looked only casually at his map with its many western states and territories, all of them void of place-names, it seemed. Now he asked how far it was to Independence. The Irishman said that this town lay two hundred miles to the west of St. Louis.

Robert felt as if he had got another kick in the behind throwing him still farther back across the American continent. Two hundred miles!

Mr. Jameson continued. It was too late for them to join the caravan of goldseekers this summer, a whole month too late. It was May now, the train to California had left Independence in April and was on its way west. A new caravan would not leave until next spring. When the buf-

224

falo grass turned green next spring, then the goldseekers would gather again.

And so Robert and Arvid discovered they must join others with the same intention. But this spring it was too late to sign up in the gold army; it had already left. New grass must sprout on the prairie before they could join. They would lose a whole year.

Their host wished them goodnight and good sleep and left. They sat down on their mattress and opened their rucksacks, still full of the bread and cured pork Kristina had packed for them, and ate. The food prevented Arvid from talking; for him to talk while eating would have been as sacrilegious as swearing in church. But Robert too sat silent now as he chewed. What he had just heard required some thought.

While peeling potatoes on the boat, they had figured that their twenty-five dollars would take care of their food and lodging for a month's travel from St. Louis to California. For they had hoped to reach the gold fields in a month, and once there they would have no further need for money.

And now this—they couldn't get there for a whole year.

When Arvid had finished eating he took hold of the nickel chain on his vest and pulled his watch from its pocket. He said that whatever else happened on this journey, he wouldn't sell his cylinder watch. They might have to go without food but he wouldn't part with his watch even if they starved. It was his inheritance and could not be touched. And Arvid's watch showed ten minutes after nine this May evening of 1851, in Mr. Jameson's manure-smelling lodging in the town of St. Louis, Missouri, where they had paid 25 cents apiece for sleeping accommodations. Gentlemen please take off their boots in bed!

Robert and Arvid, once having shared the same stable room, had sworn to stick together forever, never to separate. Now they crept under the same horse blanket: they had traveled far into the world, almost to the center of America, and they needed to stick together. Tonight they

225

felt again like comrades-in-service, sharing a stable room. They were once again a couple of farmhands—and far from the Land of Gold.

2.

Later in the summer they began to dig in the earth again—but not for gold. They got work on a farm near town whose owner wanted a potato cellar dug. Their pay was seventy-five cents a day plus board, and in the farm kitchen they could eat as much meat and potatoes and beans as they wanted. But their room was a ramshackle shed where they were worse housed than in the stable room they had lived in in Sweden. The cracks between the boards were so wide that the wind blew through unhindered. But there were no bedbugs in the walls as there had been at Nybacken, where each morning they had awakened with fresh bites on their necks; this shed was so miserable that no vermin wanted to live there.

The boys were farmhands again. They had set out to dig for gold, but when they dug into the ground they found only sand and gravel, clay and rocks. Arvid, however, couldn't help looking at his spade now and again, letting the dirt pour slowly from the blade: perhaps . . . perhaps . . . ! But never a glowworm spark of anything glittering. Robert counseled his friend to be patient, as they couldn't get any farther this year they must remain here and keep alive until spring. Next year they would find something different on their spades!

Arvid worried that they might be delayed so long that all the gold would be gone before they got there. Robert reassured him. In an American newspaper he had read that a very learned man, Mr. Horace Greeley, had said that California had at least two thousand million dollars' worth of gold. As yet only two hundred million had been dug up; there was still eighteen hundred million left. Did Arvid think that with so much there would not be enough for him? Did he want more than eighteen hundred million dollars?

When the potato cellar was finished, they were put to work helping with the harvesting and the threshing; this kept them busy during the fall, and when winter came they were put to cutting wood. Now their wages dropped to fifty cents a day, but they could still eat as much meat and potatoes and beans as before. They might have liked their jobs if they had been better housed, but when winter came the sharp wind blew through the cracks of their shed and plagued them miserably, so that they crept close together at night to keep warm.

The winter continued and the cold increased, and Arvid began to complain. Why had they traveled so far to sleep in this rotten shed? It had been warmer in the stable room at Nybacken. Had they immigrated to America in order to lie here and freeze and suffer at night? Robert comforted him; they must be patient through the winter; then all suffering and evil would be over. And what they were doing furthered their plans; they were working their way to the gold land. They had peeled their way on the river, here they had dug their way along in summer, and now they were cutting their way to California. Every single ring of the ax brought them closer to the gold land by earning money for them. And they would get there if they had to creep and crawl the whole two thousand miles!

The younger boy always found words that cheered the older one. And they continued to saw and split and stack wood in tall piles. In the evenings it might happen that Arvid asked: how much gold was still left in California—how many millions? But one evening when they returned to their cold shed after a day of work, Arvid sank down on the bunk, his hands to his face:

"I can't stand it any longer! I want to go home!"

He began to cry: he wanted to return to Minnesota, to his service with Danjel Andreasson, to the people from Sweden he knew. He had thought about it for a long while and he had made his decision: he didn't want to go on to California. He didn't care about the gold any more. He would give up the riches—it didn't matter to him if he were rich or poor. He would just as soon be poor if he only could be with people he could take to and whom he knew. He didn't want to work for an American farmer any more and have to live in this shed; he had had it much better with Danjel. As long as he must remain a farmhand anyway . . .

"But I can't find the way back . . . I can't ask in English . . . Won't you come with me, Robert . . . ? Let's go back, please, Robert!"

"No, Arvid! I won't return! Never!"

"But I can't go back alone . . . I can't manage . . . Please, Robert, come with me!"

"No! I want to see California!"

His friend's weeping and pleading bothered Robert but his mind could not be changed. He would go on; he would not return to his brother in Minnesota until he had found gold and could return as a rich man.

And he reminded Arvid of their mutual promise, a promise for all times and all circumstances: *whatever happened, the two of them must always stick together!* Didn't he remember the Sunday when they had made a bonfire at Lake Ki-Chi-Saga? They had been sitting there at the fire, warming their blue-frozen hands, and they had sworn that they would be comrades forever here in America, they would never part company!

Would Arvid now fail his comrade, and his oath?

They talked about it until late that evening—until at last they agreed again and shook hands on the promise: when the prairie was green with next spring's grass they would continue west on the California Trail.

Yes—I heard it so well: I heard you and Arvid agree. The two Swedish farm boys would never part in America.

I want to see California! you said. You wouldn't change your mind. You persuaded him to stick to his promise. You can't deny you did.

But you must know that already that first winter you had begun to doubt; your eyes had been opened, you had seen the road before you—you hesitated and thought, shouldn't we turn back? Your eyes were no longer blinded by the gleaming gold two thousand miles away. For you knew already you hadn't set out to look for gold! That wasn't your reason. You took off to get rid of mas-

228

ters, all masters in the world. But you did not know what you were looking for instead. Something you had heard in a song . . . ?

And it was that first winter that I began to buzz and annoy you—perhaps because of the cold wind in the shed. Since then you have never been able to silence me for long; you have been forced to endure my sounds. And during your woodcutting winter in St. Louis that yellow, evil-smelling fluid began to run again; it is always an ominous sign.

And I have recorded and still keep Arvid's voice: I can hear his words whenever I wish—that time, and that, and that! Please, Robert! he pleaded, like a little child. Please, Robert! Almost the same words, later. We come to that soon.

Yes, dear Robert, I have now buzzed for you so long this evening it's time to buzz you to sleep. At last you always get so tired you go to sleep. Sleep now!

Good night, goldseeker!

XVI. While the Riches Lay Hidden in the House

1.

Karl Oskar and Kristina often recalled to mind that week in June, 1855, when Robert had returned on a Monday.

Robert slept late on that June Tuesday morning of 1855, and no one disturbed him; he must be tired to death, they thought, and in need of rest. Karl Oskar had intended to do a day's work on the church building, which had been started that spring, but as his brother had just come back, he stayed at home and did ordinary small chores. Kristina wanted to prepare good and strengthening food for the prodigal, so she robbed the chicken nests of fresh eggs, and for her brother-in-law's breakfast she also made dumplings, which she knew he liked.

Robert rose at last and sat down alone at the kitchen table. After a while Karl Oskar came in; he had something he wanted to say to his brother which he should have said last night only everything had become so confused: a hearty thanks for the big bundle of bills—if now all this money was meant as a gift! He had inspected the bills, both by candle flame and in daylight, and as far as he could see they were real and must be good currency. He would put them in the bank at Stillwater at once. Nowadays so many bills were worth only half their face value, or nothing at all, that he hoped Robert would understand why they had been suspicious at first. To himself he thought that the only thing that troubled him about this money was the fact that he himself hadn't earned it with his own hands.

Robert mumbled that he hoped his brother and sister-in-law would enjoy the money. Apparently he didn't want to talk any further about the gift. He himself had little feeling for his fortune; last night he had handled the bills as if all he wanted was to get rid of them, the sooner the better.

By daylight his leanness was more marked. And his yellow skin was not a sign of health. Kristina now understood why Karl Oskar had wondered if he suffered from some gnawing disease. Perhaps he had had to sacrifice his health for the gold. And if he couldn't buy back his health with it, he had indeed made a poor bargain.

They had many questions to ask Robert, as they wanted to know all that had happened to him during his four years' absence. But he discouraged their questions; perhaps he would tell them more once he was rested. Now he was the one to ask: what had happened here since he left?

Karl Oskar and Kristina described to him the activities around the lake, the new houses that had been built, and told him the names of their neighbors, all new immigrants from Sweden. The population had increased so much they had now founded a Swedish congregation.

"We timbered up a schoolhouse last summer. Now we're hammering together a church," said Karl Oskar.

"Yes, at last," added Kristina. "They crabbed a whole year about the location of God's house."

Well, each one of the settlers had wanted the church near his claim, said Karl Oskar. People had wanted it on both the north and the south, on the east and the west lakeshore, in every imaginable place. Ten different sites had been under consideration. Those Swedes who had come here were so stubborn and selfish; what could one do with ten heads, each with a different opinion and none willing to give in? It had looked as if they might have to build ten churches, for all had the same right to decide; and only with ten churches would all have been done full justice. But at last they had been forced to agree. A site had been selected on the Helsinge farmer Lars Sjölin's claim, on a tongue of land across from Nordberg's Island. It was a pleasant location on a promontory near the lake, as nearly as possible in the center of the Swedish settlement. It was really a good place for the church, only twenty minutes' walk for them, so they couldn't complain.

"But our parish is so poor we can't even hang a bell," said Kristina.

"We'll raise a small steeple for the time being," said Karl Oskar. "We can hang the church bell when we're better off."

To build a church was a difficult and tiresome job, that much he had learned. Everything was to be done voluntarily but some sort of organization was necessary: each household was to cut, rough-hew, and deliver three loads of lumber, and each grown man was to give twelve days' labor. But no one could tell yet if this would be sufficient to complete the building. And many members were poor newcomers who barely had had time to raise a shelter over their own heads, and who must first of all see to their own needs. At least a thousand dollars in cash was needed to finish the church and as yet they didn't know if they could scrape together this sum.

"They can't agree on anything, these people," insisted Kristina. "They quarrel about the slightest nonsense."

"They had no chance to decide anything back in

231

Sweden so now they make up for it in America," said Karl Oskar.

There had been great fights about the little schoolhouse, too, before it was completed last fall. The parish elder, the Helsinge farmer Petrus Olausson, had forced them to build it on his land, half a mile from the church. The young pastor, Mr. Törner, had promised to act as teacher and kept school two months in spring and two months in autumn. During the winter there was no school as the children couldn't get out on the roads because of the cold and snow: they couldn't risk the children's freezing to death in the drifts. Johan and Marta attended regularly, and Harald would begin this fall.

This was indeed news to Robert; great changes had taken place.

The children were curious about the stranger who had brought the sweets. Robert asked if they learned Swedish in school, and Johan wanted to show him how much he knew. The boy reeled off some Swedish words. Only once did he stumble, repeating from memory. Marta too wanted to show what she had learned; she found the school's reader and read the story "The Shepherd Who Lied."

"A liar you cannot believe even when he tells the truth," she concluded her reading.

"That's an amusing story," said Robert thoughtfully. "I was asked to read that story once for Schoolmaster Rinaldo."

"The pastor says it will teach us not to lie, not even in fun," advised Marta.

In a low voice Robert repeated the last sentence of the story while his eyes sought his brother's. Karl Oskar quckly looked out through the window as if he hadn't heard.

In the kitchen a silence fell. There was a feeling that anything could happen if the two brothers now exchanged a single word.

Kristina felt the silence must be broken. "The girl has a nice singing voice. Sing something for Robert, Marta."

"What, Mother?"

"Something you've learned in school. This for example: 'We're Swedes, we're Swedes, Although we're small . . .'!"

The mother did not sing the words, she spoke them; she had no singing voice.

"That's called 'The Song of the Swedish Boys,'" said the girl. "I know a better one!" And Marta threw her flaxen braids over her shoulders, stood spread-legged in the middle of the floor, and sang in her clear, thin child-voice:

> "We go to school,
> We stand in row,
> Our hands are clean,
> Our faces also.
> Now let us listen
> With open ears,
> What teacher says,
> Or it'll be lost.
> Let's hurry and learn,
> Knowledge to earn
> Which is better than silver
> And gold . . ."

As the last words rang out Robert rose quickly from his chair; his spoon fell from his hand and clattered on the floor. He shied away as if the girl had hurt him; he stared wide-eyed at her until she backed away looking at him in fright.

Slowly he picked up the spoon. Then he sat down, silent and lost in thought. Karl Oskar and Kristina were puzzled by his behavior; Robert seemed frightened at the mere sound of a word in a song—the word "gold."

2.

In the afternoon they went out to inspect the farm. Karl Oskar and Kristina wanted to show Robert what they had tilled and planted and built while he was away. He was greatly surprised at the large field with sprouting corn, wheat, rye, and oats on the slope where only four years ago nothing had grown but weeds. And such smooth, even fields! His brother had indeed worked hard.

"If the farmers at home could see these fields they would die of envy!"

The brothers walked side by side along the edge of the field. Robert noticed that Karl Oskar dragged his left leg. "What's the matter with you? You limp?"

The older brother replied, somewhat embarrassed, that it was only the old ailment in his left shinbone; the injury he had sustained when a couple of men had tried to rob him on their journey to Minnesota; it never had healed, it ached sometimes when he worked too hard, and perhaps he favored that leg while walking.

"You slave yourself to death on your claim!"

Robert seemed serious; nothing in this world was worth aches and limps. Not even the good earth of Minnesota was worth that much.

He was a youth no longer. He had grown so old that he advised his older brother.

They looked at the fat and well-cared-for animals in the stable. Each had been bred on the place except the cow, Lady. Robert had promised Karl Oskar money for a team of oxen but now his brother had raised a team himself. And this spring one of the heifers had taken the bull, so they would soon have five cows.

"I don't want to have any more to milk," said Kristina.

They went inside the deserted log cabin, which was now used as a toolshed and carpenter shop.

"Here I stand and fix things," said Karl Oskar.

In the old log house he now spent rainy days at the workbench. The floor was strewn with shavings. On the wall, deer and calf skins had been nailed up to dry. It looked like a junk shop in there. But there they had lived for four winters. When Robert compared the log cabin with the new main house in the maple grove he could see that things had improved for his brother's family in New Duvemala.

He asked about the shanty where they had lived the first fall, but Karl Oskar had torn it down, as the old shed only spoiled the looks of the new building. He had already built three houses for his family, and now he had begun the fourth in his head.

"Next time I build, Robert . . . ."

But the most unusual thing they had acquired while Robert was gone Kristina had waited to show him last: a small tree that grew at the east gable of the new main house.

Could he guess what kind of tree it was? A little sapling, about five feet tall, its top reaching to Robert's chest. The tree had large, deep green leaves, healthy branches and foliage. But he couldn't guess. Some kind of plum tree perhaps?

"An apple tree from home!" said Kristina.

"Kristina's own tree!" added Karl Oskar.

This Astrakhan apple tree had sprung up from seeds which Kristina's parents had sent in a letter. It had grown to chest height in a few years. Now it stood here at their gable, thousands of miles from Sweden. Wasn't it like a miracle?

Robert lightly pinched a leaf of the sapling; he ought to have recognized an Astrakhan tree from its wide, thick leaves with fuzz on the underside.

Kristina said that she guessed it would take a few years more before the tree bore fruit, and no one could tell if it would have real Astrakhan apples—those juicy, large apples, big as children's heads, with clear, transparent skin that she had enjoyed at home. Their neighbors, Algot and Manda Svensson, had said that crab apples might grow on trees planted this way from seeds. Branches ought to be grafted on a trunk if one wanted to be sure of fine fruit. But she couldn't believe crab apples would sprout in America from the fine Astrakhan seeds from Sweden.

Robert stroked the branches; the leaves felt soft to his touch. "It's come from the old country . . . it too has emigrated . . ."

"That sapling is the apple of Kristina's eye!" said Karl Oskar.

From the tremble in her voice Robert had already understood as much. Everywhere on this claim, everywhere in the good earth round Ki-Chi-Saga, a great many plants

235

grew; the land was verdant with crops of wheat and barley and corn and potatoes. But of all the planted and tended seedlings, of all the sprouting, thriving growth, this sapling was obviously dearest to Kristina.

And he himself felt nostalgia as he touched the tree, he felt a strange compassion for the little life, a desire to protect and guard it. He felt as if it were a living being—as if four people instead of three were standing here at the gable, four immigrants.

"This sapling . . . it's almost unreal!" said Robert.

And when they walked on he turned back to look, as if afraid the tender, sensitive life might not be able to withstand the merciless winter cold here in North America.

3.

Karl Oskar had put out his precious copies of *Hemlandet* for his brother. Robert did not know that a Swedish paper was printed in America; in the part of the country where he had been he had hardly met any Swedes and he had never heard anyone talk of Sweden. Now he sat the whole evening and read the paper eagerly, and learned about the most important happenings in the world during the last year.

A great war was ravaging the Old World but Sweden had as yet not been dragged into it. *Hemlandet* had predicted that war sooner or later must break out in the New World also—in the North American Union—between the faction advocating love of humanity and liberty and those wanting slavery. Lately a group of courageous men in Kansas had organized the Free-States Union with the intention of driving out all slave owners. But in Georgia a white man had been fined ten thousand dollars for spreading the rumor that his neighbor had black blood in his veins. In one state slave owners were thrown out, in another it was a great crime to hint that a person was related to a Negro.

Robert said that was just the way things were in America; every place was different from every other.

236

"You must read the installment story!" suggested Kristina. "There you can see how the white lords torture the poor blacks!"

The story in *Hemlandet* was called "Fifty Years in Chains" and was an American slave's true description of his life. The story was so horrible and touched everyone so deeply that all readers were compelled to pray to God that He would abolish the curse of slavery, she said. Yes, Robert would read "Fifty Years in Chains" by and by, he told her, but for the moment he was looking for happenings here in Minnesota.

A terrible accident had occurred down in Carver County. A Swedish settler had been out hunting of a Sunday and when he returned home and started to clean his gun he was so clumsy that he shot his seventy-year-old mother-in-law to death. The paper emphasized the happening as God's warning to the immigrants; they ought to keep the Sabbath and never hunt on this day.

Cities had begun to spring up in America like mushrooms on a rainy August day. In Minnesota Territory no less than eighty town sites had been planned and surveyed during the last year.

At this Karl Oskar interrupted in annoyance: "That's cheating and swindling!"

He knew the true situation. Nearly all towns out here existed only on maps. No people lived in them, for there were no houses. The paper cities were founded by speculators who were too lazy to work the earth and merely speculated in lots. Parasitical critters who lived off honest settlers! He would like to take his gun and drive these rats and vermin out of the Territory.

Robert said that the richest cities were in California. In one of the smallest towns out there, New Home Town, lived the greatest number of millionaires on the smallest number of square feet in America.

Karl Oskar picked up the paper and read about the price of grain: winter wheat in Chicago brought a dollar fifty per bushel, while rye brought only seventy-five cents and oats thirty cents for the same measure. What he had suspected turned out to be true: wheat was the flour grain

237

valued above all else in the New World. White bread, reserved for their lordships in Sweden, was on everyone's table in America.

"I see women are allowed to write in the papers here," said Robert.

Following the example of American papers, *Hemlandet* had two articles by women. Male readers had taken exception and sent in angry letters: writing by women was contrary to the biblical and Lutheran spirit which until now had dominated the paper. The editor replied that in the future he intended to remain fearless and when he received something worthwhile written by a woman he intended to print it. He wanted in this way to encourage females who more and more were learning to write. He insisted he would still remain a good Lutheran.

"I believe he is right," said Kristina. "I can't think it's sinful to learn to write."

She felt that many Swedish immigrant women, like herself, felt inferior because they never had learned to write and were unable to communicate with their relatives at home.

"Everything is different here," said Robert. "You are a missus and Karl Oskar is a mister out here."

"Yes, I am now 'Mr.' Nilsson!"

And Karl Oskar laughed heartily: he had been elevated here! If a farmer in Sweden were called "Mister" he would take it as an insult, believe he was being made a fool of.

"You should know how trusted your brother is in America," said Kristina to Robert. "He and Uncle Danjel were elected to the parish board."

"Are you a church warden, Karl Oskar!" exclaimed Robert.

"A church warden without a church as yet. Danjel and I are 'deacons,' we're chosen to run the parish."

"Deacons?! That sounds almost like a dean or a bishop."

Kristina said she remembered that time when Dean Brusander denied the Holy Sacrament to Uncle Danjel and refused to accept him as godfather for Harald when the boy was baptized. Suppose the dean now learned that Danjel and Karl Oskar ran the parish—that in America they could select and fire ministers! Wasn't the world turned upside down out here?

This evening supper was late again because Kristina had so much to talk about with Robert. She noticed his hearing had grown still worse, that she had to raise her voice in speaking to him. And she wondered again if he weren't sick in some way; he moved about so slowly and heavily, and when he sat still and did not exert himself in any way, big drops of sweat trickled down his forehead. He was very thirsty and often walked over to the bucket to drink. He explained that he was weak after a cold he had caught on the steamboat coming up the river; that was why he wanted to go to bed early these first evenings.

And as soon as Robert had eaten supper he went to bed in the gable room.

Kristina looked after him as he closed the door.

"Something is wrong with your brother, Karl Oskar. You can see and hear it."

"Yes—he's somewhat quiet about his gold digging. And he hasn't said a word about Arvid . . ."

The old doubts were gnawing at him again; could everything be as it should with the big packs of bills his brother had given them?

Karl Oskar and Kristina remained sitting in the kitchen for a long time that evening, talking about something that had been in their minds all day long, something that had hardly left their thoughts for a minute—that something which for a whole day had been lying hidden in the bottom of the Swedish chest: the fortune that was secreted in their house.

XVII. The Second Night—Robert's Ear Speaks

You're tired and want to sleep but I must keep you awake. I am your faithful companion—I am the memories which refuse to leave you, a severe master.

You have an ear ache; you feel your heart's persistent pumping in your ear, a dull thudding. But there is nothing you can do about it, except to lie quietly and endure it. What is it that hurts me? you have asked. No being on earth can give you a reply to that question. When you were born into this world as a human being you were condemned to being hurt. You were born with this body with its two ears, one of which buzzes at you tonight! Whose decision was it that you were to be a human being? The Lord of life and death, of course, and he also created the hurt. Why did He do it?—That is the Riddle of Life you cannot solve.

During that spring, three years ago, you still had your health, without suffering. At that time you lived with an expectation which aided you to endure patiently all troubles and tribulations; you thought the only thing that mattered was to get to a certain place on this earth. Yes, I remember so clearly everything that happened during that spring . . .

1.

The buffalo grass was again turning green on the prairie, and new shoots were springing up, already three inches tall. Again there was fodder for the animals of the gold caravan, all the animals which would carry Califor-
240

nia-bound travelers on their backs and provide them with meat. The grass was fresh and green for only one month of the year, but it remained nourishing and desirable to the animals the year round.

Toward the end of March the two Swedish farmhands threw aside their axes, said goodbye to the farmer, and made ready to continue their journey westward; this spring they would not be too late to join up with the caravan on the California Trail.

Every day great numbers of strangers arrived in St. Louis on their way to Independence and St. Joseph, the meeting places for goldseekers. Here they obtained part of their equipment, food, fodder, tools which could not be bought farther west. St. Louis was beginning to look like a great army camp bivouacking for a few days. In every open place in the town, Robert and Arvid could see those strange vehicles, the Conestoga wagons, with their broad side boards and heavily forged wheel rims. From one side board to the other canvas was stretched on curved wooden bows over the wagon to form a covering. The boys looked with respect at the Conestoga wagon wheels which would turn over two thousand miles of prairies and plateaus, over mountains and deserts, and at last sink down in the sand where the gold glittered and shone.

The California-bound rode in wagons or on horses or mules and those who had neither vehicle nor animal must use the old "apostle horses"—they must walk. But even for those on foot, pack animals were necessary; no one could carry a heavy burden for two thousand miles.

Robert and Arvid counted the money they had saved and talked and figured carefully. How ought they to travel?

One morning as they walked about the town they were approached by a dark-hued stranger who carried a silver-ornamented Kentucky rifle. The man was not much taller than a young boy and wore a short red jacket with yellow stripes across the shoulders and chest. His hat was brown with a hatband of silver-white strings—the biggest hat they had ever seen on a human head. They thought it funny to see such a short man with a hat brim half as

241

wide as his height. This peculiarly dressed stranger asked them if they were on their way to California.

"Yes . . . yes! We are hunting for gold!" Never before had Robert found an answer in English so quickly.

The little man smiled, exposing long white teeth. His skin was honey-colored, and his strong, protruding nose reminded Robert of his brother Karl Oskar. His eyes were big and friendly and warm.

He too was on his way to the goldfields. He would supply them with all they needed on the journey if they would keep him company and help him with his mules. Had they any experience in handling animals?

"We are used to farm work," exclaimed Robert. "We can take care of cattle."

"Good! Let's go to a tavern for a beer."

They hung over the counter while exchanging information. Within the hour everything had been agreed upon: Robert and Arvid were employed for four months—the time needed to cover the California Trail—to serve as mule drivers for a Mexican whose name was Mario Vallejos. English was not the native tongue of either Robert or Vallejos, yet they talked with ease to each other in this language. Vallejos had been born in Texas. A few years ago the Americans had come and taken his land and now he wanted some of their California gold in exchange. A few of his friends were in the same situation and it had been agreed among them they would all meet in St. Joseph, from whence a large group of California-bound men were to start toward the end of April. From St. Louis to St. Joseph the distance was about two hundred and fifty miles; this was the road they must first travel. Vallejos figured they could cover an average of twenty miles a day so they would need about twelve or thirteen days to get to St. Joseph. They would travel over uninhabited regions of prairies and plains but he knew the road well. If the boys could leave then, he would like to start out tomorrow; he had only been waiting to find the helpers he needed.

The Mexican turned out to be the owner of eight mules, all at their peak age, between four and six years old. They were strong and sturdy pack animals, each capable of a three-hundred-pound load. Seven of them were light gray, the eighth was dark brown; this one was the largest in the herd and was to carry the owner himself.

Indian horses and Mexican mules were the toughest animals both for packing and riding, explained Vallejos. But his mules required constant attention—careful brushing and feeding and a friendly attitude.

Robert assured him that both he and his friend had always loved Mexican mules above all other animals on earth. No mules of any kind existed in their home country but they had always looked forward to the pleasure of driving and combing and feeding these wise animals. In fact, this was the reason they had emigrated to North America.

Their new boss smiled and seemed pleased with his muleteers.

The boys had never driven animals other than horses and oxen. Arvid looked apprehensively at these Mexican mules and worried about his chores:

"Asses, ain't they? Unreliable critters, I bet . . . ?"

Before he had come to America Arvid had never seen an ass except the one Jesus rode when he entered Jerusalem on Palm Sunday, and this was only a picture in the Bible. But that ass didn't look at all like Vallejos' pack animals.

The Mexican soon taught Robert all about their new duties, And Robert explained to Arvid one important point: hinnies and mules were different sorts of animals, for they had entirely different parents. When an ass took a stallion a hinny was born, but a mule was not begotten in that way; with her parents it was just the opposite: a mule had an ass to father and a mare for mother. With parents, he told Arvid, it is always the mother who is most important for the offspring, and since the mule had a mare-mother she became much more important than the hinny; she was the wisest animal on earth.

"A mare as mother and a jackass for father. Try to remember that, Arvid!"

And thus Arvid learned his first sentence in English: a mare mother and a jackass father. For he must know what kind of animals he had to take care of. Arvid had

243

heard that asses were the dumbest animals alive; on the contrary, he now learned, if you had an ass for father you were the wisest animal on earth. For all children got their sense from the mother, said Robert, and the mother was a wise mare.

"I think I got my sense from my father," said Arvid. "My mother had a poor head."

They helped the Mexican with the provisions for the journey and loaded the packsaddles of the mules with flour, hams, beans, rice, coffee, dried fruit, sugar, salt, and water in canteens. They were openmouthed at the sight of all the goods their boss had bought for the California Trail, and he said he would buy still more when they arrived at St. Joseph. During the four months required for the two-thousand-mile journey each man would consume 150 pounds of flour, 50 pounds of ham, 50 pounds of dried pork, 30 pounds of sugar, 6 pounds of coffee, 1 pound of tea, 3 pounds of salt, one bushel of dried fruit, 25 pounds of rice, 20 pounds of hardtack, and half a bushel of beans.

When Robert and Arvid saw all the food a single man would eat on the journey they began to understand how very far it was to California.

It took more than one day for even the most willing muleteer to learn how to saddle a mule and pack it properly. The weight must be evenly divided between the front and hind quarters, and the same for both sides; an even balance was required or the pack animal would fall on its nose or sink down on its hind legs. Robert and Arvid had only harnessed horses and yoked oxen—to place several hundred pounds on a small mule was a much more complicated matter. And Arvid decided this much: a muleteer must be wiser than everyone else on earth. In America a hired hand must be smarter than in Sweden.

And so one April morning at dawn, the Mexican, Mario Vallejos, set out on his journey westward across the prairie, with his two young helpers and his eight mules, to join the gold caravan—the train of the hundred thousand.

2.

The party traveled under the burning sun in daytime and camped under the chilly starlight at night. They followed in the footsteps of those who had passed here before them: soft places in the ground bore the imprints of heel irons and boot soles, of hooves and cloven hooves, and the broad wheel rims of the Conestoga wagons. But in sandy places the wind had obliterated all tracks, and on the plateaus and hard ground no tracks had been left.

The little Mexican rode ahead on his dark brown mule to locate the trail. The two youths came behind with the pack mules, each one carrying two hundred pounds for its owner. Robert and Arvid fed the mules crushed corn three times a day and watered them twice a day. They curried the animals and loaded them, followed them in daytime and guarded them at night. The longer they scratched a mule between the ears, the easier it became to take care of it.

When the mules grew hungry they folded their ears back and brayed. It sounded as if they had attacks of hiccups. The muleteers thought at first that something had got stuck in their throats; the animals wailed and hiccuped helplessly. But by and by Robert and Arvid became accustomed to their peculiar braying; they brayed when their stomachs were empty.

Vallejos considered Mexican mules most suitable for the California Trail since they required less water than horses, and in the desert they could smell water holes at a distance of two miles or more.

They were traveling across a plain and could not understand how their boss found his way. The Mexican had made himself a map for the first five hundred miles of the California Trail: from St. Joseph straight toward the Big Blue River, the first big river to be crossed. Those starting from Independence headed for Bull Creek and Wakarusa River before they reached the Kansas, the broadest and most difficult river to cross on the whole trail. He had chosen the route through St. Joseph, the northern overland route, to avoid the crossing of the broad Kansas River.

In St. Louis Robert and Arvid had begun to prepare themselves for washing gold. They had each bought a pan of good steel, which held almost a gallon of water. Now that they were the owners of washing pans, good-sized pans, they walked behind the mules and drummed with their fingers on the pans; they were ready, and they also knew how to dig.

The days were too warm and the nights too cold. At camp in the evenings they gathered dry grass and bushes and made a fire to keep themselves warm. Each in turn stood watch and tended the fire. They slept stretched out on the ground with the saddles as pillows. Arvid kept complaining of the weather in America: either it was too warm or too cold—why was it never right?

When the cold kept them both awake Robert cheered his friend by telling him what he knew about the Gold Land: in California the weather was just right the year round, and so healthy that people lived to be a hundred years old. Old people only dried up a little more for each year in the good sun, until at last nothing was left but the skin, which finally blew away over the Pacific Ocean. Out there people didn't die in the same way as in other places. In California there were no diseases to kill people. Even suicides were impossible in that state. Californians, aged two or three hundred years and tired of living, would travel to some other state, where they immediately collapsed like empty sacks and died.

Vallejos told them that nuggets had been found in the Sacramento River weighing as much as a hundred and fifty pounds, and worth fifty thousand dollars apiece.

"One single lump! Oh Lordy, Lordy!" exclaimed Arvid. And he had served as farmhand in Sweden for ten dollars a year. If he found a single nugget he could buy the manor of Krakesjö, where his old father was a cotter.

Gold was the word that gave them strength, dreaming of gold still held its power over them.

Each evening when Arvid wound his watch and one more day had been added to the California Trail he asked: "We've been on our way a whole year now—how soon will we get there?"

Robert assured him they were getting closer to the gold every day, they were twenty miles closer today. Sacramento, that was the place they were going—Vallejos had mentioned it when he sat at the fire, the map spread over his knees.

The Mexican was a good master. He didn't ask them to walk farther than they could manage each day, and they could eat all they wanted of the provisions, so they gorged themselves on ham and dried pork. Vallejos took his share of the watch, looking after the fire for a few hours every third night. He could stand heat and cold—it didn't bother him. He enumerated the dangers on the California Trail: the fording of the rivers, the desert heat, the Indians, the wild animals. But of people he feared only one man: *the Yellow Jack.* He was afraid of someone called Yellow Jack. Although he explained who this was, Robert was unable to follow his English and remained in the dark about the dangerous Yellow Jack.

At the campfire Vallejos kept himself awake by singing—always the same song, humming it, like a bumblebee's buzzing in the grass:

Oh, the good time has come at last,
We need no more complain, sir!
The rich can live in luxury
And the poor can do the same, sir!
For the good time has come at last,
And as we are told, sir!
And shall be rich at once now,
With California gold, sir!

Robert listened night after night to the dream song, the song of the yellow gold that would make him free. When at last he had reached the end of this road he would be free. He was a muleteer, he was still in service, but this service would be his last—the Mexican, Mario Vallejos, would be the last master in his life.

3.

On the ninth day after they had set out they saw for the first time the animal which had given its name to the tall grass on the prairie; at a distance they could see a herd of buffalo, an ash-gray, closed circle moving across the plain in a westward direction. It seemed to them as if the very ground were moving with this herd. The heavy tramp of the animals sounded like a muffled thunderstorm when it first rises over the horizon. So many animals in motion struck them as a revelation of the immensity of the wild regions. Several times they saw packs of furry animals—reddish, with sharp noses and long tails.

They were a small caravan of three people and eight animals. Each time the caravan passed running water—creeks or streams—the mules were allowed to drink all they wanted, but when they approached stagnant water Vallejos warned them sternly: the water holes were not to be trusted. The country grew more desolate and the ground more arid, the green buffalo grass grew thinner; the dry earth shot out from under the hooves of the mules like pelting rain. They had reached a region with no streams and they used the water in their canteens to water the animals.

In a hollow they saw a broken pair of wheels; pieces of spokes and a broken wagon tongue were strewn about. The Mexican stopped his mule and nodded meaningfully at the place, but said nothing. A few hundred yards farther on a flat white stone had been raised on end in the ground, and the stone—a foot or two in height—had an inscription in black letters:

JACK MALONEY
AGED 18 YEARS
REST IN PEACE SWEET BOY
FOR THY TROUBLES ARE OVER

Robert understood the connection between the broken wheels and the little tombstone but he did not interpret the inscription to Arvid. Nevertheless it stuck in his mind for the rest of the day.

On the eleventh day their trail crossed a desolate, sandy plain, surrounded by distant hills. The terrain was broken by stone islands in the sand and boulders of outlandish appearance. Horrible giants in animal shape were guarding this plain, petrified monsters with human heads and beast-bodies, heads of horses and lions in stone. The sun was uncomfortably warm on earth and rocks.

Vallejos said they should arrive in St. Joseph in three days.

In the evening they made camp between a split rock in the center of the plain. It was Robert's turn to guard the fire. In the night a wind came up from the west, a gusty wind that blew sand into the fire and several times almost extinguished it. He moved the embers farther in the lee of the rock; here the fire burned well and he dozed for a while, his head on the saddle.

With the first streak of daylight he got up to urinate. He walked over to look at the mules, tethered behind the rock. What he saw struck him dumb; there were only six animals. Two of the mules were gone. He hurried around the rock searching for them, but the two animals had vanished.

Arvid had tethered the mules last night when they camped, and Robert had warned him before that his knots in the halters were too loose. He shook his comrade roughly by the shoulder but spoke in a low voice so as not to waken their master, who slept only a few paces away.

"You didn't tie those mules aright! Two of them broke away!"

Arvid was awake instantly as soon as he heard Robert's words. He didn't try to deny it, he had tied the mules to some boulders—if they had broken loose he was to blame. But he didn't think it was because of his loose knots. Perhaps the beasts had pulled and pulled and the rope had slid over the rock.

Robert said it didn't matter whose fault it was; both of

249

them would suffer for this. Bad luck was the worst thing one ever encountered. If their boss should learn that the knots had been loose earlier he would never trust his muleteers again; he would fire them on the spot. As long as they were with the Mexican they had all they needed for their journey; if they were separated from him they might never get to California. They must find the strayed mules and bring them back before he woke up; they must get out and look for them at once.

According to Arvid's watch it was four o'clock. As a rule they broke camp about seven; they had three hours in which to search.

"It's my fault!" wailed Arvid. "I'm born with bad luck in my head!"

"Don't lose your head. We'll find the critters."

The boys took off over the plain on speedy legs to search for the mules. Darkness still lay thick and in this dim light a mule could hardly be seen at a distance of fifty feet. They could see no tracks of the animals however much they scanned the ground. They hollered and called the mules by all the names Vallejos used:

"Heekee . . . ! Hinni . . . ! Cheekte . . . ! Heekee . . . !"

Every few minutes they stopped and listened hopefully for the familiar braying, but there was no reply to their calls. They repeated the words without knowing the meaning:

"Hinni . . . ! Cheekte . . . !"

And no tracks were visible.

Mexican mules could smell fresh grass long distances. Robert remembered that yesterday afternoon they had passed a place between two ridges where he had seen green buffalo grass. Perhaps the mules had found their way back to this place? But it was several miles and he did not think he could find it again.

They began by searching around the campsite, tramping the ground in ever-widening circles. They wandered as if they themselves were lost in the pale light of dawn. They mustn't go too far from camp but were sure their own tracks would guide them back when they were ready to return.

An hour passed; light came slowly to the plain. They

stumbled onto a dried-out creek bed and followed its gently sloping path; perhaps there was water farther down and the mules had smelled it. They followed this furrow for a good while. Water had recently run here; there were tracks of animals, big and little ones, but they must have been made some time ago, since the tracks had already dried up. The creek wound its way in great curves but all of it was equally dry. Yet they followed it, encouraged by the many tracks in its bottom. But not the slightest glimpse of a mule tail came to their eyes, nor the faintest braying to their ears.

It was now full daylight. The wind had increased and the dust blew in clouds about them. Arvid looked at his watch and exclaimed in terror:

"It's already half past five! Shouldn't we go back?"

In order to reach camp for their usual hour of starting they must turn at once. Vallejos must already be up and about. What would he say when he missed both the mules and the muleteers? He might think they had stolen the animals and run away.

With heavy feet Robert and Arvid followed the dry creek back toward camp. The wind was increasing and they walked with eyes closed against the whirling dust.

"Where can the critters have betaken themselves?" wondered Arvid.

"We must find them!" insisted Robert.

They returned slowly, trying to follow their own tracks. Behind them the sun rose above the plain; the first rays felt pleasantly warm on their necks. But from the other direction came the wind and it was slow walking against it.

The creek they followed grew narrower and shallower; soon it branched out in still smaller furrows. Which one was the dry creek they had first encountered? They stopped and rubbed their smarting eyes. Where were their tracks?

They walked about, searching in vain. From which direction had they come? The sun flooded down on the strange rock formations and the yellow-brown hills—but which rock sheltered their camp? They didn't know; they had lost their way.

The treacherous wind had swept away the muleteers' path back to camp; Robert and Arvid were lost on the wide plain.

4.

For a whole day they wandered without rest. When night fell and darkness enveloped them they lay down, dead tired, on the sandy ground.

They had left the camp to look for the mules with nothing except the clothes on their backs. They had brought nothing to eat and nothing to drink, and they had wandered endless hours under the bright sun, through a desolate wilderness, until they were near exhaustion. They had tried to reach the mountains they saw against the horizon, but the mountains remained as distant as ever.

Where they lay outstretched on their sandy bed the stars were lit high above them. In the night's darkness the emptiness of the plain disappeared. Round and about them in the dark were rocks and hills with humps and dips on their backs, like giant caravan camels resting after a day's march. As a guardian wall around the plain the distant ridges rose like monstrous dromedaries against the heavens.

They slept but woke with limbs stiff and aching from the night cold. They opened their eyes toward the heavens. Above them the stars glittered with a cold, bluish light, like icicles under eaves. They crept closer, seeking the warmth from each other's bodies.

They slept and awoke several times during the night, and as soon as the first light of morning broke over the plain they arose and resumed their wandering. Hour after hour, they continued through this region of emptiness and thirst. The coolness of the distant hills seemed closer: they exerted their last strength, dragging their feet slowly. But the wind stayed with them, dug itself into their bodies, whirled dust into nose and eyes, into mouth and ears, accumulated it in their hair; the dust worked into their armpits, between their legs, into their groins. The dust-sand clawed and chafed, pierced and hurt; they smelled it, chewed it, tramped in it, wallowed in dust—the dusty plain had moved inside them, into their intestines, it spread before them and penetrated them, dry and consuming.

The skin on their bodies and limbs felt dried out and shrunken, it cracked and ached. The dusty wind had dried out their mouths, spread to their throats, it was about to choke them: the thirst.

There could be only one relief from this torture—one word of five letters—which they were now seeking. A few times they thought they had found it. The ground under their feet sloped, and they looked into a hole. But it was too late: it *had been* a water hole. Now it was only a hole without water; the bottom lay empty, displaying only the hardened ridges from animals' hooves. The water had dried out, the bottom mud lay dry and light gray, like ashes on the hearth.

And after these disappointments the thirst gripped their throats harder.

In the middle of the day, when the sun was at its height, the air over the plain was like burning embers in their lungs. They crept down into the shade behind a low hill, panting and giddy.

Their bodily juices were exhausted; their lips cracked and their skin peeled off in large flakes. Their feet ached and were terribly sore; they pulled off their boots: their feet were raw both above and beneath, exposing red, hot flesh, the seat of the pain which burned with its fire-flame.

Low, thorny bushes grew over the ground around the hill. Everything growing in this region was thorny, prickly, and odorless. In other places grass would grow—cool, friendly, soft. Here it was hard and sharp and piercing. The very leaves of the flowering bushes were sharp and hostile. Everything that grew here plagued them, scratched and pierced and stung them.

What kind of evil country was this they had gotten into? wondered Arvid. Here even grass and flowers tried to harm their hands.

He pulled out his leather pouch in which he kept his watch key; he opened the watchcase to wind his watch—

253

it must not be allowed to stop. He always wanted to know what time it was. Even though he no longer knew where he was, at least he wanted to know what time it was. He might be lost in the world, but not in time.

Arvid was afraid dust would blow into the case and stop the watch: "A helluva lot of dust! This must be hell's dust bowl! I'm dying of thirst . . ."

Robert said he had been looking for buffalo tracks. If they could find any they would follow them to a water hole.

Arvid swallowed, and Robert swallowed, both of them kept swallowing all the time, without anything in their mouths to swallow. But all the time their thoughts were filled with the things they would have liked to drink.

Robert stretched out his ash-dry, swollen tongue and moved it across his lips, pretending to moisten them: if they only could find a buffalo cow; then he would milk her. Buffalo milk might not taste as fresh as water, but would surely slake the thirst. And buffalo milk was said to be fat and nourishing. It would give them strength to continue. If they now had luck enough to run across a cow that had lately calved . . .

"Buffalo are wild beasts!" said Arvid. "You couldn't milk them!"

Robert stretched out full length against the hillside and immediately went to sleep. Then water came to him: in clear streams it flowed toward his face and he opened his mouth and drank. Spring-cool, refreshing water poured into his mouth, trickled down his throat. He opened his mouth wider to let in more of this comforting splendor that washed toward him. He could not open his mouth wide enough to this clear, refreshing stream.

His mouth purled like a brook. And now he recognized the stream: he was lying on his stomach near the mill brook at home, drinking its water. Into that brook he had once thrown his jacket, trying to pretend that he had drowned, for he wanted to be free of all masters and follow the running stream to the sea, to the New World . . .

But the mill brook water had no taste. He drank and swallowed and swallowed and drank but his thirst remained. The water pleased his eyes but did not satisfy

254

his taste. He saw it but could not taste it. It was a peculiar stream, this one. The water ran into him—he opened his mouth wide—it poured into his throat, down into his stomach, but he could not feel a single drop within his body: the water from the mill brook did not quench his thirst however much he drank. He swallowed whole barrelfuls but it helped his thirst not a bit. At last the water felt hard as stone—scratching, tearing, piercing, burning his tongue . . .

Robert woke up: he lay with his face against a hard boulder and his tongue dangled from his mouth, licking the dry stone as a cow licks a lump of salt.

He had drunk without anything to drink.

Arvid had pushed both his hands under a thorny bush and was filling them with sand which he threw into the air. He was digging a hole in the ground, poking, scratching. What was he digging for? Why couldn't he find it right here? A spring might exist anywhere, one never knew. If one only dug sufficiently deep. But it wasn't easy with one's hands only . . .

Robert sniffed the wind:

"It stinks of cadaver somewhere . . ."

"Yes, I smell it too."

"I wonder where . . ."

They arose and set out in the direction whence the wind brought them the nauseating odor. Almost immediately they found its origin: within a stone's throw lay the half-rotted carcass of a horse. They stopped a few paces from it and held their noses. Pieces of hide indicated the horse had been dark brown; the flesh was partly eaten away, the ribs were scraped clean, white, bent, like the peeled willow rushes of a wicker basket. The head had two deep black holes: the eyes had been picked out by carrion birds. The long teeth were exposed in a wide, eternal grin.

One hind leg had been torn apart, skinned, and lay some distance from the carcass. It was raised up, in a last, stiffened kick against the sky. The steel horseshoe glittered like silver in the sun. They noticed that the rotting horse had been newly shod.

Only a few yards from the carcass lay the broken steering shaft of a Conestoga wagon, half buried in sand. One large wheel with several inches of broad rim was buried in dust to the hub, as if suddenly having been brought to a halt as it rolled.

Sick from the stinking cadaver, Robert and Arvid were ready to turn away when Arvid exclaimed:

"Look! O Jesus my Lord!"

He shied back and pointed. Something was sticking up in the sand just in front of his feet. Something white, only an inch or two long, spindly, like a skinned birch twig— and on its end was a human fingernail. It was a finger bone poking up from the ground in front of them. Arvid had almost stepped on it.

They ran away from the place, the smell of rotten flesh pursuing them.

The boys hurried on in silence, the dust whirling round their feet. They did not walk in any definite direction, only where it was easiest for their feet. They wanted to get away from the place—away . . .

As they wandered across the plain, they felt their strength wane and they stumbled. But they must keep moving forward. They must not come to a stop. If they came to a stop they were sure they could never move on again. And one who was unable to move forward on the California Trail was also unable to move back.

Once Arvid stopped and mumbled hoarsely:

"I almost stepped on . . ." He moved his hand to his cracked lips. "Robert! It was a forefinger . . . !"

He was sure. And the finger in the sand had pointed right at them.

5.

The sun was getting low, losing its power. It grew cooler; the shadows near hills and boulders lengthened toward evening. They staggered along drunkenly, a vise of dryness and thirst squeezing their bodies. Their guts
256

shrank into a knot. Their legs flagged and bent under the increasing weight of their bodies.

Arvid stumbled into a hole; he made no effort to get up. He fell headfirst and lay still:

"Without anything to drink I'm unable to go on . . ."

Robert sat down beside his comrade, taking him by the shoulder, but felt dizziness come over him; the ground around him was wavering; he must sit there until it stopped.

Arvid rose to his knees and began to dig in the sand with his hands. He made a scoop of his fingers and dug holes a foot or more in depth. Below the surface the ground was darker and felt cooler. If he should find water here—then he could throw himself on his stomach and . . .

Robert followed the motions with his eyes, unable to understand. What was Arvid doing? What was he digging for? The holes he dug were immediately filled up and obliterated. With his scoop he caught nothing but dust, and it poured back between his fingers and became part of the ground again. Yet Arvid continued without stopping, digging in hell's dust bowl.

"It's all my fault . . . The mules ran away because my knots were too loose . . ."

Dizziness had for a moment so overtaken Robert that he did not know what Arvid was talking about. Mules that had run away—loose knots in a halter—how did that concern him? Only one thing concerned him now.

He understood their predicament but couldn't understand how they had got into it. They were in a dust bowl; they were wandering about alone in a desolate region where the ground, the hills, the boulders were nothing but dust, small whirling hard grains. Were they in a desert where everything had been burnt by the fire of the sun? What were they doing here? What were they looking for in this wide, empty space? Why had they come here? What were they looking for in a region that had nothing to offer? They had reached a land of nothingness, and it now closed in about them, terrifyingly. It had caught them in its ravenous jaws. There they sat, like prisoners in a trap.

Arvid went on scooping and scratching with his hands in the sand, like a dog covering its dung with earth.

It wasn't gold he was digging for now.

XVIII. The Missing Goldseeker

1.

Wednesday morning Karl Oskar left at the usual hour for work on the church building. A few days earlier Kristina had taken down her loom and now was busy cutting cloth for garments. As soon as Karl Oskar left, she spread the linen over the table in the big room and began to measure, mark, and baste. Seven in the family needed new clothes; no longer was she able to patch upon the patches of the old. She had been sitting at the loom during the winter, now she was sitting at the sewing during the summer. She was not an expert seamstress but the garments must do however they turned out. The children were growing fast so she measured generously in order that they wouldn't outgrow their clothes too soon. For the boys' clothing she allowed three extra inches for sleeves and pants.

When Robert had dressed and eaten his breakfast, he sat down near Kristina and watched her cutting and basting. It seemed he was willing enough to talk to her when they were alone; he was more reticent with Karl Oskar.

He said that from now on she would not need to sew and struggle; since she now had money she could buy dresses for herself of the finest cloth she could find in the stores. She laughed in reply. The first things she intended to buy with her money were not silk and velvet to deck herself in; there were a thousand things she needed much more.

Her one great concern during these days had almost

been forgotten at Robert's unexpected return. For a few weeks she had known she was again pregnant. With this certainty she had also discovered that suckling did not prevent pregnancy; she was still giving the breast to Ulrika, and yet, meanwhile, Karl Oskar had got her with child. And the birth would take place in the winter, the most inconvenient time of the year.

But after what had happened Monday night she had almost forgotten her new discomfort.

She threw a glance at the Swedish chest as if wishing to assure herself that it still stood in its place. She said that first of all they must get that great sum of money to a safe place. They couldn't have it lying here in the house. Any day now Karl Oskar would have to go to Stillwater and put the money in the bank.

Riches had come to their house, but for her nothing had changed from one day to the next. She still had her chores, which she couldn't suddenly run away from. But when she had had time to gather her thoughts about the immense bundles of large bills, she had begun to figure how best to use them. Dizzying visions about what they now could afford paraded through Kristina's mind. Above everything else she wanted help with her work, hired help to relieve her. The money would be a hedge against the fatigue which at times almost crushed her, particularly at the beginning of a new pregnancy; then she had to sit down and rest in the midst of a chore because everything turned black before her eyes.

She wished indeed to thank her returned brother-in-law for every blessed moment of rest his gift might bring her.

"You are a generous and good man, Robert."

"You have always been kind and good to me, Kristina."

Even if Karl Oskar was not entirely free from doubts about his brother's money bundles, because he did not fully trust paper money in America, no one could make Kristina waste a single thought on the possibility that Robert had returned and brought them false or useless money.

259

"I guess board and room costs a lot back there in the goldfields?" she asked.

It was unbelievably expensive, Robert told her, turning his right ear toward her. A meal cost ten dollars, the poorest lodging fifteen dollars a night, and a pair of pants fifty dollars. All were out after gold and no one was willing to do ordinary chores. The governor himself had to cook his own food and wash his dishes because his servants had fled to the goldfields. No one in California would work for anyone else, however high the pay. The gold diggers had to do everything for themselves; they couldn't get a shirt washed at any price; they sent their dirty laundry by ship across the Pacific Ocean to China. It was their only way to get something clean to cover themselves with—the people of Asia washed for the people of America, the dirt of one continent was rinsed off on another.

"To think they freight dirty laundry to China! It sounds crazy!"

She tried to draw him out of his reticence about his experiences in California:

"You must have had a hard time out there? What luck you got away with your life!"

"Got away with . . . ?" Robert repeated Kristina's words slowly, while his wide-open eyes looked at her thoughtfully. "You think I got away with it . . . ?"

Her hand around the cutting shears came to a standstill, she stopped her shears in the middle of the cloth. A quiver in his voice had startled her.

"Life, Kristina! It's worth nothing on the Trail! Nothing at all!"

"Nothing . . . ? How it that possible . . . ?"

"Life has no greater value than a grain of sand. No one cares about his life. But all care for gold. Do you know why. Kristina?"

"No . . . ?"

"I'll tell you a story."

And he began . . . A man in one of the wash gangs suddenly died. He had been in good health in the morning when he walked down to the river, but as he was cradling gold a fever suddenly overtook him and killed him, and when his gang returned home in the evening they carried his corpse on a couple of posts. They would bury him next morning. They dug a grave in the sand close to a rock and sent to the nearest camp for a minister to read and sing over the corpse. For a coffin they used an empty box which had contained smoked hams. The box was too short for the dead man, who had been tall, and they had to bend his knees. There was no lid for the coffin so they covered the corpse with a red shirt.

When the coffin had been lowered into the grave the dead man's comrades gathered around the grave, took off their hats, and bowed their heads. Everyone looked at the ground, all were silent, the way it was in a church. And the minister, who was also a gold digger, took out his Bible and began to read the ritual.

But when he had read only one short Bible verse he stopped in silence. He only stood and stared at the ground. He turned the pages of the book a little, but he didn't read any more. He only stood still and stared into the open grave. The men who had dug the grave for their dead comrade wondered what was wrong with the minister. His hesitation would drag out the funeral if he didn't read faster. They were all in a hurry, it was a warm day, they were thirsty and wanted to have something to drink as soon as it was over.

But the minister never completed the service. He read no more Bible verses. Suddenly he hurled the Bible away into the bushes, its leaves fluttering in the wind, and threw himself face down on the ground; with both hands he began to dig in the sand at the edge of the grave.

The men thought at first that the minister had had a sunstroke and lost his mind. But then they noticed he was picking up something and putting it into the pocket of his frock. As soon as they realized what it was, they too threw themselves into the grave, scratching and digging with their fingers as fast as they could. For they had discovered the same thing the minister had seen when he began reading over the corpse: nuggets were glittering down there.

The minister, when he first made the discovery, didn't know how to keep the secret from the other men, for of course he wanted to be alone with the gold. At last he couldn't hold back any longer.

Soon a great fight broke out over the nuggets in the grave. The box with the corpse was overturned and trampled to bits, and the men used the pieces as weapons. Then they tore into each other with their fists, and finally knives and guns came out. It ended with the minister being shot to death and one of the mourners being pierced through the heart with a knife. Several others were badly wounded. The survivors made peace and divided the gold from the grave among them.

So there turned out to be three funerals instead of one. The old grave was turned into a gold mine, a huge one, and the three graves were dug some distance away. Now they had no minister to perform the ritual, since he too was a corpse, and there was no reading over the graves. Instead they fired four revolver shots. The survivors wanted thus to honor and reward the dead comrades who had fallen in an honest fight for gold, concluded Robert.

While he had been telling the story Kristina had held her wool shears motionless.

"What a terrible story!"

"Karl Oskar thinks I'm always lying," said Robert. "It's best to keep silent while he's around. But I know you believe me, Kristina."

She believed every word—while he talked. Only when he had finished did wonder and doubt cross her mind.

"If this is the truth then they live like wild beasts in California."

"No one cares about his life. But all care about gold!"

"They're out of their minds if they value gold higher than their lives."

Robert leaned toward her and spoke in a lowered voice, as if confiding a great secret to her:

"The gold diggers are people who want to die."

"Ah, nonsense! They must want to live and get rich and enjoy their riches."

"But why should they give their lives for nuggets if

they didn't want to die? They would rather lie in their graves than give up the gold."

"You talk so strangely, Robert."

She forgot her sewing and looked into his drawn, wan face. The skin was taut across his forehead and cheeks and it looked as if the bones beneath were trying to push through.

"But you yourself? Did you go to California because you didn't wish to live any longer? To kill yourself?"

"I meant the others. It was different with me. My real errand was not to dig gold . . ."

And he looked beyond her, out through the window, at the tall maples outside, as he added, emphatically, *I did care for life. But I didn't know this until afterward.*"

"Afterward . . . ?"

His speech was full of riddles. But now he gave no further explanation; he rose and went to the kitchen, where he picked up the scoop to drink. The bucket was empty; he hung it on his arm and went toward the spring. He moved with tardy, clumsy steps; he no longer had a young person's quick and easy walk.

When he returned with the bucket filled, Kristina could hear him panting from exhaustion.

"You needn't carry in water if you don't feel up to it. The bucket is heavy enough for a healthy person."

"I'll manage."

She said that it was good luck they had found such a fine and large spring which gave healthy and clear water in abundance, and tasted so good. The spring was invaluable to them, even though they had to walk a good bit to it.

Robert drank and hung the scoop on its nail above the bucket. Then he came back into the room where Kristina sat with her sewing, and watched her as she forced the shears through the cloth, following the white chalk marks she had made.

He said, "You know, I don't hear well with one of my ears, Kristina. I didn't hear what you just said—what was it?"

263

She repeated what she had said about the clear water from their spring.

After that he sat silent for a long while.

2.

The intense heat of summer had started in earnest that week. In Minnesota's oppressive air the chores were performed languidly; physical motion was an effort. Kristina was using her shears and her needle—the lightest tools a person could use—but she often dried her perspiring forehead with the corner of her apron. Yet it was cellar-cool here inside compared to the sweltering heat out in the sun.

The lake water was already tepid, and Johan, Marta, and Harald—the three children she called "big"—had, after persistent begging, obtained their mother's permission to go bathing in the shallow inlet near their field. Kristina would have liked to cool her own body in this heat but she felt it could be dangerous for her to bathe in the lake while she was pregnant. She asked Robert to go with the children and see that they didn't go too far out.

After the noon meal Robert said that he would like to go out and wander about in the forest; he wanted to go and see the Indian cliff where he had gone hunting when he was home.

Kristina remembered to warn him that a fatal accident had taken place last spring below the Indian. An American settler from Hay Lake had been found dead under a boulder which had fallen on him. The cliff was cracking and new blocks were falling in big piles all the time. It took only a small stone to kill a person, if it happened to hit the head; he must be careful and not go too near the Indian.

Robert smiled, exposing his gaping gums. He was not a settler; he had not stolen any land from the brown people; he didn't believe the Indian would fling any stones on an innocent person.

Kristina looked after him as he disappeared in the

forest. He had said that he had enough, that he had freed himself of masters and need never move a hand any more. For the rest of his life he wouldn't have to do anything except enjoy his riches. He could use his time as he wanted and wander about all day long. But Robert was not calling on their new neighbors, the white settlers who had recently moved in, he was calling on the Indian, the brown cliff, where such a strange adventure once had befallen him.

Kristina went into his room to make his bed while he was out. As she turned the pillow she made a discovery: under it lay a watch, with a broad yellow brass chain coiled around it.

She stared in disbelief. Cautiously she picked up her find. Robert had not displayed a watch since his return. As far as she knew he had never owned a watch. And if he did own one, why didn't he wear it? Why did he keep it hidden under the pillow of his bed? If he had bought a watch now that he could well afford it, why didn't he dare show it?

It couldn't be a stolen watch, she felt sure. But why had he hidden it under his pillow?

She noticed it was a long-used watch; it was nickel-plated, scratched, and badly worn. She put it to her ear: it had stopped. It had stopped at fifteen minutes after twelve, whether at noon or in the night. The key to wind it was fastened to the chain. Perhaps the watch had stopped because it had not been wound, or perhaps the works were broken.

Kristina replaced her find under the pillow after she had made the bed, but her thoughts were occupied with it as she returned to her sewing.

She began basting a coat for Karl Oskar but had barely taken twenty stitches when she saw, through the window, an Indian approaching the house. At first a sense of fear hit her—just now when no menfolk were at home. . . . The Indian went to the back of the house and came into the kitchen, and then she recognized him; otherwise these brown people were so confusingly alike that she couldn't tell one from another. This one was a very old Indian

265

with thin, stringy hair, sunken cheeks, and wrinkled skin that reminded her of cracks in dried clay. Last winter during the intense cold he had come several times; she had boiled milk and given it to him. Each time he had sat long by the warmth of the fire. He spoke some kind of English and Karl Oskar had understood that he had been converted to Christianity by some missionaries who preached among the Indians. He insisted he was a hundred and fifty years old but Karl Oskar must have misunderstood him.

As soon as Kristina recognized the caller her fear vanished; this old Indian was not dangerous. He carried something which he handed her with a few grunts. It was a piece of meat, a large shoulder of venison.

The Indian had brought her a gift, and surprised and pleased she thanked him in Swedish: she had just been wondering what to have for supper—what a fine roast this would make!

The old man had carried the piece without any protection and she soon discovered dark spots on the red meat: flies. That looked suspicious in this heat. She smelled: the odor of the meat was also suspicious.

Kristina knew at once that this venison had turned bad; then she also discovered white spots: maggots. But she did not show any sign of this, she dared do nothing but accept the gift. She neither wanted to nor dared hurt the feelings of the Indian. His people did not discriminate between fresh and spoiled food; to an Indian stomach the meat was of course acceptable; the giver would undoubtedly have eaten it willingly. The brown men could stand any kind of food. In that way they were almost like their hogs, who even could eat and digest rattlers.

She smiled at the old Indian and thanked him many times, putting away the venison as if it had been a great and valuable gift. In return she gave him a fresh loaf of their new wheat bread, and he smiled back at her with his broad wrinkled mouth and uttered many grunts that sounded friendly and grateful. They must have been words of thanks in his language.

After he had left and was out of Kristina's sight, she

picked up the evil-smelling venison and carried it to the dunghill behind the stable, where she threw it as far as she could. What would the giver have said had he seen this? Probably he had carried his heavy burden a long way today.

Even though the gift consisted of unusable food it had strengthened Kristina in her belief that the brown people were not evil and heartless. She had experienced it before: if one showed them kindness, they would do the same in return. They could be as grateful as white Christian people. Perhaps there was not too great a difference in the souls of white and Indians. If the Indians were left in peace, they would leave the settlers in peace. But when they were taken advantage of they became violent and as ferocious as wild beasts. Now these hunters were beginning to suffer from starvation because their game was disappearing, for the white people had hunted and killed almost all the game in the forest. She had heard people say that the Indians would never of their own will give up their hunting grounds, since they could not live without them; in the end they would rise in a great war against the settlers.

As the afternoon wore on Kristina waited for Robert to return from his walk in the forest. Karl Oskar came home from the church building at his usual hour and then she remembered her discovery in Robert's bed and asked him to come with her into the gable room. She lifted the pillow. The moment Karl Oskar saw the watch he exclaimed:

"It's Arvid's!"

"Arvid's . . . ?"

"I recognized it at once!"

He picked up the watch and looked closer at it. "I'm quite sure. It's the nickel watch Arvid got from his father when he left Sweden. He showed it to me many times, he always bragged about the cylinder works."

Kristina had grabbed hold of her husband's arm.

"Arvid's watch! Oh dear Lord—what does it mean?"

Karl Oskar was weighing the watch in the palm of his hand. "It can only mean that Arvid is dead."

A man used his watch as long as he lived. It measured his allotted time. No one gave up his watch before his death.

"I thought so . . ."

This watch had cost ten riksdaler, twelve with the chain, Arvid had said that day when they all met and started out on their American journey. It was the sum of money his father, Petter of Krakesjö, had been able to save during his forty years as cotter under the manse. It was Arvid's paternal inheritance Karl Oskar now held in his palm.

But where was Arvid himself? Two goldseekers had set out on the California journey. Two days ago one had returned. The other was still missing. And concerning the missing one Robert had given only the vaguest information.

Karl Oskar said that while working at the church building today he had told the other men that his brother had unexpectedly returned from California. Danjel Andreasson had immediately asked about his former hired hand and had been greatly surprised when he learned Arvid had not returned. Robert and Arvid had served as farm hands together in Sweden, and here in America too they had kept together as the closest of friends—how had it come about that they had separated? And Danjel had simply echoed Karl Oskar's earlier thought when he said that with Robert returning alone one could only assume that Arvid no longer was alive.

And under Robert's pillow Kristina had found the confirmation.

She now looked at the watch with different eyes. It was connected with a human being she had known and never would see again, because he no longer existed.

"Poor Arvid! I wonder how he came to his end?"

"I'm afraid we'll never know—at least not from Robert."

"Why does he hide it?"

"Why does he hide everything from us? As yet he has barely said a word about himself. And no one knows when he lies or tells the truth."

268

Robert told stories about happenings he had been in on, said Kristina, but she had never noticed that he invented them with evil intentions, in order to hurt someone or gain something for himself. He had never hurt anyone with his lies except himself.

"This is something he doesn't want to be known," said Karl Oskar. "But I'll show him the watch. He must tell us about Arvid!"

"But if you won't believe what he says . . ."

"He has lied too much to me! And now I begin to wonder again: how about those . . . ?"

He cut the sentence off as if he had bitten his tongue. But Kristina understood: those bundles of money!

Yes, he continued, what was the story about Robert's money, those big bills he had pulled from his black satchel? And the question came back again: was the money real? And he remembered something he had noticed; two letters sewn on the satchel. First he had thought one of the letters was an N, and this would have suited if Robert also had sewn on the initial for his first name. But now as he examined it closer he thought it looked rather like an M—and that he couldn't understand since it fitted none of Robert's names. The pouch must have belonged to someone else. Who had been the owner? And what kind of money did it contain?

And now had come the discovery of Arvid's watch.

"No!" exclaimed Karl Oskar. "I can't wait till Saturday! I must know about those bills as soon as possible. Tomorrow is Thursday—I'll speak to Algot at the building—we'll drive to Stillwater on Friday."

"I don't believe Robert would deceive us with the money he has given us," said Kristina firmly. "You mustn't suspect your brother of such an evil thing!"

"What can one believe after this? What can I think?"

Karl Oskar put the nickel watch into his pants pocket.

Kristina was beginning to worry about Robert, who had wandered off into the forest right after the noon meal and hadn't returned by supper. But it was like him to wander off like that, explained the older brother. He had acted that way ever since he was a baby. Father Nils and

Mother Marta used to hang a cowbell on the boy so they could find him out in the wastelands.

Karl Oskar was hungry and tired after the day's heavy timber work and sat down to eat. There had been only four men working today; this way the building took time. A church forty-eight feet long, thirty-six feet wide, and eighteen feet high could not be finished this year. But they must try to get the roof on before winter set in. Some of the men were sluggish about showing up. Like Anders Mansson—he had put in only three days so far. He probably lay drunk in his bed most of the time; rumor had it he was getting quite bad. But Petrus Olausson, who was the inspector for the work, kept after the men and saw to it that everyone did his share; he was particular and honest in that way. And he wasn't difficult to get along with, as long as religion and godly things didn't come up. In such matters he was as stubborn and pigheaded as an old horned billy goat. However, since he no longer tried to enforce his will in their house, Karl Oskar had no trouble getting along with him.

Today during lunch hour Petrus had got into a disagreement with Jonas Petter, who had started to tell one of his bed play stories. It was about a rich farmer back in Ljuder who hired the village soldier to provide him with an heir. Jonas Petter had started telling the story at Ulrika's party, last Christmas, and he wanted to finish it this time. But he had barely begun when Petrus grew fiery red in his face and forbade him to tell lewd and obscene stories while they timbered up the Lord's house. Jonas Petter got annoyed and said Olausson wasn't his guardian even though he was in charge of the building, and the two men had exchanged some rather unpleasant words.

But Jonas Petter had stopped his story about the farmer and the village soldier, so now it might be a couple of years before he found an opportunity to finish it, laughed Karl Oskar.

It was dark, but Robert had not yet come back. Kristina felt something might have happened to him: he had wanted to go to the Indian cliff and she had warned him about falling boulders. And he wasn't well; he ought not to take off so far into the wilderness.

But Karl Oskar felt his brother could take care of himself; he knew all the paths hereabouts, and he had just returned from a much longer and much more dangerous journey.

At bedtime Robert still hadn't shown up. Kristina pleaded with her husband.

"Please go out and look for him!"

By now Karl Oskar too was a little worried. He pulled on his boots—yes, he would go out and look. But it would be difficult to search for Robert in the dark. No one knew in which direction he might have gone.

Just then heavy shuffling was heard and Robert stepped into the kitchen, where he sank down on the nearest chair. His boots were muddy and he dropped his hat on the floor; he was completely worn out and panted heavily.

"You're late!" said Kristina. "Supper is cold."

But Robert shook his head; he didn't want any food. A mug of milk would be all he wanted tonight. His stomach was upset—he had vomited a couple of times out in the forest. It might be the heat, he was better now and would go to bed at once.

He was seized with a fit of coughing; when it let up he began to drink the milk, in small swallows, while he talked.

He had been sitting, just resting, below the Indian head—he hadn't been able to tear himself away from the place. The cliff had changed since he saw it four years ago. Now the Indian had deep wrinkles in his forehead, his eye sockets had grown deeper and blacker, and all his teeth had fallen out and lay as heaps of stones below him. Yes, like Robert himself, the Indian had lost his teeth. And now he sat there, back on his rock, and looked out over all the new houses around the lake, and he seemed profoundly sad. The Indian was mourning, not a single person, but thousands of people—his people, all those driven away by the white settlers. The Indian's face was draped in sorrow, a thousand times enlarged; when one's forehead cracked to pieces, and one's eyes fell out, and

271

the teeth dropped from one's jaws—and all this in only four years—surely, such a person had gone through deep sorrow.

They listened in confusion to this speech about the sand cliff. It sounded almost as if Robert were talking about himself. He had deep furrows in his forehead, young as he was, his eyes were popping out, their gleam gone, and he had lost his teeth.

"Great big pieces have tumbled down!"

They ought to go there and then they would see that he told the truth. Big chunks from the very eyes of the Indian had fallen down. Had ever a human being in all the world wept such tears? Tears of stone, enduring tears that would remain as long as the earth stood. Those were the tears wept only during the great weeping for a whole race that was being destroyed. A thousand years from now people would still come and look at those enduring tears below the cliff of Ki-Chi-Saga's shore. The piles of stones would remain there and tell of all those who had suffered disintegration in this country—the destruction of thousands of people.

The Indian's eyes were so cracked he could hardly have any vision left. Probably he had already mourned himself blind.

Robert only wanted to tell what he had seen in the Indian's face today; it was because of this face that he was late; why he had been unable to tear himself from the place. He only wanted to explain why he had stayed out so long.

When this was done he said goodnight to his brother and sister-in-law and went to his bed in the gable room.

Kristina said, "What happened to Robert while he was away? This morning too he used riddle-words I couldn't solve."

And Karl Oskar felt for Arvid's watch in his pocket; he had meant to pull it out this evening, but had entirely forgotten about it while his brother talked of the Indian who had cried out his stone eyes. It sounded like the fairy tales he used to hear in his childhood—and all this his brother had managed to make up during the short time it took him to sit down on a chair and drink a mug of milk! That was how easily he could make up stories!

Now Karl Oskar would wait until morning to demand information about the watch's owner: the missing gold-seeker.

XIX. The Third Night—Robert's Ear Speaks

It takes no longer to die than it takes to lift the hand and point a finger. I have tried to buzz that fact into you many times. You won't believe how suddenly death can sweep a man off his feet and into his grave on the California Trail. I have impressed it upon you, and now you have seen it yourself: at sunrise healthy and red-cheeked, at sunset dead and buried. It is Man's lot, it is yours.

But I've said nothing to Karl Oskar and Kristina. No one but you can hear what I say; you can trust me. I never betray you. Karl Oskar and Kristina can guess nothing; they believe you have returned from California, and you'll hurt them least by letting them keep that belief. You could say to your brother: Gold is nothing! Nothing but deceit! But he would only wonder, and doubt you still more. He is already worrying—you can see it in his eyes when he doesn't think you are looking. He is suspicious of the great bundles of money you gave away. He's afraid they're useless. He can't get over his suspicion that you're fooling him. But Kristina believes you, you can see that.

You noticed she had found the watch under the pillow and taken it away. They want of course to know what happened to Arvid. But you have no reason to tell them, unless you want to . . . Best this remain between Arvid and you forever: no third person would understand. And

273

never a sound from me; all you hear, when I buzz you all night long, are your own sounds.

You don't think you can sleep in peace tonight? Listen now, how I buzz and whiz, like the howling wind that lured two muleteers to a dust bowl and thirst—that treacherous wind on the plains that covered their tracks and prevented them from finding their way back. Tonight you're tired—and the more tired you are, the stronger my buzzing, the better you hear me:

Listen, goldseeker!

Why are you wandering about, out there on the plain? What are you looking for?

1.

The sun's fire had burned down toward evening. The ashes of coolness spread across the plains. The dusty ground, burning in daytime, cooled during the night. The oppressive dust-laden air gave way, and less effort was required to move.

Robert and Arvid continued to wander. They must not stay in one place, must move on, forward. They managed to keep their feet moving even though every step hurt. They stumbled across the plain, they held onto each other's arms for support, to keep upright. Two twisting bodies straggling along, held together in a firm grip; two bodies walking steadier than one. Two boys walking arm in arm, like a couple in love, like a boy and a girl walking across the grass of a blooming meadow on a cool June evening.

For they were inseparable and would never part.

A few times they saw creatures moving over the plain, red-furred, sharp-nosed animals sweeping by in small packs. They were the size of small dogs and moved as quickly and softly over the ground as the very wind. They must have been carrion beasts, feeding on the dead horse.

Dusk was falling; no longer could they see holes and crevices where they stepped. Arvid fell down. Robert grabbed him under the shoulders and helped him to his feet again, even though he would have preferred to stretch out and lie on the ground. He brushed the dirt from his comrade's neck, but he could not get rid of the grains of sand that chafed under his eyelids.

As they walked on, Arvid pulled out his watch; before it got too dark he wanted to know what time it was. His father had instructed him to keep the cylinder watch well cleaned at all times. Now he was afraid that sand might have got into the vest pocket when he fell; if a grain of sand got into the works it might stop the watch.

Arvid held the nickel watch against his swollen, cracked lips and blew on it as it dangled from its chain, blew away the sand. Then he turned the lining of his pocket inside out and brushed it well with his fingers before he put the watch back in again.

Around them cliffs and sandhills donned the black cape of night and assumed nocturnal shapes. Once again they became monstrous creatures: a buffalo ox's horn-crowned royal head was placed on a mule's narrow, spindly body, and a desert wolf with a thirty-foot tail opened its deep cliff-jaws in front of them. And the wall of distant hills underwent its metamorphosis and produced camels and dromedaries with humped backs and swaying necks. After the caravan day the desert's beasts of burden had lain down to rest in a circle under the stars.

They had gone out to search for a pair of stray mules, but a little while ago they had come across another animal:

"The horse had just been shod!" said Arvid.

Robert too had noticed this. The horse lay dead, and half eaten away, but his shoes had glittered brilliantly in the sun. It was doubly evil to meet death with new shoes on one's feet. They gleamed like silver above the rotten flesh. And the separated, lone hind leg had stiffened in the sand in a final vain resistance. It rose in an accusing kick against the Lord in heaven. Poor lone hind leg in the wide plain!

But Arvid had seen something still more lonely than the hind leg; he had almost stepped on it.

"It was a forefinger! It pointed right at us!"

The evening coolness had cleared Robert's head and he could again think clearly; his thoughts were circling around one single object, one only—the one they were now looking for.

He had thrown away his shoes and the sand felt cooler when he walked barefoot. But inside he was filled with dry, hot, burning embers which had plagued him for more than a day now. In the blisters on his lips this fire burned and stung; his tongue grew into a swollen, smarting lump, tasting of hard, gray earth from the dried-out water holes. It had to be somewhere, somewhere they must find it. It couldn't have dried up everywhere, somewhere it must still well forth. They must go on searching, they would find it at last.

Before they got lost they had seen water in many places, and the holes had not been dry. It couldn't have dried up all at once. If they only could find some grass again, then surely they would be close—that short, thick grass, the buffalo grass. . . . Only yesterday they had seen it on their journey—or was it the day before yesterday? Which morning was it he had awakened and found the two mules gone? Was it yesterday, the day before yesterday, or the day before the day before yesterday?

Somewhere they would find it.

They had traveled many hundred miles to join the gold caravan, the train of the hundred thousand. Now they were looking for something very common: *water*.

2.

Over the biggest dromedary's dark hump the moon rose. From the moon disc—three quarters filled—a pale, clear light was diffused over the sandy plain. Now they could continue their search, they would be lighted by the night sun.

They had walked only a short distance when they found themselves in a hollow. Arvid was the first one to discover it: something gleamed in the moonlight at the bottom of the hollow. He saw it only for a second—then he let out a hoarse howl.

Violently he pulled his hand from Robert's, rushed forward a few paces, and threw himself headlong on the ground. Robert had seen nothing as yet, as he came stumbling behind, half asleep. What was the matter with Arvid? Did he see water again? Twice before he had seen it, but only in his imagination; as soon as they had reached the place they found only dry sand.

But now Arvid was lying on his stomach, drinking from a small pool in the bottom of the deep hollow. It had been a big water hole, but had now narrowed to a small pool. And Arvid was guzzling and drinking. It was not imagination this time; at last they had found water.

Robert not only saw the water, he could hear it from the noise his friend made. But when he came closer he could see in the clear moonlight that it was no fresh, gushing spring they had found. It was a mud hole with stagnant, thick, dirty, opaque water. It did not look like good drinking water. In the ash-gray mud around the pool were deep, hardened tracks from animals.

He threw himself on his knees beside his comrade to drink. But such a nauseating odor filled his nostrils that he pulled back. The pool stank from something rotten, cadaverous. His desire to quench his thirst was checked by a feeling of nausea.

But Arvid was stretched out full length on his stomach, his whole chin in the pool, like an animal that drinks by putting its snout into the water. He was lapping and drinking in long swallows—puffing, panting, snorting, drinking. He got water in his windpipe, he coughed, it bubbled in the pool.

"It stinks like hell," mumbled Robert.

Arvid did not worry about the odor; he was not using his nose; only his mouth and throat were open. He continued to drink, sucking in the water like a cow, gorging himself drinking. For each swallow he let out a deep, muffled, satisfied groan.

"Is it all right? It smells like stale piss."

Robert again bent down over the pool, driven by his insufferable thirst. His mouth touched the water—he must overcome his nausea, he must drink. Anyone as thirsty as he must drink anything fluid, however nasty it smelled. But in the moonlight it seemed as if the water was cleaner and clearer on the opposite side of the pool. He crawled on his knees away from Arvid to the other side. Here it did seem less nauseating.

Beside him a post had been driven into the ground, with a piece of board nailed to it. There were letters on the board, clumsily written in chalk. After one look at the board Robert was on his feet again:

LOOK AT THIS
DON'T DRINK—THE WATER IS POISON—THE DEATH

The post with the narrow board across it rose beside the water hole like a cross on a grave. Robert looked at the wooden cross for one long, frightened second, then he yelled, "Stop, Arvid! It's death!"

In his fright he was using English words which his friend did not understand.

"Come, Arvid, and look at this post! It says the water is poisoned!"

And at once he could hear what the Mexican had said: the water holes along the trail were not to be trusted. Someone had drunk of this water before and discovered it was poisonous and put up the sign to warn others.

"For Christ's sake, stop drinking!" He grabbed his comrade by the shoulder to pull him from the water. But Arvid had already raised himself up on his knees. He had drunk a lot, he had satisfied his thirst. Water trickled in big drops from the corners of his mouth; his chin with its scraggy beard looked like a dripping muzzle. He wiped his mouth with the back of his hand and belched.

"Helluva dirty water. Don't quench the thirst much."

"It's poisoned!"

Robert pointed to the sign where the warning could be read in large letters. But it was in English and meant nothing to Arvid.

278

"For God's sake, don't drink any more!"

"Well, it wasn't very good water. It's stinky!"

"Arvid—you must puke it up!"

"The hell I must . . . ?"

"Don't you hear—the pool is poisoned! You've drunk your death!"

"Well, it couldn't be that bad . . . ?"

Robert pulled Arvid away from the water, into a thicket of low bushes at the edge of the muddy pool. His friend must not be tempted to drink any more.

"Puke, Arvid! Put your fingers in your throat! Get rid of the water!"

But Arvid refused to think that he had drunk death into his body. His belly was full of water, brimful, but he felt no discomfort. He refused to put his fingers in his throat, he didn't want to vomit. All he wanted was to lie down and go to sleep. His stomach felt a little heavy after all the water, a rest would be good. And with a tired sigh of contentment he stretched out on his back under the bushes.

"Please, Arvid—listen to me! You must get rid of the water!" Robert tried to put his own fingers into Arvid's throat and make him vomit.

"Let me alone! I'm all right! Let me sleep now . . ."

There was nothing more to be done with Arvid. He just wanted to sleep, right in this spot. He refused to move an inch. Why should he put his fingers in his throat? He wasn't sick. All he wanted was sleep; it was the middle of the night and he was more tired than any person on earth had ever been before.

Arvid pushed his head under some low branches as if he wished to hide it. He went to sleep at once, snoring noisily.

Suddenly it became very dark; a great cloud had crossed the moon and cut off its light. The contours of the landscape with its cliffs and boulders and sharp grass and buses were enveloped in darkness. Somewhere under that black mantle lay the chewed-off horse shank with a new shoe, and near it a white finger pointing from the sand.

Robert sat beside his sleeping comrade, staring out into the desolate night. His vision could not penetrate far in this darkness. He could not see the pool, even though it must be less than thirty feet away. He could not see the wooden cross that was raised beside it. But it was there all right, the words remained where they once had been chalked on the wood: *Look at This—The Death.* Death remained, it was near. It had only hidden itself. Perhaps it did so at times, to fool one. But it was there, and kept close to them.

He had two names for death, each sounding very different to his ear: the Swedish word sounded hard and frightening and threatening: *Döden!* It would be the clarion call over earth on doomsday morning: Döööden! That word cut like an ax through bone and marrow. Its echo was fear, a sound without mercy, a wailing without comfort. But the English *death* sounded soft and peaceful, quiet and restful. It didn't call for an end to life in threatening and condemning sounds. Death was soft-voiced, merciful, it approached silently, kindly. It brought comfort and compassion to a person at the end of his life. Death—it was a whisper in the ear, it didn't frighten or terrify. It said in the kindest of words how things stood; it said in all friendliness: *Now you will die.*

But it was only due to the softer word that the English death sounded kinder than the Swedish, and words were nothing but foolery and cheating. The English, lurking back there in the dark only a few paces from them, it too had no mercy.

Arvid had drunk of death's water and now he slept and was satisfied. Robert had not drunk, he still had the thirst that consumed life in him. If he drank from the pool he would die. If he didn't drink, he would die.

He moved his dry, swollen tongue; he said something to God. He wanted to tell the Lord over life and death that he did not wish to die. He wanted to explain that life was dear in the moment it was to be taken away. Never was it dearer. Never had it been dearer to him than during this night in the wilderness. How could his creator demand of him that he, only in his twentieth year, be

280

consumed by an unbearable thirst, his body to disintegrate until only whitening, clean-gnawed bones would remain? Like the rotting hind leg of the horse, helplessly kicking toward the heaven? No, he wanted to keep his body intact, walk on his feet over ground that was covered with soft, fresh, green grass—and he wanted *to drink of the clear, fresh, running water on earth!*

Water, water! He must find it!

Exhausted, Robert sank down against the body of his sleeping comrade. Confusion entered his thoughts, his head grew dizzy, and he sank into a hot, febrile slumber. As he slept he wandered about on green paths, and found running brooks that streamed over his face, filled his nose and mouth, and watered freely a verdant earth.

He dreamed deep, wonderful, purling water-dreams.

3.

He was awakened by a groan; first from a great distance, then closer, until at last it was close to his ear:

"Ooohhjj—ooojjhojj! My guts! They kill me!"

Arvid was rolling over in the sand, pulling his knees against his chin, twisting himself into a bundle, stretching out again, throwing himself to and fro, rolling over. He fumbled for Robert, got a cramp-like hold on his arm. Robert's hands found his and their fingers twisted together in a knot. Their tied-together hands held them together:

"It's killing me! It's tearing the guts out of me! Help me, Robert! Please, help me! Help . . . me . . ."

Two great swollen eyes stared in the dark from Arvid's face. He held his hands against his stomach and rolled over again. Then, violently, he pulled away his hands and dug them into the sand, scratching wildly, kicked the sand with his feet until it whirled in a cloud around them. He was digging a hole where he lay, poking himself down into the earth, as his cries became a howl.

"Oooooh! Ooooooohh! God . . . help . . . me . . ."

Death had arrived—Arvid had death in him. He had unsuspectingly opened his mouth and in deep swallows let it enter his body. Now it tore at his guts, and he screamed out his pain as loudly as his voice could manage.

Robert felt in the dark for Arvid's flailing hands. If he only had had some medicine, a few drops to give him, some salve to put on, any help. But he had nothing to offer.

"OOOOHHJJJ! Help me! Please! Help! OOOJJJ!"

Arvid dug, beat wildly about him, yelled until his voice and strength failed. As he weakened, his wail sank to a pitiful whine, a quiet whimper, a feeble sound like a bird's peep.

The intense pain continued for a few hours. At last Arvid emitted only a weak, slow complaint. In his pain-ridden impotence he groped again for his comrade's hands and crept close to him on trembling limbs. They lay twined together. Robert could feel Arvid's burning breath panting in his face; against his chest Arvid's chest pumped like a smith's bellows.

"Don't leave me . . . please . . ."

The two comrades lay close together. They had come together from Sweden to North America, they had started out together on the California Trail, they had traveled together thousands of miles, and now they were still together. They had sealed with a handshake their intention never to part.

"Don't . . . leave . . . me . . ."

Arvid had once wanted to turn back from the California Trail, but had kept his promise and stayed with his friend. Now he could trust Robert to stay with him. The two of them would never part—how many times hadn't they repeated that. And Robert said it here again:

" . . . never leave you . . ."

Arvid could trust him—they would never part. But as his cries gradually died down there was nothing to keep Robert entirely awake. He slid into a sort of doze, between waking and sleeping. He felt Arvid's fingers fumbling for his, and he held on to them even harder. A cool wind swept under their clothing—he moved closer to his comrade, who now lay almost silent, his breathing sounding choked. Something inside him was closing his windpipe.

It was still dark and Robert did not notice when Arvid unhooked his watch chain from the buttonhole and pulled the watch from its vest pocket. But his ear registered something he had grasped in his slumber: Take good care of it . . . good care . . . good . . .

But just now Robert wasn't listening, he was where he wished to be, tossed high over mountains and deserts, up to the stars and the sky. Up there he met an immense river that flooded out of heaven. In that river he sank down, sank down to the bottom, to the bottom—and the bottom at last turned into the sand where he was lying. He lay there thrown down from heaven.

And then it was morning.

The sun stung his eyes with its ray-spears and awakened him. His eyelids smarted from sand. He rubbed them, looked about, and got himself together: everything came back.

"Arvid . . . !"

Arvid lay close to him, stretched out on his stomach. He lay on his face in the hole he had dug with his own hands. His hands lay beyond his head, the palms turned up, full of sand. He did not move, he lay still, like the ground under him. His face was turned down, his nostrils in the sand. Robert stretched out his hand, felt his comrade's cheek lightly, and turned the face toward him. Arvid's eyes were glassy, their vision broken, yellow sand grains clinging to the eyeballs.

Robert called Arvid's name several times, but he did not reply.

As he turned Arvid's face something stuck to his fingers; his fingers were red, bloody. Arvid's chin was furrowed with wide, red streaks. He had vomited blood in great quantities. In the corners of his mouth it had coagulated into thick, blackened lumps, it had spread across his cheeks like blossoming flowers.

Robert could not grasp or understand it. He had blood on his hand; he must have pricked it on a thorny bush

283

until it bled. All the bushes tore like claws, the grass was sharp, the very ground tore wounds in one's feet. He called Arvid—he called louder but received no answer. He noticed that Arvid's fingers were bent like scoops; he lay there unmoving but it looked as if he were trying to dig his own grave. Or what was he digging for?

And over the golden brown hills the sun's flame flared again. A new morning had dawned in the land of dust and stone, heat and thirst.

4.

Robert's dizziness returned and he lost consciousness. He again heard the sound of approaching water; new rivers streamed over him and he lay down to drink. But into his mouth ran a hard, crunching water which hurt his swollen tongue. He spit out the sand he had been chewing

Arvid had found a water hole and had hurried to drink. The hole stank of old urine but he drank and felt no discomfort from it and then he lay down to sleep. He awakened and called and called, but he was still lying there. They were not separated.

They had set out together to look for gold, for they wanted to be rich and free. And there lay Arvid on his stomach, digging with his hands. Help me! he had cried, and dug as if this would relieve him. He was digging for gold but the only thing he dug up was potato peelings, whole piles of them, a whole heaving boat full of them. And their boss had been angry and called Arvid a son of a bitch. What luck he didn't understand English—it might have hurt his feelings. Arvid had once been accused of going after a heifer and had been given the name "The Bull of Nybacken." He had emigrated to get away from that name, he had traveled all the way here, to dig this hole where he now lay so quietly.

Beside his comrade's arm lay something that glittered. It wasn't gold, it was Arvid's watch, and it was only nickel-plated, with a brass chain. It was the chain that glittered. And Arvid was so careful with his watch. Why had he thrown it away like that? It could easily get sand in the works. He must retrieve it—he stretched out his hand for the watch and held it to his ear: it had stopped. Sand must have gotten into the works then. It had stopped a little after eleven, but now it was early in the morning.

So nice Arvid was still here, they weren't separated. Arvid lay still, he had covered his face with flowers. There lay two big roses right over his mouth, dark red now in the sun. Robert stared vacantly: where had Arvid found those beautiful flowers on his face?

"Comfort me! Help me!" And he had comforted him and said: "I won't leave you . . ."

Arvid had drunk and sated his thirst. But Robert was still thirsty; he must drink, or he wouldn't manage to get to California. He must get up and look for a water hole. Must move on, mustn't stay in the same place; the one who couldn't move forward couldn't move back either.

Oh—back there the stream is spurting forth! A spring must suddenly have opened up. But the water is running in the other direction, it's running away from him; it's out of his reach. He must run to catch up with it! Water—water—now at last he had found it!

He yells until he loses his breath, he cries out in wild joy:

"Arvid! Arvid! Hurry! Come here and let's drink! Water! Come . . . Come . . . !"

He rose on wobbly legs. But Arvid remained still.

But this was a running spring, with clean, clear, healthy water. It wasn't a pool, stinking old piss. And he ran after the water that streamed over the sand. It was a broad, gurgling stream; it ran faster, he followed, he hurried his steps, he ran as fast as he could, used all his strength. He was barefooted but didn't feel the sharp ground grinding against his sore feet as long as he saw the stream in front of him.

But it ran faster than he could run. And all at once it was gone. He scanned the broad plain—where had it gone to? It had gushed forth from the earth—and it had run into the earth again.

He stopped and stood there like a hunter who looks disappointedly after escaping game.

Robert wandered alone in the wilderness. The world was nothing but a plain, a sun above it, and a firebrand in his throat.

In his confused mind one thought remained: he and Arvid had promised to stick together. But where was he? He was alone now. They must have lost each other. He must find his way back to Arvid. He knew where he was lying—stretched out in a ditch with two red roses on his mouth. He must walk back to that place. There was a thicket of low bushes there, with thorns on them, and next to them a water hole with deep tracks in the gray mud from animals that had come to drink.

He scouted, he fell, he rose again. The sun burned and he crept into the shade under cliffs and boulders. He sat down to rest. But the stream came running by right in front of him. He rushed up and staggered after it until it was gone.

He chased many running streams which he could not catch up with. He walked until the sand under his feet disappeared and turned into grass. It felt different—softer, nicer. He tramped through short, withered grass, buffalo grass. He recognized it easily; their mules liked that kind of grass. And wasn't he looking for a pair of mules that had strayed? And didn't he just hear their names called? He listened. No, he must have been mistaken.

It was good to go barefoot on grass instead of sand. Especially with sore, chafed feet. Something thundered and roared in his ears—was it water streaming? It was far away. But the sound of a call again penetrated through the din in his ears, clearer now. There it was again—the names of the mules. He remembered their names—or what was he hearing?

"Heekee . . . ! Hinni . . . ! Cheekte . . . !"

He himself had called those names only a little while ago, when he and Arvid looked for the strayed animals. It
286

must be the names that now echoed in his ears. Heekee—Hinni—he and Arvid did not know what those words meant, for they had not named the mules. It was someone else calling now. He had heard that same voice call animals before, and the animals had been dirty gray, as big as heifers, long-eared and spindly-legged. They had coal-black eyes and braying voices. They carried heavy packs, moved slowly on their spindly legs, the sand whirled softly around their small hooves as they crossed the plain. They were tame, sluggish, trustworthy riding and pack beasts one could talk to and scratch behind the ears: *Mexican mules*—that was their name.

"Hinni! Cheekte . . . !"

Mexican—now the call was clearer, sounded closer, and he recognized the voice. He had heard it sing round the campfire:

Oh, the good time has come at last,
We need no more complain, sir!

It was because of this that he and Arvid now were walking about here, side by side:

We shall be rich at once now,
With California gold, sir!

The singer of this song had packed huge gourds, enclosed in woven straw, and from those vessels he had often drunk. Drunk . . . ! What did the Mexican call those containers . . . ? He searched in vain for the word, the name. And what was the name of the man who had sung at the campfire? A small man, in a red jacket and brown pants with yellowish tassels and the broadest hat any man in creation had ever worn.

Oh, the good time has come at last—he tried to repeat the words and answer the singer, but his swollen tongue produced only a hoarse croaking. His reply did not reach far enough, did not reach his master—yes, that was his boss's voice. And he was calling his strayed mules, not him. He was Robert Nilsson, a farmhand from Sweden,

287

on his way to the land of gold. If he only managed to croak and bray, perhaps his boss would think it was his mules replying. But he needed water—he had drunk before from his master's gourds . . .

The voice came closer. It was next to his ear. But at that moment he himself was removed, slid away, fluttered out into the distance without being able to stop it. In the very moment when the familiar voice spoke into his ear, he was pulled away, flew into the air over the plain; he swam high above sand and grass, over the earth, above hills and cliffs, he was lifted all the way up into the heavens and all the stars gleamed and glimmered before his eyes. Now he was so high above everything that never more would he come down to earth.

But up there in heaven stood a very little man in a red jacket and broad hat; he leaned over him, and he had black eyes, kind mule eyes, and a nose that was almost as big as Karl Oskar's. Judging by the nose it could be Karl Oskar, his brother. And he spoke like a brother.

"Poor boy! My muleteer . . . I've been looking for you . . ."

And he was on earth again and lay on his back in the buffalo grass. He had fallen down from the heavens and the stars and he held something in his arms, held it hard: with trembling hands he held onto the straw enclosure of the gourd—the calabash.

"Oh, poor fellow . . . Just in time . . . My muleteer . . ."

Robert drank. He drank a water that stayed with him. It couldn't flee, it was shut up in a bottle, in a gourd which he had caught in his arms—*this water did not run away from him.*

You can figure it out if you wish. Arvid had been dead now for three years. Of the cotter's son from Krakesjö manor there is no longer any sign in the sand. The wind has long ago covered him with sand.

He emigrated a long way to his grave. He found a quiet place, a silent and peaceful room in the earth.

REST IN PEACE SWEET BOY
FOR THY TROUBLES ARE OVER

But the cries of his death agony, his calls for help, his wailing—all these I have saved for you in here. How did you like it when I let you listen to them again a moment ago? Didn't they sound as real as ever? Piercing, penetrating like that time? Haven't I kept them well? Could you hear any difference in the cries from that first time?

"Help me, Robert! Please help me—I'm dying . . ."

How many ears do you think have heard this pleading before me on this earth? But not all, by far. have kept it so well as I. Each time you hear this pleading sleep comes late to you. It was during your wait for sleep that you began to ponder your lot in life.

It's nearly morning but you are still awake, tossing your head back and forth on the pillow, trying all sides, unable to find the one which will silence me. I understand so well that you want to get my sounds out of your head. But I assure you: I'm your most faithful comrade. You and Arvid had to part at last, but you and I shall stay together. I will never leave you!

Listen! I buzz for you through the long hours of your waking! Listen, goldseeker, where you toss on your bed!

I have preserved the sound of the wind over that plain—can you hear how it roars across those empty spaces in that country of stone and dust and thirst? And the wind roars over the earth at will throughout the night! It quickly obliterates a wanderer's tracks and covers in short time a wretched, naked, lone finger pointing accusingly from the sand.

XX. Wildcats of Many Breeds

1.

On Thursday morning—as on every weekday morning—Karl Oskar was up and about before daylight. As soon as he was dressed, he raised the lid of the old

Swedish chest against the wall and took out two bundles of money, which he held in his hands for a few thoughtful moments. He had done this each morning since Robert's return.

Cash—to him it was the most annoying word in the English language. Cash—it was what he lacked. No cash, Mr. Nilsson? You must pay cash, Mr. Nilsson! How many times hadn't he received that reply like a humiliating box on his ear when he had asked for credit in a store. *No Cash?* Those two words could be used to sum up a settler's situation in Minnesota.

Yet here he was, handling two bundles of crisp cash—four thousand American dollars, fifteen thousand Swedish riksdaler! After five years on the new place, these bundles would now end all his worries about cash. But these bank notes had fallen in his lap too unexpectedly. How could a man, from one day to the next, grasp that he had become rich? That was why each morning he needed to feel his riches and see the money with his own eyes.

Karl Oskar pinched the black and green bills. Were they worth their stated value? Could he trust the gift even though he could not trust the giver?

For only one more day must he control his impatience. Tomorrow he would get the information from the bank. Although he had agreed with his neighbor to drive to Stillwater on Saturday, after the discovery of Arvid's watch in Robert's possession his suspicion of his brother flared up anew. By going to the bank on Friday he would cut down his uncertainty by one day; by tomorrow he would know the truth!

Karl Oskar would have to be a little late for his work on the church building this morning; he must have a talk with Robert before he set out. He put the money back in the chest and went out to do the morning chores in the stable.

Meanwhile, Kristina began to prepare breakfast. She had been thinking over what Robert had said to her yesterday, and the more she thought of it, the greater riddle it became. She had known her brother-in-law for ten

290

years but yesterday he had seemed to her an utter stranger.

She wondered that Karl Oskar and Robert could be brothers. How could two people of such opposite natures have been begotten by the same father and carried in the same mother's womb? As long as she had known these two men Karl Oskar had been the big brother and Robert the little brother, but there was a difference even greater than the ten years that separated them. It was their natures—their characters and dispositions—that made them so unlike. Karl Oskar was like most of the hard-working, enterprising settlers out here, but Robert was not like any other person she had ever known. There was something both stimulating and disconcerting about him; he held his own with his clever talk but at the same time he was unpredictable—no one could guess one moment what he would do the next. And at times he behaved as if he himself didn't know what he ought to do here on earth—as if it didn't matter one bit how he whiled away the time, as his life flowed to its end.

Karl Oskar had often said that he regretted having brought along his younger brother to America; Robert fitted this country like a square plug in a round hole. He was too soft and lazy and lacked persistence, insisted the older brother. But Robert had succeeded so well that he had become rich before any other settler from Ljuder! What would Karl Oskar now say about the little brother he had considered useless? Monday evening Robert had silenced Karl Oskar with the black pouch; as soon as he had displayed his money, the roles of the two brothers were reversed. The older one could no longer reproach and scold the younger one. Now it was Robert who did the talking, now it was he who knew what was what. The younger had become more important than the older, and who could now say that Robert didn't fit in America?

Since last Monday evening Robert had been the big brother and Karl Oskar the little brother. It was strange the way things had changed between the brothers!

Yet Robert, this new big-brother who had returned from the gold-land, had not said twenty words about his

291

riches. No one could say that he bragged about them, no one could accuse him of big talk. And Kristina—like Karl Oskar—felt that there was something wrong and perhaps frightening about his silence.

On Thursday morning Robert was up earlier than had been his wont since his return, and he came into the kitchen before Kristina had put the food on the table. His eyes were pale and bloodshot as if he hadn't slept. She had noticed that he slept badly; a few times she had heard him go to the kitchen to get a drink.

She put the food on the table and called Karl Oskar, who was surprised that his brother was up already; this was the first time since his return that he had shown up at the breakfast table. He yawned broadly, exposing the tooth-empty upper jaw. His appetite was poor; he chewed slowly and had trouble swallowing. Kristina urged him time and again to eat some more; he ate less than the little boys, Johan and Harald, who ate their breakfast standing up at the table—children were said to grow faster if they ate standing upright. For Robert's sake Kristina had baked a big corn omelet but he took only a small piece of it on his plate.

It was unusually quiet around the table in the kitchen this morning. But when everyone had finished Karl Oskar pulled the nickel watch from his pocket and placed it beside Robert's plate.

"Why do you have Arvid's watch?"

Robert showed no surprise or confusion when he saw the watch, which appeared near his plate like an extra dish of food that he must eat before he left the table:

"I put it under my pillow. I noticed it was gone."

"Why do you hide the watch? Why don't you dare tell us the truth? Why don't you dare tell us that Arvid is dead?"

That was three questions at one time. But Robert only replied:

"You have a right to ask, Karl Oskar. That you have."

He was interrupted by an attack of persistent, hollow coughing.

"The first evening you said Arvid had remained in the goldfields."

"Yes, I said he remained out there. He did." Robert's coughing spell was over.

"But you didn't say he was dead. That he had sacrificed his life."

"Who doesn't sacrifice his life on the Trail? Everyone does—one way or another . . ."

"You talk in riddles! Tell us the truth right out!"

Karl Oskar was getting impatient and loud, but his younger brother remained calm. He picked up the watch and coiled the broad brass chain slowly around his forefinger. Kristina rose and began to clear the table; without interfering in the conversation between the two brothers she was listening intently. She told the children to leave the table.

Robert twisted the chain of Arvid's watch tightly around his finger until it resembled a thick golden ornament. He squeezed the watch inside the palm of his hand. Kristina noticed his elbows were beginning to tremble.

Robert's eyes looked so big and glassy today; she felt his forehead with her hand.

"You're burning hot! You have a fever!"

Karl Oskar had sounded angry and she whispered to him not to cross-examine his brother in this way; they could see he was sick.

Her cautioning had its effect. Karl Oskar rose, and put his next question in a milder voice.

"We two are brothers—why don't you confide in me?"

"The very first evening I came home you said to me, 'Stop lying!' I had just begun to confide in you. But you didn't believe me. You said, 'I know you're back without a single nickel!' "

Robert had risen too; he straightened his narrow, caved-in shoulders. They stood shoulder to shoulder and as Robert straightened up it was apparent that he was a couple of inches taller than his older brother.

Not even physically was Karl Oskar any longer the big brother. And his cheeks reddened slightly as he remembered that on Monday evening his "little" brother had got the upper hand: This is just a little pocket money!

"But couldn't we be honest with each other again? Why did you hide the watch? No one is going to think that you killed Arvid to take his possession!"

Robert turned his face quickly toward Karl Oskar and his reply came as a sudden thrust.

"Maybe you have guessed it! Perhaps I did kill Arvid! Perhaps it was my doing . . ."

"Are you out of your senses?!"

"He wanted to return . . . once . . . but I . . ."

Robert stopped suddenly, his shoulders caved in again, as if he were defending himself against a blow. He pressed his hands against his head and panted:

"I can't . . . Leave me alone . . . I'm not strong enough . . . Please, Karl Oskar . . . leave me in peace . . . dear brother . . . forgive me . . . I can't stand it . . ."

He rushed to the door and opened it with a heavy jerk of the handle. While they stood there, perplexed at his sudden outburst, he ran out of the kitchen as if he were pursued. They looked after him through the window—he had thrown himself face down on the ground near the newly planted gooseberry bushes. There he lay, unmoving.

"Leave your brother alone," advised Kristina. "You can't do anything else . . ."

"No." Karl Oskar sighed irresolutely. "What else can one do? Nothing, I guess . . ."

He knew that Robert would never take back a single word of what he had said, never admitted one of his lies, never would admit that he did lie. Would they ever know the truth about Arvid? Would they learn what had happened to the two old farm hand friends after that day four years ago when they set out on their journey to California?

But one piece of clear information they would get—by tomorrow they would have the truth about the goldseeker's riches.

2.

Karl Oskar left to work on the church building. A few moments later Robert came back in, like himself again. Today, once more, he wanted to take a walk to the Indian, he said. And Kristina watched him stroll off through the pine grove to the west.

She went into the gable room to make up his bed and there she discovered large dark red spots on his pillow slip which hadn't been there yesterday. The spots could be nothing but blood oozing from his bad ear during the night.

She began to wonder if Robert didn't suffer from some consuming inner illness; he had a nasty cough, and sometimes he couldn't eat their food—such troubles were not caused by a bad ear. Did he perhaps have chest fever? When she was alone with him she would ask him about this; he seemed to confide in her rather than in his brother. For the moment the red spots on his pillow slip told her more about him than he himself had done so far.

Kristina sat down to her sewing and picked out the basting from a pair of pants she was making for Johan. It was still early in the day but the heat was already pressing perspiration through her skin. The older children had gone down to the lake and must be splashing about in the inlet. Outside the chickens cackled; she now had a score of laying hens, all from the eggs of the hen Ulrika had given her two years ago. The cow, Miss, had lately calved but was not yet recovered and stood tethered down in the meadow. She had already had time to fill her belly and sought shade under a tree where she stood and chewed her cud.

Just then the oppressive, heavy stillness of the summer day was broken by loud cries from the children. Kristina dropped Johan's pants on the floor and was outside in a second.

Johan and Marta came from the lake carrying Harald

295

between them. Harald's face was red and his eyes wild-looking, as he screamed loudly. The mother took the boy in her arms, carried him inside, and put him on the bed in the gable room. There was no use questioning the little one—he couldn't talk; he panted for breath, groaned and puffed, bubbling foam escaping from the corners of his mouth.

The mother felt a sudden pressure across her chest.

"What happened to the boy? Did he fall and hurt himself?"

"It's the wildcat! A great big wildcat!"

Johan and Marta were talking at the same time. While they had been out in the water Harald had crept in among the bushes on the shore. Suddenly he had come rushing back, yelling at the top of his voice, and they had heard a horrible growling and hissing: Harald had come across a big wildcat that was hiding in the thicket. They too had seen the evil critter that had frightened Harald; it was gray and had a thick cropped tail and thick legs. They had seen his head sticking out from the bushes, an enormous head with long whiskers—exactly like an ordinary cat but much bigger.

Johan and Marta had been so scared when they saw him they too had yelled, and the screaming of the three of them frightened the cat, who sneaked back into the bushes again. They had rushed home but had to carry Harald, who was so frightened he couldn't walk by himself.

Kristina pulled off the boy's clothes to see if the wildcat had wounded him, but she could find no claw marks on the little one's body. It must have been the scare that affected the boy. But she felt sure the littlest of the brats had been in danger of his life; these big cats were said to kill children of his age. She had heard that those treacherous wildcats got right into houses. Karl Oskar had once shot such a beast down at the lake.

Kristina went to fetch some sweet milk from the spring where she kept it sunk in a bucket to preserve it in this heat. She tried to make Harald drink.

"Dear sweet love, don't be afraid—that ugly cat . . ."

A little child could lose its voice from sudden fright. But by and by the boy's voice returned; he stuttered a few syllables; soon he managed an occasional full word.

"The cat . . . he groaned . . ."

"Horrible creature!"

After a while Harald seemed all right again and could talk fairly well, but she had better keep him in bed for the rest of the day. Kristina warned the other children not to go near the lake. The big wildcat might still be there, lurking in those heavy bushes that hung over the water in the shallow inlet.

Kristina had barely sat down to her sewing again before she was interrupted by a caller—a dear caller: Ulrika Jackson had come to visit New Duvemala.

Ulrika was on her way home from St. Paul, where she had caught a ride on a cart and decided to stop in since she was so close. She hadn't seen her namesake for several months. Kristina's naming her lastborn Ulrika had pleased her more than a proposal from the President of the United States would have—if she had now been unmarried.

The first thing she asked was how much the girl had grown since her last visit. Ulrika herself had had a new baby last winter, her second child in wedlock—again a girl. It seemed to be her lot to mother females only. She still hoped to bear a male who could be consecrated as a holy preacher. Why didn't the Lord wish to make her worthy to carry in her womb a future servant of his church? She supposed she had in some way annoyed God. But in what way?

Today for her journey to St. Paul she was wearing a new dress, with big puffed sleeves and a wide collar.

"Miss Skalrud says I deck myself in too much lace and flowers and embroidery," said Ulrika. "The Norwegian says, 'If you don't get to be a priest's mother it's only a punishment for your vanity!'"

Kristina inspected the new dress: all upper-class ladies in America had puffed sleeves and wide collars, and they were not considered sinful or blasphemous decorations. Or did they tempt the menfolk to fornication? Ulrika's new

297

dress fit her well and was most becoming to her. Kristina couldn't believe that because of puffed sleeves and lace and embroidery the Almighty would make Ulrika unable to bear male children.

"I would be glad to dress in potato sacks if I thought it would help," exclaimed Ulrika. "But I keep hoping for next time. I'm only forty-two—I'll be fertile still for a few years!"

Kristina explained why she was keeping Harald in bed and told Ulrika about the wildcat lurking in the bushes. When Ulrika also heard about Robert's unexpected return her curiosity was aroused and she showered Kristina with questions: What had happened to Karl Oskar's brother in California? How much had he told them? Had he earned any gold to bring back? Kristina replied evasively. Robert had gone out but Ulrika herself could ask him as soon as he came back. So far he hadn't said much. She looked askance at the Swedish chest and was sorely tempted to confide in Ulrika about what lay hidden in it, but she dared not because of Karl Oskar. Nothing must be said to anyone as yet.

Robert did not return for the noon meal. Ulrika took his place at the kitchen table once she had thwarted Kristina's attempts to set the table in the big room in honor of her guest.

"I've been to St. Paul to visit Elin."

"Elin? Has your girl left Stillwater?" asked Kristina in surprise.

"Yes, she has a new job." Ulrika became so serious that it surprised Kristina. She went on: "It was a hell of a thing. There are worse wildcats than those on four legs." And Ulrika began to talk about the two-legged ones.

A great scandal had happened in the Baptist congregation in Stillwater. For more than four years Ulrika's daughter Elin had been maid to Mr. Paul Hanley, the most prominent and richest member of their church. Hanley and his wife had been kind and generous to Elin. But a few times during the last year Elin had complained that Mr. Hanley acted peculiar toward her. She was asked to help him pull off his boots, she was told to sew buttons on

298

his clothes while he had them on, and when his wife was away he called Elin to his room after he had gone to bed and asked her to make the bed while he was lying in it. These were chores he had thought up for the innocent girl, who wondered what it was all about.

And a few weeks ago she had come running home crying. He had tried to lead the girl astray and fornicate with her. His wife was at a party; he had called Elin to make the bed again—and then he had pulled her to him and thrown her down on the bed under him. Only with the greatest effort had she struggled free—luckily Elin was a sturdy, strong, full-grown girl—and, scared to death, she had rushed home to her mother. Ulrika realized at once what great danger the girl had been in: six or seven hooks had been torn loose from her petticoat.

Ulrika had gone straight back to Mr. Hanley and called him all the names he had earned, both in English and Swedish: adulterer, seducer, virgin-robber, *horkarl, knullgubbe.* He denied everything and called Elin an inveterate liar. But Ulrika had walked right into the elegant bedroom of Mr. and Mrs. Hanley and, as luck would have it, happened to see four of the torn-off hooks and eyes from Elin's underskirt right on the floor next to the bed. She recognized them at once, she had sewn them on herself when she had made the petticoat for the girl. She picked them up and stuck them right under Mr. Hanley's nose: she had sewn those hooks and eyes to her daughter's clothes—how did they happen to be in his bedroom, next to his bed?

At that the hardened seducer admitted that he had fondled his beautiful girl servant, but it had not been with any sinful or lewd intention. On the contrary: God himself had sent him the thought that it was his fatherly duty as her master to test the girl's chastity. She was so attractive and thus constantly exposed to temptations and to the desire of men wishing to seduce her. As a true Christian it was his duty to guard the innocence of his girl servant. He had seen men approach her with decidedly dishonorable intentions, and he would hate to see her led astray by immoral men, into death's destruction, so often the lot of beautiful servant girls. But the girl had not understood that with his fondling he only wanted, in a fatherly way, to test her chastity. And for this he was very sorry, since he had only touched her with pious intent.

But Ulrika had replied bluntly to his false excuse: Elin had a mother who guarded her maidenhead. And he—married as he was—what kind of guardian of girls' chastity was he? Searching so forcibly in their underwear that hooks and eyes were torn off! Instead of leafing through petticoats he ought to leaf through the Bible and find the verse where it says: adulterers and those who break the vows of holy matrimony God will judge.

She demanded the balance of Elin's wages on the spot. The girl would not come back to a service where she would fear to be raped by the master the moment his wife left the house. A wildcat might be a hairier beast than Mr. Hanley but hardly more dangerous. Ulrika had long been aware that that elegant gentleman suffered from secret desires for women; his pants protruded as soon as he heard the rustle of a skirt; such things an experienced woman knew by instinct.

She had told everything to Henry to make him get after the adulterer. And finally Mr. Hanley had confessed privately to the pastor, saying he was crushed with remorse. And Henry, who loved a human being more the greater a sinner he was, had given him absolution. They would keep the incident quiet and Mr. Hanley would remain as one of the trustees of the church—he had, over the years, contributed great sums to the congregation. And Ulrika, who once in her old body had been a great sinner, felt that he should be forgiven this time. But this she had said to Henry: if Mr. Hanley made any more attempts at rape, then she herself would openly tell the whole congregation about his try at Elin, and to prove it she would show the hooks from the girl's clothes which she was keeping for that purpose. That would quickly push him out of the church.

And Mr. Hanley, although he was on secret probation, had already engaged a new girl who was almost as good-looking as Elin. So it didn't seem as if the man was trying

300

to avoid new temptations to sin. And now Ulrika wondered: would the hooks hold in the new girl's petticoat when the master undertook his chastity test?

Elin had immediately got a fine position with the chief of police in St. Paul and was paid three dollars more a month than Mr. Hanley had given her. Ulrika had visited her daughter in St. Paul and was glad she liked it so well with the new people. After all, perhaps Mr. Hanley's chastity test had been a good thing as it might contribute to her luck in life; as a servant to the chief of police himself, her maidenhead should be safe from two-legged beasts in pants.

Kristina had listened to Ulrika without interrupting her. Now she said, "There, you see—American men too are not to be trusted!"

"Yes, a beautiful woman is in trouble anywhere in the world," sighed the experienced Mrs. Jackson.

Kristina tried to persuade her guest to stay overnight; they had plenty of sleeping places in their new house. But Ulrika was in a hurry today.

"No, I'm sorry, but we have speak-meeting in the church tonight. And Sunday we have love feast and bread-breaking, and that kind of meeting has to be prepared for days in advance."

Ulrika would return home on the lumber company ox wagon, passing along the road near Sjölin's claim, opposite Nordberg's Island, where the men were just building the Lutheran church. She had been to that spot before, and even though she was a Baptist she must say the Lutherans had found a nice and pleasant place for a Lord's temple there on the crest of the hill, with all the foliage around it. But however nicely a church was situated, false teachings could be preached in it.

Kristina said that Ulrika must also take a look at their cemetery, which had been consecrated last fall, a short distance farther on along the shore. As yet no grave had been dug in the cemetery.

Little Ulrika was having her noon nap, the other children were taking care of themselves, so Kristina walked

301

with her guest almost to the edge of Olausson's claim, where the ox team would meet her.

Ulrika's visit had stimulated and cheered Kristina, taking her mind off the things that had been disturbing her. As she walked back it struck her that she never was on intimate terms with the neighbor women even though she often saw Manda Svensson and Johanna Kron and others. They talked only of daily chores, children's troubles, their pregnancies and births—those they had experienced or were anticipating. These women came to her with all the troubles she had enough of, was in the midst of, which almost overwhelmed her, and therefore a visit with them did not especially enliven her. Nor was she able entirely to open herself to them and confide in them. Perhaps she had changed during her long isolation; she herself had been separated from people for so long that she could not admit anyone to her innermost thoughts.

Even Karl Oskar had once asked if she had grown shy of people. Whatever the reason, Ulrika was and remained her only intimate friend among women in America.

3.

Robert had returned from his walk in the forest and was lying on his back in the shade of the huge sugar maples outside the house. Kristina was short of breath after her walk in the heat and sat down on the stoop for a moment. She said jokingly that she never knew where Robert kept himself during the day. Even though he was a grown man she thought they should still hang a cowbell on him so they would know where he was.

Robert smiled back. It was true—he had run away many times but he always came back.

He had a book in his hand which he showed her. It was *The History of Nature* he had brought with him from Sweden. He had left it here and he had just found it among the junk in the old log house. The book was torn, the pages held together at the back by a few thin, twisted threads; it wasn't much to save.

"But I just ran across an amusing chapter. Listen to this, Kristina!"

And Robert read aloud:

"About Gold and Gold Coins.

"Gold is always found as a metal, sometimes mixed with silver. It is found in mountains, embedded in pyrites or quartz; but most gold is found in the earth, usually in fine grains. Then it is mixed with sand. Sometimes bigger lumps are found. Because the gold grains are so much heavier than the sand grains one can wash away the sand with water leaving only the gold; this is called washing gold.

"Gold cannot be changed either by air or fire if it is pure; that is why gold is called a noble metal.

"Pure gold is more than nineteen times heavier than water . . ."

He looked up from the book: "Did you hear that, Kristina? A noble metal! Nineteen times heavier than water! And worth more than human life! This last isn't in the book, of course, but I'm going to write it there!"

Kristina listened abstractedly; at the moment it was hard for her to concentrate on gold and gold washing. She was thinking of her boy inside in bed; she must go and see how he was.

"A wildcat almost scared the life out of Harald this morning, down at the lake. Why don't you take Karl Oskar's gun and shoot it!"

"Why should I kill a wildcat?" asked Robert, looking up from his *History of Nature.* "He has the same right to live as you or I."

"But it's a dangerous and beastly critter!"

"There are no beasts except white-skinned people."

"Now you're poking fun at me, Robert. I meant it seriously."

"I'm not fooling. I have never seen any beasts except

303

people. The wildcat only eats his fill, but people steal everything they see. They are worse than the wild beasts."

"May God protect us if that is true!"

"It is true, Kristina. I should know."

He had used a lot of English in his talk when he first returned, but after only a few days he spoke his native tongue as purely as before. His hearing, however, seemed to grow worse; when she spoke to him he always put his hand behind his right, healthy ear and turned it toward her.

Now that they were alone she must try to make Robert confide in her about the ailment he suffered from.

"There was blood on the pillow from your bad ear last night."

"It's been out of use for a long time. But it's a good sign when it bleeds—then the ache stops."

"They were horrible spots."

"I'm sorry, Kristina, if I ruined your pillow slip."

"How silly of you! I wasn't thinking of the slip. But I do feel sorry for you if it aches in the night."

And Kristina shuddered to think that when his ear bled it no longer hurt.

She told him that Karl Oskar and she were really worried about him. They were afraid he had picked up some dangerous sickness in the goldfields. Why didn't he tell her what was the matter with him? He must try to find some remedy.

He replied in a low voice that it was very kind of her, but she mustn't worry about him. As soon as the buzzing and the noise stopped in his ear he would be entirely well again. Sometimes, when the ear was quiet, he immediately felt better.

"There is nothing the matter with me, in any way."

Robert sounded full of confidence that he would soon be well again. He was lying on his back in the grass, holding the *History of Nature* above his face. He turned back to the chapter "About Gold and Gold Coins:"

"Are you listening to me, Kristina? Did you hear that gold is nineteen times heavier than water?"

"I heard you."

Now he lowered his voice as if he wanted to confide a great secret to her and was afraid someone might be listening.

"But it's only dead weight. Do you understand? The weight of the yellow gold is dead . . . dead . . . dead . . . !"

From the gable room Harald was calling his mother. The boy had heard her come, so she rose from the stoop and walked away from Robert. But she turned twice and looked at him where he lay in the grass, holding his old, torn book above his face.

His explanation of the chapter in *The History of Nature* had filled her with inexplicable anxiety and sadness.

XXI. The Fourth Night—Robert's Ear Speaks

You push your head so deep into the pillow tonight. Do you think you can shut me up in that way? Do you think you can choke me, get rid of me forever, by pushing me down into the pillow?

No, you should know better after all the years we have been together. You know it doesn't help to press me into the pillow. You might soften my sounds a little, perhaps. But only very little. Yes, you have tried to silence me in every way. What all haven't you figured out during the many nights we have been together! You've turned and twisted and tried various positions doing what you thought would help. Sometimes you've behaved like a fool—like the time you poured a spoonful of whiskev into me! I choked a little, but not for long. You wanted to get me drunk! Ha, ha, ha!

I heard what you told Kristina today: your ache eases

when I bleed a little. I know it. Sometimes I feel sorry for you and show it that way. Kristina has changed the spotted slip and now you have a new, clean one to rest on.

But these blood spots of mine do not tell anything to Karl Oskar and Kristina about the things that happened to you on the California Trail. You can trust my silence. But sometimes I think you're going to tell on yourself—at least when you are alone with Kristina. Both yesterday and today you almost told her—shouldn't you be more careful? Your ailing ear isn't so bad that it can't hear when you're about to spill over.

I don't have much to tell about your separation from Arvid at the water hole, because you didn't understand at the time that your parting was final. But I've all the sounds stored away. You're familiar with my good memory. But much of this you're not interested in any more. You lost something that time—you know best what it was. That's why so much from those days is of no importance to you any longer. Then why should I keep repeating it?

But that time when you were lying on your back in the withered prairie grass I heard a well-known voice calling the mules. It was the mule owner. And with him came succor—water, which gave you back your life.

1.

"My poor boy! I take care of you! You get well . . . !"
Mario Vallejos had gone out to look for the lost ones from his caravan—two animals and two muleteers. Since none of his provisions were missing, he did not believe the two boys had fled with the mules, and after two days of searching he came across Robert, far gone from exposure and lack of water and food. The Mexican questioned him and what he had assumed was confirmed. He never found his two lost mules.

Robert was well taken care of by his master, who assured him he would soon be well again. Within a few days he had recuperated sufficiently so that they could continue their journey. He still felt weak and was bothered by dizziness but now he need no longer walk; he rode on one of the good Mexican mules instead. The mule lent him its spindly legs and small, hardened hooves, which moved quickly through the whirling sand. His own feet were covered with blood blisters and worn to the bare flesh.

The caravan was smaller now—only two men and six animals. One man and two mules had been left behind along the road.

The caravan now covered a shorter distance each day than before, since six animals had to carry the burdens previously distributed on eight. The pack mules had thinned down during the trip from St. Louis. Their hindquarters grew more sinewy each day. Their owner claimed that on the California Trail mules became so skinny that two animals were required to throw a shadow.

Robert wondered what happened to people before they reached California. How many goldseekers would be needed to throw a single shadow?

For more than a year now Robert had been on his journey toward the Land of Gold, and as yet he was only at the beginning of the road. But in the grave Arvid had dug for himself, and where he remained, Robert too had left something of himself; when he resumed his journey he felt empty inside. Life had returned to his thirst-plagued body but he felt like a pod without a kernel. He rode the mule and watched his accompanying shadow on the ground. He still had enough life in him to supply a shadow, something visible that moved along with him. But could he catch it with his hands? Was there any substance to this shape that slid along on the ground beside the mule? What he saw was something dark and thin and empty. And this nebulous, vague something was from now on to be his comrade and companion on the California journey.

Vallejos, his good master, talked to him about the land they would come to at the end of the journey, where the sand was mingled with gold. Gold! Vallejos spoke of gold,

307

he sang of gold, dreamed of gold. He saw the "Pillar of Gold" which showed them the way through the desert. Mario Vallejos lived in the faith of gold.

The little Mexican feared none of the things they might encounter on the two-thousand-mile journey: not dangers of the desert, poisoned water holes, prairie fires, wild beasts, or Indians. Only one name did he still mention with fear in his voice—*The Yellow Jack*. Who was he? What was it? Vallejos sometimes spoke his native Spanish and often used English expressions Robert did not understand, and among them was this one. This much Robert understood: that this yellow Jack had killed a lot of people. He was the most dangerous encounter the gold-seekers could expect on the California Trail. But was he a bandit, an Indian chief, a human or an animal, a hurricane or a prairie fire?

Vallejos tried with gestures and signs to explain to his muleteer. He held his hands to his head as if suffering torture, he contorted his face, felt his back as if hit by a blow from a whip, he shook his hands, opened his mouth, and stuck out his tongue much as if he wanted to spit it out: this was Yellow Jack! But Robert was unable to interpret the signs. Perhaps Yellow Jack was the name of some terrible weather condition they would meet in the desert regions further west? When Vallejos described this monster by trembling in his whole body, Robert thought he was trying to describe an earthquake in its upheaval.

Robert was now alone with his master and soon he could resume his old chores. He was employed by the Mexican and he stayed with him and followed him. He no longer cared where the journey would take them. He rode his mule during the day and rested his head on the saddle at night. And he listened in silence when his master talked of the California country and described the banks of the Sacramento gold river.

Sometimes it might happen that he stuck his hand into his pocket and felt the nickel watch. It was as though he sought in his pocket for the hand which for a thousand evenings had wound the watch. Now it had stopped; it remained stopped. But Arvid no longer needed to know when it was time to rise in the morning, when it was mealtime, or time to go to bed in the evening. As he had twisted his body and tumbled about in the grave his hands had dug, he had pulled out the watch and put it in the sand beside him. He had no more use for it; what use could he have for a contraption that showed time when there was no more time for him?

One winter evening after cutting wood all day long they had returned to their miserably cold shed and Arvid had started to cry. "I don't care about gold any more! I give up riches! I don't care if I'm rich or poor! I want to go back!"

That evening, as he cried so miserably in their shed, there had still been three months of time left for him. He was still to rise from his bed a hundred mornings, still take out the key and wind his watch on a hundred evenings.

Robert would never wind that watch again. He didn't care any longer about the time needed on the road to California. He was not in need of anything to measure and point it out, it was lost to him permanently.

In a grave he never again would see, he had lost his dream of gold.

2.

Twenty days out from St. Louis a train of two men and six mules arrived in St. Joseph, one of the starting places for the train of the hundred thousand.

It was now the last week of April 1852. It was the beginning of the long-journey season; the plains were green, and the army of goldseekers congregating at St. Joseph was ready to take off for the West. During a few days the last preparations were made for a two-thousand-mile move, for a life of travel during the next four months. For the last time the vehicles were tested and tried out, the provision sacks inspected; guns and revolvers tested, and guides and lookouts who rode as a vanguard to the train were chosen with discrimination.

In St. Joseph, Mario Vallejos had arranged to meet two friends from his own country who were to accompany him to California. He looked for them for several days among the hordes of people that filled the place but was unable to find them. He sat silent and sad in their tent until late at night. At last he said that his friends were reliable; there was no explanation for their failure to show up except that they no longer were alive. And he felt sure that no one except Yellow Jack had killed them.

They had raised their tent in a hickory grove in a small valley; round about them spread the immense camp of the California farers. It was a camp of noises, the abode of a thousand sounds, where commotion reigned, cries and complaints rising at all hours of the day. Here an enormous horde of humanity was in motion, here great herds of cattle had been rounded up, and the noises that all these living creatures emitted could burst one's eardrums. The camp seemed to Robert like a fair in his home country, a thousand times enlarged, a fair that went on day and night—a giant fair that would last four months without interruption. Drunken men hollered, angry women yelled, children cried, horses neighed, oxen bawled, cows lowed, sheep bleated, mules brayed—not for half an hour did silence rule during the whole twenty-four hours of the day.

New arrivals came every day. One night Robert was awakened by a piercing scream outside the tent:

"Water! For God's sake gimme some water! Water . . . !"

He rose and went outside in the half dark, where he could see a shape crawling on hands and knees, begging for water. Two men came and picked him up, one by the shoulders and one by the legs, and carried him to a tent. The man had just arrived from the plains.

Robert had seen a reptition of his own rescue. But now his blistered feet were well on the way to healing and he could again walk. Life had been given back to him—if not the desire to live.

He was back at his job—he curried, fed, and watered Vallejos' mules; he ate and drank and slept. Most of the time he kept to the tent, knowing little of what took place in the camp around him. He listened to the sounds around him day and night and guessed what was going on. He heard new songs from the goldseekers:

> No matter whether rich or poor,
> I'm happy as a clam;
> I wish my friends could look
> And see me as I am.
> With woolen shirt and rubber boots
> In sand up to my knees;
> And lice as big as chili beans
> A-fightin' with the fleas.

It was the last refrain that caught Robert's attention, the lice, big as chili beans. He himself had got lice in this camp; his shirt was creeping with the critters. They were round, fat, shiny lice that bit into his body like gadflies on cow udders. However many he picked from his shirt and skin it seemed just as many were left even though he deloused himself for hours each day. The Mexican was constantly rubbing and scratching his body but Robert never saw him pick away any lice.

Robert himself was now a victim of the song's vermin; the shiny lice were not unlike gold grains. His mother used to say: if you got lice that bit into the skin you would soon get rich. The sign was considered sure. In that case he would reach the gold land and become a rich man.

One day as he was walking some short distance outside the camp he saw a group of men digging in the ground beneath some tall trees. He stopped to watch. Were they already digging for gold? Couldn't they wait till they got there? Why were they digging? The men were in a great hurry and shoveled quantities of dirt and sand from holes in the ground. But they didn't dig to pick up something; instead, something was to be put into those holes. Behind them lay a row of bundles, wrapped in blankets, six feet

311

long. He easily recognized that measure: the height of a person. And from one blanket he saw a human foot protrude, with long, dirty black toenails.

He walked on. Now he knew what went on at the encampment in St. Joseph; here the men were not digging *for* something; here a different labor in the earth took place.

On another occasion he stopped and listened to two men who were felling a hickory tree; the wood was used for repairs of the ox wagons. In their conversation they had used an English word that he had recently seen on a wooden board near a water hole: death. One of the men was leaning against his ax handle for a moment; death had taken twenty-seven people yesterday, and several hundred lay sick in their wagons and tents.

In the Train of the Hundred Thousand the men practiced to dig graves before they had opportunity to dig for gold.

Then one day Robert's master entered the tent, fear in his eyes, stuttering, "Yellow Jack has come! Yellow Jack is in St. Joseph!"

And Vallejos explained to his muleteer who the Feared One was, but he used so many incomprehensible words, in rapid Spanish; when he grew excited his mother tongue would spurt from his mouth. And now Robert understood that Yellow Jack was not a person, nor an animal, nor one of the Lord's tempests or earthquakes: the feared one was an invisible murderer who had sneaked into the goldseekers' camp; it was because of him they already had been forced to dig while on the road.

At last the day of breaking camp dawned, and on one of the first days of May the gold army moved out of St. Joseph. Mario Vallejos was excited and happy that morning as he sat up on his mule. He kept singing, "The good time has come at last!" He was anxious to get away from Yellow Jack, he wanted to ride so fast that the pursuer would be unable to overtake him.

The road from St. Joseph, Missouri, to Hangtown, California, was about two thousand miles. At an average
312

speed of seventeen miles a day they would reach their destination in September.

Now the march was headed for Big Blue River. The animals were rested and the first day twenty miles were laid behind them. The second day they were down to eighteen. The same distance was announced the third and fourth day. But after one week the caravan moved barely fifteen miles a day. The animals were getting tired and a day of rest was decided upon. Because of the good speed of the first few days they still held to the average.

At the camp, each evening a few of the dead were buried. The men threw lots among them to decide who would dig the graves. It sometimes happened that a man who helped dig one evening was buried the next.

The dead animals—horses, oxen, and mules—were left along the wayside and no one counted them. Close on the track came flocks of red-furred animals with sharp noses and long tails. They were the only animals that grew fat on the California Trail.

After two weeks they reached the first great obstacle—Big Blue River. All the belongings and all living beings who could not swim were taken across the broad river on floats, which had been left behind by goldseekers who had crossed before them. The crossing delayed them two days, but on the west bank of the river the endless plains lay before them. This prairie was wider than any they had seen before, it was like eternity—had it no end?

Now they were crossing Nebraska, the land of the big buffalo herds, the great plains. As they moved along under the open sky with its burning sun, and rested under the clear stars of the prairie, their train grew ever smaller: their army diminished as it encountered this immense expanse; like a long worm it crept its way over the ground.

Robert was carried along without asking where, his life one of the thousands which made up the worm crawling along the ground.

While crossing the great plains they managed their seventeen miles almost every day. Here the road had no hindrances and was easy to traverse. The next big road sign

313

would be the fork of the Platte, which was supposed to be twelve days from the last river crossing.

On the fifth day out the plain was broken by a mountain range. In the evening the California farers had reached Spring Creek, a recently established trading post, and here they made camp to rest for a day. Plenty of healthy drinking water was available here, and buildings of a sort had begun to go up. They chose a camping site near a stream with such glitteringly clear water that it shone even after dark, as if an unextinguishable light burned at its bottom. Robert stood for some time in the evening, looking at this stream. He had always had a liking for streams.

Next morning when Robert rose to attend to the mules, Vallejos remained in his bed. The master's look struck fear into the muleteer. Vallejos held his head between his hands and complained loudly:

"The Yellow Jack! The Yellow Jack is here . . . !"

After Robert had listened to him and watched his contortions he knew who Yellow Jack was.

Vallejos' limbs trembled and shook in fever; he felt his back while he screamed, he grabbed his head in both his hands as if he wanted to tear it from his body because of the burning ache inside. And from his mouth streamed blood and foam—black and sticky like crushed blood. The vomiting went on until he almost choked; congealed blood stuck in his throat and interfered with his breathing.

Now at last Robert understood what his master had been trying to show him: arms and legs shaking with fever, the contortions of the body, pain in the back, the twistings of his head. He recognized the sickness that had attacked the Mexican: a lurking, treacherous, contagious disease. It had been after them in St. Joseph, it had followed them when they broke camp, it had all the time been in their train, swimming with them across the broad river, pursuing them across the prairie. It attacked people without warning, like a way-laying bandit; it threw itself over them, like a tearing wild beast; it lit immediately its consuming fire, and that fire did not go out until life was out. It was because of this disease that the men each evening drew lots for grave-digging.

And now Vallejos had been overtaken by this pursuer whom he had spoken of and feared from the very beginning, the pursuer he himself had fled from and who had taken the lives of his friends: Yellow Jack.

Yellow Jack was a fever. Mario Vallejos was on his way to California to seek yellow gold. Instead he had found yellow fever.

3.

Close to the Indian trading post at Spring Creek a big tent had been raised in which a great many people lay sick. It was a makeshift hospital. Here lay the sick left behind by earlier caravans. Most of these earlier people had already died, less than twenty were still alive. To this make-shift hospital the Mexican Vallejos was now brought, accompanied by his Swedish muleteer who was determined to remain with his sick master and take care of him.

In this wilderness emergency hospital the victims of yellow fever lay on beds of dry prairie grass, looked after by an old half-Indian woman, tall, with a red-brown face and white hair. The sick were not expected to get well; the nurse was there only to look after them during their remaining days. They couldn't be left to die alone. Here lay those who were too weak to continue on the California Trail and too weak to go back.

Vallejos was often unconscious, although intermittently he would babble in his incomprehensible Spanish. Delirious people usually speak their mother tongue. His face had turned yellow as a chamois. It was easy to see whose stamp he bore.

Sometimes when his mind was clear, he recognized his muleteer and shouted out to him:

"Leave me! He'll take you too! Get out! Hurry away! You're young! You still have your life! Leave me! Save yourself while you still have time!"

But Robert remained beside his boss. He made a bed next to that of the sick one. He carried water from the clear stream and was always close when Vallejos wanted to quench his fever thirst. He wouldn't leave his boss; he brought his master water as the master once had brought him water.

After a day's rest at Spring Creek the gold caravan continued on its way. That morning Robert stood outside the hospital tent and watched the camp break up. All desire to go with the train had left him; it was his boss he followed; the other people did not concern him. He remained with Vallejos. The old nurse explained yellow fever to him: This disease was terribly contagious! If he cared the least bit for his life he must leave this place at once! She could not understand why a healthy person would come into this tent of pestilence. "The yellow fever will sweep you off your feet! Tell me your name, boy, so I can notify your people!"

He told her his name but said nothing about relatives in this country or in the homeland. He wasn't afraid of contagion, he did not fear Yellow Jack. On this journey he had become acquainted with death only too well to have any fear of it. What use was there in worries about one's life? Moreover, as long as the lice kept pestering him he knew he was all right. The vermin grew fat on his body; he was still well supplied with gold lice.

The old woman—she must have a name although he had never heard anyone call her anything but Missus—insisted on getting his address in good time so she could notify his relatives that he had died on the California Trail. But Robert thought he would in time himself return and tell them of the death he had experienced.

He told the old woman that he must remain and look after his sick boss and see to it that he got all the water he wanted.

On the sixth day after taking sick, Mario Vallejos died during a violent fit of vomiting which choked off his breath. He passed away, steadfast in his faith of the gold, aged thirty-two, mourned only by his muleteer.

That same day Robert Nilsson from Sweden became a rich man.

During the last day of his life the Mexican had been clear in his mind and had talked at length, coherently, to Robert. The deathly ill man was grateful that his young companion had stayed at his side and cared for him. He handed over to Robert a small pouch he had carried fastened next to his body. The contents of this pouch, the mules, the provisions, all he owned, he now gave to his devoted muleteer.

"Farewell, son!"

Only a couple of hours later the last seizure of vomiting had overtaken him. Yellow Jack had completed his work on one more human being.

Robert had not earlier been chosen as a grave digger. Now he alone dug a grave under some trees for his master and put his body in an empty packing box in which the nurse had kept smoked ham. She was with him when he buried Vallejos, and sang a psalm in an Indian language, Robert repeated a Swedish funeral psalm he remembered from Schoolmaster Rinaldo:

> . . . and me in earth you offer
> a cold and narrow bed . . .

Something had to be read at a grave; this short psalm fitted well because the coffin was narrow, for Vallejos was a small man. Here a ritual of Indian singing and Swedish reading was performed over a dead Mexican who would not have understood a word of it. But the Lord over life and death understands all languages equally well since he made the people who spoke them.

Only some days after the funeral did Robert think of looking at the contents of the small pouch with the letters M.V. sewn onto it. In it were gold and silver coins, in five- to fifty-dollar denominations, a total of $3,150.

The sign had proven true: if many lice congregated on a person, then he was slated soon to become rich.

All Vallejos' provisions and equipment Robert gave to the nurse's emergency hospital, and in return for the great gift, the old woman permitted him a corner of her own "bungalow" behind the hospital tent where he could sleep. She told him he could stay as long as he wanted.

He took his mules to an Irishman who supplied the trading post with buffalo meat, and the man promised to slaughter the animals immediately; Robert had become attached to them and wanted to relieve them of further suffering on the California Trail. After this he had only the pouch left of Vallejos' possessions, but in it were gold and silver—$3,150.

Robert had lost his last master, he had buried him with his own hands. He had been left behind on the California Trail, and now he was alone.

He was free and independent, he had no animals to look after, no chores to perform for another human being, no master over him. He was alone, he was rich, he was free, and he had his life. The nurse was a good woman who fried buffalo meat for him, offered him grapes and other fruit, and gave him pills and medicines against yellow fever. He was alive and all should have been well.

But his appetite for life had not returned.

Robert remained in Spring Creek and sank down into a bottomless pit of fatigue and listlessness. The days passed without his counting them or remembering their names. People spoke to him and he replied, but the words he used were meaningless. Nothing of what took place in his surroundings concerned him. Days and nights followed each other, washed over him, one much like the other, as similar as the billows on the sea. Everything came and went as it pleased, happened as it chanced. What could he do about it? Why should he do anything about it?

Nothing hurt him any more, nothing pleased him particularly. He could neither be happy nor sad. He did not care where he lived; he neither liked nor disliked it. His body was given what it required, and it was satisfied. He had food and drink and a bed to sleep in, and he ate and drank and slept and attended to his bodily needs. What was there beyond this? Perhaps there was something, but he was unable to do it.

But now and then a feeling came over him: there was something he was supposed to be looking 'for; he was neglecting it by staying here. This feeling began to frighten him; everything in his life was wrong, topsy-turvy. Why didn't he do something about it? And why didn't it bother him?

From the mountains came a stream that flowed through Spring Creek with the cleanest and clearest water he had ever seen. It was so transparent it was almost invisible; if it hadn't been for its motion and purling sounds a casual observer might not have noticed it. The stream glittered with light even after dark; it was filled with life, a life of light. In the evening Robert stood at the edge of the creek and watched the moving stream. An ever moving light was running away and yet remained. He came to the same spot the next evening. The stream purled and glittered, it was there before him, and at the same time it was hurrying away to mingle and mix with a greater body of water.

The stream ran by clean and empty as a young person's days. Robert Nilsson stood beside it and simply watched. He had no strength to do anything else. It was too late for him to retrieve his life.

The summer ran past him; the prairie was already red with the sun-scorched grass. He saw how those passing through Spring Creek rested for a day and a night, then moved on. There came buffalo hunters, fur traders, and settlers, landseekers, merchants, Indian agents, swindlers and cattle thieves, honest people, and escaped murderers. But on all these men he saw the same face. It was the face he had seen on every member of the hundred-thousand train to the West: the *goldseeker's face.*

What were they after, all these God-created creatures? They were on the same errand, all of them. All of them searched for the same, on direct routes, or indirect; they wanted to grab for themselves everything of value in this land—animals, the earth's growing plants and trees, everything of value on the ground and below it. They straggled and struggled, they rode, they walked, they suffered hunger and thirst, they tortured themselves, they suffered a thousand plagues, they killed themselves and others. They were after riches. They lived in the faith of gold. They were heroic—they were the resurrected gospel martyrs, they were ready to die for their faith. Each day they gave their lives to spreading the gospel of riches on

319

this earth. They believed all people in all lands should be their disciples.

Daily Robert saw one single face, the face of Man made in the image of the creator. This was barefaced Man, fighting for his one and only true religion, the one he confessed honestly in his heart.

And none of these men he saw pass through Spring Creek that summer knew that it was *water* alone Man could not be without.

During your stay in Spring Creek you thought you would never again have a master. You yourself had buried the last one, you alone had dug his grave and filled it with your own hands. You laid his body in a packing case and read a psalm over it. But you still had me. I am with you tonight, three years later.

Once you read in a medical home adviser: Ear diseases are often accompanied by so-called buzzing of various strengths and types. They may be experienced in daytime as well as at night, but they are especially strong at night when silence reigns. Then they can become a terrible plague...

That fits me, doesn't it?

You wanted to get rid of all masters and that was why you set out to dig gold. But you discovered on the Trail that gold was the most severe of all masters. Even more exacting than I. Long before you reached the gold land it demanded your life, so merciless is gold. Was that something to search for?

You gave to the gold what you were forced to give; it was too late to refuse. The disease now consuming you entered your body that summer, as you guessed. But some diseases are in no hurry as they ravage and destroy a body. Sometimes they take many years for their work. They lull a person into hope in the meantime. But they are not slow because of mercy when they take years to turn a living being into a shell.

You're a shell, Robert. That much you have at last realized while turning and twisting at night, trying to escape me; you have squandered the creator's gift. How could you have acted so foolishly? You think you have a good
320

answer: you didn't know any better; your intelligence didn't allow you to know better. Who else could have told you? No one, except the creator himself. And He failed. He let you waste your life while still a youth. He had made you such that you could do no better, knew no better.

The creator gave you strength to dream an immoderate dream—but he did not give you the strength required by an immoderate dreamer. And what can a weak person do? What did you do?

It is clear to you that what has happened was inescapable. You fought your lot in life. Your life is fated, Robert! Only thus can it be explained.

You never thought you could get free, you didn't have the strength. You were caught, enclosed in the cubicle of your fate. There is a truth about this, and you are familiar with it: Concerning imprisonment in the Fate that is common to all creatures: only in imagination do they break free: all remain in their cubicles and live out their interminable days, one after another. They make their abodes there for all the days of their lives, until the last day comes and the weight of the earth, of which they are a part, covers them.

You've been lying now for several hours without the peace of sleep. You have been lying so long on your back. You ought to turn on your side for a change—onto the left side—your evil side—your pursuer's side. If you turn on your side and dig me as deep as you can into the pillow, perhaps you can silence me a little.

And I will be kind to you tonight and relieve the bursting ache in here. I'll pour out a little blood, only a few drops. Now you'll feel how it helps. There now—can you feel the warm fluid? It feels as if someone had squirted tepid water into your ear, doesn't it? And now it drips red on the slip, the new, clean one that Kristina put on today. Nothing feels as wonderful as the end of pain.

Now you'll soon sleep! Again tonight you'll sleep on a spotted pillow!

I don't begrudge you a deep, wonderfully purling water-dream!

XXII. The Unget-at-able

1.

On Friday morning Karl Oskar was up before day-break, greased his oak-wheel cart, and made ready to drive to Stillwater. Already at sunrise it was evident the day would be very hot. It would be the first time he had undertaken a long drive with his young ox-team. Animals were greatly plagued by the heat and the mosquitoes, and although his ox team by now was well broken in, he was afraid they might be unruly and hard to handle in this heat; that was why he wanted to get under way while the morning was still cool. He hoped to be back again with oxen and cart intact before sundown.

Last evening Kristina had gone through the two bundles of money, removing spots from the bills and iron-ing out those that were wrinkled. A few grease spots re-mained, but on the whole the bills now seemed clean and neat; they were at least as nice-looking as other American paper money they had had in the house.

Karl Oskar pushed the two bundles down in the sheep-skin pouch Kristina had sewn for him when they left Sweden and which had served as a hiding-place for their Swedish money. In this pouch—worn as a belt under his clothing—he had, during the crossing from Sweden, se-creted five hundred *riksdaler*, all he had owned after sell-ing the farm and the cattle. Now it hid thirty times as much in American money, sufficient to buy ten farms as big as Korpamoen. This according to the value printed on the bills. Today he would ask the bank in Stillwater if the money was acceptable.

While he was yoking the oxen Algot Svensson, his com-panion for the journey arrived. He was always punctual. Today Karl Oskar was to be a witness for his neighbor at the land office, concerning Svensson's right to his claim in section 35 of Chisago Township.

Before Karl Oskar got into the cart he said to his wife that today he was setting out on the most important errand he had undertaken so far in America. And he had almost the same anxious expectation as on that day when he had gone to her father's home in Duvemala to ask for his daughter Kristina as bride: no one could tell in advance what the reply might be.

Then he stepped up into the cart and it started on its clumsy, thudding way down the road along the lakeshore. The sheepskin pouch was under Karl Oskar's shirt; his riches were on the way to a better place of safekeeping, a right place of safekeeping.

2.

This Friday turned out to be the summer's warmest day in the St. Croix Valley. The heat bothered Kristina as she sewed and she had to lie down and rest for a moment now and then. She had a burning headache and she saw black every time she tried to thread the needle. Her discomfort from her pregnancy increased with the hot weather; all smells became vile, nauseating her, and if she saw a blowfly light she wanted to vomit. A woman was only half a person during the first months of this condition; taste, smell, and appetite were completely awry.

Robert had found a cool place to rest under the sugar maples near the house. He was not going to visit the Indian today; it was too hot in the forest. She had also noticed how tired and short of breath he became after his walks. Kristina picked up her sewing and went outside to sit in the shade with her brother-in-law. The heat was not quite so oppressive here as inside the house. Robert was reading the latest issue of *Hemlandet*. He had just discovered an advertisement:

HELP WANTED

Youth for Hemlandet's Printing Office. Applicant should be able to read Swedish; if he also can write, so much better. If he has a good head, lack of knowledge can gradually be remedied . . .

"Do you think I should apply for the job, Kristina?"

"You with your riches needn't work any more!"

And she reminded him that the very first evening he had said that he had done all the work he intended to do and had had his last master.

His bad ear was turned toward her; probably he didn't hear what she said; he was absorbed in his reading.

"Here is something for you, Kristina."

He read aloud:

"*Hemlandet* has been considering the printing of a nice, neat Swedish A-B-C book. For this, however, several Swedish letters and decorative signs will be required, and the readers are asked for contributions of fifty cents each which can be sent to the printing office. We have also decided to print Luther's Little Catechism, word for word according to the Symbolic Books, and without the improvements or worsenings which have been made to this little bible, in this country as well as elsewhere. This Catechism will be the first Swedish book printed in America."

"That's good news!" exclaimed Kristina.

"Yes, you said the other day Johan and Marta did not have any A-B-C book or catechism."

"We need those books! I'll tell Karl Oskar to send in money at once!"

She sat on the ground, the cloth she was sewing on on her knee. Robert was lying in the grass, reading. He had returned last Monday; today was Friday. He had been in their house four days. But she felt that during these four days as much had happened as during the four long years he had been gone.

If there was anything else of importance or interest, would he be kind enough to read it to her, she asked? He replied that there wasn't much in the paper today except for a funny piece about a false Swedish priest—quite a long article.

Hemlandet warned against a self-styled minister who traveled about among the Swedish settlements in Illinois and Minnesota. He called himself Timoteus Brown, but it was a false, assumed name. He was not ordained, only a former student with a whiskey flask in his bag. But he preached, married couples, baptized children, and gave the Holy Sacrament. He had an unusual gift of speech and could entirely at will turn his listeners' heads, and that was why many Swedes had been fooled and availed themselves of the services of the false priest. Timoteus Brown had such remarkable gifts that he could preach in any religion he chose; one teaching was as easy to him as another. If he came to a Lutheran settlement he preached the Lutheran teachings, but among the Methodists he was an accomplished Methodist preacher, and among the Baptists he preached the Baptist doctrine better than anyone they ever had heard. And he did call himself "the cleverest minister in America."

Nor had Brown hesitated to falsify the Holy Sacrament: not one drop of wine had been added to the fluid in his cup; only water, into which fruit juice and vinegar had been mixed with syrup to make it sweet. In some settlements the participants had been seized with stomachache and diarrhea from his false sacramental wine. The self-made minister himself insisted that he gave the sacrament according to Christ's ordinance which forbad alcoholic spirits. But this, the paper said, was a false interpretation, exaggerated temperance zeal. He not only hurt people's bodies, but more important, their souls when he married trusting couples without being ordained. In the Swedish colonies, in Illinois and Minnesota, many otherwise honest and decent people now lived in sin and fornication, not knowing how deeply they had fallen in sin and iniquity.

Hemlandet urged the Swedish settlers to drive away Timoteus Brown, this blasphemer and derider. He was described as a wolf gifted with a sheep's mild appearance which aided him in bewitching people.

Robert was interrupted in his reading several times by his persistent cough. Now that Kristina sat close, she looked at his face: it was caved-in, ravaged, wan. And his body was barely skin and bone; he had never appeared so worn-out as he did today. He must surely be suffering from a much more serious ailment than his bad ear.

She must try again:

"Have you never been to see a doctor, Robert?"

"Hadn't thought of it. I'm only twenty-two. I can't go to a doctor—I'm supposed to be healthy!"

"You have caught something dangerous. I don't know—but it might lead to your death . . ."

"Death . . . ?"

The word escaped him in a quick breath.

Robert pulled up his upper lip in a great smile, or sudden surprise, and exposed decayed teeth in the back of his mouth. He turned from the paper to his sister-in-law.

"Kristina—you don't believe I'm afraid of death?"

"All people fear death!"

"Not I!"

"You too—now you only brag!"

"No, I mean it. Death cannot really do anything to me. It cannot touch me."

"Stop! That's blasphemy!"

Kristina's body had straightened up with the last word, now she fumbled with the needle so that it pierced her thumb instead of the cloth.

"Do you mean you are above death? Above the Almighty?"

"All I said was, death cannot touch me."

Robert threw down *Hemlandet* in the grass and rose to a sitting position. He leaned his elbows against his knees and bent his long, lean torso toward Kristina.

"No, not even death can hurt me or get at me any longer."

"That's terrible of you to talk like that! It's arrogance! Conceit!"

Kristina stuck her thumb into her mouth and sucked a few trickling drops of blood. She sat and stared at Robert, horrified at his talk; was his mind affected? Even yester-

326

day she had wondered if he wasn't out of his head at times.

"Nothing touches me any more. Neither good nor evil affects me. Do you know why?"

"No, you must explain it, Robert!"

"I'll try . . ."

The cough prevented him from going on. She sat in suspense, waiting for his explanation.

When Robert at last had finished coughing, it came slowly and simply:

"I have reconciled myself to my lot. That's all."

He had pulled up a few tall spears of grass and began chewing them. As he looked back on his life, he told Kristina, he understood everything that had happened to him. It was the way he was created that explained his life. If he had been an obedient and willing farm hand, he would never have tried to steal rest periods while he dug ditches, and then he would not have been given a hard box on the ear by his first master, and would have escaped his earache. And if he had had the temperament of an obedient and satisfied farm hand he would never have emigrated. And even if he had emigrated, he would have remained with his brother Karl Oskar and worked on his claim in Minnesota and been satisfied with that life. Then he could have lived his whole life in one place, in constant peace of mind.

But the way he was born prevented him; he couldn't stay in Sweden, he couldn't stay with his brother in America, he couldn't stay in service. He himself drove peace and tranquillity from his mind, although without wishing to do so, since deep in his heart he wanted to live a peaceful life. But he couldn't take a claim and be a settler; he might as well try to reach the moon, or walk across the water out there on the lake. He had been given those ideas about gold and riches and freedom, and he was forced to get out and pursue what was in his mind. This brought him into one bad situation after another. His misfortunes and sufferings were his own doing, as he himself had once caused the box on his ear. He was often accused of lying, but he never knew when he did lie, and if he did lie it was because he was forced to. All his hardships in life he himself had caused. Like yesterday—when he got into a fight with his brother—he alone had caused it. Everything that happened to him was because of the way he was born.

To him, as to everyone, a certain fate had been given, which he couldn't escape however much he tried. At his creation it had taken charge of his body and soul. He had carried it through his whole life, in his head, in his mind, in his heart. He couldn't escape it as long as life remained in his body—no more than a person could tear out his heart and remain alive.

It didn't help to pray to God that he would re-create him and make another person of him. No living being was twice born into this world. He would remain, unchangeably, Axel Robert Nilsson with a sick, buzzing ear which spoke loudly to him in the silence of the nights.

Such was his fate. And there remained nothing for him to do except adjust himself to it. The most difficult and most bitter thing he had experienced was adjustment—adjustment to himself, adjustment to the person he was, from whom he could never escape, who forever remained unchangeable, who was the same until the end of life, who eternally was *he*. He had suffered for many years—intensely, patiently—but he had come through at last. He no longer fought his fate, he no longer was bitter about it. He had accepted his impotence. He had adjusted himself to this: that nothing could be done, and so found harmony with his lot in life. And after that—what more could happen to him? Because to his fate belonged also the end, death.

Robert knew he was someone very little who had thought himself to be someone very big. For a long time he had demanded the measureless, but at last had been forced to be satisfied with the person he had been created and accept the fate chosen for him. It had cost him a great deal—oh, what hadn't it cost him to submit to the Lord of Life and Death! But there was no other comfort for him, or anyone for that matter, except this, to say to the one who reigns over creation: I cannot fight you! I might as well try to lift the earth on my shoulders and tear down the heavens above me! Why should I fight you, when I know in advance who will win? Do with me what you want! It suits me! Then I will have peace and be unget-at-able by death. By accepting it it no longer concerns me!

"Do you understand me, Kristina?" he ended. "I'm not being conceited. I'm not boasting. I'm full of humility instead. I am reconciled."

He had spoken slowly and calmly, as if fearing to say too much or use the wrong word; as if, in this way he could tell her everything clearly and honestly.

Kristina had listened in silence, and when he finished she remained silent. It was Robert's voice she had heard, but the words were the experience she herself had lived through and felt; they had sprung from her own heart, as it were. How many times hadn't she asked herself: Is everything that has happened to me decided by God from the beginning? Did the creator decide on the emigrant's lot for me? As Robert talked about himself, he was explaining her own eternal questioning and pondering and wondering. Now for the first time she knew something about him—now, when she recognized herself in him. One couldn't know a person before one discovered him in oneself—and oneself in him.

"Robert . . ." she stammered faintly. "Now I understand."

It was during this talk, that she truly began to know him. And that conversation would remain with Kristina forever afterward.

XXIII. The Fifth Night—Robert's Ear Speaks

You had intended to sit up and wait for Karl Oskar this evening, he is returning from Stillwater. But he is delayed, you're tired and it's getting late. Well done of you to listen to Kristina and go to bed! You'll see him in the morning.

I understand—you would have liked to speak out with your brother already tonight. It would have been right—after what happened yesterday morning.

Karl Oskar has looked so crushed ever since you opened your black pouch Monday night. Then, for once, he had nothing to say. Never before have you seen him so embarrassed. But he has always been suspicious of you and he doesn't trust your gift. He's afraid you're fooling him with false useless money.

But today he'll learn he hasn't been cheated. And tomorrow he'll shake your hand and say, Forgive me, Robert! Forgive my mistrust! From now on I'll always trust you! We must be as good and intimate brothers should be!

When you and Karl Oskar have talked together these last days it has been one continuous cat-around-the-hot-milk business. From now on that will be over. All will be different between you as soon as he learns that you haven't lied to him.

You had wanted Karl Oskar to offer you his hand this evening. But you must wait till tomorrow. And now you want to sleep. I know; you've only one wish left—to sleep. And this you do wish like hell. And your intense weariness closes your eyelids but you don't go to sleep. You lie awake and wish and pray. You call on sleep, the only good thing you've left in life: come, come to me! But it doesn't come. For with night and silence I come instead.

Perhaps you should sing an evening psalm, calling on Sleep; a waking person's praise of Sleep. You, the dearest One I know! Sleep, you lovely Comforter! Where are you? Come, come and take me with you! To that place where no suffering is! Come and save me from my sleeplessness! Carry me off! You know the place where it is good to be! I have been there and I want to go again and stay there! Blessed Sleep! Take me in your arms! Hold me to your soft bosom! Where there is no more suffering!

But you know your prayer is in vain: I'll keep sleep

from your eyes a long time tonight also. Night and its silence—that's when I reign! I yet have much to tell you, and you must stay awake and listen. I'll tell you about the ghost town on the sandy plain where you stayed so long. How long was it . . . ?

It began with a voice you thought you recognized . . .

1.

It happened in Spring Creek one day in September.

Robert was walking past the trading post where ox teams were resting and people always congregated. Several trains had just arrived from the prairie. He walked among the vehicles as an idle bystander when he heard a voice he thought he recognized. The speaker was just jumping off a big double-team wagon which was piled high with buffalo hides. A cloud of flies swarmed over the load. The hides stank like entrails at slaughter. Robert looked closer at the red-faced man jumping off. He knew in advance that this man had the goldseeker's face, like all men passing through Spring Creek. There was something in this face, something he recognized: puffed-up, rosy-red cheeks, flat nose, blood-streaked eyes under heavy, swollen lids. It was a goldseeker's face all right, but so ugly it was easily recognizable. And it was well-known to him— it belonged to a countryman.

The man with the load of hides wore a flaming red shirt and light yellow deerskin breeches with black fringes along the sides. But as Robert recognized his face he also remembered him in different dress: a light brown large-checkered coat with pants of the same big-pattered cloth, fitting tightly around his legs, a voluminous handkerchief dangling from his lip pocket, black patent leather shoes; he remembered the man standing on the deck of a sailing ship, leaning on the rail and spitting into the ocean while entertaining the other passengers with his stories. And one of the crowd around him was Robert.

The "American"! The American on the *Charlotta!*

Robert had recognized the voice he had heard tell so

many stories about the New World during their crossing to America. And the face—he had seen thousands of strangers but this face was not like any other, this one he recognized.

He walked closer and asked in Swedish, "Aren't you Fredrik Mattsson?"

The man in the red woolen shirt turned, and opened his mouth as if ready to swallow some of the fat blowflies that buzzed over his load of buffalo hides.

"God damn! A Swedish fellow!"

"You are Mattsson who crossed on the *Charlotta,* aren't you?"

"That's right! And I believe I met you before, boy?"

"On the ship . . ."

"Oh yes, we traveled on the same ship. I remember you now. Well, well—what was your name . . . ?"

Robert told him, and Fredrik Mattsson shook his hand so hard that the finger joints snapped.

"Very glad to meet you again, Robert Nilsson. It's not every day you meet a countryman in this territory!"

Fredrik Mattsson was from Asarum parish, in the province of Blekinge, Sweden, and he had been nicknamed the "American" on the *Charlotta.* At their landing in New York he had disappeared. None of the other passengers knew where he had gone. Robert had eagerly listened to his stories and often wondered what had become of him. Now they had unexpectedly met again, deep in America, all the way out in Nebraska Territory.

Mattsson said that since landing in America he had never run across any of his many companions on the ship. And he was glad at last to have found a young friend from those days at sea.

"That old tub *Charlotta!* She must have sunk by this time!"

"After the landing, where did you go, Mr. Mattsson?"

Robert felt he must call his older countryman mister.

"Where did I go? I'll tell you, boy! But call me Fred. All my friends in America do. And I'll call you Bob. Now we can talk Swedish together!"

And Fredrik Mattsson from Asarum leaned against the tall wheel of the ox wagon and continued in the language

332

he called his mother tongue, although Robert noticed that a great number of the words he used were English, or a mixture of English and Swedish, so common among his countrymen in America.

"I took a ship in New York, a clipper ship to California. She was a beautiful ship, loaded with gold-seekers . . ."

"The *Angelica*?" said Robert.

"Oh, you noticed her too, boy!"

And Robert did indeed remember the sleek, copper-plated *Angelica* with her pennant fluttering in the wind: *Ho! Ho! Ho! For California!* Hadn't he wished he could have boarded that ship where the men danced and sang and had a good time! They were on their way to dig gold and become free.

"I took the *Angelica* to Frisco," explained Mattsson. "I stayed a year in the goldfields, but no luck for me. The best days in California are over. It's hell to live out there. No sir! No diggin's for me! I've left gold behind forever! Last year I was traveling about and happened to come here to Nebraska. Now I live in Grand City. I have a bar, and a hotel—Grand Hotel in Grand City. Now you know, Bob. And call me Fred!"

"I will, Fred!"

The hotel owner from Grand City had been out on a business trip and was now on his way home with a load of buffalo hides. He was in big business.

"What do you do around here, boy?"

Now it was Robert's turn to explain. He and a friend from the *Charlotta* had also started out to dig gold in California. They had taken a job with a Mexican to look after his mules. But his friend had remained on the plains and the Mexican had died of yellow fever. Last spring Robert had lost both his friend and his boss. He had been left behind in Spring Creek, where he had stayed alone through the summer. His employer had left him what he owned; Robert had enough to live on.

"You are lucky! Did you make any money?"

"I have enough."

"Good! Then you can live as a free gentleman in America!"

Fredrik Mattsson thought for a few moments. When he continued, his voice was even friendlier than before. He put his hand on Robert's shoulder.

"I know what, my Swedish friend! You come with me to Grand City! You stay as my guest at the Grand Hotel!"

"Where is Grand City?"

"Fifty miles from here. Toward the east. You come with me! We Swedes should stick together! We'll have a good time together!"

Robert could live wherever he wanted. He didn't care where he went.

A few hours later the load of hides started out from Spring Creek with a new passenger. Robert was traveling back across the Nebraska plains. He had given up going west, he was now traveling east.

He had turned his back on the land of gold.

2.

They drove for two days across the prairie. On the afternoon of the third day they came to a deep valley whose bottom they followed, and at dusk they had arrived at Grand City.

The town had been founded a few years earlier by a group of Mormons. The Mormons had been chased out of Missouri, said Fred, and sought freedom in Nebraska. Grand City had flourished, but soon troubles had arisen between the Mormons and new settlers of other sects who had moved in. When the inhabitants began to shoot each other, the town had stopped growing. Last summer the Mormons had been chased out of Grand City too, and since then life had been calmer. Last winter a tornado had moved most of the houses far out on the prairie. Since then business hadn't been very good in Grand City.

As they came closer Robert saw that the town had been built in a gravel pit; the walls of the pit surrounded Grand City on all sides. It was a place fortified by nature. The houses, all along one street, were of varying shapes and construction: some of stone, some shed-like, some covered with tent roofs, even shanties of branches and twigs, roofed with leaves and turf. And the street at the bottom of the pit had caved in in many places; in one such hole lay a pile of boards that once must have been a house.

Robert also noticed big caves in the gravel walls surrounding the town. Someone had been busy there—what kind of digging had taken place?

"The Mormons kept poking for their Bible," explained Fred.

Their first prophet, Joseph Smith, had found the Book of Mormon, written on plates of gold, while he was digging in a sand pit in Vermont. An angel had shown him where to look for the truth concerning the last revelation. Smith had been a capable man with a good head; a pity that he had been lynched up in Illinois by people who were jealous of him. While the Mormons were in Grand City their local boss had received a revelation from an angel; the tablets Smith had found did not contain all the truth; several chapters of the Book of Mormon, indeed, the most important chapters, were buried in the sandhills hereabouts. And on this prophet's instigation the Mormons had started to dig. They dug day and night, they poked through every hill near town. They sifted every grain of sand but had not found a single written word. It had been a false angel, a liar angel, who had fooled the local prophet.

A cloud of dust enveloped the wagon as they drove their lazy team along the one street of the town. Robert looked at the sand pit walls: the upper layers hung far out beyond the lower ones; at any time they might cave in. And the walls were pierced by holes which the first settlers had dug in their search for the eternal truth about life and death. The undermined walls could cave in and in a few moments bury the whole of Grand City.

One house in the center of the town had a sign painted on it in somewhat shaky letters—GRAND HOTEL. The house was built of stone with a rather flat roof of bark. It was so low that it resembled a cellar house. The door had a sign in chalk: *If you want anything, walk in!*

335

Fred Mattsson jumped down from the load; he welcomed his old friend and countryman, Bob Nilsson to the Grand Hotel in Grand City; he had all kinds of guest rooms for gentlemen—his was not only the biggest hotel in town, it was the only one.

The hotel had been closed while its owner was away on business. Now he opened the door with some caution; the upper hinge was loose and dangling, and in spite of his care it fell on his boot as he stepped across the threshold; he kicked it aside.

They walked through a narrow hall, dark as a cellar. The hall ended in a few stone steps which led up to a bare room. This was the Grand Hotel's best guest room, and here the Swedish guest could stay. Inside was a real bed, nailed together of heavy boards, with a mattress and fairly clean sheet, pillow, and blanket. The only other furniture was a table and a chair at the window. The walls were decorated with buffalo horns; even this room indicated they were in buffalo country.

A room for a gentleman, said the host, a room for a man of means in America. Now Robert must rest while he went down and cooked dinner for them. They would have their dinner in the main dining room. Unfortunately, the Grand Hotel was without personnel at the moment. Before he left on his business journey he had been forced to let his chef go, his last employee. This man had been ordered never to get drunk until after dinner, but he had never obeyed. The host himself had always had to save the steaks from burning. And one day the cook had taken the wrong bottle and poured castor oil in the bean soup. The guests had all spent the night in the privy. In the morning they had all moved out, accusing him, the owner, of trying to poison them, and refusing to pay their bills. That was why he had kicked out his chef; that bean soup had cost him two hundred dollars.

About an hour later Robert came down to enjoy Fred's promised dinner. The "main" dining room was a widening in the hall with an iron stove in a corner. It had a long table at which twenty guests could sit down to a meal. Fred was frying buffalo steaks on the stove and served them with a red, peppery sauce; he called it chili colo-

336

rado. The meat was good but the sharp sauce burned Robert's tongue. The host had put both knife and fork at his plate; almost every day, said Fred, some guest arrived who asked for both these tools. After the buffalo steak he served pancakes which he called tortillas. He had learned to cook these in the California goldfields.

Fredrik Mattsson from Asarum poured whiskey from a fat bottle and handed his guest a large tumbler of the dark-brown fluid.

"Let's drink a Swedish *Skol!* Good luck, boy!"

Robert was not accustomed to the strong liquor, which scratched like a scrubbing brush in his throat and burned in his stomach afterward. The hotel dining room had a closed-in and dank smell. Robert couldn't help saying that he felt as if he were sitting in a cellar.

"Yes, Grand Hotel was built for a potato cellar!" said Fred proudly.

And the host told him the story of his hotel, an amazing and proud story. The house itself was a historical building; it was the oldest house in town, four years old. He intended to put a sign on the front of his house indicating its venerable age.

When Grand City had been founded, four years ago, the first inhabitants had needed a place to store their potatoes. This house had been built for potato storage. But as the town grew and attracted cattle thieves, ruffians, and murderers, it had become more important to have a safe place to put them rather than the potatoes. It was worse to have thieves on the loose than to eat spoiled potatoes. By and by they were hanged, of course, depending on time and opportunity, but it usually took a day or two before official execution could be performed, and in the meantime the criminals were kept in this jail. In this very spot where they now were sitting, many men had spent the last hours of their life.

Then had come a time in Grand City's history when law and order had been set aside. There had not been enough men to attend to that business; no one could expect men to jail themselves and stay in prison. For a year or so the jail had been abandoned for lack of officials.

The last prisoner had been strung up, or perhaps he had escaped, and no new criminals could be supplied.

Then came the church period of Grand City's history. After the Mormons, a group of Seventh-Day Adventists had arrived. They needed a church and rented the empty jail. The potato cellar was turned into the Lord's temple. The pulpit stood here in the dining room; when Fred tore it down he had used the planks for a counter in his bar. Here in this old potato cellar the Seventh-Day Adventists had once made themselves ready to ascend into heaven—the Last Day, they had decided, would occur on New Year's Eve 1850, and all members of the congregation had gathered in here. They had sold all their possessions, everyone was dressed in white muslin robes; they had done their earthly chores and were ready for the ascension. But the Last Day had been postponed indefinitely, and since the Seventh-Day Adventists already had given away everything they owned on earth without gaining admittance to heaven, some problems about money had arisen. The confusion increased when the pastor ran away with the wife of the church warden.

And the crafty Mormons, who preached their doctrine forcefully, took advantage of the other sect's predicament: they drove them out of the church and used the building themselves.

After a time of great strife in Grand City's church life a period of peace and order reigned. Even though the town at that time was without jail or potato celler it had five church buildings, all Mormon.

The host inhaled deeply, spat to the left and then to the right, and poured more whiskey for his guest and for himself before he continued.

This peaceful period was nearing its end when he came to this town. He had arrived in time to attend a Mormon wedding here in the church. A rich and highly trusted member was marrying eight women at one time. It was an average Mormon wedding and he had participated in the festivities.

The eight brides had been lined up in a row outside on the street, decked in white clothing, their hair curled, all ready. In front of the brides sat the bridegroom, like a

338

company commander on a fine horse, in tails and stovepipe hat. The congregation had raised a triumphal arch across the street, and back and forth under this arch men rode among the guests and fired salutes with rifles and revolvers until the whole town was enveloped in a cloud of powder smoke. When the ceremony was about to commence the brides walked under the arch to meet the groom. Each bride in turn walked up, the groom pulled her up beside him in the saddle and rode off to the house where the bridal chamber had been prepared. After a time the groom came riding back alone; now his first wife was no longer a maid but a Mormon wife. The marriage had been consummated. Then the groom picked up his next bride, rode away, and turned this maid into wife.

In four hours the groom had finished his ride—eight times back and forth. In four hours he had consummated his marriage with eight wives. And that Mormon was a small, weak-looking man, but he had been gifted with heavenly strength to perform his manly duty. He could almost be compared to Brigham Young himself.

But this wedding turned out to be the undoing of the Mormons. It caused bad blood among other men in town, who had long envied the Mormons their women. There was already a great lack of women in the West before this sect had come with their polygamy. One man could take ten wives while a hundred men couldn't get a single woman. A small war broke out in Grand City. The Mormons used Colt revolvers and could fire five shots without reloading, but some of the other men had Sam Colt's newest invention, which fired six shots. And with Colt's six-shooters they drove the whole Mormon group out of town.

Now the churches stood empty and Fred had used the opportunity to take over the biggest building in town. He had opened a hotel and bar in the old Mormon temple, and the onetime potato cellar was now really in its glory.

Well, wasn't that a proud history of this house? In three years it had been potato cellar, jail, church, and hotel! Could Robert name any famous building in the world that had had so glorious a past? And in so short a time! This house was an example to newcomers of progress

339

here in the West. It took brains, of course, and some fighting, but survivors did have a future.

That was how Fred Mattsson had become the owner of the Grand Hotel in Grand City.

"I can thank Sam Colt's six-shooter, of course," he added. "Sam is the greatest living American. Do you know that he made his first revolver when he was fourteen! Think what the West would have been without him! It simply wouldn't have had any future at all if men had had to stop and reload at every shot!"

Robert's head spun from the whiskey he had drunk; suddenly he felt drowsy and listened only vaguely to Fred.

But then a tornado had hit Grand City last year, Fred went on. Three fourths of the houses in town had blown away—thirty, forty miles out on the prairie. And in many cases the inhabitants had sailed away with their houses. The town had again come to a standstill; indeed, it had gone through difficult times. But Grand Hotel remained and it was one house the West would boast about in the future.

Robert was yawning; the sturdy meal and the strong liquor had practically put him to sleep in his chair. His host urged him to go to bed and rest for a while. After all, he was a guest in the hotel. Fred himself would now open his bar for the evening. His return had been awaited impatiently in the town, and his old steady customers would begin to arrive any moment now. He had been closed for two weeks—tonight there would be a throng at his counter.

3.

Robert slept a few hours and awoke with a burning thirst. He was not accustomed to American whiskey; he had a taste of stale herring brine in his throat.

He walked down the black cellar hall, feeling his way along until he found a side door which opened as soon as he touched the door handle. He saw at once he had happened on to the bar. The room had a low counter made of rough lumber. In front of this, on a long bench, sat a dozen or so men with their hats on. In there, too, it smelled musty and sour, like an old cellar with sprouting, half-rotten potatoes; or perhaps it smelled from sour beer. The dirty floor had not been touched by broom or scrubbing brush in many a moon.

"Hi, Bob! Welcome to my saloon!"

The host of the Grand Hotel now wore a large white apron which turned him into a bartender. He stood behind the counter rinsing glasses in a bucket of water. The wall behind the counter had shelves with bottles and mugs, and the top shelf had a red painted sign: Fred's Tavern.

It was strangely silent in the bar; the men sat motionless and did not offer to make room for the newcomer on the bench. Fred rolled up a chopping block and poured a glass of whiskey for Robert; then he started talking to him in Swedish.

The saloons Robert had seen before, or passed by, had always been noisy with the din of many voices and he wondered why it was so silent in here. He looked at the customers: they sat still and solemn, as if this house still were a church. What was the matter with them? Presently, as his eyes became accustomed to the dim light, he understood: the men were asleep; they were drowsing, or had passed out more or less; a few rested their heads on their arms on the counter and snored contentedly; some slept less heavily and winked and nodded now and then. Some stared glassy-eyed at the bottles on the shelves, as they might stare out across the plains when they had discovered something far away, some game that was entirely beyond their strength to reach.

Silence and drowsiness reigned in this saloon, because the men at the counter were already drunk. From time to time Fred's annoyed look scanned his dormant guests. No one was drinking; the ablest customers confined their activity to a vague look at the liquor they ought to have been drinking.

"Those devils drowse off in here!"

The host spoke in his homeland dialect.

"Time to stir up my business again!"

Fred stooped under the counter and found a small hand spray which he filled from the wash bucket. Then he walked three times back and forth and sprayed the befogged heads of his customers.

"They need a shower once every hour."

The row of slumbering, dazed guests came to life again; they wiped their eyes, began to talk and yell; they discovered their glasses were empty, or gone, and shouted to the bartender, shaking their fists and calling for new drinks.

The bartender put away his sprayer, its purpose accomplished, and attended to pouring whiskey instead. Business in Fred's Tavern had resumed its normal speed.

After a while the owner again had time to speak to his new guest, his young countryman. He leaned on the counter that had been made from the torn-down pulpit.

"You mentioned a fellow who was with you, Arvid, did you say? And he kicked the bucket?"

"Yes. From thirst. He drank poisoned water, we couldn't find anything else . . ."

"I see. Last summer ten thousand people died from thirst on the California Trail."

Robert said that he had never thought of it before, how impossible it was to get along without so simple a thing as water.

"In my hotel you needn't go thirsty! With Fred you won't miss a thing! You can have anything you wish to drink, my dear friend!"

"I like it here."

"Good! A friend of mine runs a whorehouse across the street—would you like a woman tonight? A good *knull* would do you good!"

Robert had never been with a woman. He had only imagined how such a thing would take place. He had never had sufficient courage to try. Now he asked, from pure curiosity, how much it would cost at this house across the street.

"It's Wednesday today," said Fred. "You can have a *knull* at a special rate today."

"Special rate? What's that?" Fred had been using the American expression.

"I mean it costs less."

342

"Oh—I thought it was a disease."

"No, you needn't worry about that! The whores are healthy as hell! But business is kind of slow in the middle of the week. You can get a piece of ass for half price. They have awfully nice girls—and Saturday it costs twice as much!"

Robert sat silent; perhaps he was contemplating whether or not to go. Fred understood fully; he might be too tired tonight. There was no hurry, he was to remain at the Grand Hotel, and the house across the street was open twenty-four hours a day, at least until the next tornado. The big storm last year had after all left the whorehouse standing; the good Lord had so far been as careful of the place as if he were a partner in the business.

The bartender poured whiskey for those customers still able to ask for refills; then he resumed. The goldseekers passing through Grand City on their way to California were the best customers at the whorehouse. They took advantage of this stop, they knew how few women there were in the goldfields. He too had known. There was only one woman to each hundred men, and she was well used. And the women in the goldfields were horribly expensive and demanded payment in pure gold, big nuggets. Never before in the history of the world had there been such an opportunity for women to get rich by lying on their backs. A woman in California could gather a fortune within three months, if she was decent and capable.

And the men out there, in their loneliness, grew so soft-hearted and weak they would often faint at the mere sight of a woman. Many gold diggers couldn't stand being without and used their mules. These animals didn't always smell so good so the men sprayed them with costly perfumes; after that they smelled like women. Men always wanted pleasant smells about the business, something grand—the gold diggers were soft that way. So some bought the finest silk and velvet they could find and spread it over the mules; they hung lace on the mule ears, embroidered linen and garlands around their necks, and often pieces of expensive jewelry. They decked the mules as if they were beautiful women before they mounted them. For everything must be beautiful, as it should be; the goldseekers were that way.

And Fred wanted to point this out: men were good and kind and fine deep inside, even when they were forced to use animals. In whatever circumstances men were found themselves they longed for the beautiful.

Silence had again descended over Fred's Tavern; only a soft snoring was heard. The customers were going to sleep again; one after another lost his voice and passed out. Occasionally a belching, a snore, or a clearing of the throat was heard, but spoken words had given out.

And the host explained to Robert all the advantages for his guests: Grand Hotel of Grand City offered all the things in the world a man could ask for. And in the house across the street a gentleman could satisfy his further desires.

It had grown stuffy and close in the bar and Robert felt sleepy. He rose and said he would go to bed.

Fred nodded. "Good night! Sleep tight! I must attend to my business . . ."

He looked in annoyance at his customers and bent down for his spray can again to get life into his business.

4.

Robert stayed on with his compatriot at the Grand Hotel in Grand City. During the day he would wander about and look at the place. There were remains of many houses that once had stood along the street: foundation stones, heavy timbers, caved-in chimneys, an occasional iron stove—the heavy objects the tornado had been unable to carry out on the prairie when it had struck last year. Robert thought that if the big storm had hit the town on the night the Seventh-Day Adventists waited in their church for the Last Day, they might have thought they were being taken bodily to heaven on the hurricane.

Here were places where people had lived; the people themselves were dead or had moved away. Even the rats were dead—furry, flat, dried-up rat carcasses lay strewn on the old sites like lost mittens. This was a ghostly place; people and animals had lost their lives here—their ghosts might return at night. Who knew? The town in the sand pit was a ghost town. It suited Robert to live here.

But after dark he hardly dared move about in Grand City; it was too easy to fall into holes. And the gravel walls hung over the city as a constant threat, as if they could bury the town at any moment.

The ghost town had only one-tenth of its original population but there were still a few hundred inhabitants who might ask each morning: Will our town cave in and bury us all before evening?

The guests at the Grand Hotel were travelers who passed through Grand City and needed a place to rest for a night. But for days on end Robert was the only guest in the house. The saloon gave the owner his income. After a few weeks, Robert offered to pay for his lodging. He made the suggestion one day when only the two of them were eating in the main dining room. But Fredrik Mattsson threw up his hands: there was no hurry about that. Moreover, he wanted to treat an old friend from Sweden to lodging for some time. Countrymen must stick together. Robert insisted he wanted to pay for himself—he had plenty of money.

Fredrik Mattsson's swollen, bloodshot eyes fluttered about a moment, he turned away as if suddenly embarrassed, he didn't want to snoop into other people's affairs, but would Robert feel hurt if he asked how much the Mexican had left him?

"Not at all, Fred. You are my friend—I'll show you!"

He went to his room and fetched the small pouch of soft black leather with the letters M.V. embroidered on it. He had so far used only a little of the contents. He really ought to count the rest of it. He poured the gold and silver coins onto the table. His host eagerly helped him count the money. He divided the coins into piles according to their value; he knew American money, he conducted big business.

Robert still had almost three thousand dollars, two thousand of which was in gold.

Fred threw his hands up as if wanting to call on the high one in heaven.

"My dear boy! Have you entirely lost your mind! How are you using your money? Do you just hide it away?"

Robert said he used the money as he needed it. What was wrong about that?

"My poor fellow Swede! It's criminal, that's all! You can double your money, many times! Have you never met a sensible person in America before? Has no one advised you about money?"

And Fredrik Mattsson's voice sounded truly sad when he heard how foolishly Robert had handled his fortune: to leave all that cash in a pouch! That was called dead money! And a businessman like himself could only feel sad when he saw how dead this money was. Money must be put into something to earn interest. Money must be kept alive, multiplied—a hundredfold, a thousandfold, like seeds in the ground. If he had put his money into a business when he got it he would have had ten times as much by now. He would have had thirty thousand instead of a mere three thousand. It was indeed a crime to handle money this way. It was not only a crime against himself, it was a crime against humanity! To keep all this money uninvested! For humanity, in order to survive, must keep business going.

"Bob," said Fred, and patted Robert's hand in deep compassion: "Bob, you do indeed need a good friend."

And in his solitude, after Arvid's death, Robert had often felt he did indeed need a friend.

Fred's eyes could not leave the piles of gold and silver coins before him on the table. At last his face lit up.

"I got it! I know what to do, Bob! You and I should be partners!"

Robert looked puzzled; he didn't understand. But Fred was jumping up and down in joy over his bright idea.

"Damn me! Why didn't I think of it at once!"

"What do you mean? What should we do?"

"You put your capital into my hotel! You'll multiply your money! You can retire as a rich man! You and I will be partners! In my hotel!"

"Would this money be enough for that . . . ?"

346

"It will help in the business, and I'll pay good interest! You can't handle your money yourself, Bob!"

Robert knew he couldn't handle money, he had never had any to handle. This was the first money he had ever had. And he felt the coins could easily be stolen from the pouch; he had been thinking about finding a safer place.

Fred continued. He had in mind expanding his hotel business and could use some more capital—first of all they must find a staff of servants. Suppose Robert put some money in the hotel, say two thousand dollars—the rest he could keep for spending money—then he, Fred, would pay the highest interest ever paid in the New World, half the profits! They would share as brothers what they took in. The Grand Hotel was already a fine business—it would be still better with more capital to modernize it. And since they were from the same homeland he felt they were practically relatives. With the two of them partners they would have a family business, as it were.

Robert had never thought of his money working for other people and at the same time increasing for him. But as his friend had such a great understanding of business, he could see no harm in following his advice.

He said, "You take care of my money. If it isn't too much trouble for you?"

He was grateful for Fred's suggestion; his only worry was that the handling of the money would be too much of a nuisance to his friend.

"Hosannah!" exclaimed the host of the Grand Hotel. "From now on we'll do *big* business! Boy! Will you be rich one day!"

Fredrik Mattsson took charge of the two thousand dollars from the black pouch. Thus Robert became a partner in the Grand Hotel in Grand City, the town's largest and only hotel.

5.

The liveliest time of the week in Fred's Tavern was Saturday evening between eight and nine. At that hour the members of the Whiskey Club met, the largest and most important club in town. They met to drink Kentucky Straight, and their bylaws stated they must meet for one hour, between eight and nine. During this hour they could, and must, drink all the whiskey they could down. The cost per member was a dollar and fifty cents. The one who consumed the greatest quantity during the evening hour need not pay the week's membership fee. The rush in the bar during this hour was enormous; Fred couldn't draw an even breath until the meeting was adjourned and the members had retired to the saloon floor, in more or less resting positions.

After the meeting of the Whiskey Club, Fred would devote Sunday to cleaning his saloon.

Even before Robert became a partner in the hotel business, he had helped Fred a little during the Saturday rush. He washed glasses, helped to serve, and kept track of drinks consumed. During the hour of the club meeting the consumption of liquor was as great as during the rest of the week. After Robert had become a partner he felt it his duty to assist the host whenever he could: he helped with the cooking, peeled potatoes, cut firewood, ran errands, swept up, and washed dishes; mostly he washed dishes. But Fred did not ask his partner to work.

"You shouldn't work as dishwasher here, Bob! It's below your station!"

But Robert said it wasn't too much if he helped with the dishes and did what he could. Fred mustn't do all the work by himself; he wanted to do his share. And since he was a partner in the business he felt a certain responsibility about the running of the hotel.

Fred said he would look for help—a big staff of people, he said. But for a few months ahead he was so involved in big business he didn't have the time to look for servants.

For days it would be quiet about the place, with only an occasional guest, or no guest at all. Then Fred had spare time in which to tell Robert about his experiences in California and Robert also had time to walk about and explore Grand City. He would stand for long periods and look into the holes which had been dug in the sandhills

348

around town where people had searched for eternal truth; they had dug for an answer to the Riddle of Life. Here tablets were said to have been hidden, containing words of ultimate truth, the last revelation. And people had dug and dug, for many long hours; it must have taken a terribly long time to dig all these holes. But they had found nothing, received no information. All their labor had been in vain: they found nothing but emptiness, all had been an illusion. They had been tricked by a lying angel.

On business errands for Fred, Robert had visited a number of the houses in town but as yet he had not been to the house across the street. He had seen the sign on the door in letters too large to be missed: Welcome, Gentlemen! Come Right In! And in the evening after dark a yellow lantern was hung at the door. He had asked Fred about the inmates, whom he had never seen, and he was told that they did not go out in daylight; they were mainly sleeping and resting then. But they were available all night through. And in the evening, and late into the night, varying noises came from that house.

Inside the women waited. They were ready night and day. All men were equally welcome, everyone who came was given what he desired. The price was two or three dollars in the middle of the week, double on Saturdays and Sundays.

There was still something Robert had not experienced in his life, and it was available to him in that house. He had wondered greatly how it would be, how it would feel. And he must find out. Indeed, he wanted to know, he must know.

But he had heard that if you visited a whorehouse you got sick. You caught venereal diseases. The poison crept into the marrow of one's bones, one rotted inside. Sores and boils broke out, one's limbs were eaten up and fell off. And the poison multiplied from generation to generation. A whore's body was full of poison, and her life lasted barely four years.

Could this be the truth? The truth about something one would never know until one found out. So it was with the gold, and it was the same with the house across the street. In there the women gave something great to the visiting

349

men—they let the men penetrate into their own bodies. A greater gift could hardly be offered a man. And it cost only three dollars. For this price the man could do what he wanted with the woman. Why did she sell her secret parts at so cheap a price? And why did the man value it so low?

Only one house in town had on its door the sign Welcome! And this very house he always passed by. It held a promise for him, something new and unknown. It was a house with a kind word on its door, a house that offered something generously.

Two evenings in succession, after he had washed up and had nothing more to do in the hotel, he walked across the street and stood for a moment in the yellow light of its pale lantern. Then he walked back.

He had been on the California Trail, he had experienced a great deal—yet he was afraid, he was a coward. He wanted something and it was within easy reach, and he dared not take it. The following evening, to bolster his courage, he drank a tall glass of Kentucky Straight: this would make him bolder. Then he crossed the street for the third evening.

Come Right In!

This evening the door stood ajar; another sign that a caller was welcome. He found himself in a large, dimly lit room; only a few small candles in wooden sconces high up on the wall spread a light that hardly reached the floor. A group of women huddled at a table in the far end of the room, with beer mugs and whiskey glasses in front of them. These were the dishes that he washed every day; often he got tired from standing on his feet for hours. He could barely see the women's faces in the dim light, he couldn't make out if they were beautiful or ugly. But he could see the color of their clothing, a pleasure to his eyes. And it didn't smell of dank cellar in here; a sweet odor came to his nose, the odor of refined women.

He had stopped at the door.

"Hello there! Come on in!"

One of the women called out to him. Her voice sounded kind, and clear as a bell.

"Come on in!"

Women's voices encouraged him, yet he stayed where he was. His whiskey courage was beginning to fail him, he had crossed the threshold of the house, but what ought he to do now? He felt deeply embarrassed, and the consciousness of his inexperience embarrassed him further.

One of the women rose from the table and came toward him. She was tall, almost as tall as he when she stood beside him. She had on a flowing robe which fluttered gently like a sail in a light wind. She walked softly, soundlessly. Her shoulders were bare, and he could see the furrow between her breasts. A pair of big black eyes were resting on him: he was among friends, he must join them, wouldn't he come with her?

But he remained standing at the door as if his legs were paralyzed. The women at the table began to laugh, hard, rasping laughs, like a saw in dry wood.

With some effort he turned to leave. But the tall woman had got a steady grip on his arm and held him inside.

"Don't be so bitterly shy!"

She turned to the others and said something he didn't understand, and then they laughed even harder and more derisively.

He had almost decided to leave; these women made fun of him, laughed at him. But he must stay, he must show them he wasn't afraid of women. And the one at his arm assured him that all she wanted with him was something very nice and that nothing in this house would hurt him. If he just followed her, they would undoubtedly get along and be good friends.

"Come along, my little sweet potato . . . !"

She had a purring, caressing voice that pleased his ear. It was like the soft down of a pillow. The voice had power over him. She put her arm across his back and guided him, silently. They crossed to the other end of the large room, where she pulled aside a hanging; behind it stood a low, broad bed. Then she pulled the hanging in place behind them; it fell down over his shoulders and back like a cape.

They were separated from the others in the house.

351

Here behind the hanging he was alone with the woman and the bed.

Her robe was green; the cloth rustled against his own clothing. He had barely seen her face and as yet he had not said a word to her. She alone did the talking. She lit a candle, then she bent down and poked in the bed. She would make it soft and good for him, as soft a bed as he had ever felt before. He would be wonderfully pleased, she had never cheated a man of anything, each one had left her satisfied and well pleased.

And again she called him her little sweet potato.

She smelled sweet, terribly sweet. Her black eyes glittered in the flickering light, but her cheeks were gray-white, like rye flour. He turned away his eyes, he dared not look her in the face. He was tempted, but now that they were alone he was seized with fright.

He did not know how a man acted with a woman in bed.

He stood rigidly, his limbs clumsy. His arms limp, he remained motionless at the bedside. With one quick, accustomed movement the woman turned down her robe, leaving herself exposed to the waist. And then she asked in her husky voice: wouldn't he like to have a peek? Didn't she have beautiful breasts? All men liked them. She wanted a dollar extra for the breasts; they ought to be worth it out here in the West. There were no breasts like hers in all of Nebraska, nay, not in all the West!

He looked at her breasts; they hung limp and flat and dangled so low they almost touched her stomach. They looked like an udder between the hind legs of a cow.

And he swallowed with an effort; he felt nauseated. What did he want with that woman? He wouldn't want to mix himself with her . . . He was in a whorehouse and she was a whore. A whore's body was filled with poison and her life lasted only four years. This one here—how much poison did she carry in her body? How long a time had he left to live . . . ? Why had he come in here? Had it been because he had no desire to live any longer . . . ? Suddenly he wanted to live . . .

His fear made cold perspiration break out on his body. But the woman sat down on the bed and pulled him down beside her. All right? An extra dollar for the breasts? The finest breasts in the West. White and pure like the rose and the lily. He could have the whole business for three dollars—if he gave the money to her now they would be ready in a jiffy. But why didn't he talk? Why didn't he say a single word?

Her hands found their way under his clothing. They were at home on a man's body: with sure, experienced motions the hands opened his pants and felt toward his groin.

Now at last he spoke. He forgot himself and spoke Swedish to her: She must let him alone. He didn't want anything of her. He had only come out of curiosity—he was staying at the hotel across the street. He would be glad to give her the three dollars. But he didn't want to do anything with her. He wanted to leave at once . . .

But she of course did not understand him and her hands felt his body and took hold of his testicles. Now she was talking in a caressing, silver-clear voice that tinkled like a bell; she laughed heartily as one hand held on to the scrotum.

What a dear sweet potato! She would squeeze the honey out of it!

He heard himself talking in Swedish and corrected himself in stuttering English. But the lure of the unknown experience and his fear kept him paralyzed and he let her go on.

She burst out laughing again.

"What should I do with this kid?"

She tightened her hold on his testicles until it hurt him. The pain brought him back to himself and at once he recovered his ability to move, he pushed her aside and jumped up, pulling the hanging apart so violently that it fell to the floor. He ran through the room where the other whores were still sitting at the table, reached the door, and got out into the street. He heard the women laugh behind him.

Outside the whorehouse he tumbled over in a hole in the street, in spite of the lantern light, and hurt his right knee. Limping badly he reached the hotel door, moving as fast as his injured knee permitted. He felt his way through the dark cellar hall, found his room, and threw himself on his back on the bed, his limbs trembling. His knee ached and his groin hurt. The derisive laughter of the women had followed him across the street; they were poking fun at his innocence. Now they must be talking about him, the sweet potato who wanted to but didn't dare. They were laughing at him, making fun of him: what to do with such a fool?

But the sweet potato had run away, they had not squeezed the honey from his pouch.

He lay on his bed, trembling. His testicles hurt from the woman's grasp. Now he knew why the prices were so cheap over there. What they offered was false. Their gift was false. It was right that their wares cost two dollars only—with an extra dollar for the finest breasts in the West. They weren't worth any more. He had had the experience now; the glory over there was only something he had imagined. Nothing to long for. He had been made a fool of in that house and it had served him right.

He had wondered how it was to mix with a woman. He had learned tonight. He didn't want to know any more.

6.

Robert stayed in the sand-pit ghost town for over two years.

Each day he felt that the pierced gravel walls might cave in and bury the town and its people. It seemed to him a miracle that they still stood. And he asked himself if he wasn't staying in Grand City only to see its burial. Perhaps he secretly longed for the big cave-in to take place and end life for all of them.

Or a new tornado might come and carry off the remaining houses—hurl the Grand Hotel and the whorehouse far out on the endless prairie. To be buried as a crushed worm or wafted as a feather through the air seemed much the same to him.

After his experiences on the California Trail, Robert felt that death was the only sure thing in this world, the only thing that *really* happened, and the only thing that

354

could change anything for him. And he believed himself separated from death only by a transparent film, thin and sensitive as the retina of the eye. He could see through it clearly, and he wondered constantly why it didn't burst. He lived a life of pretense—the happenings of life did not concern him.

A winter passed, and a summer and a second winter, but the big cave-in-burial did not take place in Grand City. Nor was there another tornado. The houses were neither buried nor blown out on the prairie; they still stood, and the people in them remained, among them the two Swedes who ran the Grand Hotel.

Fredrik Mattsson lived his life in great earnest, in great hurry. He was involved in *big* business, bigger than before, whatever it happened to be now—his partner never asked. Robert was hotel owner and servant in one person and did the heaviest chores. Fred intended to hire necessary personnel—he had already decided how many people they needed—but unfortunately he never had the time to see to it. His days were entirely taken up by other, more urgent activities. And since his partner had brought in new capital, the hotel was to be enlarged and improved. In the beginning he discussed his plans with Robert.

One evening he asked, "Bob, can you hang paper?"

At first Robert did not understand what he meant.

Well, in the morning Fred would begin the great improvement: they would paper the hotel walls. Could Robert do this? Fred had come across a big pile of light-blue wallpaper rolls, very cheap. For several weeks Robert boiled glue, measured and cut and hung paper over the naked walls of the old potato cellar. The work amused him, because he could see results. He changed the color of the naked hotel walls from dark gray to light blue. He felt he was making the days brighter for the strangers who would stay in the rooms.

But the hanging of the light-blue paper—at fifty cents a roll—was the only improvement undertaken at the Grand Hotel.

7.

It was during Robert's third winter in the ghost town
that his illness began. It started as a persistent fatigue
which did not disappear with rest, a hollow, empty cough,
and sometimes tearing pain in his stomach. He lost his
appetite, couldn't keep down the food he swallowed; he
lost weight, grew wan. Already before this he had grown
thinner, and the fat gold lice had long ago deserted his
body; now not the smallest nits could find nourishment
there. He stayed in bed for a while and felt a little better.
For short periods he felt almost well. But the illness came
back, and then his teeth began to fall out.

When he looked in a mirror he didn't recognize himself.

Fred often would say to him: "Your face is pale as
hell, Bob!"

Because his partner looked so yellow Fred wondered if
Robert hadn't perchance caught the yellow fever while he
looked after Vallejos. Perhaps it had entered his body and
not broken out until now? Robert didn't think so, but
then he knew nothing about disease. He had never had
any ailment except his bad ear.

By spring he had recuperated enough to be up and
about but he felt far from well; the oppressive fatigue remained in his body, and he was almost unable to do anything. He no longer could assist Fred in running the hotel.
And he had grown tired of the ghost town and wanted to
get away from it as soon as he felt strong enough.

He had told Fred that his older brother had taken up a
claim in Minnesota, and now Robert hinted that perhaps
it would be best for him to return to his brother.

Fred replied enthusiastically. Since Robert didn't feel
well he ought to be where he could get care and rest. He
himself could not look after his friend and countryman in
the manner he would wish. But Robert's relatives would
surely do so and help him regain his health and strength.

"Bob, you needn't be a burden to your brother. I will

of course return the money you put into my hotel! I'll not only pay back the capital—I'll pay interest as well, the highest interest in North America."

Fredrik Mattsson from Asarum would, in every detail, keep the promise he had given his countryman. And Robert in turn assured him that he had always trusted his friend in their mutual business. He had never heard of one Swede cheating another in America.

"Of course not! I've increased our money! I know how to handle money in America, Bob. I know how to pay out the capital and still have it!"

From his vest pocket he fished up a five-cent coin and held it before Robert's eyes.

"See this nickel? With this one single coin I paid for my food a whole winter in Chicago!"

"You couldn't!" exclaimed Robert. "Unless you were a magician or something . . ."

Fred explained that it had nothing to do with tricks or miracles; it was pure business ability. That winter in Chicago he had had no cash except this coin. He had lived with a woman friend, free of charge, and he had eaten all his meals at a saloon on Clark Street where every customer who bought anything for at least five cents could eat a free meal. Each morning he had gone to this saloon and bought a five-cent cigar. Then he had eaten his breakfast. But he did not smoke his cigar—when he emerged onto the street he sold it to anyone he happened to meet for the same price he himself had paid. In that way he got back his five cents. At dinnertime he went back to the saloon, bought a fresh cigar, ate the dinner he was entitled to, and then went outside and sold his cigar for five cents. In that way he retrieved his nickel so he could buy a new cigar in the morning and have his breakfast, and so on.

He had lived in this way the whole winter through buying and selling two cigars a day and eating two solid meals. And when he left Chicago in the spring he still had his nickel, even though it had paid for his food for a whole winter.

Fred threw the coin into the air and caught it on the downfall.

"You see, I know how to handle capital! I pay out and still have it! I've done the same with your money, Bob. I know the tricks. Life is easy in America if you know the tricks."

Up to the very last moment of Robert's stay, the host of the Grand Hotel was helpful and generous to his friend and partner. He arranged for his trip home: an ox train would soon be due in Grand City on its way east to St. Louis, and from St. Louis Robert could take the paddle steamer as soon as the northern Mississippi was open. Robert remembered the route; it would be his third journey on the broad river.

"You must get yourself some decent clothes, Bob," insisted Fred. "You must return as a gentleman!"

A few hundred dollars in silver were still left in Robert's black pouch—enough for his trip home, a suit of clothes, and a new rucksack. Now anyone could see he was returning from the goldfields, said Fred.

Thus one day in April 1855, the younger partner in the Grand Hotel, Grand City, was ready to leave the business and the town. The ox train for St. Louis had arrived. The two friends stood at the counter in Fred's Tavern, and the one who would stay behind solemnly opened a bottle of Kentucky Straight. With controlled emotion Fred said they must drink the painful *Skol* of farewell. For the last time they would use the beloved Swedish word of greeting to each other. From then on the word *Skol* would never more be heard in this room.

And now at their parting the moment had come for him to repay Robert's loan as he had promised.

"My dear friend, after two years your capital has doubled. In this way you are getting 100 per cent interest. I owe you four thousand dollars!"

Fredrik Mattsson put two heavy bundles of bills on the counter in front of his friend; he had of course changed Robert's gold into bills. This had to be done before money could circulate and grow, and he was repaying him in bills.

He looked at his countryman, as if to see his reaction.

"Have you ever seen or heard of wildcats out here?"

"Wildcats? Do you mean those wild animals . . . ?"

"No. I mean free money in America. What you see before you on the counter is four thousand dollars in wildcat money. You get your capital back in sound, free money."

For the first time Robert saw wildcat money and he liked the name; to him it had something to do with freedom and liberty; the bills had probably been given that name because they in some way echoed the freedom of the wildcats in the forest.

"Here you are, Bob. One hundred per cent interest!"

Robert was overcome by the great generosity his friend displayed at their parting. Was it right for him to accept these big bundles of money, four thousand dollars? He felt like a miser, a usurper. No, he couldn't accept all this money—he hadn't earned it. And he said if he accepted it he would ever after feel he had skinned a countryman and friend.

"No, Fred, you're too generous to me!"

But Fred forced him to take it, he himself pushed the bundles into the black leather pouch. He knew how Robert felt, but after all, it was only his own money that had doubled in two years by constant, careful handling. He paid back in wildcats—sound, free money that would double again if handled wisely. They were as good as gold in the right hands. Up in Minnesota, where there were few banks, these bills might be worth even more than out here, probably more than gold.

Robert gave in. He now possessed four thousand dollars of this money that had been named after the free forest cats who had no masters, and who roamed at liberty wherever they liked. Instead of the heavy, exacting gold, he had now liberty's light and sound money in his bag. And wasn't this the kind of money he had always been looking for?

His partner, this competent businessman, had doubled his fortune. And that very moment Robert decided how he would use this great sum of money.

He thanked his countryman with all his heart, thanked him long and well, not only for his great help in increasing his money, but also for all the stories about the gold land he had listened to in the Grand Hotel when undis-

359

turbed by guests. What he had learned he would not forget.

So the two friends emptied their farewell *Skal* to the last drop; for the last time the Swedish toast was used in Fred's Tavern.

Later, in the street outside the hotel, Fredrik Mattsson from Asarum, Sweden, waved a cheerful goodbye to Robert Nilsson from the same country, as he left the Grand Hotel in Grand City on the ox wagon, the wildcats in his bag.

You're listening, but you haven't heard Karl Oskar return; you don't hear well—it's I who ruined your hearing.

It's been a long night for you—I've had much to tell, have tried not to forget anything of importance.

But now my story nears its end.

It was during your last winter in the ghost town that I came back to you. Since then I've left you only for short intervals. I've buzzed and throbbed and banged and hammered so intensely that you have been forced to listen to me. And you can say what you wish, but you can thank me for the fact that you began to ponder your lot in life. I've kept you awake at night and given you time to think in peace when all is silent.

And at last you have returned and can play the gold-seeker who struck it rich! The sound, free money in your pouch hadn't been touched when you returned. You had decided not to spend a single dollar of it, for you wanted to give all your riches to Karl Oskar and Kristina.

Thus your trip has not been in vain, my dear gold-seeker. Your money will help your brother and sister-in-law. Who could deserve the money more? Who could use it better? Who could need it more? Your brother is still young, but he has poked so hard in the earth here that he already limps—even though he won't admit it! When he has cleared one field he begins with another, and another, and so on. He loves it. But however big his fields he will never be satisfied. Yet he too, in the end, must be satisfied with a handful of earth—as much as the mouth of a dead man can hold.

And Kristina is not nearly as strong as your brother.

She is only thirty, yet soon she will become bent and broken on this claim if she doesn't get help. She has five brats, and will have more, she has her big household to care for, all the livestock—constant chores inside and outside. She is like a ship at sail: never entirely still, always driven by some little gust of wind. You see how worn out she is in the evenings. You can be pleased that your money will help a little to ease her burden.

You've returned with riches to the home of Karl Oskar and Kristina. You've kept the promise you made them when you left four years ago. But it cost you mightily. You returned a whole life older. And your return was not what you had imagined when you left; you expected to return with your life unspent. But now you've learned what life is and what death is. You've experienced them both, and these two ought to be the title of the story that now draws to its close.

Dear Robert! You've been lying awake for long hours tonight. We won't part, you and I. Don't think so for a moment! You yet have one master left! But now I shall release a few great drops of comfort, a few drops to ease your pain, so that you will have a few hours' rest. This much credit you must give your sick, buzzing ear: it has taught you to value sleep as the greatest gift the Creator has to offer. When fatigue and despair rob a person of life's strength, it is restored with sleep.

Farewell now for the moment. Sleep well, goldseeker—you who never saw California!

XXIV. Wildcat Riches

1.

Karl Oskar had expected to return from Stillwater before nightfall on Friday, but at bedtime he was not yet back. Kristina put the children to bed while she herself stayed up and kept a fire going to keep supper warm for her husband.

As yet she wasn't worried. Karl Oskar had been late on several occasions when returning from Stillwater or Taylors Falls. On the wretched, recently cleared forest roads so much could happen to delay a ramshackle ox cart, and their oxen were young and barely trained. Then it was so hot during the day with swarms of that summer plague, the mosquitoes. No one could get a moment's peace in the forest because of these pests. She felt sorry for Karl Oskar, who must drive the team such a long way in this heat, when even well-trained animals sometimes bolted and took off because of the stinging critters.

A young ox might easily bolt in this weather, and then the driver might get hurt also. It comforted her that Karl Oskar wasn't alone on this trip. Their neighbor, Algot Svensson, was a capable and reliable man.

Robert had gone to bed at his usual time. There was no need for him to stay up and wait for his brother. He was weak and sickly and needed his rest more than anyone else in the house.

A couple of long hours passed as Kristina waited. On the hearth stood the pot containing the corn porridge she had cooked for supper, which was beginning to smell burned. She must prepare something else for Karl Oskar, something she could make ready quickly. She found some eggs and poured water into a pot to boil them; she also cut a few thick slices of pork. Then she waited again.

It was close inside, so she went out and sat down on the oak bench near the kitchen door where it was cooler. The crickets squeaked and chirped in bushes and grass all around the house. She had become accustomed to this sound of the night's whistle pipes, but tonight she wished the screech-hoppers would keep quiet; their noise distracted her and prevented her from hearing the rumble of the ox cart down the road.

It was almost midnight before Kristina heard the sound she had been waiting for. She went back into the kitchen and blew fire into the dying embers; the food would be ready as soon as Karl Oskar had unyoked the oxen and stabled them. She heard no voices; their neighbor must have left below the meadow and taken a short cut to his home.

After a few moments she heard the familiar footsteps outside the door. Only a few minutes more and the eggs would be boiled and the pork fried. Karl Oskar came in.

She greeted him with the words that many times before had met him when he returned:

"You're late . . ."

He flung his hat unto its accustomed nail on the wall, drew in his breath, and said that on the way home they had hit a stump in the road, turned over the cart, and broken the axle. Algot Svensson had gone to the new homestead at Hay Lake and borrowed tools so they could cut a tree and put in a new axle. This had delayed them several hours. His cart wasn't good enough for long trips.

She was just lifting the boiling pot off the fire and she turned around quickly; his voice sounded strange. He spoke with an effort, in short, stuttering words as she had never before heard him talk. What was the matter with him? The broken axle couldn't have affected him that seriously.

He walked past her into the big room before she could see his face, and now she remembered his most important errand today. But she had not intended to ask him anything before he had eaten; hungry men needed food first of all.

Karl Oskar usually went directly to the table and sat down to eat when he came home hungry. Wonderingly, she went into the big room after him. He had lit a candle; his face was stern, his features frozen.

"What is it, Karl Oskar. . . ?"

His face was spotted, marked by his dirty fingers wiping off perspiration. He had driven his team a long way on a hot day and he had turned over, but he was not hurt. Why, then, wasn't everything all right?

Kristina noticed that he held something in his hands. With a sudden, angry thrust he threw it away—flung it all the way into the fireplace corner toward the old spittoon she had just cleaned. It was a bundle of paper which fluttered in the air as it flew past her; around and inside the spittoon a heap of green bills lay strewn.

"We can throw those on the dunghill!"

"The money. . . ?"

"Wildcat money!"

"Paper money. . . ?"

"Useless! Money for wildcats!"

"Aren't they real. . . ?"

"This money isn't worth a shit! 'Good for nothing' they said at the bank!"

Karl Oskar sat down on a chair, heavily.

" 'These bills ain't worth a plugged nickel!' the man at the bank said!"

He tried to repeat what the man had said, the English words of the banker that still rang in his ears.

Today, he told her, when he had gone to the bank at Stillwater, one clerk after another had come to inspect the money. At last they had called out the head man of the bank and he had inspected the bills at length. It was he who had said: *Wildcat money! Good for nothing!*

The Indiana State Bank of Bloomfield, which had issued the money, had long ago gone broke. That was probably why its name hadn't been on the list in the Swedish newspaper. Bills on that bank were no longer in circulation in this part of the country, the banker had said, only far out in the wild West. And he had added, that even there it must be Swedish immigrants and other newcomers who were cheated by that kind of money.

He had said he was sorry for Karl Oskar, and the clerks had said the same, but they couldn't accept his money. They had advised him never to take bills unless he knew about the bank that issued them. And he had stood there like a fool when they handed the money back to him. He suspected the American bankers had had a good laugh behind his back, laughing at a trusting, ignorant Swedish settler.

He was seldom with business people and he had never heard of wildcat money; it was money issued by banks that lacked securities and were unable to redeem it.

Kristina was glued to the spot staring at the fireplace corner, which was covered with the bills. Only last night she had ironed out these bills and removed the spots from them.

364

She tried to understand; how could the bills be false? Anyone in Sweden making false money was arrested by the sheriff and put into prison. She asked: Were such swindlers allowed to be on the loose in America? Had the banks themselves the right to cheat people with useless bills?

Karl Oskar replied that as long as there was no order in currency anyone could start a bank and print bills. There was full freedom in this country. And wildcat money was a suitable name; the bankers who had printed these bills were of the same ilk as their namesake; they were robbers, as treacherous as the wild beasts lurking in the bushes, endangering their children.

Kristina sank down on a chair, her head filled with a throbbing confusion. Dazed and bewildered she tried to understand. Last Monday evening a fortune had come into their home. This was Friday—and here it was back in the house again. But now the money lay strewn like refuse in the spittoon in the corner.

It was a false fortune, wildcat riches.

She had forgotten the frying pan—an odor of burned pork came through the door from the kitchen. It had entirely gone out of her mind that she had been preparing supper for Karl Oskar.

But he smelled it.

"You're burning the pork!"

He rushed to the kitchen and pulled the pan off the fire, then returned to her in the big room. He didn't care enough about food to eat; he wasn't hungry tonight. He started walking back and forth across the floor, he pounded his fists against his chest; it was as if he wanted to punish himself for his foolishness.

"I had made up my mind I wouldn't let him fool me any more! I had my doubts all the time! But he won—he made a fool of me!"

"Do you think Robert meant to cheat you?"

"See for yourself! He tried! Look in the corner! His hellish lying! He's unable to say a single word that's true! Where do you think he has his gold? It's inside his head—where no one can get to it!"

365

"I can't believe Robert had some evil intent in mind when he gave us the money," said Kristina firmly.

"You still think well of him?" exclaimed Karl Oskar in a hardening voice. "A liar can just as easily cheat! Don't you know Robert by now?"

Kristina had just begun to know Robert. She had never thought of him as being evil or deceitful, and after her talk with him today under the sugar maples she knew better than before that he was not a bad person who wished to cheat them with false money. Even though he did lie he was not a cheater. He was not one who would want to skin anyone. On the contrary, he himself was trusting and easily cheated. She wondered if it wasn't possible that Robert himself had been cheated by those bankers who had printed the bills.

"He must know they're useless!" said Karl Oskar. "He must have tried to use the same kind of money himself! He must have found out the bills were useless and then decided they were good enough for us!"

"No! I don't believe that of Robert!"

"He felt ashamed of returning empty-handed, of course!"

Karl Oskar looked toward the gable room.

"I'm going to call him—then you can hear what he has to say for himself!"

"It's the middle of the night!" She took him by the arm. "He's weak and ailing—leave him alone till tomorrow morning."

"Well, as you say . . ."

"You need to calm down too . . ."

"But you can be sure I'll have a talk with him in the morning!"

"Don't do anything rash," Kristina pleaded. "Robert might have an explanation for his wildcat money."

"I'm sure he has! He can always dream up some lie. That's easy for him!"

Karl Oskar walked back and forth, flailing his long arms; the movement of his body gave him some outlet for his anger. But Kristina sat crushed and silent until the corners of her mouth began to twitch.

"Is there anything one can trust here in America. . . ?"

"We mustn't take this too hard, Kristina . . ." He lowered his voice, changing his tone completely. Looking at his wife he could judge it was now time to talk differently.

"No—no more crying about this! We aren't richer than before, but neither are we poorer. We haven't lost anything! Not a single nickel! Nothing has changed for us."

He could also have said that in one way he almost felt satisfied. He had been right when he refused to believe in easy riches in America. For five years he had struggled and been harassed by his lack of cash—and the first time he had gone to a bank to put in some cash he had been told it was worthless. It was as though justice today had been meted out between the settler who improved his lot through honest work and the good-for-nothing speculator, or whatever his name, who tried to get rich without work.

Kristina heard the words; as rich or as poor as before—no change . . . But for her something had changed. She had never for a moment doubted but that their fortune was real, and she had already speculated on what the big bills would bring them. During those days and nights since Robert's return she had thought of how their life on the claim would change. Stimulated by the thought of riches she had already begun to live this new life. She had filled their naked rooms with new furniture, with new clothing for all of them, of better cut and fit than she could manage by her own sewing. She had traveled to visit her friend Ulrika in Stillwater on a new spring wagon pulled by horses; she had already engaged a maid to help in her chores—she had indeed found aid for her overwhelming fatigue. She had bought thousands of things for the house and her dear ones during this wonderful June week when for four days she was rich.

The time of wealth had lasted from Monday to Friday. And now? Through the open door came the everlasting complaint of the crickets squeaking like an ungreased wheel, that turned at dizzying speed out there in the grass. This familiar sound of the summer night seemed at this moment a sound of derision: Monday night—but now it's Friday! Where are your riches now, Kristina? In the spittoon? Have you so much money in this house that you spit on it? For four days, Kristina, you were rich, but it was not yours, it belonged to the wildcats—perhaps they are enjoying it now, tearing it to pieces in their lairs and holes! Tearing to pieces all the things you had counted on. For a wildcat is much stronger and smarter than you. You're only a poor woman! Trusting Kristina! So sorry for you! But you have known all along that this wilderness is full of evil, lurking creatures.

Yes, for Kristina something had changed. It was true, all they had gained out here during five years remained. They had not lost anything. Yet she felt as if this night she had suddenly become terribly poor.

2.

Saturday morning Robert entered the kitchen as Kristina was busy starting the fire. His hair was ruffled and stood straight up, his cheeks were gray in the early morning light. He went over to the water bucket and took down the scoop from its nail on the wall. Just as he had finished drinking, Karl Oskar came in from his chores in the stable. He took his brother by the arm.

"Come, I want to show you something."

They went into the big room, Kristina behind them. Now it would come—she had been lying awake during the night, anxiously worrying about the morning meeting of the two brothers.

Karl Oskar pointed to the fireplace corner with the bills spread over the spittoon; they lay where he had flung them last night on his return.

"Here! You can have your spending money back! It might be useful when you go to the privy!"

He spoke loudly, anger vibrating in his voice, but Robert did not seem to understand what he was driving at. He put his hand behind his healthy ear and turned it toward his brother to hear better.

"Keep your rubbish! Pick up the shit! I can get along without your useless money!"

Karl Oskar stood straight and strong and stern as he
368

faced Robert. Now they had resumed the old order: Karl Oskar was again the big brother scolding his little brother.

But Kristina could not see that Robert showed anything but puzzled surprise.

"I don't understand, Karl Oskar. . . ?"

He recognized his bills in the corner, all over the spittoon. Why were they there? Who had thrown them there? Wasn't his brother going to put them in the bank at Stillwater yesterday?

"Are you crazy, Karl Oskar? Why do you throw away all that money?"

"Shithouse money! Not worth a plugged nickel! All of it isn't worth one Swedish penny!"

"Not worth. . .? No! You're crazy . . . Karl Oskar . . . Impossible . . ."

Robert insisted on his innocence, both in words and gestures he denied knowing what it was all about. His eyes, his open mouth—all insisted that he was honestly innocent:

"It isn't true! I don't believe a word of what you say!"

"You still deny? You still persist in your lying, you . . . you damned cheater!"

Karl Oskar seldom grew angry, but when anger overtook him it came fast and furiously. His hands shook, he closed and opened his fists, he rubbed one fist against the open palm of the other hand. But even his bodily motions were no longer sufficient outlet for him. His fury at Robert burst out violently as he shouted with all his strength, "You're a hell of a liar! Why did I ever let you come with me to America! There isn't a decent thought in your heart! Here you've poured lies on us all week long! But now at last it's finished! Finished! Do you hear!"

Kristina stepped between the two brothers.

"Stop shouting, Karl Oskar! You and your brother can at least talk to each other like decent people!"

Several times Robert had tried to say something but each time he had been interrupted by coughing. At last, in a weak, hoarse voice, he managed, "I always thought the money was good. I remember, though, they call it wildcat money in English; that means free, sound money. And I told you the first evening . . ."

369

"I knew it!" interrupted Karl Oskar. "I knew you knew it all along!"

He turned to Kristina.

"There, you hear? He knew the money was no good! Wildcat money! He did it purposely! He wanted to fool us . . ."

But at this moment the little brother did not listen to the big brother's accusations; he heard another voice that had spoken long ago: Have you heard of wildcats? They're just as good as other bills, if they're handled right. The wildcats are as good as gold—up there in Minnesota . . .

Could it be that one Swede had cheated another Swede in America. . . . ?

"Calm down now!" Kristina pleaded with Karl Oskar.

"He wants to get rid of his useless money with us!"

"I—I didn't want to cheat anyone . . . please, listen, Karl Oskar . . ."

"Shut your damn trap!"

Karl Oskar was rubbing his right fist ever harder against the palm of his left hand; his features had hardened, his eyes had grown so small they looked as if they had receded into his head.

"You're a hell of a brother! All my life I have to go and feel ashamed of you—my own brother! Ashamed . . . ashamed!"

"But listen to me . . . I didn't think . . . I didn't know . . ."

"Shut up, I said! If you don't shut up, you damn liar, I'm going to shut your trap for you!"

It happened in a second. Karl Oskar's right fist was raised against his brother. He hit him on the mouth.

Robert stumbled backward from the impact, against the wall; he almost fell, but the wall supported him.

"Have you become a wild beast yourself?" Kristina had grabbed hold of Karl Oskar's right arm with both her hands; anger flamed up in her also and gave her strength. "Have you lost your mind? Watch yourself!"

"I'll shut his trap for him. . . !"

"Are you hitting your own brother? Sick and ailing as he is! Get hold of yourself, man!"

370

Karl Oskar tore himself free of her and stalked back to the corner.

"Attack an invalid!" Kristina's lips were white with anger.

Leaning against the wall, Robert managed to stand upright, but his legs still shook under him. Just as his brother's blow hit him he had been ready with his explanation: You must realize that I have been cheated first! I had never meant to cheat you, brother! I would never be low enough to cheat a brother!

But instead of his own voice all he heard now was the ear mocking him in a painful throbbing: What did you bring home? Useless money! How about your health and your life? No riches and no life! What is left for you?

From the kitchen the children had been listening to the commotion, and the two smallest boys were crying with fright. Kristina quickly closed the door. Karl Oskar remained in his corner, staring silently at the floor. He had not answered Kristina's rebuke. His senses had returned, he stood with his head bent.

"Attacking a brother! Acting like a lunatic!"

Kristina approached Robert.

"Did he hurt you?"

"Not seriously . . . It's nothing . . ."

His hand moved to his sore upper lip. His brother's fist could not knock out teeth which he had lost far out West, in buffalo country.

His fingers moved slowly across his lips.

"It's nothing at all! I'm not even bleeding! The liar hasn't even blood to give!"

"I want to talk with you calmly, Robert," said Kristina. "Won't you tell me the truth now . . ."

"Dear Kristina—I didn't want to fool you, I wasn't trying to cheat anyone . . ."

He turned to his older brother.

"I am not lying . . . I didn't know . . . I had never tried to use the money . . . I had saved it for you and Kristina . . . I wanted to leave everything I owned to you and her . . . And I expected you to come back from Stillwater and offer me your hand . . ."

He stopped. He continued to himself: You did offer me

371

your hand, brother. But it was a fist, hard, and struck my face. It hit instead of thanked. Such is our fate, brother. Our lot in life.

Karl Oskar had acted in a fit of anger. But now he had had time to control himself and knew that he had gone too far, that he had committed an outrage against his brother. He had given free rein to his anger, and in so doing he had also given his brother the upper hand.

"Forgive me, Robert," he stammered.

"You had a right to hit me. It was my fault. I lived so long with that wildcat . . . I was blind to him . . ."

"I blew up," said Karl Oskar. "Will you forgive me?" He had raised his head.

"I forgive you, of course. You're already forgiven! You're my only brother . . . I should have asked you to forgive me . . . But it's too late now . . . everything is too late . . ."

Robert sounded submissive, as if he had earned the blow, as if it were a well-deserved punishment. His legs felt steadier now, and he walked slowly away toward the gable room.

Karl Oskar remained in his corner; the blow he had given his brother seemed to have dazed him instead.

Kristina was silent and reproached him no longer. When she heard him apologize to his brother she felt a strong compassion for her husband; anyone could make a mistake.

Robert had gone to his room. They stood and waited, silent, confused after the flare-up. He came out again, and now he had put on his boots, coat, and hat. He moved quickly and resolutely.

"Where are you going?" asked Kristina, surprised.

He did not reply to her—he turned to Karl Oskar.

"I'm off again. I don't want you to feel ashamed of your brother. Goodbye! Forgive me the embarrassment I've caused you."

"Take it easy, Robert! Wait a minute!" Kristina had grabbed hold of the back of his coat. "You can't go off again! You aren't well! You need care. . . !"

"Goodbye, Kristina. You've always been kind to me . . ."

He walked toward the door, passing the fireplace corner where the green-black bills lay scattered—wildcat money. As they caught his eye he stopped, as if a vision had appeared to him, revealing all, explaining all. He exclaimed, "As good as gold! No! As false as gold! Bills or gold, all money is equally false! 'As good as gold'! Ha, ha! As rotten, as deceitful, root of all evil! Dead weight! That's what gold is! Now I can laugh at it all . . . Ha, ha, ha!"

And as Robert hurried out the door he began to laugh, a high, piercing laugh, echoing through the house after him.

His laughter caught his brother and sister-in-law unawares; it frightened them as much as a sudden attack on their home with shot and shell. They were completely perplexed. And they made no attempt to stop him.

They stood and looked through the window after the fugitive, who was already some distance from the house. He walked along the edge of the field, down the slope, toward the lake; he crossed the narrow creek and continued westward.

He was headed for the forest. Soon he would be swallowed up by the pines and the thickets.

"Hurry after him!" Kristina urged her husband. "Hurry as fast as you can—don't let him get away!"

Karl Oskar replied that he knew his brother. Better to leave him alone when he took off. Robert had always run away. He had fled many times in his life, but he had always come back. He was sure to return this time too.

Robert's tall, narrow body disappeared among the pines, whose trunks were gilded by the early morning sun. He walked with hurried steps until he vanished from their sight.

XXV. A Stream That Runs Toward Greater Waters

1.

Robert walked without any definite course, around thickets, avoiding holes and swamps, choosing the easiest path. He detoured, walking sideways, between tree trunks, around boulders and hills, across glades and clearings. He walked without knowing where he was going, cut through the forest without a goal.

It was a sizzling hot day. The bark of the forest pines exuded a scorched odor. Tinder-dry branches cracked underfoot. No one had ever cut or removed fallen and dead trees from this wild forest: they stood where their roots held them, rotting down aboveground. Their dry boles had darkened in the bark and stood there covered with gray peelings; the dead trees appeared to be covered with dust and ashes, buried standing up after their death.

In forest openings he waded through tall, coarse grass which crackled against his knees. And wherever he walked, mosquitoes in great clouds kept him company. One thick swarm circled his head and followed him faithfully in all his turns and detours, stinging him angrily, whizzing, buzzing their eternal hum. They were like wild beasts thirsting for his blood.

When his legs grew tired, he sat down on the ground on a soft spot. But he took only short rests; soon he rose again and walked on; the pursuer inside his head forced him to keep moving on. He must stay on the move, must get away. He must keep walking for as long as he found ground under his feet.

His master kept him awake when he wanted to sleep, awakened him if he nodded, got him to his feet when he sat down to rest. His ear ached terribly. This morning again there had been a big red spot on the pillow.

He wandered about in the forest as the day passed. A dry branch knocked off his hat; he left it behind. The swarm of buzzing mosquitoes followed him on his wandering. He walked with a singing wreath of mosquitoes in his hair, he carried a crown of bloodsucking insects on his forehead. He wandered through the forest crowned like a king, crowned by a cloud of stinging, plaguing mosquitoes, and in the center of the cloud was the aching ear.

In the afternoon the skies grew overcast; with the sun hidden the air cooled off, and toward evening it began to rain. Soft drops wet his skin, they fell more heavily, and at last drove away the mosquito wreath around his head, and its monotonous song died away. It was a relief to be rid of this crown of bloodthirsty insects.

With dusk the rain increased. The drops no longer caressed his skin, they were sharp, whip-like. Wet grass and leaves soaked his skin, his pants clung to his legs, water splashed in his boots. For a while he looked for shelter. Then he crept into a thicket of mountain ash. He tore leaves from the lush foliage and spread them on the ground. He would make a bed; he covered himself with a branch and stretched out on the leaves. He lay hidden by the foliage, and the thicket was hidden by darkness.

Night fell with urgency over the forest. Here there were animals, and his good ear registered the night sounds of living creatures, sneaking, creeping, hissing, wings fluttering. A few times he heard persistent calls, perhaps Indians, perhaps birds. But his left ear heard only the usual sound, accompanied by pain.

He picked up a few wet leaves and tried to press them into his ear. They felt soft and cool, seemed to relieve the ache for a moment. He went to sleep but woke up immediately. His pursuer had awakened him. He pushed fresh leaves into his ear. Then he went to sleep again.

His night in the thicket passed in a continuous sleeping and wakening, and during both he heard his pursuer's voice: I'm with you wherever you go! I'm inside your head and you can't get away from me! You can run away from other masters but not from me!

At daybreak a clear summer morning dawned over the wild forest. The clouds opened their portals for heaven's

375

sun, which shone into even the densest thickets. He rose from his bed of leaves, a few of them revealed red spots where his head had been against them. He was struck by the old saying that leaves spotted red when a bird coughed. When he tried to move, he felt as if he had heavy weights on his limbs. He trembled and shuddered; this warm morning he felt cold inside.

He walked on, slower now, his steps unsteady, unsure. The oppressive heat returned, and the swarm of mosquitoes with it. Again he became a king with a mosquito crown; but the bloodsucking creatures ruled over him.

He felt thirsty and began to look for water. His stomach was empty but he felt no hunger.

His ear hummed and throbbed and drove him on. He must get away, he must flee to some place where he would be unreachable. Only the unreachable one could enjoy peace and rest. He did not recognize this part of the forest, did not know what time of day it was. In his pocket he carried Arvid's watch, but it had stopped three years ago and had not been wound since.

Snails in great numbers had come out after last night's rain, enlivening the ground with their beautiful houses— blue, yellow, red, and brown—striped in all colors. But the rain had already been sucked up by the earth, the holes and creeks were empty. He must quench his thirst, he kept looking. In a clearing he found some wild strawberries and picked and ate them. They tasted to him of summer at home in Sweden, when children removed their stockings and shoes and ran barefoot, but they did not relieve his thirst.

Suddenly he realized where he was; above him rose the green brow of the Indian, the sand-cliff king, crowned with a stunted growth of greenery. The dethroned ruler of the forest looked out over his lost kingdom. His face was petrified in sorrow, his eyes so deep they appeared bottomless. But proudly the Indian turned his brown-yellow forehead to the east and called to the intruders who swarmed over the valley like bloodthirsty beasts: Fill this deep valley with gold! We do not accept your gold for the graves of our fathers!

Gold! A great mocking laughter filled his ear, it echoed

through the forest, it echoed through the whole world. A farmhand had started out for California to dig gold. He peeled potatoes, dug cellar-holes, cut wood, fed mules, washed dishes. And in between he dreamed a dream that had nothing to do with the yellow gold, and that was the true dream, the dream of running water. But now he was confused by words he recollected, scenes he had witnessed, songs he had partly heard: Oh the good time has come at last—the best time in California is over—they're digging like hell for gold—Corn and pudding and tapioca pie—Hi and ho and off we go!—and a heart torn from a carcass of ribs, and a decaying horse-leg kicking futiley against the heavens with a silvery shoe . . .

For some time he followed a winding deer path, until he came to a bog with a narrow water hole in the center. But this was stagnant water and he dared not drink it. In that hole lay fevers and ills and the poison of lurking death. One careless swallow of that water, and death would enter his body. Stagnant waters spoiled quickly and no one could trust them.

Drinking water must be running water. The dream-water must be in motion, pouring forth, purling and swirling in freedom; it must flow free as the river that ran to the sea.

> We will be free, we will be free,
> As the wind of the earth and the waves of the sea.

He walked around the bog without attempting to drink, his feet sinking deep in the mud. He left clear tracks behind him. Indians never left any tracks when they passed through the forest. An Indian's foot moved lightly and quickly as a wing above the earth. Now he was back at the place where his boot tracks indicated he had been earlier.

He thought now and then that he had run away again. As soon as no one was looking he ran away to the woods and hid. This he had done ever since he was a small child. But this time no one had hung a bell around his neck, this time no one would find him. He would remain unreachable.

He saw a great body of water shining blue among the pines: he was back at Ki-Chi-Saga. Many people had lately come to this lake, cutting the trees, timbering their houses. But in this particular spot the shoreline still lay wild and untouched as far as he could see. He walked slowly along the shore, looked down into the water which clearly reflected the skies above him. He could see the reeds growing upside down, stretching their heads toward an open sky which undulated at the bottom. He could see two skies, two heavens, the one above him and the one below in the water, and between them lay the earth on which he himself wandered about, lost.

Striking fins made circling ripples among the boulders; near the shore the lake bubbled with fish. If he had a fishing pole he would immediately have a bite. And if he could make a fire and if he had a pan . . . For a moment he thought about the taste of good, fried fish; but he felt no real hunger.

On a flat stone in the sand lay a fish, washed up by the waves; it had a big head with two horns, a long narrow tail. Its whiskers told him it was a catfish. But its skin was white, perhaps it had been lying here dead, in loneliness, drying for a long time in the sun. He picked up the fish by the gills and held it to his nose; it smelled disgusting, making him want to vomit. It had already spoiled. With a jerk he threw the fish away, far out into the lake.

His feeling of hunger entirely disappeared as soon as he smelled the fish. But his burning thirst remained. His tongue felt dry and thick and squeezed. His ear throbbed and ached. He walked along under the tall pines near the shore, it was cool in their shade; under them the water lay black as tar. In several places he found fish skeletons, gnawed clean by animals; and in the sand were the round tracks of fox paws.

Weariness came over him, dulling his senses. The pursuer hammered and buzzed, hurting. It felt as if something had swelled up in there and wanted to get out; it knocked and thundered and pounded on the closed door: *Open! Open! I want to get free!*

But he moved on, wandering about in circles, in wide

arches. No bell around his neck tinkled and disclosed his path as he searched for a place where he would be un-get-at-able.

2.

It was late afternoon but the sun was still above the tree crowns when he reached a small stream that wound its way among the thickets. The stream had shrunk in the summer heat, and clean-washed boulders rose from its bottom, but the water purling around them was crystal-clear, and the thick bushes and trees had helped to keep it cool.

He threw himself headlong on the ground and dipped his face in the stream. The water ran into his wide-open mouth—he swallowed, he panted, he drank. It gurgled in his throat. He drank for a long time. When he had quenched his thirst he sat down to rest near the stream, water still dripping from his chin. The foliage formed a thick mantle over this brook. Close to him an elder bush spread its branches over the water.

He gave in to his weariness and sank down. He remained still as the ground itself, as he watched the running stream. His mind cleared.

Once before he had sat here. He had seen this narrow stream swell with the spring rains: it was that day on which he had first set out in the world, on his way to his first job as farmhand. But he did not wish to have any masters, and to escape from service he had thrown his coat in the water and pretended he had drowned in the brook. That had been his first attempt to become free and un-get-at-able.

Now he was back. He recognized the place, it was well known to him. Before his eyes he saw every detail: the smooth, shiny stones at the bottom, the lush vegetation on the banks, and the fresh, purling water with its bubbles glittering like water-lily pads. Everything he saw was the same. He had been here before; beside this little stream—so free in its course—he had rested during the last hour before he became a servant.

He had come back to the mill brook.

He took off his boots and socks and dangled his bare feet in the stream; he had always done this here when he was a young boy. The water purled and bubbled between his burning toes. It cooled his legs mercifully. It felt so good.

This water never stayed in the same place. It never had time to grow stagnant and rotten. The foam-pearls whirled on their way and he followed them with his eyes. The brook threw itself over obstacles, twisted hurriedly past bushes and roots, cut a course with its own strength. It was headed for the sea and when it reached the great body of water its way lay clear across the world. Then this little stream would mingle with the great billows that carried the ships on their broad shoulders, lifting them up toward the heavens, and lowering them again into the ocean's deep valleys. On the ships grew masts, the tall pines that held the sails. With great white wings the ships flew across the ocean to the New World. The farmhands who had felled and cleaned the masts were not allowed to go with the ships on their journey; they must stay behind in their dark rooms, peering out through dirty windows, chained to their service and their masters.

But two farmhands had accompanied the tall pines from their homeland across the great sea. And one of them had returned from his long journey.

He sat dangling his bare feet in the cool water as he had done so many times before in this brook. He had strayed far before he reached home. He had roamed widely, he had been in the train of the hundred thousand, led by the Pillar of Gold, and he had almost perished in that evil place of sand and stone and thirst. He had lived years in a ghost town, full of rat cadavers and desolate sites where people once had had homes. He had not thought he would ever return again, he had not imagined he could return. But at last he had found his way home. He recognized everything. Here he had rested the day he set out into the world. Now he had come home.

He needn't walk any farther, and that was good, as

tired as he was. He hadn't rested well for a long time. But here he could rest—he was at home.

What time of day was it? He had no watch—except the one that had stopped three years ago. He would have liked to know what time it was when he returned.

He lifted his feet from the water and stretched out full length on the ground beneath the wide elder tree. It was good to be home, to rest here at the brook and watch through the foliage how it hurried on its way. And here he could go to sleep and dream again the water-dream, the good dream.

8.

Once he woke up and lay and listened, greatly surprised. His ear was silent, it didn't buzz any more. His left ear did not ache, did not buzz, did not throb. It gave no sound at all.

He lay quite still and listened intently, but could hear nothing. The world had grown completely silent. Then his left ear must be well. He felt no pain. And he felt released and refreshed and deeply satisfied. His torturing companion had disappeared. His pursuer had at last deserted his head and left him in peace. He was rid of his last master. He needn't run away any more. He was unreachable, un-get-at-able, he was free.

He noticed it was evening, the day was over. He could just lie here and go to sleep again. Now that his ear was silent perhaps he could sleep the whole night through. He no longer had a master who would call him at a certain hour. And a drowsiness that was good and irresistible soon closed his eyes, pulled his lids shut.

All was silent in the world. His ear did not awaken him.

Close by the goldseeker's still body the stream in its course hurried on its way to mingle with greater waters.

4.

A search party found his tracks near the bog, and from there on they followed them to the edge of the brook where he lay under the foliage. They thought he must have been dead for two days when they found him.

Karl Oskar Nilsson made the coffin for his brother. He was buried one evening on the out-jutting point at Lake Ki-Chi-Saga, where the Swedish settlement had chosen and consecrated their cemetery. Karl Oskar put an oak cross on the grave, and carved in the wood his brother's name, with the usual dates, and a line from a psalm he remembered:

Here Rests
AXEL ROBERT NILSSON
Born in Ljuder, Sweden, 1833
Died in Minnesota, North America, 1855
Let me have a Pleasing Rest

His was the first grave to be dug in the cemetery on the point. Robert Nilsson was the first of the Swedes in the St. Croix Valley to be buried under the silver maples.

Part Three

BLESSED WOMAN

XXVI. The Queen in the Kitchen

1.

Karl Oskar caught sight of her in the window of Newell's Hardware Store on Third Street between Jackson and Robert streets; he was walking by and she was displayed in the window. Her name—"The Prairie Queen"—was lettered on the front. She was well polished; her shiny iron surface caught the eye from a distance. The Queen showed herself in all her glory to those on the street and many persons stopped to look at her. A poster, praising the Queen, also hung in the window, and recommended her to buyers: "Undersigned, James Boles, certifies that we use the Prairie Queen in our home and that she is better than any other we have had." "J. Blien's Post Boat Company certifies that the Prairie Queen is also suited for boats." "Undersigned, Nicolas Dowling, certifies that I like the Prairie Queen better than any other make." "The undersigned, Mr. and Mrs. John O. Andersson, certify that the Prairie Queen is superior to any of her competitors."

But the price asked for her was high: thirty-three dollars.

Karl Oskar had driven to the pork market in St. Paul with four of his slaughtered hogs. In Stillwater pork brought only four cents a pound, but in St. Paul the price was six cents; thus it paid to drive the longer distance. The buyer had counted out forty dollars in silver to Karl Oskar. He could pay cash for the Prairie Queen and take her home with him on the wagon.

After a moment's hesitation he stepped inside Newell's Hardware Store and negotiated his purchase.

Three weeks before Christmas the Queen arrived secretly at the New Duvemala settlement. She was se-

385

creted in a wooden box, nailed shut, which Karl Oskar smuggled into the woodshed when no one was around. He put the box in a corner and, to be on the safe side, covered it with some old sacks; here she was well hidden.

The Prairie Queen was not to be moved from her hiding place and into the house until Christmas Eve. She was to be a Christmas present for Kristina.

Karl Oskar mused that the Prairie Queen was an excellent name for a cookstove. The Prairie Queen, which had gulped down all of his income from the sale of four great hogs, was made of cast iron and came equipped with four utensils: a roaster, a kettle, a coffeepot, and a frying pan. It had the reputation of being more convenient than any other stove in the world.

In order to prepare food at their hearth, a pot was placed in an iron ring which stood on three legs in the center of the fireplace. Only one pot could be used at a time and care must be taken lest the ring holding it turn over. All their cooking and frying had been done this way until now. But it was not ordained that for all time people should prepare food on a hearth. In America a time of constant invention of new machines and utensils and gadgets had begun. Then the Nilssons had read in *Hemlandet* that stoves of iron were now for sale, stoves that were not built into the hearth and anchored to the chimney but could be moved like any other piece of furniture. Kristina had wondered what such a cookstove would be like. Now she would see one with her own eyes.

Karl Oskar let Johan and Harald in on the secret of the hidden box in the woodshed. On the morning of Christmas Eve, while Kristina was busy with the milking, the two boys helped their father carry in the heavy iron object and place it in the kitchen on the old hearth, from which the ashes had been swept out. They arranged the four cooking utensils, each one in its proper place on the removable rings and lids of the surface. Karl Oskar broke into the chimney; the iron pipe at the back of the stove was pushed into the hole, and the smoke outlet was ready. Finally he went over the whole stove with a woolen rag, dusting and polishing until the cast iron shone and gleamed.

The Prairie Queen now sat in her proper place in the kitchen. She sat in a queen's seat, elevated on her throne, lighting up the whole kitchen. As soon as one stepped across the threshold one's eyes fell on it.

When Kristina returned from the stable she stopped dead and stared at the stove. What in the world was that sitting back there? What had they put on her hearth? Her husband and sons stood silent, winking at each other as she exclaimed. She had noticed earlier that they were snickering about, giggling over some secret doings.

"What in all the world. . . ? What is that in the fireplace?"

An important guest had come to their house this Christmas, explained Karl Oskar. A queen had come to them in their kitchen. She would always sit there on the hearth, and would help the mistress with her cooking chores.

Kristina walked closer to inspect the Prairie Queen. Her hands stroked the shiny iron, took hold of the pot handles, lifted up the kettle and the coffeepot as if to feel how heavy they were.

"A new cookstove of iron!"

"Of cast iron," said Karl Oskar.

"Have you bought it. . . ?"

"Yes, it's bought and paid for. I'm not in the habit of stealing things."

"Oh my—what a stove! How pretty it is!"

"The stove is a female, by the way. Called the Prairie Queen. The name is stamped on the front of her."

Kristina sat down on the pile of wood beside the stove, overwhelmed, while Karl Oskar described the cast-iron stove with a pride that couldn't have been greater had he himself been the inventor.

Into these holes with doors one put the wood. And here, covered with lids and rings, were the cooking holes. The rings could be removed according to the amount of heat required under the pots and kettles. To keep food warm only, no lids were removed. It was a clever contraption, for sure. And that big door on the side was the baking oven, not for real baking, of course, but for smaller cakes. An explanation of how to use the Prai-

387

rie Queen came with the stove, in English, unfortunately. On the iron stove food would cook much faster since it held the heat.

"And all these cast-iron utensils come with her," he added. "Aren't they fine?"

"They are like the glory of heaven!" She lifted the coffeepot again. "The Americans are so clever. But why do they call it the Prairie Queen?"

Perhaps some settler from England had thought up the name for this superior invention, suggested Karl Oskar. The young queen of England was supposed to be the greatest majesty of all those in the world, thus the name "Queen" for this splendid stove.

"The stove is a beautiful decoration for our home!" said Kristina.

She stood before the shiny, cast-iron Prairie Queen, admiringly and respectfully like a dutiful subject before a majesty of flesh and blood on a silver throne. She could not have been more surprised had a living royal person entered her kitchen this Christmas Eve. But this queen was crowned with four gleaming utensils. What woman in a kitchen could watch that crown without being seized with desire to use it.

"Can you light the stove?" she wondered.

"She's connected, ready to go. You can begin cooking at once."

Karl Oskar had cut wood of the right size for the Prairie Queen's firebox. In no time he had a fire going in the new stove. It smoked a little, but he blamed this on the heavy air and fog they had on this Christmas Eve; it caused a poor draft in the chimney.

When the Prairie Queen was ready, Kristina prepared the first meal on the new stove: the Christmas Eve dinner, the greatest festival meal of the year. It was their third Christmas in the new house, and their seventh in North America.

2.

The children were allowed to eat as much as they could of the delicious Christmas food and then they went to sleep in the gable room, sated and tired.

Since last Christmas a new life had come into the house; in February Kristina had borne a boy, christened Frank Aldo Hjalmar. They called him Frank, the first of the children to be given an American name. When they came to their third American-born child it was their new homeland's turn to be remembered at the baptism, thought Karl Oskar. Now their brood had grown to half a dozen, and of her surviving children, Kristina had given life to three in Sweden and three in America; one half of their children were Swedes, one half Americans. In their home the two peoples were equally strong, half of their children represented the old country, half the new. When Frank was born, Karl Oskar had said: Now it's just right!

After Frank's birth Kristina had been so weak physically that it was several months before she could fully resume her chores. And during the recent exhausting Christmas preparations she had felt that her strength had not yet fully come back.

Before the children were sent to bed this Christmas Eve, Karl Oskar had read the Christmas gospel aloud to his family, as was his custom. Now that the parents were alone Kristina read a few psalms from the prayerbook about Christ's birth, beginning as usual with Luther's words of greeting and rejoicing on the blessed day. The message of the Savior's arrival here on earth was comforting to her anew each time she heard it.

By and by their talk turned to worldly things, and, naturally, first of all to the new iron stove.

"Thirty-three dollars!" said Kristina. "What an expense!"

"The stove will aid you in your work," said Karl Oskar. "It's worth the price."

In a sudden burst of emotion Kristina put out her hand to him across the table.

"Thank you, Karl Oskar."

It was she he had thought of when he bought the Prairie Queen. This she had of course understood at once, but it was good to hear him say it. He never failed in his concern for her. It seldom expressed itself in words; he was shy and retiring in such matters. But they knew each other so well that words between them were not required; it was unnecessary to say the self-evident. And from their deeds they knew each other's thoughts. What people said need not mean anything. What people *did* meant everything.

How much work and worry he had had fattening those four hogs which had paid for the Prairie Queen! How many steps he'd taken so that she might have an iron stove! Nothing could have been more timely than this help in the kitchen. Yet, she felt that he could have bought something they needed more for those thirty-three dollars. There were farm implements invented here in America, that could have aided him in his work. Hadn't he several times spoken of a reaper and a threshing machine?

The reaper and the thresher were still too expensive for him, replied Karl Oskar. He would surely get himself both these machines, by and by—he knew how many days' work they would save him in a year—but lately he had been thinking of a horse. He couldn't raise a horse since he didn't own a mare. He had had it in mind to put aside this hog money for a horse; he had felt he almost had it by the halter. But just then he had caught sight of the Prairie Queen in the store window in St. Paul—and he had let go his hold of the horse.

"I thought of you, Kristina. It's too much for you—you need a little rest."

She felt his concern, both in voice and look.

Sure, she needed a long rest. Her strength diminished as her chores increased. The older children were growing up and could begin to look after themselves, but those of tender age required care in their stead. She had always had three babies who depended on her: one in her arms, and two hanging onto her skirt. This predicament had been her lot as a mother. And at regular intervals she had had to retire to childbed, from which she arose more tired each time, her body turned into a supply room for a new life, her thin breasts sustaining a hungrily sucking mouth. Karl Oskar had known what he was doing a few years earlier: he had made a solid cradle of oak. That cradle rarely stood empty.

Karl Oskar himself pulled such a heavy load that he could not take on any of hers. But his willingness to help was in itself a help. And the chores with the children she could never have managed except for the great mother-comfort: she had carried them in her body; she had borne them in pain; but when she had them around her—all healthy and without blemishes, chirping like morning birds—in such moments she felt a joy so great that she only wanted to thank God for the lives he had created through her. She ought to be still more grateful since all their children had been born well developed and without deformities.

She said that she must try to get through each day in turn. But after a moment's silence her thoughts turned to other things.

"I wonder how they have it at home this evening?"

"They must be on their way to the early morn Christmas service," answered Karl Oskar. "The Swedish clocks are six hours ahead of us."

Kristina had wondered greatly about this difference in time. It showed that Sweden and America were two entirely different worlds, each with different time and hours. While it still was evening here, dawn broke at home. The two countries were given their days—their light and their dark—at different times.

During a few evenings before the holidays Karl Oskar had busied himself with his letter to Sweden. Tomorrow he would take enough time off to finish it. What more was there to put into the letter? He had told in detail about the iron stove he had given Kristina as a Christmas present, he had enumerated the cooking utensils that came with the stove, and he had written that the price in Swedish money was about one hundred twenty-five

391

riksdaler. Father and Mother would feel he had paid a senseless sum for it. A mason in Ljuder parish would build a whole fireplace for ten riksdaler. But he had added in his letter that he felt sure it would be many years before an iron stove would be put into a farm kitchen in the home parish.

The last letter from his father had come during the fall; it had been short, yet difficult for Karl Oskar to read. The lines wriggled up and down like a snake; the letters in many places crept into each other, making them impossible to decipher. His father, Nils Jakobsson, wrote that his hands trembled, but he need not have written this: every word in the letter indicated the condition of his hand.

His father had replied to the message about his son Robert's death in America: "It was Sad for us Old ones to learn of our youngest Son's demise in youthful years. It was difficult for Robert to be satisfied with anything in this World. You wrote your Brother traveled widely. Wither can Man Flee that Death shall not o'ertake him?"

The letter was barely ten sentences long, and Nils had written only these few words about Robert. It seemed as if the trembling hand had been unable to manage any of sorrow's outpourings. When Karl Oskar read the letter to Kristina, she told him what she had heard his father say that April morning when they left home and started their journey to America: "I must step out on the stoop and behold my sons' funeral cortege." The words touched Karl Oskar deeply. His father had felt his sons were dead while they still lived. Thus when the message of Robert's death reached him he had submitted to his loss in advance.

The old parents did not know the circumstances of their youngest son's death. Karl Oskar had only written that Robert had died suddenly and from an unknown sickness.

Surely, no age has a promise of the morrow. When Karl Oskar had gone to inspect the maple-studded knoll near the lake for a cemetery, who would that day have thought his younger brother, a young man of twenty-two, would be the first to be buried under the silver maples?

Since then a new summer had come and gone; the silver maples had twice shed their leaves over the first grave of the new cemetery. And Robert was no longer alone in the Swedish burying plot at Chisago Lake.

You raised your hand against your brother the last time you saw him in life! Such had been their last meeting: one brother had struck the other. Karl Oskar had struck his brother, flesh of his own flesh—what wouldn't he give to have that deed undone. He had regretted his action at once, and Robert's assurance of forgiveness was some comfort to him when they found the body a few days later. But his brother's forgiveness was not sufficient for Karl Oskar; he could not forgive himself for what he had done. Kristina had not again mentioned this burst of temper, except to say on the day of Robert's funeral that this was a warning, something to learn from, the thing that had taken place when two brothers met for the last time in life: people should always act toward others as if their meeting were the last.

The gold-seeker returning from California had been a short-time guest in their house. He had arrived on Monday evening, he had left on Saturday morning. During five nights he had slept under his brother's roof—then he had taken off again, but had not gone farther than the brook a few miles away in the forest. There his body was found.

If they only had known that Robert was deathly sick when he returned . . . But Karl Oskar guessed that Robert himself had not known this. And so the sick one had been forced to end his life like a wounded animal seeking a hiding place in a forest thicket. Such an end would have been spared him had they known about his mortal illness. But the wise man who knew everything aright—his name was Afterward.

Robert's own reticence was at fault, but concerning his illusory fortune, he had convinced them he had acted in good faith and had believed the useless bills were worth their face value. And it was good, at least, to know that he hadn't wanted to cheat them but had himself been cheated. Karl Oskar had later thrown the whole bundle of bills into the fire, and as he did so he had felt an intense hatred for the notes: these bills had been printed and circulated to destroy people. Because of these damned bills

393

he had abused his brother! He had wished the wildcat money had feelings; he wanted it to suffer in the flames as it burned to ashes.

What had happened on Arvid's and Robert's California journey would now never be clear to them. The goldseekers' own mouths were closed for eternity. Arvid's watch, which they had found in Robert's pocket after his death, had been sent to the boy's father, the cotter Petter of Krakesjö. Karl Oskar had enclosed a letter saying Arvid had perished in North America, in an unknown way, in an unknown place, and that no one knew his grave. The father received back the inheritance he gave his son at the emigration; the patrimony returned to its source in Sweden.

On Christmas Eve they always thought of their relatives, both living and dead. Kristina remembered that already a year and a half had passed since Robert was buried on the beautiful hill near the lakeside. But he was far from forgotten; Kristina often mentioned his name, and she did so tonight.

"My brother—I never understood him," said Karl Oskar. "I wonder if he ever would have found peace in this world had he lived."

"Robert was already finished with life," replied Kristina. "He was reconciled to his fate."

She had several times told her husband about the talk she had had with Robert under the sugar maples on the Friday when Karl Oscar was in Stillwater; it had been her last talk alone with Robert. Now she repeated it again to her husband, and he wondered how she could remember Robert's words in such detail after so long a time. She explained that his words had had a special meaning after he was dead, and she had thought of them so much because they were uttered at a time when he had only a few days left of life. She had been talking at the time to one who had already completed his life span.

"Do you suppose he knew he didn't have much time left?"

It was not the first time he had asked this question, and she replied now as before. Robert was sure to have felt

394

that his life would not be long. But his words could sometimes be interpreted one way, then again another way. He
had also said that he didn't suffer from any disease except
the old earache he had had since his farm service in
Sweden. And when *Hemlandet* had printed a notice seeking a young man to learn printing, he had asked her if he
oughtn't to reply to the advertisement. Then he had
sounded in good health, with no expectation of imminent
death.

Karl Oskar nodded: Robert had been a master of
secret, always talking in riddles.

"I suspect he had consumption," said Kristina.

"Probably so."

"But Robert wasn't afraid of death. He was unreachable, he said."

"Unreachable? There again he spoke in riddles!"

"It's no riddle—I understand what he meant."

"You do?" Karl Oskar raised his eyebrows and looked
at his wife in surprise. "What do you suppose he meant?"

This time Kristina was slow in answering, and when
she spoke her voice had changed; it was tense and re-
strained. In vain she tried to suppress a tremble.

"He was through his. We have ours ahead of us, we
do."

Karl Oskar's eyes still rested on her inquisitively; he
did not understand.

"I just said Robert was reconciled to his lot in life," she
resumed. "We are not."

What is this all about? he asked himself. A few words
by Robert, a year and a half ago, she had taken so seriously that time and again she came back to them and repeated them. What did it mean? He began to suspect that
she was keeping something from him.

"What is it we must be reconciled with, Kristina?"

Now she quickly turned her eyes away as if she were
found out. She seemed to feel she had said too much and
was now regretting it. She replied that she didn't want to
talk about it tonight. It was time to go to bed. It was awfully late, she was quite worn out this Christmas Eve.

How deeply Robert's statement concerning his fate had

affected her she did not divulge to Karl Oskar. It concerned her own life, the lot of the emigrant. And each new day posed this question to her: How would she manage *her* lot in life?

3.

Beginning on Christmas Eve 1856, Kristina had a good and faithful assistant in her kitchen. On the Prairie Queen she was able to prepare food for the large family in half the time it previously had taken her. After a few months with the new stove Kristina could not believe she had been able to manage her household without it for so many years. The new invention saved her so much work it became the most useful object in the house.

Kristina loved her stove as if it had been a living being. She looked after it carefully, dusted it every day, and polished away spots and grease and soot. The Prairie Queen always sat shining clean in its elevated place, an enduring, elegant decoration for their home. And it was the first object a caller's eyes would light upon when entering the kitchen. She always received her homage: what a beautiful stove!

The only name they used for it was the Queen: Have you fired the Queen? Has the Queen burned down? Did you empty the Queen's ashes? The potato pot is boiling over on the Queen! Get some wood for the Queen! And they were proud they had a stove they could speak of as royalty, even though it was their servant.

Karl Oskar said that of course an Englishman must have named it; an American would have called it Mrs. President of the Prairie. But he himself was a man who insisted the real truth be known in his house.

"You, Kristina, *you* are the queen in our kitchen!"

To this she laughed heartily, her hands and face sooty. Pastor Törner had once said something similar when she mended the seat of his pants; he had said that with thread and needle and nothing else she could turn herself into a queen and their house into a palace. But she had never before heard a man use such fair and poetic speech to his own wife.

Karl Oskar insisted. No one but she reigned in their house. While he had his domain outside, she was the absolute ruler inside their timbered walls; he made the decisions in stable and barns, in forest and field. And neither one ever interfered in the other's rule. In this way their power had always been divided, both in Sweden and America, and it suited him well, and he hoped it suited her too.

The fine stove was queen in name only—Kristina was a queen in reality. She stood faithfully at her stove, she kept her house in order, she managed to make new clothes for all of them and kept their clothing clean. She milked their cows, churned butter, made cheese, spun and spooled yarn, wove and sewed, and during the rush seasons she helped Karl Oskar in the fields with sowing, mowing, and harvesting.

But every day she fought her fatigue. Each day there came a moment when she was tempted to give in to it and suddenly drop what she had in hand, when in the midst of a chore she wanted to lie down on her back and do nothing except this: only rest quietly. How rest tempted her—she longed to taste the wonderful rest! She forced herself to go on; this must be done! It was her work, her duty and no one else's. No one in the whole world would do it for her. If she didn't do it, it remained undone. There was no recourse, no grace. It was necessary, and what was necessary a person always managed.

Kristina was not yet an old woman; as yet she had not earned the right to sit down and rest during the day. Only after another twenty or thirty years as the household ruler would she be permitted this. Then she could abdicate her queenly kitchen affairs and surrender to her great wish: rest.

The depressing evening fatigue, with worry in its wake, was nothing new to her; it was part of the lot of every working person. But in the past the fatigue had disappeared after a night's sleep and rest, and a new day had brought its gift, new appetite for work and new assurance. In this respect it was now different for Kristina; the morning no longer brought back her courage and confidence.

XXVII. The Year Fifty-seven

1.

During the open-river seasons in 1855 and 1856 the steamboats carried sixty thousand passengers up the Mississippi to settle in Minnesota Territory. Because of the great immigration, a steamboat costing $20,000 returned twice this sum to its owner within a year.

A story is told of one ship which paddled up the Mississippi with two hundred passengers who had already in New York bought, through a real estate broker, land for their settling in Minnesota. They asked the captain to put them ashore at a town called Rolling Stone, located on the river.

The captain pulled out his charts with all the landing places along the river. There was no place called Rolling Stone. He found a later map of Minnesota Territory on which all towns and places of settlement had been marked. It showed no town called Rolling Stone. He pursued his investigations further, he inquired from old river captains whose boats they met and who had traveled this route for years, he asked early settlers who came down to meet the boat at the piers: no one had heard of a town or place called Rolling Stone.

And the captain turned regretfully to his passengers: he could not put them ashore at a place which did not exist.

However, the two hundred passengers, having bought lots in the fair city of Rolling Stone on the beautiful shores of the Mississippi, showed the captain their maps and descriptions of the new town. The real estate man in New York had supplied them with these papers. The pictures showed tall houses in the town, churches, hotels, shops, and taverns. All the streets in Rolling Town were well marked. The captain could see the market place. The passengers pointed to the city hall. They had been given the name of the mayor, they knew the number of inhabitants. They showed pictures of the beautiful surroundings. Anyone seeing these pictures must be caught by an irresistible desire to own a home in this wonderful town. And each one of the two hundred passengers had paid three hundred dollars for a lot in Rolling Stone.

The captain replied: Rolling Stone was without doubt a beautifully situated and well laid out city. It was only that the city was missing. If Rolling Stone had ever existed in Minnesota Territory, it must now have rolled to some. other territory.

The captain regretted it sorely, but he was forced to put his passengers ashore where they could continue their search for the town in which they had bought lots for their new homes. They could themselves choose a place along the wild shore where they would leave his boat; it couldn't house them for the rest of their lives. And so they were put ashore. They built themselves brush huts along the bank; they dug themselves down near the river, they were seized with cholera, dysentery, fevers; the greatest number of the lot-owners in the non-existent town died; the survivors gradually scattered and were swallowed up by the great country. But none of them ever found his way to Rolling Stone. Because this town had never existed, except on paper.

This incident took place in Minnesota Territory in the year 1856.

In seven years seven hundred towns were surveyed and laid out in the Territory, and the number of inhabitants increased from six thousand to one hundred and fifty thousand. After the 1851 treaty with the Sioux the whole country west of the Mississippi lay open to settlers. In the capital, St. Paul, there were ten thousand people in 1856. The settlers called this town the Pig's Eye. Close by, at St. Anthony Falls, the new town of St. Anthony was growing up, later to be renamed Minneapolis.

Not all of the one hundred and fifty thousand inhabi-

399

tants had come to Minnesota to farm. In the tillers' wake came the speculators who would become rich without tilling the earth. To these, land was a commodity, to be bought one day, and sold for a profit the next. The speculators' only implement of labor was paper. They printed bank notes and swamped the country with wildcat money; wrote sales contracts and obtained deeds to land; drew maps and built towns on paper. Thus, a large part of the country came into the hands of people who never touched the handle of an ax or a plow.

Under the speculators' hands, land quickly rose in value. The price of a lot might double overnight. Claims were staked out with feverish haste: "Take what you can, and take the best!" The man who came yesterday obtained a better piece than the one who arrived today. The speculators sold their land and bought more, farther west, which in turn was sold when it was time to raise the price. Those who handled paper became rich on the backs of those who handled the heavy tools of labor. Money men grew rich, while the ax and plow-men remained poor.

Exploiters and exploited have existed in all countries in all times. This was a country and a time for one who saw the opportunities, for one who was handy with paper.

Minnesota Territory had been established in 1849, and its blossoming during the next seven years was amazing and without precedent. Everything rose in value, all kinds of objects—including the solid ground—were sold and bought, money was abundant, and new stacks of bills were issued as required. There was immeasurable prosperity in the country.

But what was the foundation for this great prosperity?

The foundation can be found in the story of Rolling Stone.

2.

After the prosperous years came the year 1857.

It began with a disturbing occurrence in the East: New York banks closed. This crash quickly spread westward;

the Chicago banks toppled. By the autumn of 1857 it had reached Minnesota—St. Paul and Stillwater. The banks in these towns closed. People who had been rich in the morning were destitute before the sun set. People with no property except money were penniless. The paper bills no longer had any value. There was no gold and no reliable bills, no acceptable currency. No one could buy without money, and no one could sell. Business came to a standstill.

New bills, warrants and scrips, were issued by the authorities; these would take the place of currency but were accepted with suspicion, and soon were worth only half the printed value. The people in the Territory had lost their confidence in bills.

What could money be used for when it was no longer trusted? What could money men do without money? The speculator's twilight was at hand; the great revolution in money matters swept them from the Territory; those who had hoped to get rich by buying and selling had nothing more to gain here. The great horde of speculators, brokers, and jobbers left Minnesota. In one year St. Paul's population dropped by four thousand.

The farmers had for a time been eclipsed by real estate speculators. With the upheaval of '57 a threatening danger to those settlers who had come to make their homes in the Territory was removed. It was the money men who now were pushed out, while the ax and plow men remained in possession of the earth.

And the future state of Minnesota was to be built by those who remained.

3.

During 1855 and 1856 the weather had been favorable for the crops, and the fields at Duvemala, in Chisago Township, had brought good harvests. Each fall, as soon as Karl Oskar had done his threshing, he noted down in the old almanac the number of bushels harvested. And in the fall of 1856, recording his sixth harvest in America, he looked back at the earlier figures. He saw that his crop this year was half again as great as last year, and his corn alone had brought him ten times as many bushels as his first year's crop. Now he was planting the Indian grain on a quarter of his fields; corn might give up to forty bushels per acre and wheat was almost as generous in the deep soil. These new grains were blessed in their growth. And from the figures in his almanac he could follow the improvement on his claim from year to year.

But the following year was to be a year of adversity. Already in spring a severe drought set in which lasted the better part of the summer. The crops withered before they headed. The corn was best able to withstand the persistent drought but the other crops were a failure. Then, about harvesttime, came the locust plague. There had been no grasshoppers in Minnesota since 1849, and the settlers were in hopes they would never return. One day, however, they appeared in immense, ravenous swarms. Like a rain of living black-gray drops they fell over the earth. These repulsive creatures showed an unbelievable hunger, unlike the hunger of other creatures. They consumed everything green in their path, and in their wake left only the black earth behind them.

While these ravages took place, the legislature in St. Paul offered a bounty of five cents a bushel for grasshoppers. Johan and Marta earned two dollars each for catching them. Governor Ramsey proclaimed a day of prayer in the churches against the locust plague, and the authorities also urged the observation of a fast day against the disaster. Few listened to this; the settlers felt they would probably have to starve enough during the winter after the hoppers had eaten their crops.

In Chisago Township the hopper plague was less severe than in other parts of the Territory, but Karl Oskar's crop was still only a quarter of the previous year's. Fortunately, having something left of the old harvest they could manage to get along through the winter.

Then in the late fall of this memorable year came the currency catastrophe.

Karl Oskar had already learned that money was nothing but paper. During 1857, many others were to share his bitter experience; they were stuck with bills the banks could not redeem. During the last years wildcat money from banks in Wisconsin and Nebraska had also been circulating in Minnesota. Few were the settlers who hadn't one time or another been fooled into exchanging a load of grain or a fatted hog for worthless bills. And thousands of gullible settlers who had trusted the sly wildcats found themselves destitute, their faith in paper money gone. This worthless paper ruler was dethroned. The frosty fall wind of '57 blew away the speculators who exchanged land plots as Gypsies exchanged horses.

How hadn't Karl Oskar's anger been stirred by these parasites! They were like the rats that fed off the grain and food in the cellar; however well they guarded and hid their food they could still see the teeth-marks or the dung of these pests. "If you won't eat where I bit, you must eat where I shit," the rat seemed to say. And it was not easy to separate its droppings from grain and flour bins; with cats, poison, and traps he had tried to rid himself of the vermin. And here were these other thieves the settlers must feed—the speculators, humanity's rats who grew fat on the crops others had harvested for them. It was more important to root them out than it was to destroy the pests in the granaries and cellars.

The great money upheaval—as long as it lasted—freed the country of them, but, like the rats, they left dung behind. The settlers had a difficult time when business came to a standstill; they couldn't sell anything, no one had the money to buy. For his grain and pork Karl Oskar would accept nothing but gold or good bills, and neither were available this fall. Thus he was without cash for the purchases he wanted to make. And when he occasionally could sell anything for sound cash, the price offered was pitifully low. Pork was down to two cents a pound; after fattening a hog for half a year until it finally weighed two hundred pounds he received four dollars for his labor. He might as well lie down on his earth and kick himself.

But Karl Oskar grew neither poorer nor richer during 1857. What did it concern him that the banks tumbled? He didn't have a penny in them. His claim was his possession, and the fields lay where they had always been.

For months on end they didn't have a coin in the house, but they had a roof over their heads, heat from the stove, bread, milk, butter, eggs, pork to eat. What did it concern them that money had disappeared? They had a home and food.

Karl Oskar had come as a squatter to his claim, one of the wooden-shoe people from Sweden. Other settlers in the Territory, with more elegant shoes, had often looked down on and pitied the poor squatter who must make his own shoes from the wood of the forest. But the man in the wooden shoes sat safe and comfortable on his claim after seven years, while thousands of other settlers became destitute in the great depression of 1857.

Each fall since Karl Oskar had got his own team, he had broken at least five new acres of the vast meadow below his house. By now he could look out on thirty acres. Next spring he would seed four times as much land as he had owned in Korpamoen, and this land was three times as fertile as his old farm. In favorable years he now harvested larger crops than any farmer in Ljuder parish.

He liked to sit at the window and look out at his fields; this was the land he had changed. When he came the whole meadow had been covered with weeds and wild grass. Now it produced rye, wheat, oats, corn, potatoes, turnips. The wild grass had fed elk, deer, and rabbits; now the field yielded so much there was enough for them as well as for other people. And it was *his* hands that had held the plow handles when this fertile earth was wrested from the wilderness. The cultivation was his work and no one else's, it was the labor of his own hands.

If he should call his clearing his own created work, Kristina would undoubtedly say that he boasted and call him arrogant. A creator, to her, was only one who could make something out of nothing, and only one could do that, the Omnipotent himself: he had created the fertile field at Lake Ki-Chi-Saga on the third day of the creation, when he bade all water gather into one place under the heavens so that dry land appeared. Yet he, Karl Oskar Nilsson, sought his sustenance from the earth and had changed it so that it would give bread to people even after him. Couldn't he at least consider himself a handyman to the creator?

Kristina was intimate with the Almighty and always trusted him. But Karl Oskar could not be like her in this trusting. Ever since the years of adversity at home in Korpamoen he had been suspicious of God's help. Whatever a person did, he couldn't be absolutely sure of God's aid in his enterprise. He himself had been forced to trust himself and his own strength. Our Lord let the crops grow, but how many grains would he have harvested if he hadn't cleared the land, plowed and sown? Who would have tilled the field for him if he hadn't done it himself for himself? Could it be sinful arrogance in him to look out over his fields and feel: this is the creation of my own hands!

And he would continue his work; he would clear wider fields, raise more cattle, cut down more trees in the forest, and build bigger houses. He would from day to day improve his claim until he was no longer able to do so. Soon enough his arms would grow old and tired.

To struggle on, each day in turn, to feel and use the strength he had—that was a settler's lot and purpose in life.

XXVIII. The Letter from Sweden

Akerby at Ljuder parish, August 16
Anno 1857

Beloved Brother Karl Oskar Nilsson:

The Lord's Peace and Blessing upon you.

I am about to write you a message of Sorrow. Tears of bereavement are falling as I pen these lines. Our Father, Nils Jakobsson, parted this life the 4th inst. and He was brought to the earth in the Parish Churchyard the 11th inst. His life's span amounted to Sixty-two years and a few months. He suffered a long deathbed but did not Complain. Our new pastor gave him the Sacrament three days before he died, he managed to put himself in order for the pastor and combed his Hair himself.

It was Our Father's wish to pass on and have Peace. He had some fever attacks and dizziness toward the last and his mind wandered. The last Night he mentioned you and Robert in North America, he heard your wagon drive out of the yard on your journey to America and he rose from his pillow and said Now they are leaving. He said few words in life after that.

We must all one day pale in Death. Our strength will not suffice against Him. But there is much to do when He is a guest in the house. We are settling the estate and I ask you to send me your power of Attorney, then we need not have an auction after our Father. Send also an attest that our Brother Robert is dead and then we won't need a Power of Attorney from Him.

We are in good health in our family except that I have a boil on a finger of my right hand. I have a kind husband, we have now 2 sons and 1 daughter. I have forgotten how many children you have, Write and tell us. I guess you've forgotten the people hereabouts—Dean Brusander is dead, he had a stroke in the Sacristy Whitsuntide morning, he asked about you a few years ago when he Baptized our oldest boy.

Mother greets you as she can't write to you herself. Our Mother is getting old and worn-out—when our strength is gone all joy is over.

It is not easy to write down my thoughts on paper, I am poor in composition, excuse my poor spelling. Don't forget us in your new Homeland.

God Bless you, Brother, and hope your success continues.

> Written down by your devoted Sister
> Lydia Karlsson

XXIX. The Letter to Sweden

New Duvemala at Taylors Falls Post ofis
North America, october 3 Anno 1857

Beloved Sister Lydia Karlsson,

Your letter received, I could not help but shed a few tears as I held it in my hand and read that our Father had passed through the Valley of Death. I mourn him here, far from His bier.

I had hoped to see Him once More, I had a good Father but was not always an obedient Son at Home. I feel though that Father forgave me my emigration, I did the best for my Own, our Father couldn't think anything else.

Now my Father is in that Land where I no longer can reach Him. Peace over his Grave and Remains. Yes, Death mowes his sharp scythe and makes no exception among us. When He comes we must go with him, whether we want to or not. I am however, glad that Father had one of his children with him as a comfort on His Deathbed.

My kind parents looked well after me when I grew up but out here in my new land I have been of little Help or comfort to them.

I enclose a paper which assures you that you my beloved Sister Lydia Karlsson shall have my inheritance after my demised Father Nils Jakobsson. You shall have my share for looking after Our Mother as long as She is in Time. I believe it cannot be a large sum of money.

We have lately had some trouble with money matters in America but it is getting better. Many people have moved in from Sweden this last Summer and they are still coming daily. Even from Ljuder Parish people have come to this Valley. I see that the Dean is Gone, how did he like it that his parishioners followed me to North America? But he couldn't blame me, I like the land here but have never boasted in order to lure people here from Sweden. I urge no man to emigrate; each one must do so at his own risk.

The number of our children is 6 up to date, if I haven't written this before. Our youngest is a strapping son, we call him Frank, it is an American name. He runs and plays on the floor, He was one year last February, the little American let go his hold and walked by himself 14 Days before he was a full year. Our Children have grown fast in their new Homeland it's a Joy for us to see.

I enclose my dear Greeting to our Mother. I know you take good care of her. You are my beloved Sister and we must write each other more often. Before each Day reaches its end I have some thought here in America for my old Home,

Your Devoted Brother

Karl Oskar Nilsson

XXX. Karl Oskar's Followers

1.

They had seeded and planted and harvested and threshed this year as all other years, but the weather had been unfavorable and contrary at all seasons. In the fall came a flood; it began as a sudden shower, but the shower lasted a week, two weeks. The rain did not fall in drops, it streamed down in sheets. Days on end it hung outside the window like a striped curtain. No settler had ever seen such a persistent rain in Minnesota. The autumn sowing was delayed because of the wet weather, and the rye did not begin to sprout until the winter frost had gone into the ground.

On one of these long days, when the rain prevented all outside work, the Lutheran pastor came to call. A memorable rainy night four years earlier Pastor Erland Törner had come to the settlement at Duvemala for the first time. This rainy day he came on a last visit—he had come to say goodbye.

There had long been rumors that he wanted to leave the Swedish congregation in the St. Croix Valley, and now they were confirmed by his own words: he had accepted the call as pastor to the new church in Rockford, a new town down in Illinois, where there was a sizable Swedish colony. He was going to get married and this had influenced his decision to leave. He was engaged to a Swedish girl in Rockford and she wanted to remain in her hometown after her marriage.

Before the pastor arrived, Kristina had felt her nose itch and she had sneezed three times in succession, a sure sign that important callers would arrive. But the minister's visit today was of little joy to her, as he had come to say farewell to them.

He was no longer the pale, spindly young man who had warmed himself before the fire in their old log house, dressed like a scarecrow in Karl Oskar's roomy clothes. Since then he had put on weight and his body was firmer; his face was weatherbeaten and his looks rugged. The hard life of traveling about in the wilderness had left its mark on him so that now the young pastor could be taken for a settler. And his life was not unlike that of his fellow countrymen.

During the first two years they had gathered for services in the schoolhouse; only last year had the new church been ready for use. Since then Kristina had failed to attend services only four or five times: if a child lay sick, or if she herself lay in childbed. Karl Oskar and she had also attended the Sacrament each time the Holy Supper was given. Pastor Törner's sermons had been a comfort to her soul; they had quieted her anxiety and helped her overcome her worries about eternal damnation. This minister did not enter the pulpit like a stern judge—he was a mild gospel preacher, on equal footing with the sinners. He did not wish to judge anyone, he only wanted to comfort all. He was the only minister she could think of in their pulpit; he was *The Minister*.

And now he was to move away from them. She couldn't pray God to leave him for her sake. She mustn't be ungrateful, but rather, grateful. She only wished she could give him something in return for all the comfort he had brought her.

Yesterday Karl Oskar had shot a wild goose with black neck and brown wings; she had plucked the white-breasted bird, drawn it, and prepared it for the pot. The goose was as fat as a grouse and had so much flesh there would be sufficient for all of them. She had planned to save the delicate bird for their Sunday dinner but it was as if God had designed that she must roast the goose today and invite Pastor Törner, since it would be her last opportunity.

She set the table in the large room, and invited her guest to sit down on the new sofa they had recently bought. Karl Oskar and she sat on either side of him. The children were not allowed to sit at table today, they would eat afterward in the kitchen.

"My first night in the St. Croix Valley I slept in this home," said Pastor Törner. "In this home I preached my first sermon in this valley, and here I gave the Lord's Holy Supper for the first time. Memories make your home dear to me, my friends!"

He spoke his native tongue better than any other Swede she had met in America, thought Kristina. It was balm just to listen to his voice. Most of the immigrants had begun to mix up the two languages dreadfully so that she could hardly understand them. Even Karl Oskar's language had changed; she noticed the mixture sooner than others because she herself never used English.

The children peeked in through the kitchen door while Karl Oskar and Kristina sat eating with the minister. To the three oldest he had been their teacher and they had great respect for him; they were unusually silent and well behaved as long as this caller was in the house.

In the beginning Pastor Törner had acted as teacher for

410

the Swedish children as well as minister for the congregation, but after great effort the parish had last year managed to get a teacher from Sweden, a Mr. Johnson—he was quite particular that they call him Mister. He had brought good recommendations from previous positions in the new country, but childless parents had not been anxious to share the burden of the salary for the new teacher—which would indeed have been unjust—and thus the parents of the schoolchildren alone paid him. The teacher was remunerated according to the number of children he taught, receiving one dollar a month for each child. A room had been prepared for him in the school building and he was also given free firewood. The parish contributed ten bushels of rye flour a year, and thus he had his bread free.

Besides instruction in the Christian Lutheran religion, Swedish, and English, the settlers' children were taught writing, arithmetic, history, and geography, and Mr. Johnson had proved to be a competent teacher; he had graduated from high institutions in Sweden. But after he had been here for some time it was discovered that he drank. According to the children he sometimes told funny stories to them during school hours instead of going on with the lesson. Once he had danced in the school, jumped about, and sung for the children, and it had definitely not been psalms he had sung, either. He had apparently been drunk. Some parents had become greatly disturbed and insisted the parish must get rid of Mr. Johnson. Other parents would rather have a drunkard than no teacher at all. At Karl Oskar's suggestion the parish council had deferred the question. Now he wished to ask Pastor Törner's opinion.

"Should we keep the schoolmaster?"

Mr. Johnson did drink in excess, said the pastor, but there was no evidence that his lamentable weakness had made him neglect his duties. During this first year he had taught the children well. They would probably not be able to find a teacher of Johnson's ability to replace him. The salary was not high enough to attract a graduate teacher from Sweden. As long as the teacher's drinking did not

411

hurt the children, Pastor Törner thought they ought to keep him on.

The Swedish teacher was no longer a young man, and the pastor had spoken seriously to him and made him promise not to take any whiskey until after school hours. Then he would have a whole night to sober up before his next day of teaching. He hoped Mr. Johnson would keep his promise.

For his three children of school age—Johan, Marta, and Harald—Karl Oskar paid the teacher three dollars a month. Next spring when Dan—their first little American—began school, Karl Oskar would have to pay four dollars a month.

He said that Mr. Johnson had a good head, but it was too bad he spent his salary for drinks, which undermined and ruined a person, body and soul. Among the settlers they had an example to warn them: Anders Mansson of Taylors Falls. He had several times this last summer come drunk to church.

Yet Pastor Törner felt that less drinking took place among the Chisago settlers than in other new settlements. And concerning morality, during his time among them only two illegitimate children had been born, both of whom had been begotten in other Swedish settlements.

Pastor Törner praised the delicious goose several times, and Kristina guessed that God himself must have directed the bird in front of Karl Oskar's gun yesterday to give her this opportunity to treat their pastor to a farewell dinner.

After the meal, coffee was served, and Pastor Törner distributed gifts to each one of the six children. Happiest of all was Harald, who received a Swedish book—*First Reader for Beginners*—which the pastor had sent for from the old country. The pastor had instructed Harald for a few months and he remembered what a good head the boy had.

"He reads Swedish like a minister!" said the mother proudly. "As soon as he has read a piece once he can repeat it by heart!"

The father added that they had sent for the *Little Catechism* from *Hemlandet* and the boy had learned it by

412

heart in a few evenings. And when he found anything printed in English he read it as well as an American.

Pastor Törner looked from Harald to Karl Oskar.

"Of all your children, this one particularly takes after his father."

"You mean he has my nose!" smiled the settler.

"His nose is assuredly the most apparent likeness!"

Harald was the only one among the children who had inherited the Nilsa-nose, this enormous rutabaga that disfigured Karl Oskar's face. But there was a belief in the family that its bearer would have luck in life. When the children teased Harald because of his nose, Karl Oskar would comfort him by saying: "Remember that your father's nose was the best luck he ever had!"

And now the father said to the pastor that he hoped Harald would propagate this rutabaga in his own children, and to their children and children's children, so that the big nose, a hundred years from now, might decorate a great many American faces as a living memorial to the Nilsa family. In that way, perhaps, he would set his mark on America.

2.

The new-timbered Swedish church had been built in the spacious oak grove on the peninsula opposite Nordberg's Island, a mile and a half from Karl Oskar's place. From the center of the roof a steeple had been raised whose ever-narrowing timbers rose upward fully thirty feet toward the sky. The builders had gone to a great deal of trouble with this spire, the timbers carefully hewn and planed, but now, seen from the ground, it looked as if it were made of ordinary fence posts. Thirty feet seemed to diminish into a puny distance up there; it was but a snail's pace on the road to the firmament vaulting so high above their new church. From the ground, thirty feet seemed like a pitiful attempt at a steeple. But none of the builders had raised a church before, none had put up a spire over a Lord's house. And God must realize that these were awkward builders who had raised his church at the old Indian lake, and therefore God must be forbearing. But in any case this was the first Lutheran church in the St. Croix Valley, and even if the steeple rose only thirty feet into the air it pointed the way to the Lord's heaven.

Even though services were being conducted in the new church it was far from finished inside. There were only a few pews and most of the participants must stand during the sermons; church bell and organ were missing, for the parish was short of cash. Concerning the color of the exterior paint for the building, a long-drawn-out argument had arisen among the parishioners.

Three different groups each wanted a different color for the new Swedish church. The first group wanted the church washed red to remind them of Christ's blood and wounds which had redeemed Man from eternal condemnation and effected atonement with God. The second group wanted to see the temple walls green as grass, the color of sweet hope, leading their thoughts to the eternal joy of heaven, helping them to find comfort in the Father. Finally, the third group wanted to paint the church white, the color of purity, innocence, and angels' wings. This would always remind them of Christ's saying: Even though your sins be blood-red they shall be washed as white as snow.

For a year and a half the arguments had gone on among the reds, greens, and whites. Many stormy meetings were held, long speeches and heated arguments were heard. Pastor Törner regretted this disunity but he himself took no definite stand. He tried to calm the stirred-up emotions by pointing out that their salvation in no way was dependent on the color of their church. In the end the third group gained a majority, mainly because the parish business manager, Petrus Olausson, was the leader of that group. Consequently the new church had been painted white.

Later, a rumor had it that Olausson, long before the strife began, had happened to buy a large quantity of white paint.

"The settlers fight about any little thing," exclaimed Kristina. "The Swedes are hopeless that way!"

"We must follow the American order of things," said Karl Oskar. He approved of that order, however cumbersome and time-consuming it might be to make many heads agree. At least here they ran their own church without interference from high lords. What did the congregation have to say when churches were built in Sweden? The bishop decided almost everything. And Ljuder parish was run by three or four mighty men. Here three or four hundred people took part and made decisions about their parish and their church. It might take more time, but individuals should have the right to put their fingers in their own pies.

As a member of the parish council, Karl Oskar had suggested the erection of a lightning rod as a protection for the new church; since it was built of wood it could easily burn should lightning strike it. Long ago in Sweden, his meadow barn, filled with hay, had been destroyed by lightning fire; he had never forgotten it. In this country lightning seemed to be more frequent and of greater intensity than in Sweden, and he had put up lightning rods on both his main house and barn. It would be very simple to have a similar protective rod for the church. A copper wire would follow the side of the steeple down and into the ground; if lightning should strike, it would run along that wire and disappear into the earth.

Petrus Olausson was immediately against Karl Oskar. To put up a lightning rod on the church would be to show disrespect and suspicion toward God. A person who failed to believe that the Lord would be capable of averting lightning from his temple and would rather trust a copper wire, such a person could not be a faithful Christian. A true Lutheran must trust God, not a copper wire. If they put up a lightning rod they would commit the grave sin of weak faith. They should trust in the Almighty himself to protect the church they had built for him.

Karl Oskar replied: Was a person then not to use the protective remedies invented? That meant one couldn't use warm clothing against the cold. Nor could a person swim to shore if he happened to fall into the lake. It meant they could not harvest their crops in the fall but must starve during the winter. If this were the Lutheran religion, then he was no true Lutheran.

"Yes, we know," agreed Olausson with sad finality. "You and your wife harbor sectarians and evil preachers in your house. The soul fiend has put it into your head to use the lightning rod in an attempt to make us give up the true religion. When the devil wants to snare a person, a thin copper wire is quite sufficient."

Olausson thus having raised a doubt in the mind of other council members concerning Karl Oskar's religious beliefs, one by one they refused to vote for his motion. Only Jonas Petter stood by him. Because Karl Oskar and Kristina still opened their door to the wife of the Baptist minister in Stillwater, no lightning rod was erected for the new church. The parish left it to the Lord to protect his temple against lightning.

There was still much disorder and confusion in the Swedish Lutheran parish in Chisago Township. There were members without any respect for the church's holiness, who acted within its walls as though it were a worldly house. Who could rebuke the impudent and shameless since no one had a right to give orders? The pastor himself was hired by the parish as its servant. At last it was agreed that vulgar behavior in the church would be punished with fines. To avoid hurting anyone's feelings it was called a tax, a nuisance tax. If anyone brought dogs into the church during the service he must pay a dollar for each animal. A gun was allowed if put in the corner, but dogs were not suffered since they disturbed the service by growls and barking. If one entered the temple with dirty boots and made marks on the floor he paid fifty cents for this offense. But most expensive of all was to come drunk to the service: this was taxed at two dollars. It was difficult to decide when someone was to be considered drunk; if one was quiet and orderly he need not pay this so-called nuisance tax, however much whiskey he had consumed. But if anyone raised his voice in talk or laughter, or interrupted the minister at the altar or in the pulpit, it was considered a two-dollar sin.

During the first year the nuisance tax was in effect, it brought the parish forty-five dollars. This money was kept in a special savings box; in time it would be used for the purchase of a church bell. Thus evil was turned into good: the more disorder in the church, the sooner church bells would peal for the Swedish settlers at Chisago Lake.

3.

The colony grew with each year's immigration. The newcomers were mostly relatives and friends of earlier arrivals, lured here by the description of the fertile country. They would arrive during the spring and summer and their log cabins would be built by fall. The immigrants came from various countries, but the majority were Swedes. In Chisago Township there were now five hundred Swedes, and fifteen hundred in the whole valley: a good-sized parish had moved from Sweden to the St. Croix Valley.

The settlements sprang up ever closer to the new church. On the peninsula opposite Nordberg's Island, that had been named for the first landseeker at this lake, a new town site had been surveyed and named Center City. It was a rather boastful name but the settlers felt the town would in time live up to it. The site was at the center of the settlement and was planned to become the county seat of Chisago County.

A group of houses rose quickly in Center City. A few enterprising Swedes built a sawmill and a flour mill, both run by steam. The settlers need no longer drive long and difficult roads to have their timber sawed or their grain milled. An Irishman opened a lodging house where travelers could sleep and obtain food; a German wagon-maker built a shop with a lathe and other machinery. An American opened a tailor shop, a Norwegian blacksmith arrived with his tools. The Chisago people could now obtain clothing and implements near home.

One day the Nilssons heard that a young Swede had opened a general store in Center City.

The first time Karl Oskar went into the store he thought today he wouldn't have to use English to make his purchases. The store was so recently built and opened that piles of shavings still lay in the corners. Counter and shelves had not yet been painted, and there was a smell of pitch from newly sawed pine boards. From the ceiling hung a number of implements, harnesses, lanterns, coils of rope, and other objects, but most of the shelves were still bare.

Behind the counter stood a young man with a firm, narrow face and open, light-blue eyes. His blond hair was cut short and neatly combed. No one need ask in what country the new storekeeper had been born: his boots of thick, greased Småland leather alone gave Karl Oskar the information.

He greeted the man in his native tongue and was about to tell him who he was when the young man behind the counter said, "You must be Karl Oskar from Korpamoen?"

If the store ceiling had fallen on his head, Karl Oskar could not have been more surprised. The new storekeeper not only used the Ljuder dialect, he also spoke to Karl Oskar as if his name had been in daily use at home.

"Why—yes! But how in all the world . . .?"

"I'm Klas Albert Persson from Ljuder. My father was Churchwarden Per Persson of Akerby."

"You must be his youngest boy?"

"I am."

"Well!"

Karl Oskar stared in disbelief at the younger man who was claiming that they were from the same parish in Sweden. And indeed, his ears testified to the fact that the young man spoke the Ljuder dialect.

"You certainly surprised me. I hadn't expected one from home to be the new store owner."

"I came to America three years ago," said Klas Albert. "I've worked recently in a store in St. Paul."

Klas Albert—yes, Karl Oskar remembered the boy, who had been of confirmation age when he himself emigrated; now he looked to be in his early twenties. He remembered him as a boy in Sweden; now he saw him as a grown man in America. In Klas Albert's change he

418

could measure the time he himself had been out here: enough for a boy to grow into manhood.

Many people were said to have come to America from Ljuder but he had not met any of them. And now the first store in the new town of Center City in Chisago County was run by a son of churchwarden Per Persson of Akerby. In some way it seemed the old and the new country had come closer through this meeting.

This countryman he must greet warmly. He offered his hand. "Welcome to us, Klas Albert."

"Thank you, Karl Oskar."

Karl Oskar had learned through letters from home that the churchwarden had been killed when his horses bolted, the summer after their emigration. The son now told him that his oldest brother had taken over the homestead. They were seven brothers and sisters, and the six younger ones must find their way in life the best they could. Since there was nothing to do at home, he had come to America to find his future. More and more people at home did likewise.

But the farmer from Korpamoen had never imagined that a son of the rich churchwarden would ever emigrate.

"I recognized you the moment you came in," said Klas Albert proudly.

"Hm. My nose, I guess?"

And Karl Oskar smiled broadly. The churchwarden's boys must often have seen his big nose when he drove by on his way to church or to the mill.

Klas Albert's look indicated that this was so. "But you've changed a lot since I last saw you."

"Grown older, of course. We age faster in America than in Sweden."

"Something in your face is different," explained the younger immigrant. "Your skin looks like American people's, they get so sunburned it stays with them the year round."

"Well. How did you happen to come to Chisago?"

"I heard they had planned a town here, and I thought, as soon as they lay out a town they'll need a store."

Klas Albert had wanted to be a storekeeper ever since he was a small boy. But there was no opportunity in

Sweden. All the old aldermen sat there and decided who was to be admitted to their group; they wouldn't let in an outsider with no experience. Anyone wanting to start something new ran into red tape and great lords to stop him at every corner. So he had felt North America was the place to start a business unhindered. It was of course bad luck for him that he had had to start in this depression while all these money troubles still were unsettled. Wasn't this a strange country, where anyone who wanted could start a bank and print his own bills? It was confusing, and certainly was apt to make people lose confidence in paper money. In Sweden only the government had the legal right to depress the value of money.

But this town had a good location; as more people came business would soon improve. He had heard that a German had arrived who would open a second store in Center City. "But I'm sure I'll get along," concluded Klas Albert with youthful confidence.

And Karl Oskar encouraged the new businessman.

"There're lots of Swedes around here; you'll get along, Klas Albert."

He talked so long with the Akerby churchwarden's son that he almost forgot he had come to do some shopping. Before he left he invited Klas Albert to his house next Sunday. It would be hard for Kristina to wait to meet him.

When he came home he told her about the new storekeeper in Center City who was no one else but the youngest son of the Akerby churchwarden. And the following Sunday Klas Albert arrived and was greeted as the most welcome guest they had ever received. Kristina had eagerly been awaiting the visitor and she began at once to question him about the home parish. She asked about people she remembered and wanted to hear of; hour after hour she questioned him about their home village. As it happened Klas Albert had left Sweden three years earlier so his news was not entirely fresh, but his brothers and sisters had written him about what had happened after he left; North America was spoken of in every house, and more and more people thought of emigrating.

Kristina learned a great deal she hadn't known, and it

was especially pleasing to her to see the face of a person who had been in the home places later than she.

Klas Albert was impressed with the fine house they had built to live in, so Karl Oskar took him out on an inspection of their other buildings and the fields; his new home could stand inspection and he wanted to show his guest from Sweden how things were with him in North America.

It was the nicest time of year, early summer; the verdant fields were fresh with the new crops. Karl Oskar didn't want to boast of his great fields, but Klas Albert guessed he must have over twenty-five acres—which was a good guess. The fat oxen and the cows with their swollen udders wallowed in the meadow, healthy hogs filled the pen, thick-wooled sheep bleated contentedly. Stables, barns, threshing and wagon sheds were examined, and American tools and implements—so work-saving for a settler—were inspected in detail. Then Karl Oskar showed Klas Albert the huge sugar maples. Every year Karl Oskar drilled holes in the trunks to release the sap, which gave them all the sugar and syrup they needed. He asked the guest to taste the product; didn't those blessed trees give them good sweetening?

The more Klas Albert saw the more his respect grew for the farmer from Korpamoen who was responsible for this thriving farm. Time and again he asked: *When* had Karl Oskar done all this? *How* had he had time? The reply was short. He had not wasted a single working day during his years on the claim, and that was the way it had happened.

Kristina showed the young man the Astrakhan apple tree, grown from a seed that had been sent from her Swedish home. The tree had shot up so fast it was now a head taller than she herself. Every fall she dug around her tree and covered the roots with an extra foot of soil to protect them against the cold. Her tree was in its early youth; as yet it had had no blossoms.

When the inspection had been completed and they sat down to the dinner table, Klas Albert said, "Not one of the big farmers at home in Ljuder is as well off as you, Karl Oskar and Kristina!"

He knew Karl Oskar had been the first farmer in the home parish to sell his farm and emigrate to North America. Now he wanted to say how much he looked up to him and respected him for having taken this initiative. He always admired the first ones, those who dared something new, those who were courageous enough to move. Karl Oskar had indeed been bold in taking off for such a distant country.

Karl Oskar looked at the floor, embarrassed at all this praise. "When I started to talk emigration, the whole parish felt insulted. It was as if I had done something evil. People thought I should be punished for my arrogance."

"Now you can laugh at those hecklers!" insisted Klas Albert.

"They poked fun at me and said my nose would be still longer when I came to America."

"Well, is it?"

Karl Oskar laughed. "I guess it's about the same, within a fraction of an inch!"

"That I must write home about!" said the young storekeeper.

They had so much to talk about that their guest remained until late in the evening. When he finally left, Karl Oskar said to Kristina with pride that now Klas Albert would write home and tell them he had met the Korpamoen farmer in Minnesota. He would tell them about the Nilssons' situation after starting a second time in life. And what he wrote would be spread over the whole parish, and people would talk about them and about their fine home, New Duvemala, on the beautiful lake. And what now would those people think who once had talked so cruelly about him because he left his old home. They had predicted that his arrogance and pride would be punished with an evil end. His deriders would of course be hoping to hear that he and his family lived in poverty and misery in the new country. Instead, they would hear from the son of the churchwarden himself that Karl Oskar now had twenty-five acres of the most fertile land in America and harvested better crops than any farmer in the whole of Ljuder parish!

"There'll be a great sickness in Ljuder for some time,"

predicted Karl Oskar. "People will be sick with jealousy!"

Kristina had noticed his eagerness to show Klas Albert around. "I think you boasted a little too much," she said.

"To point out the truth is not to boast!"

Now many more would follow the example of the one they had belittled and derided. His old neighbors had already started to come here; Ljuder parish was being transplanted to this valley. And he felt sure the settlers would in time outshine the home parish. The looked-down-upon emigrants—that pack of Gypsies—would win out over their slanderers. And he began to realize he had shown his countrymen the road to a new and greater homeland.

4.

About the same time that Karl Oskar from Korpamoen and Klas Albert, the churchwarden's son, met in America, the successor of Dean Brusander sat in his office in Ljuder parsonage every day and handed out emigration papers which his parishioners came to ask for. On the top line of each page in the parish register he wrote after the emigrant's name: *Moved to N. America.* But those words he only wrote once on each page; below, on the following lines, he wrote *Ditto.* It was sufficient. From the first line to the last there were many dittos. And every line of every page of the large parish register was filled with the names of Karl Oskar Nilsson's followers.

XXXI. A Blessed Woman's Prayer

1.

Ulrika had given Kristina a mirror which she had hung on the long wall above the sofa in the living room. In that position the mirror could be seen from any place in the room and was convenient to look into. A red rose had been painted on the glass in each one of the four corners, and when Kristina sat on the sofa and turned her head she was confronted by her own image.

As a girl Kristina had often been told that she was beautiful. And perhaps it had been the truth since so many had said it. But where now was the girl who so many times had blushed at the words, "You are beautiful!" Where now were her full cheeks with the soft little dimples of laughter? What had become of her nicely rounded chin? Where was her blossom-tinted color? Where the young girl's quick and clear glance? What had become of the lips once full as wild strawberries?

The flower of her youth had passed and was gone. The mirror showed her a face already marked by age. It was always there, reflecting back at her; she could not escape the face of a woman getting on in years.

Every day she met this depressing sight. Was this she? She herself? These gaunt, wrinkled cheeks, this pale-gray color, this sharply etched chin, these tired, fading eyes without a glint, this caved-in mouth with teeth missing— this was she herself, what was left of the once beautiful girl Kristina of Duvemala! And the face seemed to her doubly old and doubly pale as it looked back at her between the four red, cheerful roses in the corners of the mirror; they should instead have served as a frame for a youthful, blossoming girl's face.

424

Kristina no longer wished to acknowledge her face. She would be just as pleased if she never saw it again.

"How silly of me to put up the mirror," she said to Karl Oskar. "I would know anyway that I look worse each day."

"We all must age," said Karl Oskar comfortingly. "But the years are harder on us emigrants; we age faster than others."

The years had set their mark on him too; he no longer moved about with such quick steps and easy gait as before, and at times he complained of the old ache in his left leg which made him limp occasionally. But she had fared worse than he; the neighboring wives had guessed she must be older than her husband, even though she was two years younger. The burden of childbearing fell on the woman; that made the difference.

Frank, the youngest in her flock, had come as a birthday present: he had been born on her thirty-first birthday, two years ago. She had barely been twenty when she had her first child, her daughter Anna, who had died at an early age in Sweden. In the eleven years between her first and her youngest, she had endured seven childbeds and borne eight children. During that time she had also gone through their emigration to a new continent, the building of a new home. All the things that had happened to her were bound to leave their mark on her.

"I want to put away the mirror," she said, "somewhere in a dark corner."

"But it's a nice decoration," said Karl Oskar. "And when Ulrika comes here she'll need it to look at herself."

"She doesn't age," said Kristina, with a trace of jealousy of her best friend.

"No, that is remarkable."

"Her color is like fresh cream even though she has had six children."

"Six?" he wondered. "I thought it was more. But those bastards she had at home I guess she didn't count very carefully."

Kristina tried to tell herself that it was childish to regret that she no longer looked like a young girl. And deep in her heart she knew that her vexation was not primarily directed against her changed face; she regretted her youth which had run away from her during her isolation in a wild and foreign country. Her youth was suddenly gone before she had had time to enjoy it. And she blamed the emigration which had devoured her joyous years. As a young girl—with great expectations for the future—she had not counted on a change of home and homeland.

It seemed to Kristina the great majority of people enjoyed much good and experienced much happiness in life which she had been denied. Most of them had participated in wonderful experiences that she would never have. She had been denied so much and she felt it was the emigration that had robbed her of this. Thus she had never been able to adjust herself to her lot as settler.

But this she had never told Karl Oskar. Nor had she told him that if, at the age of nineteen, she could have seen herself in labor seven times before she was thirty-one, she would probably have said no to his proposal and remained a spinster.

Ulrika had given her a real scare by saying that she could go on and bear children until she was forty-six: half of a woman's fertile years still lay ahead of her. She could expect to give life to as many more children as she already had.

She had said at the time that she couldn't survive that many births, of that she was sure. Each time she was more worn-out, more tired. She still felt the results of the last birth in her body.

Frank was now two years old, and as yet there had been no signs of a new life beginning. It was her strongest wish that he might remain the youngest. Kristina feared she could not survive one more childbed.

2.

Scarcely had their church been built when they lost their minister. Before Pastor Törner left he promised to find a replacement for the Swedish parish in St. Croix among the Lutheran synod of Chicago. But there was a dearth of Swedish ministers in America; few churchmen wanted to exchange their comfortable lives in Sweden for the dangers and privations of Minnesota. And there were those ministers who felt that these ungrateful people who had left their homeland were lost to God anyway and condemned to eternal damnation.

Meanwhile the emigrants at Chisago Lake must get along with visiting pastors from other parishes in the Northwest, and even though these came at frequent intervals there were many Sundays without a serivce.

One evening Karl Oskar came home from a parish meeting with sad news about their schoolmaster. Pastor Cederlöf, the Lutheran minister at Red Wing in Goodhue County, who had preached last Sunday and remained for the parish meeting, had told the members something greatly disturbing. In Mr. Johnson, their schoolmaster, he had recognized a false priest, Timoteus Brown, who had long traveled about in the Swedish settlements and—according to momentary suitability—pretended to be a Lutheran, a Baptist, a Methodist, or a Seventh-Day Adventist. Even the name Brown was false; the man's real name was Magnus Englund, a drunken student from Uppsala, sent by his parents to the New World to cure his drunkenness. Once it had become known that he was a self-made minister he had given up preaching and taken to teaching school. As a teacher he was probably less dangerous. Pastor Cederlöf had not told Englund that he had been discovered, but he wanted to warn the parish council that their teacher was a wolf in sheep's clothing; the Swedish paper had long ago published warnings about him.

Consequently, said Karl Oskar, the parish council had today sent for the schoolmaster to examine him, but that bird had already been warned and had flown from his nest in the school building. Someone had seen him board the steamboat in Stillwater.

The Swedish student Englund-Brown-Johnson, who for some time had given good instruction to the settler children, had disappeared and was never again heard of in the St. Croix Valley. So the new parish was for the time being without either minister or teacher.

Several weeks might sometimes elapse without a service in the new church, and Kristina stayed home even on Sundays. Then would come a Sunday with a new minister, always a new and unknown pastor, in the pulpit. It wasn't as it had been earlier. To her, the services in the new country had been linked with the churchman who had given her the Sacrament in America for the first time and who had turned their old log house into a temple. Without Pastor Törner before the altar or in the pulpit, the church did not seem the same God's house to her.

And Kristina had not yet heard church bells ring in America. An empty and silent steeple rose from their church in the oak grove at the lake, and no organ played inside. Their temple stood there mute, mum, and silent, as if not daring to voice a sound before the Lord. Each time she looked up at the empty steeple she thought: Like the bells at home, here too the peal from on high would have inspired reverence in the congregation; the Lord's own voice from above would have opened the hearts of people before they entered his temple.

One Sunday it was announced that a well-known minister from faraway Chicago would conduct services in the new church. But when Kristina left her bed that morning she told Karl Oskar that he would have to go to church alone; she did not feel quite well today.

What was the matter with her? She couldn't tell definitely, and he wondered. Was she lying to him about her sickness, he asked himself. He hardly remembered a single instance during their marriage when he had caught his wife lying.

During the night Kristina had dreamed that she had borne a child. It had been a very short dream but much had happened in it. She had been sitting in their new church and suddenly felt she was pregnant. She remembered it was her eighth time. The child in her womb felt well developed and she could not understand why she hadn't felt her pregnancy before. When at the end of the service she was leaving the church, labor had overtaken her and she had borne the child on the steps outside, in view of all the worshipers. The child dropped naked on the top step and wailed loudly. At that moment Samuel

428

Nöjd, the heathen fur trapper, whom she had never seen in church before, approached her with an evil grin. He picked up the child and ran away with it, carrying it by the legs, head down, as he would handle a dead rabbit. Then she herself had cried out, she tried to run after the kidnapper but was unable to do so and fell headlong down the church steps. On the top step she could see a big red mark: her own blood.

At the sight of this she had awakened. Her shift was drenched through with cold sweat, but a joyous relief filled her: only in her dream had she been pregnant. But today she was unable to mount the steps where she had experienced her birth dream.

Kristina had never believed that dreams came true or were a premonition. But the birth on the church steps had shaken her more deeply than any dream she could remember. What could it mean? She knew at least why she had dreamed this particular dream; two months in succession her bleeding had been delayed a whole week beyond the expected day. Twice in a row she had suffered a week of anxiety, waiting for her body to give the sign which meant comfort and peace for another month. And when the sign at last appeared she felt wild with joy for a few days. Fear of a new pregnancy had disturbed her sleep so that in a dream she had experienced what she feared. That must be it. That the repulsive heathen and whoring man Nöjd stole her child added to the horror of the dream.

For years now she had carried within her the fervent wish that God would make her barren for the rest of her life. But she had not dared voice her desire and pray to him to grant it. She had often wondered about this: a woman who refused the blessing of fertility and prayed for the curse of barrenness—didn't she sin against God's commandments?

In her fear of a new pregnancy, increased by the dream birth on the church steps, the old temptation returned to her. She thought it over, hesitated, doubted. She decided to ask the advice of Danjel Andreasson, and the next time she saw her uncle alone, she asked, "Would I commit a grave sin if I prayed God to relieve me of further child-births?"

Danjel was accustomed to his niece talking intimately to him in matters she would not even mention to Karl Oskar, and he was not surprised at her question. He replied that the Almighty could see into the hearts of all his creatures. He knew all her thoughts, wishes, and desires. If she wanted to be relieved of bearing any more children, then this wish must already be known to God. And it was assuredly permitted for each person to pray according to his understanding; if she were praying for something that was good for her, then the Lord would grant her prayer, otherwise not.

Kristina interpreted her uncle's opinion to mean that a woman's prayer for barrenness was not a sin against any of God's commandments. Of course Danjel was only a poor sinner himself and could not with assurance tell her when she sinned and when she didn't. But if she transgressed with this prayer, then she must already have committed the sin in her heart. Wasn't she courageous enough to do in word what she already had done in thought?

In every need a person must turn to his creator, every worry, great or small, must be carried to him. God demanded simply that a worried person turn to him, ask his aid.

And now she was a worried and deeply frightened person. Why did she hesitate? Why did she delay? Why hadn't she been bold enough to offer this prayer long ago? But now she would do so.

Not at the same time as her evening prayer, however, which she read every night in bed before going to sleep. Not so much because Karl Oskar would lie awake in his bed across the room and listen, but mostly because this was a prayer of great importance to her. This urgent prayer must be said secretly, alone, with no one looking on. She wanted to feel entirely alone with the Almighty. And if she sought out a lonely place for the prayer, then he must understand how important it was to her, how fervently she sought its granting.

And this prayer would always remain a secret between the creator and her.

On a light, balmy July evening Kristina stole up the hill to a grove of immense oaks a few gunshots' distance from the house. She had been careful to see that no one noticed her leave; she sneaked away like someone on a forbidden errand. God saw her, and he would listen, but no one else must see or hear her. She felt she was on her way to a sacred meeting—which she was. Tonight she was meeting God in his own beautifully created oak grove.

Below a mighty oak she fell down on her knees to offer her secret prayer.

Her knees in the lush grass, her forehead against the oak trunk, Kristina prayed to him who had all power in heaven and on earth. She prayed for that which was good for her. A seven-times blessed woman prayed for barrenness for the rest of her life; she prayed the Lord to have mercy on her tired, worn-out body, and not create any more lives in it.

"Dear, dear God! Don't let me become pregnant again! I am unable to endure it! Think of me, dear God!"

The tall oak crowns swayed above her head. The wind, rustling in their leaves, was the only sound in the grove up here tonight. The silence and the stillness aided in making her feel alone— alone with God. The soft wind she heard in the crowns of the trees she took as a touch of the creator's own soft hand, as a breath of confidence from the heaven above her; the father in heaven touched his praying child.

After the prayer a great calm came over her. When she rose from her bent knees, she felt sure her prayer had been heard.

XXXII. Partners of America

1.

On May 11, 1858, a new star shone on the flag of the United States of America. On this day the Congress admitted a new state, the thirty-second, into the union. The state was Minnesota.

But a great distance separated Washington from Minnesota and it was two whole days before the 150,000 inhabitants of the far-away territory learned that they now lived in a state of the Union. On the beautiful May day, when the decision was made, the settlers were busy with the spring planting of their fields, unaware of the transformation of their status: in the morning they went to work as territorial residents, in the evening they returned as citizens of the greatest and mightiest republic in the world.

Up till now the Minnesota settlers had felt that the government in Washington was their guardian: the representatives they had sent to congress had no voting rights. Washington had appointed their governors, made up their budget, and generally supervised their activities. This had made the people feel that they weren't trustworthy. And they had waited a long time: congress had more than once denied the territory state rights. The southern slave states would admit Minnesota unless Kansas too were admitted. But since the Kansas constitution permitted slavery it was not acceptable to the Northern states. However, after many bitter debates in Congress, both territories had now at last been admitted.

As soon as the decision was made in Washington, the great news was dispatched by telegram to the Minnesota legislature. But the telegraph wires reached only as far as Prairie du Chien, Wisconsin, and from there the telegram had to be carried by steamer up the Mississippi. On the morning of May 13, when the new state already was two days old, the steamer arrived in St. Paul. There the papers spread the happy message with the biggest headlines ever seen in the territory: GLORIOUS NEWS! MINNESOTA A STATE! BRING OUT THE BIG GUN! And half the front page of the *St. Paul Pioneer* depicted a cannon being fired under a flag with thirty-two stars. BRING OUT THE BIG GUN! The letters above the cannon were so large the readers could almost hear the firing.

Fort Snelling at St. Paul fired all its guns, with the consequence that people who hadn't yet heard the news, thought the Indians were on the warpath and began to leave their homes in panic. But as soon as the word spread, each owner of a firing iron added to the noise and celebration. Every settler with a gun fired a shot of joy. For several days one would have thought war had broken out in the new state of Minnesota with battles in every settlement. Old breach-loaders and blunderbusses were fired, Kentucky rifles and Samuel Colt's new revolvers, repercussion rifles, English guns, Scottish shotguns, Irish carbines, German cavalry pistols, French bird guns, and—not least—old Swedish muzzle loaders. In the Minnesota forests, the salutation of all its inhabitants thundered in unison. No gun had a report exactly like another; each rifle and gun and revolver and pistol had its own voice: European people fired their different weapons, uniting into one many-voiced greeting and salutation to the free land of the new world where they had become citizens.

BRING OUT THE BIG GUN! Now they could choose their own government. Now they could elect representatives and have a voice in Congress, could participate in the great decisions! Minnesota's settlers now had a right to sit in the Capital, at the table of great deliberations.

The echo of great expectations rose with the salutation in the clear May sky. Those who fired were themselves fired of a great expectation: their territory had grown up, had become a state. Now more immigrants would arrive, to break more fields, build more houses, more churches

433

and schools, built better, more passable roads. Railroads and telegraph lines would now be built, mail-service would improve; the one-time territory would be drawn closer to its older brethren-states in the Union. Money matters would be regulated; new laws concerning printing and issuing of bills would destroy wildcat money forever. Reliable currency would make business grow again, and prosperity would return to the young state ruled only by the settlers themselves.

Joy reverberated in the spring air, this spring which had brought good weather for sowing and growing. The sap in the sugar maples flowed more abundantly than ever before, grass and flowers and all the plants of the earth sprang up in a profusion such as no one had previously observed—this spring when Minnesota became a state.

2.

In the settlements at Chisago Lake, the news of statehood was celebrated joyfully. Here no one could afford to waste ammunition but this time everyone was generous with his powder. Karl Oskar shot off three salutes from his old muzzle loader—the only shots he ever fired just for fun in America. His gun was old but it had been made by the most famous gunsmith in Småland and it made more noise than any of the other guns in the district. Karl Oskar said that since he was the first one to settle at this lake he must fire a shot loud enough to be heard all the way to Washington by the President himself!

This same spring Karl Oskar and his family received their papers as American citizens. There were five of them to get such a paper—he, Kristina, and the three children born in Sweden. Each paper cost a dollar. It cost him and his family five dollars to become citizens of the United States. The American-born half of his flock were citizens as soon as they left the mother's womb; because of this they saved three dollars.

Since they had left Sweden and were stricken from the Ljuder parish records they had not belonged anywhere;
434

they had not had papers that they rightfully belonged in any country; they had in a sense been vagrants in the world. Now they had printed papers to prove they belonged to a new homeland.

When Karl Oskar a few years earlier had assured the court in Stillwater that he wanted to settle in America and become a citizen, he had been asked to forswear all allegiance to foreign rulers and potentates. Without a moment's hesitation he had forsworn Oskar I of Sweden all obedience and allegiance. He forswore the Swedish king with an easy conscience since he could not remember that he ever had taken an oath to uphold that ruler.

In order to become a citizen of the North American republic you were also supposed to renounce your nobility status and all titles and prerogatives adhering to your status in the old country. Because in this country no one had greater rights and advantages because of his birth; counts and barons and similar lords were forbidden. In whatever mother-womb one had lain meant nothing here; it did not make one a ruler over other people, as in Sweden. But Karl Oskar need not renounce any patent of nobility or inherited rights; from his homeland he had only brought the title of farmer, and this he could keep in America as long as he wished.

Karl Oskar spent several evenings reading their citizenship papers; with the aid of his son Johan, who had learned English at school, he searched out the meaning of the words and interpreted them for Kristina. Their names were now incorporated in the official papers of their new country; they would forever remain recorded in official American records as citizens of the United States. They were now equal to the families who had lived here for a hundred years or more. And it was printed on paper that they had changed from Swedes to Americans.

"Are we no longer Swedish people?" wondered Kristina.

"We're stricken out at home. We're American citizens. We're partners of America. We have renounced Sweden for eternity."

"In case of war between the two countries—will you go out and fight against Sweden?"

He laughed. "I guess I must if I'm asked."

"Never have I heard such craziness!"

"But the Americans have once and for all gotten rid of the English king and will never again fight the old country. They have better sense."

Kristina eyed the citizenship papers without understanding a syllable. In her, America had acquired a citizen who never used the language of her new country. She kept to her resolution not to try to learn English. Yet Karl Oskar insisted that through these papers she had been turned into an American.

Kristina felt it couldn't be that easy to change a person. This paper couldn't change her, even though it was large and thick and decorated with stamps and ornaments around her name, which was printed in large letters. In this paper it stated that she was an American citizen: "Wife of Charles O. Nelson." But what did this new name mean to her? It changed her neither inside nor outside. She was sure to remain the same as she had been since her birth: Kristina Johansdaughter of Duvemala, Algutsboda parish, Sweden. And however much her name was changed on American papers, she would continue to think as often and as longingly as before of her old homeland.

She had noticed that Karl Oskar had changed these last years. Not in clothing or external things but in his speech and his way of thinking. He accepted the customs here, he felt that Americans were clever and industrious, he approved of most of their ways and tried to ape them.

He himself testified to this change as he now asked his wife: Should he begin to use the name on the American citizenship paper, should he call himself Charles O. Nelson? What did she think?

"I don't like it!" said Kristina. "You may renounce the Swedish king, but if you change your Swedish name I'll laugh at you! For then it means you're getting to be uppity!"

This was a clear reply and he said nothing more. Kristina was really right, he thought. And he continued to write his name in the old way; he was still Karl Oskar Nilsson.

3.

The powder smoke of the May festival days blew away, and plans for the new state's government took its place. Liberty always brings with it great concerns and much trouble, and liberty is most troublesome to those who are unused to it. It now fell upon the shoulders of Minnesota's inhabitants to agree on how to govern their state; they must prepare and agree to a state constitution.

In the old territorial days, Democrats and Whigs had fought for power. But in 1855 a new party had come into existence, founded in Michigan the year before. Its members called themselves Republicans. They promised great advantages to the settlers and wanted to give land free to newcomers. They became the party of the settlers. Alexander Ramsey, the territorial governor, previously the Whig leader, joined the new party and became its leader. The Democratic leader was Henry H. Sibley, earlier the government's Sioux Indian agent. The Democrats were soon outnumbered by the fast-growing Republican party.

Republicans and Democrats met in St. Paul to work out a constitution for the state of Minnesota. But the differences between the two parties grew ever wider, and soon made it impossible for the delegates to work at the same table. It turned out to be very difficult to work out *one* constitution for the new state; on the other hand it was very easy to arrive at *two*. The two parties sat in different rooms and each made up a constitution. The two documents differed in about two hundred points.

In the Old World people shot each other when they disagreed about forms of governments, but Republicans and Democrats in Minnesota agreed on one thing: this must not happen among them! They must come to peaceful agreement. And after long and tiresome negotiations the two constitutions were finally fused into one, acceptable to both sides.

Now the young state must elect its first governor. But

437

its inhabitants had come from countries in the Old World, where they never had been permitted to select their rulers, and their highest lord—the king—had always been appointed by God, Who never asked their advice. The selection of a governor would be the first test of the people's ability to govern themselves.

Both parties nominated candidates: Alexander Ramsey on the Republican ticket and Henry S. Sibley on the Democratic. A bitter campaign ensued.

In the Swedish settlement at Chisago Lake many immigrants who never before had participated in choosing representatives for governmental posts, must now for the first time in their lives learn to handle a ballot. To the Swedes, this participating in their own concerns, seemed a strange and novel business. Most of the Swedes at Chisago Lake wanted Ramsey. His party promised aid and easing of taxes, while the Democrats advocated raising taxes for farmers. And Ramsey's personality and background inspired confidence. Born to poor people he had been orphaned at ten, from which time he had supported himself, often through manual labor. He had worked as a carpenter and forester and like themselves learned to get ahead in the new country. He was the right kind of governor for men who wielded the ax and the plow. In Sweden one must be born in a castle to reach such a high position, in America a log cabin sufficed.

Colonel Sibley was a businessman, one of the higher-ups in The American Fur Company, the richest and most powerful business venture in the territory. Sibley, the Democratic candidate, had grown wealthy from dealing in furs; he would be a governor for money-men. About him his opponents said: Sibley is honest in this way, that he never makes any promises except those he won't fulfill.

In Red Wing, a Swedish paper had been started, *Minnesota-Posten*. While *Hemlandet* was intended as an organ for all Swedes in America, the *Minnesota-Posten* directed itself especially to the immigrants in Minnesota. The new paper was more American than its predecessor and championed the new homeland above the old. In its first issue it explained that the Swedes in America would never really have a chance until they were entirely inte-

438

grated with the Americans. "*Minnesota-Posten* aims to devote itself to the new generation and wishes particularly to be a friend of young people and a guide for their transition from Swedes to Americans . . ."

The Red Wing paper came out for the Republicans and urged the Swedes to take advantage of voting rights to support the good and the right by casting the first ballot in their lives for the Republican candidate for governor.

Long before Karl Oskar had become a reader of the *Minnesota-Posten*, he had decided to vote for Ramsey. In this he listened to the best advice available: he followed his own common sense. The Democrats had been in and misused their power until they had almost ruined the country; the money situation indicated it was time for a change. Only those who earned easy money stayed with the Democrats and were for Sibley.

Karl Oskar was shocked at the shameless behavior of the party members against each other during the campaign. In each issue the *Minnesota-Posten* called the Democrats "this dishonorable pack." To express such an opinion right out would be libelous in Sweden. But apparently what was considered a crime in Sweden was a civic duty in America.

The Democrats said the Republicans were playing false by promising the settlers free land. The Republicans accused the Democrats of having bought five thousand gallons of cheap whiskey to be used for vote buying; they were sending agents around with whisky kegs and offered up to ten gallons for a vote. A rumor was spread about Colonel Sibley that while he was an agent for the Sioux he had led such an immoral life that he had had thirty-five children by squaws. A man who in this way increased a warring tribe—was he suitable as governor? A few days before the election, a Republican paper raised the number of Sibley's illegitimate children to forty-two, while the Democratic papers published attests from well-known people, assuring the public that the Colonel had not a single brat among the Sioux.

The Democrats won the election, and Colonel Henry S. Sibley became Minnesota's first governor. In some quarters it was felt that the rumor about his many children

439

among the Indians had won him the victory. Those who held it to be false were greatly angered at the dastardly attempt to dirty an innocent man—that was why they had voted for Sibley. Those who considered the rumor true regarded his forty-two-fold paternity as proof of superior manhood, not at all derogatory to a governor of the young and fast-growing state—that was why they had voted for him.

Most of the Swedish immigrants voted Republican: in Chisago County 409 votes were cast for Ramsey, with only 192 for Sibley. And the honest *Minnesota-Posten* greeted the new governor with the following words—in Swedish: "This old fox will now be our governor for the next two years!"

The Republicans blamed their loss on the whisky; a great number of the Democratic voters had been drunk. The Democrats accused the Republicans of ballot stuffing. One man could only have one vote, but in several Republican townships it appeared that more ballots had been cast than there were inhabitants; indeed, in two districts the number of ballots was twice the number of voters. The election turn-out, consequently, exceeded all expectations.

The difference between the number of votes and voters was difficult to explain, but apparently some non-existent persons had participated. The majority of these votes were discarded, but the incident could not be held against the voters: it was self-evident that the new citizens had overdone it a little when they used their new rights for the first time: it was probably purely an expression of joy which had made them produce more votes than voters. These people had for so long been suppressed and without rights in their respective homelands that it was quite excusable if they exaggerated a little when they celebrated their coming-of-age. Their action showed they were people with life in them; they would be able to take care of themselves.

In view of the fact that these immigrants and other settlers out here lacked all experience in self-government, they merited this praise at least, that they had proved they could vote for a governor.

440

4.

About this time, when men got together in Minnesota, there was talk about a lawyer down in Illinois whose name was Abraham Lincoln and who was at the helm of the new Republican party. But the man was seldom referred to by his name. He was called Old Abe, or Honest Abe. It was known of him that he was a settler's son and had been born on the floor of a log cabin in Kentucky. Honest Abe came from the deep forest, his ax under his arm; he had been sent by God to be the settlers' leader in the Northwest. His body was said to be as large as that of the biblical Goliath, and the strength of his arms was fantastic: he could drive his ax deeper into the wood than any timberman before him. In wrestling no one had ever been able to press Abe's shoulders to the floor; both as wrestler and fighter he was unbeaten in all the states and territories of the Union. And the creator had endowed him with spiritual gifts of the same immense proportions. He studied while he performed his daily labor; as a store clerk in New Salem he read a book with one eye while he weighed up coffee and tea for his customers with the other. Ever since he was thirty he had been called *Old Abe*—this because of his great wisdom. In him friends and foes could trust: he would always satisfy the former and disappoint the latter.

The settlers in Minnesota were sure that Old Abe was capable of thinking for all of them. At last a great leader had been born to the men of ax and plow.

The stories about him changed and grew ever more amazing with the years. One day he had short-weighed tea for a customer by three ounces, and he rode twenty miles to the customer's house with the missing amount. Another time Honest Abe walked five miles to give ten cents back to a customer he had overcharged. Soon it was ten miles Abe had walked and five cents; as the story spread the distance grew greater and the sum smaller.

When Honest Abe himself opened a shop he soon lost

441

out; he was unable to lie or cheat and consequently showed no head for business. Now this remarkable man had become a lawyer in Springfield. It was a great distance to that town in Illinois, and to the settlers in Minnesota Old Abe seemed like a saga giant—good and strong beyond the measure of ordinary mortals.

In the *Minnesota-Posten,* Karl Oskar and Kristina saw a picture of their new leader, "taken," the paper wrote, "in the most complete likeness in which a human being can be taken." They studied Honest Abe's picture closely, and Karl Oskar expressed his satisfaction with the long, forceful nose.

"His nose is almost as big and clumsy as mine!"

"Not quite that bad!" insisted Kristina.

"Well, it's more shapely, perhaps. Wonder if Abe's nose will give him luck!"

"Why do they call him Honest Abe?" wondered Kristina. "It sounds as if honest men were rare in America."

The man in the picture—with a nose almost as big as the Nilsa-nose—wanted to liberate the three million slaves in the southern states, those people who, like cattle, were listed among their owners' possessions and valued at three billion dollars. From *Hemlandet*'s serial, "Fifty Years in Chains," Kristina knew of the cruel lot of the Negroes in the South. Must people be treated like that only because God had made their skin black instead of white? It would only be fair if owners and slaves were to exchange skin for the rest of their lives, she thought.

Sheriffs from the South had been all the way up to Taylors Falls looking for runaway slaves, but people there had hid them from the pursuers and helped them on their flight. Kristina had hoped runaway Negroes would come to their house so she could give them lodging. Their own white skin, which protected them from being hunted like animals, had been given them as an unearned gift; they ought to pay something for it.

Karl Oskar cut out the picture of the man who wanted to abolish both masters and slaves. Old Abe had said: In this country one man is as good as another, and sometimes better. This wonderful expression the settlers heard
442

often, laughing heartily and proudly each time. It was a good slogan for free men in America, especially for those who handled ax and plow.

5.

In the following year's general election, the Republicans won and Alexander Ramsey was elected Governor of Minnesota by a majority of more than 5,000 votes. The people's self-governing ability had developed since last year: only a few hundred nonexistent voters participated this time, and only a few votes were bought for whisky— and a much better whisky at that than the year before.

The settlers' own party was at the helm in Minnesota and would hold it for many years to come.

The Republicans had won with a great majority in all the counties with Swedish settlers, especially Chisago, Marine, and Goodhue. "Minnesota has shed the Democratic yoke!" was the jubilant expression of the *Minnesota-Posten*. But shortly after this the Swedish-language paper died an early death. Unlike people dying of old age, the paper died of youth. The number of Republicans had increased, but the number of subscribers had decreased. The paper was often late, which the editor excused by saying he had been on long journeys and delayed by bad weather, which had prevented him from getting the paper out on time. But people grew tired of a paper whose editor never traveled in good weather.

Hemlandet was again the only paper in the Duvemala settlement. They need no longer fetch their paper in Taylors Falls, and it now came to Klas Albert's store in Center City. Klas Albert was usually referred to as Mr. Persson, but the old Ljuder people continued to call their storekeeper the churchwarden's Klas Albert. His first months had been rather hard, but gradually his business flourished. He served his countrymen well, buying a horse and wagon to deliver groceries to his customers, summer and winter. And the young man understood how to treat his women customers so that they always came back; many of them, it was rumored, not to make purchases, but to propose marriage to the young businessman. The number of women in the St. Croix Valley had during the last years increased so much that there now was one woman to seven men—but seven for Klas Albert, according to the rumor.

One humid summer day, during the hay harvesting, the young storekeeper drove up to Duvemala with his load of groceries. He was waving their copy of *Hemlandet*, and called out before he stepped down from the wagon:

"The king is dead!"

Karl Oskar was busy stacking hay, aided by Johan and Marta. He thrust the hayfork into the ground and leaned against the handle.

"What king, Klas Albert?"

"Oskar, of course! Our Swedish king!"

He handed the *Hemlandet* to Karl Oskar, who read: "An electric telegraphic dispatch from Stockholm July 8 announced that His Majesty King Oskar I's valuable life had flickered out this date at 8 A.M."

Karl Oskar said he would take a few minutes' rest and they walked into the kitchen, where Kristina lit a fire in the Prairie Queen and put on the coffeepot. She was greatly moved by the news that Sweden's king had died; her eyes grew moist and she dried them intermittently with the corner of her apron.

"But he was no longer our king," said Karl Oskar.

"It is sad anyway. He too was a human being."

"Even a king can't escape death—that might be some comfort for us."

She reminded Karl Oskar that he had been named after Oskar's father, Charles XIV John, who had reigned at the time of his birth, and that his second name had been given him after Oskar, who was then Crown Prince. He could thank the dead man for one of his royal names.

"A name doesn't honor a man," said Karl Oskar. "The man must honor the name."

Later, at the table, Klas Albert read from *Hemlandet*: "Oskar I was a gracious father to his subjects and wielded a prosperous scepter. During his reign he fostered liberal-

444

ism among his people to the comfort and advantage of every inhabitant. Therefore all his subjects now mourn the loss of a king who won the affection and love of his people through his mild and just rule . . ."

"King Oskar I's High Remains will lie in state in the Serafimer Hall for three days where the mourning subjects can view it."

Karl Oskar Nilsson, the Swedish-born settler with two royal names, listened skeptically as he sipped his coffee. "Well, well, so is there really such an awful weeping in Sweden!"

"It sounds like a great funeral wailing throughout the country," said Klas Albert.

"It says all his subjects mourn him—that's a lie that we won't fall for out here in America!"

"Perhaps they put that in to fill out the space in the paper," suggested Kristina.

But Karl Oskar said further that if everyone in Sweden had been so happy and satisfied during Oskar's mild and just reign, why, then, had so many thousands of his subjects emigrated to North America?

"Do you understand it, Klas Albert?"

"No. I know as well as you, Karl Oskar, how miserable things were at home."

"The king was probably a kind man," said Kristina, "But perhaps he didn't rule alone."

"He became king the same year I took over Korpamoen. He has reigned ever since I became a farmer, fifteen years."

"The new king is Charles XV," said Klas Albert, and turning again to the paper, he read: "In the fullness of his manhood Charles XV has inherited the glorious scepter which his father's weakened hand relinquished even before his death. Charles XV has assured his subjects that he wants to be their most gracious king, that he will discharge well the duties of his high office which Providence has entrusted to him, and that he will pursue a mild and just reign."

At the last words Karl Oskar nodded in recognition. "Yes, the government in Sweden has always been mild and just! The new king has already learned that by heart!"

Yes, of course. All the people in Sweden had donned their black mourning clothes and were weeping for their king from morning to night. Except the peasants, of course —they must get in their hay while the sunshine lasted.

Karl Oskar added that he expected a still greater immigration after this. All the Swedes unable to endure the loss of their king would probably show up in Minnesota, sooner or later.

XXXIII. If God Doesn't Exist . . .

1.

The fire burned and crackled on the hearth in the big room where the Nilsson family sat within the circle of light this November evening. Kristina was carding wool for stocking yarn while Marta, who had just learned to spin, picked up the wool wads as they came from her mother's carding combs. Johan sat like a man reading the latest issue of *Hemlandet*, while Harald spelled his way through a chapter in his *First Reader*. Dan was working on the runners for a sled he was building; with some help from his father he hoped to have it ready for the first snow. Ulrika was dressing a doll, given to her by Ulrika Jackson; when the doll was dressed she removed all the garments and began to dress it again. Of the children, only Frank was not with them; he had been in bed for a few days with a sore throat, although he was improving. Karl Oskar, too, was missing from the fire-lit circle this evening. He had gone to St. Paul to look at horses; a drove had just arrived from Iowa. He would be away for the night and was not expected home until tomorrow evening. The children were in a state of great anticipation at the prospect of their father returning with a new horse.

Undisturbed by the din of loud child voices, Harald went on reading his lesson, the same piece over and over:

"All things are made by God. He has made me. I am only a child but I know I am more than a dog or a horse. What has a child above a dog or a horse? A horse or a dog can stand and walk as well as a child. Horses and dogs have sight, smell, and taste like me. But I have a soul. I can see my body. But my soul I can't see. My body will die. But my soul will never die. It ascends to God when my body dies.

"God is with you in good and evil days. He is your comfort in sorrow, he is your support in need, if you only pray to him. He wants to be your help . . ."

Now and then a burned-out log broke and the pile of firewood caved in a little. The crackling of the fire, the screeching from Kristina's wool combs, and the buzz of the spinning wheel mingled with the boy's singsong reading.

But not one word of the lesson escaped Kristina's ears. It was truly astonishing how much those short simple words contained.

Harald resumed: "He is your comfort in sorrow, he is your support in need, if you only pray . . ."

The words rang in her ears, piercing like a sword in her heart: "He wants to be your help." No—she didn't understand it, it didn't agree, it had not turned out as she felt it must. It was not as these words promised; she had known this for some time now.

On the evening last summer when she had prayed under the huge oaks up on the hill, she had felt confident her prayer had been heard. This confidence had grown in strength for four months. Now it was completely shattered; for two weeks she had known she was again with child.

The Kristina who sat here this evening combing wool for her children's stockings was for the eighth time a blessed woman. And the lesson in the *First Reader* with its short words seemed to her a raw and inhuman parody on the prayer she had prayed last summer.

"Listen, Mother!" It was Johan, who had discovered something in the paper.

"A report from New York says that engineer Elias Howe's sewing machine with shuttle sold to the number of

447

twenty-five thousand last year within the United States. Wouldn't you like to have a sewing machine, Mother?"

She continued her carding without a reply. The boy repeated his question: Didn't she want a sewing machine?

"Why . . . Yes . . . yes, of course!"

A machine with hands that could sew, thereby saving one's own hands. Well, that was really something.

Johan looked askance at her and wondered what was the matter with Mother lately. Often she was so slow in answering that he must repeat his questions. Mother seemed to be losing her hearing. And she was so silent these days—she hardly spoke to anyone unless she had to. Was she sad about something?

Johan went back to read to himself about the comet with the growing tail which the Italian stargazer Giambattista Donati had discovered last summer and which had caused great consternation throughout the world. In June the comet had no tail at all, but by August it was a million miles long, by September four million, and now in November six million miles long. Soon the tail of that comet, it was said, would stretch across the whole firmament. Johan had been out looking for it on several evenings but it had been cloudy and he hadn't discovered the smallest tail spark of the terrifying heavenly body.

Kristina could not stop listening to Harald: ". . . if you only pray . . ."

Who could have prayed more fervently than she? But God had not heard her. He had remained deaf to her prayer. He had given her neither reply nor sign—unless her new pregnancy was the reply? During the very moment of prayer she had felt the Almighty's mild hand upon her forehead, but she had made a miserable mistake. He was unmoved, unresponsive. It was not the fatherly hand she had felt stroking her brow during the prayer last summer—it must have been nothing but the wind.

"He wants to be your help."

But now she knew the truth: God did not wish to help her.

She must go through it all again, all she had prayed to be relieved of: first the sick and miserable feeling for a few months, then carrying the increased burden of her body, shuffling about on heavy feet, and at last the terrifying labor, her strength spent, and the great weakness and fatigue afterward with her limbs heavy and aching. And just at the time when most was required of her, she would have to get up nights to give the breast to the baby, stay up till all hours when it was sick or fretted, caring constantly for the tender life day and night. All this she must go through again; for the eighth time since her twentieth year it was demanded of her. And this time she met the pregnancy with less strength than at any of the other seven times. Her weariness was great when she went to bed in the evening, it was almost as great when she arose in the morning.

God was omniscient; he knew that her strength was barely sufficient for all her chores, for the care of the children she had already borne. He knew she was worn out, young in years though she still was. He knew she would not be able to stand another birth, another child, and to make sure, she had told him so in her prayer last summer. Yet he was creating a new life in her. Why did he do this to her? Why hadn't he heard her prayer?

She had waited as long as she could to tell Karl Oskar. She had told herself she might be mistaken. Her period had been late before. No need to hurry with this information—she must be sure. And now she was sure. And this morning before he left for St. Paul she had told him. It was her time again; she must go through it once more.

No one could expect him to be happy over it. When Frank was born he had said, "Now it is about right." Six had not seemed too much for Karl Oskar, but a seventh would be. And then the seventh was announced. What would he say now when it was more than about right, when moderation was exceeded?

He said just about nothing. He stood silent for a moment at first. If he was disappointed, he didn't show it. Never had he shown any disappointment at this sort of news. Already? he used to say in the old days, his joy perhaps a little forced. But this time he just said nothing.

"Well, hmm, time again? Well—if we can feed six

449

brats, I guess we can feed seven! As long as you can take it."

That was all he had said this morning, and it was about what she had expected him to say.

In Korpamoen in Sweden she had been afraid to bear too many children lest she couldn't feed them. Then she had said to Karl Oskar, "If we could leave each other alone, then we wouldn't have any more." Now she felt this had been a childish suggestion; in a true Christian marriage the mates belonged to each other physically also. And this physical need for her husband had grown stronger with the years, that was the strange thing about it. To Karl Oskar it had been a necessity from the very beginning.

"All things are made by God."

But Kristina couldn't endure hearing Harald read the piece any more tonight. There was one way to silence the studious youngster.

"Get to bed now! All of you!"

The children were a little surprised at Mother's sudden and firm command and obeyed hesitantly. She gave each a lump of sugar to urge them on. For little Frank was already in bed and for him Kristina warmed a cup of milk, stirred some honey in it, and fed it to him with a spoon. Yellow mucus still came from his infected throat and this mixture eased the soreness.

Frank was a lively and keen boy. His soft, flaxen hair curled all over his head and his eyes were a clearer blue than those of any of the other children. But he would not remain the little one much longer—only till midsummer next year. By midsummer a new childbed would be awaiting a blessed woman.

2.

Kristina was unable to finish her prayer that evening.

She began several times: Our Father in heaven, let me this night rest within thy protection! But after a few sentences the words choked in her throat, clung to her tongue. She stopped. She began again, but couldn't get any further. The prayer remained stillborn in her thoughts, unspoken by her tongue. She lay awake, her eyes wide open against the room's darkness.

The hours passed, it was close to midnight, and as yet she had not said her evening prayer.

What was the matter with her tonight? She wasn't worried because Karl Oskar was away and she was alone with the children. Karl Oskar had been away many nights during the last years and she wasn't afraid; the Indians hereabouts were by now so few that no one feared them any longer; besides, they now had neighbors all around them. It was not fear that kept her awake. What was it then? She always said her evening prayer before she went to sleep. Now she couldn't go to sleep because she had been unable to finish her prayer.

Something lay heavy on her chest, choking her. She began to imagine a pair of forceful, hard hands held her throat in a vise; she sat up and took a deep breath to rid herself of this feeling of imminent choking, then eased, she lay down. After a short respite the sensation returned.

Finally she rose from her bed, put on a skirt and jacket, and stuck her feet into her soft deerskin moccasins. The choking in her throat was still there. She gasped for air like a fish on dry land. What had come over her tonight? She had never had these choking sensations before. The house felt unbearably close. She must go outside so she could breathe fully.

Cautiously, silently, she unlocked the front door and stepped out on the stoop. It was midnight and so dark she seemed to have stuck her head into a big sack. She could not see the sky or the moon or the stars. It was black at her feet, black above her head, and black all around her. Night had lowered its deepest darkness over the earth. It was as dark as it could possibly be on a November night in Minnesota.

It was cold, perhaps near freezing, but the cold felt fresh and dry; the clear night air rinsed her throat and she breathed more easily. Vaguely she discerned the tall sugar maples, stretching above the roof. She stepped down from the stoop and walked along the side of the building, grop-

451

ing about for the house timbers. The wall guided her through the deep darkness. She felt her way, stumbling a few times, but walked on. She turned the corner; now she was at the back of the house. She was wide awake but moved stiffly, as if walking in her sleep. Her hands lost touch with the wall, but she walked on. She felt the soft ground under her slippers; she was walking through her flower bed. She raised her hands in front of her, fumbling, groping, like a blind man.

She walked a little farther, until her foot hit a large tree stump. Here Karl Oskar had felled the big elm that shaded the field and sucked nourishment from it. The huge stump was all that was left of that tree—it seemed to her now a comfortable seat. She sat down, slumped forward, shivering in the cold; she huddled over bundling inside her jacket.

It was a silent night, without wind. Above her she could see no heaven, around her no earth. All she was aware of was emptiness and desolate silence. This autumn night was without sound of any kind. No leaves rustled in the trees, not a single crackling noise came from the stripped cornstalks in the field, not one monotonous complaint from the crickets. Even the screech-hoppers' eternal wailing was silenced. Sitting on the stump, enveloped in night's black mantle, her eyes could see nothing, her ears hear nothing.

She was inside a black, empty hole. She was abandoned, alone in a desolate world.

She was lightly dressed and she pulled the jacket tighter around her, her limbs trembling: Kristina, what are you doing? Why have you left your warm bed this night to walk out in the dark, to sit on a stump behind the house? You had trouble with your evening prayer, something pressed at your throat and stopped the breath in your windpipe. You could not go on praying to God, who does not listen to you, won't answer you! Your faith failed you, doubt drove you from your bed into the night.

And out here the same questions assail you:

Why didn't God listen to you when you prayed to be spared another childbirth? Why didn't he listen, why didn't he grant your prayer? If God exists, why doesn't he hear your prayers, Kristina?

If God exists . . .! For the first time in her life Kristina caught herself putting an *if* before God.

What she had done shocked her. The heavenly father—did he not exist? This had never been possible for her to imagine before. It would never have entered her mind. It would have been absurd, something one never even thought of. But suddenly she was sitting here and thinking: Suppose God didn't exist?

Here was an answer to her questions. It would explain all. It gave her a definite answer. If it were true, she need not wonder and question and worry any more. Then she need not anxiously ask herself why her prayer hadn't been granted. If God didn't exist, then he could not hear the prayers she addressed to him. She would have prayed all these years to a heavenly father who wasn't in heaven.

Tonight a frightening answer confronted her. Every evening she had prayed: Our father in heaven . . . *But if he weren't in heaven . . .?*

If God didn't exist . . .? Was it reasonable to believe this: *that God didn't exist?*

Darkness engulfed her mercilessly as she sat there on the stump. In this November night, heaven was invisible to her, the earth was invisible. The world around her was completely empty. Silently, without a single sound, the night enveloped the lone settler wife. Even the interminable wailing of the crickets had died down. Perhaps they had grown tired of their persistent complaint when no God heard them. This night was only silence and emptiness and darkness. There was no heaven and no earth—and no God.

Kristina, the mother of six living children, carrying still another life in her womb, sat on a stump outside her home in the middle of the night instead of lying asleep in her bed. She was a blessed woman but she felt tonight as if God did not exist.

3.

The night air chilled her body; she shivered, her arms and legs trembling. She had come out without a shawl. But she did not go in, she was not aware of the cold. Tonight she was oblivious of her · body. She was only aware of her disturbed soul.

What could she do if God didn't exist? In whom could she trust? Who would help her? Who would protect her against danger? Who would in the future give her strength to take care of her home and her children? Who would help her endure life in this new country, which to her always remained *away* from home, never home? And who would in the end receive her after death?

If God didn't exist . . .?

No, she couldn't become reconciled with that idea. She could not be satisfied with the answer that came to her tonight. All the strength of her soul rose in defiance; the answer was unacceptable. The least a person could ask of God was that he existed. It wasn't something she wished—she demanded it, she required it more surely than any other being on earth could.

She demanded of God that he exist. The creator must assume the responsibility of looking after his creation, as a father was responsible for the children he begot. Without a father in heaven she could not endure living her life on earth.

Stiffly she folded her hands trembling with cold, she clasped them tightly in prayer. She began in a low voice, haltingly. But after a few words, new life informed her tongue. Her voice grew strong, the words flowed from her mouth clear and sure. Her soul's need was the power driving her to prayer, and she was able to pray again:

"God, you must be! Listen to me, you must! Haven't you created me? Then you must not abandon me! Without you I would be a miserable creature—lost and alone in the world."

Kristina addressed her prayer to the black desolation of

454

the November night, she called into the dark loudly, her prayer became a cry of anguish: "You must exist, God! I cannot fulfill my life's lot without you!"

But when her voice had died down, silence again took over. Nothing more was heard, not even the faintest echo. No answer came; the night around her remained still. The night had devoured her prayer. It was as though she had hurled it into a black, yawning abyss. Her call to God had been devoured by a bottomless emptiness. The darkness around her kept silent, the desolation did not reply, nothing answered her.

4.

She did not know how long she had been sitting on the stump behind the house when something startled her. She rose as if suddenly awakened from a deep sleep. Why was she here? She felt stiff and cold through and through. She strained her ears and listened; she could hear something. A sound had reached her ears, a very faint sound, the first sound her ears had caught out here tonight. It did not come from the leaves rustling in the trees, not from the dry cornstalks, not a screech from the crickets—it was the sound of a voice, however faint it seemed. And she felt in her heart someone was calling her.

She held her breath while she listened, her face heavenward.

Didn't it come from up there? Wasn't it God replying to her? Didn't he call her: Kristina! Kristina! I hear you!

But no sound came from above. And it wasn't her name she heard. Yet—she did hear a voice and she felt that it called her.

Someone near here was replying to her prayer of a moment ago. She heard a creature with voice and tongue. She was not alone in the world.

Just then her ears caught the sound clearly; it came from inside the house, a baby weeping, faintly, pitiably, and only one word was she able to understand: *Mother!*

It was one single word, and it was uttered faintly, but it was enough for her.

Heaven above her remained silent, deaf and dumb; it was not the father in heaven who called to her, it was her boy who lay sick with his throat infection. He had awakened and he missed his mother and now he called for her.

A wholesome, comforting calm descended on Kristina as she hurried in to her child. Tonight she needed to flee to a living creature who was more helpless than she.

XXXIV. Prayer Granted

1.

Spring this year was the earliest since the Nilssons had settled in Minnesota. Already in March the powerful flow of sap in the sugar maples had risen, and Karl Oskar pushed his auger deep into their trunks to collect more sap than he had ever tapped before—fifty gallons during the spring of 1859, as he recorded in his almanac. And early in April the fields were dry enough for sowing.

And this spring Kristina's Astrakhan apple tree bloomed. She had watered, weeded, fertilized her tree, but however much she cared for it, it grew too slowly for her. She wanted to see wider boughs, heavier foliage, more height from year to year. She felt the severe winters were hard on the roots and delayed the tree's growth. Karl Oskar jokingly suggested she move the apple tree inside during the cold season. But now it had developed enough to bear fruit; unexpectedly it was covered with blossoms, a cope of beautiful white flowers lightly tinged with pink. Suddenly, at their east gable, a most decorative tree gladdened their eyes.

Next fall they would be able to gather a precious crop of juicy apples, refreshing apples with such transparent skin you could almost mirror your face in it. Astrakhan apples had a wonderfully fresh taste and a fragrance that filled the room; it was an apple as pleasing to the eye and nose as to the tongue.

In a few months Kristina would be able to eat apples from the tree that she had grown from a seed. Over the years she had tended the seedling as if it had been a living, feeling being. She felt close to this tree that had begun in one country and moved to another, sharing her fate.

Each morning, as soon as she awoke, Kristina looked out the window to enjoy the blossoms. The tree from Duvemala, blooming so beautifully here in North America, gave her new comfort and confidence in her own strength.

But the tree bloomed for only a few days. Unexpectedly, one night there was a severe freeze; in the morning the ground was covered with frost, the flowers hung limp and dead. There remained nothing for Kristina to see other than how her tree shed its cope, how the wilted blossoms flew away with the first morning wind like a swarm of butterflies.

The Swedish tree had blossomed too early, but the tree itself was healthy and green, and it would grow and branch out and bloom again another spring.

The time had come for Kristina's great spring washing, which she took down to the lakeshore to pound and rinse. It was her heaviest chore of the year, and her body felt stiff and clumsy already even though she was only in the beginning of her sixth month. Her back ached from being on her knees at the beating board and her washing dragged on longer than usual.

Toward the evening of the third day, as she was about to rinse the last few garments in the lake, a sudden pain cut through her back so sharply that she had to sit down and rest on the beating board.

She must have strained herself lifting the heavy washtubs or some other burden, she thought. If she remained sitting quietly for a few moments perhaps the pain would subside. Instead, it grew in intensity and spread from the small of her back through her whole body. And then she recognized it; it was not the first time she had experienced it: it was labor pain.

Johan was fishing in the reeds a short distance from her. She called to the boy: he must go and fetch Father, who was sowing wheat in the field.

The pain forced Kristina to lie down on the steeply slanted beating board, which was far from comfortable as a bed. As she lay on the board she suffered a sharper pain than any she had ever experienced in her seven childbeds. Afterward, she believed she must have fainted.

Karl Oskar came running; he would help her get inside the house. She bent double when she tried to walk; her legs failed to support her. He had to carry her to her bed. Once there she pulled off her clothes and discovered red runnels on the inside of her legs: the bleeding had begun.

Karl Oskar hurried to his nearest neighbor, Algot Svensson, to fetch his wife Manda to come and help. Meanwhile Kristina had another hemorrhage, and before Karl Oskar returned with their neighbor she had borne a lifeless child.

For a few days before this happened she had noticed a faint bleeding. She had not realized that this, and the backache, were the signals of an imminent miscarriage.

2.

Ulrika sat at Kristina's bedside. It was the day after her miscarriage, and Mrs. Jackson had hurried to New Duvemala as soon as the message reached her.

Kristina lay spent, badly worn. A great weakness had come over her after the hemorrhaging, which had continued long after the stillbirth. Today the bleeding had finally stopped and now she felt as if she were torn to • pieces inside. She was uninterested in everything about her and had only one desire: to lie still in bed.

"This was my first 'lost journey,'" she said. "My time was more than half gone . . ."

"A miscarriage is harder on a woman than a natural birth," said Ulrika. "It can be fatal to lose a brat before its full time."

She asked how much blood Kristina had lost. Approximately how much—she knew Kristina couldn't have measured it, but couldn't she tell almost how much? It was difficult to judge, even approximately, said Kristina, but she guessed she must have bled at least a quart last evening and during the night. For a while, during the night, the blood had run as it does from a stuck pig.

"A hell of a lot! That sounds bad!" Ulrika was deeply concerned. "I read somewhere a person only has about three quarts in the body!"

"Well, I guess then I have only about half left." Kristina's pale lips attempted a smile.

In Alex Turner's drugstore in Stillwater, Ulrika had bought several kinds of medicines, pills, and powders for her friend, which she arranged on the bedside table. She knew what was needed for a woman who had lost blood from a miscarriage. Here were the excellent blood pills; no one less than Mrs. Sibley, the governor's wife, had written a testimony to their excellence; they had healed her. And this was the blood-rejuvenator-power, discovered by a Swedish Methodist priest in Chicago; his pills were really miraculous even though he was lost in religious matters. And then she had brought a bottle of medicine called Gift of Blood, which had been manufactured in Washington, and she felt sure anything made there, especially medicines, must be first-class, for undoubtedly the President himself was sure to test and try the products of the capital.

But Kristina felt better from Ulrika's presence alone. She looked at the label on the bottle: Gift of Blood. "Gift!? Does it mean the medicine has poison in it?"*

"Oh no! Not a drop! I wouldn't want to poison my best friend!"

Kristina was overwhelmed by her thoughtfulness and concern. Tears of appreciation came to her eyes: "My dear Ulrika—you've gone to a lot of trouble for my sake . . ."

"You never take care of yourself, Kristina. I've told

* *Gift* in Swedish means poison.

459

you before: you have too much to do. You wear yourself to a frazzle!"

Now she must rest and gain strength after her miscarriage, emphasized Ulrika. Staying in bed was utterly important. And she mustn't do any heavy work for a long time. She would send Miss Skalrud over to take care of the household for a while. That Norwegian was a stubborn, bullheaded woman, but very capable if you left her alone and didn't interfere with her work. Norwegians were easy to get along with if you let them have their way.

"Skalrud helped me through my last childbed."

Last winter Ulrika had borne her third child since her marriage to Pastor Jackson. This time the ministerial family had been increased by a son.

Kristina asked, "How's your little one?"

"My little priest! He's wonderful! He weighs twenty pounds already. He eats like a pig, my boy. He's as fat as a bishop. Who knows—perhaps the Ljuder parish whore has borne a bishop for America! Wouldn't that be something, Kristina!"

The Lord had finally heard Ulrika and given her a male child, whom the mother long in advance had dedicated to the Church. She had been granted the deep grace to carry in her womb for nine months a man of the Church, and she enjoyed the honor, several times a day, of offering her breasts to a future dignitary of the Church. Only now did she feel fully recompensed for having once been denied the Holy Sacrament in Ljuder and excluded from the Swedish Church. By giving her a son, God had meant to poke the Swedish Church in the nose, give it a hell of a poke.

One of her wishes, however, could never be fulfilled. She had wanted to write Dean Brusander of Ljuder and tell him that in her marriage to an American minister she had herself given birth to a minister. Then Karl Oskar had told her the dean had died, and there was now no earthly post office where she could direct her letter. The dean had died before he knew whom he had pushed out of his church. Anyway, she was willing to let bygones be bygones and forget about the old insults and let them rest in their grave in Sweden. Perhaps God, too, was willing to forgive that devil's ilk, the Swedish priests.

"Well, I guess I mustn't be too proud and vain because I've borne a son," added Mrs. Jackson in quiet modesty. "A human being mustn't blow himself up till the skin bursts."

Before she left she took Karl Oskar aside and warned him that undoubtedly Kristina's misfortune had been caused by her heavy work. Why couldn't he help her with the worst chores from now on? By now he ought to be Americanized enough to scrub the floor, milk the cows, and wash dishes.

And Karl Oskar retorted that quite often it happened that he milked the cows and washed dishes. But he was still Swedish enough so that he had never scrubbed a floor. Perhaps he had better rid himself of this Swedish trace.

3.

Kristina enjoyed eight days of bed rest while Miss Skalrud took charge of the house for her. Meanwhile, Ulrika returned at intervals to see that her friend followed her advice and took the blood-giving, blood-strengthening, and blood-renewing pills, powders, and medicines. But rest itself was Kristina's best medicine. Her births had become more difficult each time because she didn't have the strength for them, thought Ulrika.

Kristina as well as other settler wives ought to learn from the Indian women; they lay down on their backs and rested completely for two days each time their period came. That was why they had such easy and quick labor. It was quite simple for a squaw to have a child: she simply squatted down to expel the infant, in the same way as she took care of her needs.

The wife at New Duvemala was soon on her feet again, but she was still weak and tired. She must do only lighter chores for some time. Karl Oskar lugged in wood and water and milked the cows for her; she need not do any outside chores this spring. Marta, now twelve, was willing and handy and quite a help to her. After some weeks Kristina again felt fairly well physically, but her spiritual welfare was far more important to her at that time.

A killing frost had this spring ravaged her apple tree and her womb. A life that had grown and increased for more than twenty weeks inside her had suddenly left her body. As it left, she had felt as if part of her inner organs had gone with it, a part of dead, bloody tissue. She had managed to give it only one horrified look; it appeared as if the life had been choked by her own blood. While the child was still within her, she had felt it move many times. It had been alive in her womb, but it could not live outside it. A human being had begun its life inside her but had been forced from its mother-shield too early and had perished. And the mother who was unable to become a mother to her child did not even have a grave to tend. The child in her dream, born on the church steps, had also been taken from her, but it had been alive, and its cries, as Samuel Nöjd carried it away, still echoed in her ears. Her stillborn child had been mute, a lifeless lump of flesh and blood. Thus the dream had come true in one way, but not in another: a half-true dream, as it were.

After her miscarriage, Karl Oskar had taken the child away, and she realized he must have buried it somewhere in the forest. Where was the . . .? she had once asked. He would never tell her, he had replied. And perhaps it was as well. She knew herself: *the child had been returned.*

One secret remained between God and her. She had prayed to be relieved of another birth, and she had been. He had granted her prayer. He had taken the child back. He had not dared trust it to her, for she had prayed to be relieved from fertility and wished for barrenness, she had rejected blessing and prayed to be cursed. Now it was clear to her: she had sinned with her prayer in the oak grove on the hill that evening last summer.

And she had committed a still greater sin with her dark doubt in the night last fall. She had doubted the Almighty—in a moment of great weakness her faith had faltered until she had doubted that God existed.

She had been given her reply; she had been rebuked. He had taken his creation away from her womb.

Thus Kristina had encountered the father in heaven in all his severity. His punishing hand had fallen on her that her blind eyes might be opened and she might see what she had done. A blessed woman had received the answer, both to her prayer and to her questions of doubt in a moment of despair. God had shown her that he existed, and he had shown it to her in such a way that she never again need doubt.

Now there remained for her only to submit.

4.

A Settler Wife's Evening Prayer:

Tonight again I pray for forgiveness, as I did last night and the night before, and all evenings since I lost my child. I have confessed my sin and endure my punishment with patience but soon I hope to feel that you have forgiven me a little. I want so to feel that you haven't turned your face away from me. Otherwise my despair will be great. I have no one to turn to, no one but you. Karl Oskar is kind and thoughtful about me, but my husband can be my staff only in worldly matters. When I worry about my soul, then he can't help me—no, no more than any other wretched human being.

I'm a simple and ignorant woman but I have repented and wish to better myself. From now on I will patiently endure the life which you in your grace and blessing give me. I will take care of the little ones with all the strength you give me. I shall try as well as I can to look after the other children you have given me. But you know how tired I get at times; in the evenings I feel worn out, and in the mornings I wonder if I will be able to get up.

Sometimes I feel I would be glad to die, because then I

would have the enduring rest which I long for. But I worry lest I die before my children can take care of themselves. If I should leave Karl Oskar he would be unable to handle the little ones alone; this you know. Ulrika is barely five years old and little Frank isn't three yet. Therefore, I pray you, my creator and Lord, let me live still a few years, at least five years more, if you could grant me this. By then Johan and Marta will be nearly grown and can look after the others. Then I'll be satisfied to die, if only you will receive me in your wonderful rest and peace.

I think often about the words of Robert, my brother-in-law: I'm unable any longer to fight against him who rules creation—I might as well try to lift the whole earth onto my shoulders or tear down the heavens above my head. Therefore, do with me as you wish! I am reconciled to all. Like him I submit to the lot destined for me. Then nothing ill will happen to me in death.

But dear Lord—I cannot think of being dead alone; in time I want Karl Oskar and the children with me in death. I do not wish to be alone in eternity.

Give me strength to last a few years more! Dear God, the first thing and the last I pray for this evening: *Don't make my children motherless too soon!*

Bless and keep all of us who sleep under this roof and all the settlers who have come to this foreign land! Amen!

5.

It was Kristina's habit, during this season of the year, to lie awake in the evenings after she had gone to bed and peer into the dark for that land where the evenings in spring were light.

In her thoughts she traveled the road back, piece by piece, mile after mile, down the rivers, across the prairie, over the sea. But the road each time seemed longer—she never reached the end, not even half or a quarter of the distance. She never reached her goal, she spent all her time on the road. And each time she journeyed a shorter distance, while the land receded farther.

By and by, as the land of her childhood and youth faded into a distant memory, it was transformed in her mind's eye. And as she remembered it in later years, she no longer longed for it: she was already there.

As a small girl she had lost her doll one day, the first doll she had ever had, a china doll in a blue-flowered dress; it had fallen into the farmstead well at home in Duvemala. She was inconsolable over her loss and cried and begged her father and brothers—wouldn't they please get the doll out of the well for her? But the well was too deep; whatever was lost in it once remained there. So her doll had stayed at the bottom of the well. On clear days she could look down into the well and see the doll's dress like a streak of bluing in the water. She would climb up on the fence around the well so that her parents had to forbid her to go near it. But whenever they were out of sight, she would steal back to peek in. She could see the rose cheeks of the doll fade away and the dress fade in the water. Her lost doll existed, and she knew where it was, yet it was lost to her forever.

At the next fair her father had bought a new and much bigger doll for her, with a still prettier dress, but this didn't help; she could never forget the other one, her longing for the lost one was as great as ever. She talked only of her lost doll, she re-created it, put new dresses on it, envisioned it as the largest and most magnificent doll ever to be bought at a fair. At last it had become a doll no one had ever seen or ever would see.

So it was with her native land. She had lost it in a well so deep that she never could retrieve it. At first she had at times caught a glimpse of it with her inner eye, but during the past years it had sunk ever deeper and farther away from her. The land was there, and she knew where it was; she stood staring after it in the daytime, she had stretched her arms out to it in her dreams at night. But she would never reach it, never get it back. And she had no hope ever on this earth of seeing her beloved ones there at home.

But as the years passed and drew the homeland farther

465

and farther away from her, the memories of that land came ever closer, and the light over them became clearer.

Thus, the same change had taken place with regard to her homeland as with the doll of the blue dress down in the well-bottom. She made a Sweden out of her own longing, a Sweden she carried within herself, a homeland that was hers and no one else's. In so doing, she built recklessly from anything she could get hold of: all of childhood's light and happy experiences in her home village, as they appeared across memory's bridge; the dreams she had dreamed of her home while in this foreign land; happenings in Sweden she had heard others speak of; memories from the reading of the Bible and the saga books. She gathered up experience and dreams, guesses and suppositions, truth and fiction—from all these she wove a land that no one had ever seen, and no one ever would see.

Kristina often told her children about Sweden. The two oldest had some faint memory of an earlier home far away, but to the other four, Sweden was only the land where Father and Mother had been born and where their grandparents lived. The mother often told them of her own childhood, her sisters and playmates, of schooling and games, about the seasons—a cooler summer and a warmer winter than here—about the first day of spring when she ran barefoot, about the first wild strawberries in summer and the first apples that fell from the tree in fall, about the wastelands' blossoming heather in August, of the ripe-red lingon tussocks in September, the winter's sleigh rides and the ice on the pond, about the Christmas morn journey to the early service in the light the crackling pitch torches cast over the snowy night.

She told it as it came to her, as the moment supplied her, and she changed it from time to time, added to, or depleted from it. Sometimes the children might find her out: But Mother, you told it *so* the last time! And now you tell it this way. Which way was it? And she couldn't reply except to say that it was the way she told it, and that was the right way and it couldn't be any other. Because that was how it was in Sweden where she was born and had lived as a child.

But her own children listened to her in the same way as they listened to fairy stories. To them, Sweden at last became one of those wonderful countries they read about in storybooks, where only good and pleasant things happened to the inhabitants—a country well suited for children. Once little Ulrika asked her mother: Did Sweden exist in reality? Was it actually a country on earth? Or was it, like that country with the proud prince and the beautiful princess, somewhere east of the sun and west of the moon?

The mother, of course, replied that it did indeed exist and was on earth. Neither to herself nor to her children could she admit that she had described a country which no one beside herself had seen and no one ever would see.

Only one homeland is given to a person. Kristina had lost hers. But she had no home-longing any more, she no longer missed what she had lost; she had won it back in the only way possible to one who has lost her dearest possession.

Now when Kristina lay awake during the dark spring nights in Minnesota, her longing soul sought another land in which there was no difference between night and day.

XXXV. To Reconcile Oneself with Fate

1.

The whitewashed fireplace was trimmed with fresh leaves and a young birch had been placed in each corner of the big room; outside, a birch had been raised on either side of the entrance door, and above them the lush foliage of the sugar maples spread its greenery. Above the door, between the birches, hung a wreath of cornflowers, poppies, morningstars, and bluebells. The path to the door had been well swept, and great leaf rushes had been

467

placed on either side, forming a festive arch over the pathway.

It was Midsummer Eve and Karl Oskar and Kristina had raised the summer festival's green arch before their home. Following the custom of the homeland they had wished to create a holiday air by decorating with young leaf trees and fresh summer blossoms. But they could not make it entirely like the homeland; the light northland's summer night was missing.

They sat behind the birches on the stoop while the short moment of twilight sped by. Today was a great day of remembrance for them: their new Swedish almanac, printed by *Hemlandet*, was dated 1860; the brig *Charlotta* of Karlshamn had landed them in New York on Midsummer Eve 1850. Ten full years to the day had passed since they took their first steps on American soil.

And now Karl Oskar and Kristina went over their memories of the long years they had spent in their new land. They went through it all from the beginning: their first shanty of boughs and twigs where the storm in the late fall had been so hard on them, the first long and severe winter when they often went without food. Then came their first spring when Karl Oskar broke ground and planted their first crop. They recalled the first autumn they had a crop to harvest, the smallest ever but the most important of them all; they took the first sacks to the mill and baked the first bread from their own rye flour. It had been one of the greatest joy days in the new land when this bread was taken from the oven, steaming and warm—what a taste!

And they remembered also the heat of their first summers, and the intense cold of the winters in the log cabin, snowy winters that seemed as if they would never thaw out in spring. Their thoughts lingered on the good crops and the poor, on the births of their children, their baptisms, the first Sacrament in their house, the first service in the new church, Robert's return with the wildcat money, his death and funeral—on all the happenings which during ten years had varied from their daily routine. Three new lives had been added to the family and there would have been still one more, if the birth had taken place in its right order. This one would have been about a year old now at Midsummer, ready to try its first steps across the floor.

But the greater part of the thousands of days encompassed by their ten years in America were gone and lost to their memory. Those were the quiet working days when nothing had happened, nothing except the labor of their hands, the innumerable days which were only work days, work from morning to night, each day confusingly like the next. Now, in retrospect, these uncountable laboring days seemed like one day, one single long day of patient struggle. And that day was of greater importance than any of the others: during its course they had started out, from the very beginning, for a second time in their lives, and for the second time built a home.

That Midsummer Eve when, tired and spent from the long voyage, they had walked down the gangplank in New York harbor was now part of a distant past that seemed incredibly long ago. The ten years of their lives that belonged to America had lengthened in their minds and seemed so very long because they had been years of great changes.

Kristina looked down toward the lake, out over the water which sparkled peacefully in the sunset; her eyes lingered along the shores.

"It has changed since we first came. I can't recognize a single spot."

"That would have been hard to imagine when we settled here," said Karl Oskar. "And that it would change so soon!"

All around the lake the shores were now cultivated. On every surveyed claim stood a house in which lived a settler and his family. The very name of the lake had been changed: the heavy Chippewa word, Ki-Chi-Saga, was almost forgotten and was never used by the settlers when they spoke of the old Indian lake. The metamorphosis of the wilderness where Karl Oskar and Kristina had settled in 1850 was complete.

Karl Oskar sat on his stoop and looked out over the slope where his fields, bearing beautiful growing crops, stretched away; nearly all of the meadow had been turned

469

into cultivated land, almost forty acres of it. And next to this field was a piece of ground with heavy oaks where the topsoil was equally deep; before he was through he wanted to cultivate that piece too, even though it would require heavier labor and take a longer time because of the large oak stumps he would have to dig out.

He was pleased with the work accomplished during these ten years. They had arrived practically penniless, bringing only their poverty. All they owned now they had won for themselves on their new farm. They were far from well-to-do but they had earned security, they got along well. Still it had taken more years than Karl Oskar had thought it would to reach their present situation.

Work itself was as hard and as heavy in the new land as it had been in the old. But there was one great difference between America and Sweden: in America your struggles brought some return, here you were rewarded for your labor.

"We have improved since we settled here, don't you think so, Kristina?"

"We are better off than I dared hope for when we slept in that shanty the first fall."

Karl Oskar appraised the sturdy walls of their house, built with seasoned pine of the finest kind obtainable in the forest, fine-hewn on both sides. But this house would be six years old this fall. Next time he built . . .!

"But everyone does not improve his lot here in America," added Kristina.

She could have enumerated several of their country-men. She could have mentioned the names of two youths, men who had emigrated to find early graves in America. But she needn't—Karl Oskar knew this as well as she.

And he admitted that the success of an immigrant did not depend on the country alone, it depended as much on the man.

A short silence ensued. Out here on the stoop it felt comfortable this evening; a light breeze from the lake caressed their cheeks. The real summer heat had not come yet—it seldom made its appearance before Midsummer.

"At home the youngsters dance around the Maypole on

470

Midsummer Eve," said Kristina. "All the old folk dances—'I weave you a wreath,' 'Find the shepherd,' 'Catch your partner.' "

It was as if now she had given utterance to the thoughts she had had all the time they had been sitting out here.

"Well," said Karl Oskar, "I guess everything is as it used to be there."

He could not imagine that much had changed in his home village during the ten years since he left it forever. In Sweden no changes or improvements ever took place. There people lived as they had always lived, performed their chores over and over as their forebears had performed them. That ancient kingdom was ruled by the Law of Unchangeableness. In the United States new ideas were tried and greater changes took place in one year than happened in a hundred years in Sweden.

Karl Oskar could still see his home village as it had been that April morning when they stepped onto the wagon to drive to Karlshamn. The years had brought no change in the picture he carried in his memory. He saw his parents as he had last seen them from the wagon—his farewell look: Father and Mother standing side by side on the stoop, placed there, immovable as stone monuments, looking after the wagon with their sons driving through the gate, leaving their old home, their village where the family had lived through endless generations. The wagon swings out into the road, the team begins a slow trot, he himself turns once more and sees his parents stand motionless as before, Father leaning on his crutches, Mother beside him, tall, her back straight, perhaps straighter because of this farewell moment. They remain in the same position, until the road turns and they vanish from his sight for time and eternity.

In that position their son in America had seen his parents for the ten years his eyes could not behold them.

Already, Father had been decaying in his grave in the churchyard for three years, but to Karl Oskar he still stood on the stoop beside Mother, supported by his crutches, looking after his departing sons. There Nils

471

Jakobsson would remain standing as long as his son had a memory.

Father had been against the great decision of Karl Oskar's life; he had never reconciled himself to his sons' emigration. The last night of his life he had heard the sound of their departing wagon. To the memory of the dead one belonged something that still hurt Karl Oskar. But it did not change his conviction: he had done the right thing, even though he had acted against his father's wish.

But how was it now with Kristina? He had harbored through the years a question he had never managed to direct to his wife. Perhaps he feared the answer, perhaps that was why he had never given it voice.

Their emigration, from the very beginning, had been his idea and it was he who had driven it through. His wife was against it for a long time—only the brutal famine winter, when he had been forced to make a coffin for his oldest child, had changed her mind, so that she said she was ready to go with him. Since then it had seemed to him many times that she had accompanied him half regretfully. What did she think now, ten years later, about the decision which had affected them and their children's lives so deeply?

This memorable day might be the right moment to put the question to her.

"We did the right thing when we emigrated—don't you think so, Kristina?"

She turned her head and looked at her husband; he could see her face only faintly in the dusk. Kristina seemed surprised at his question, as if it had taken her unawares.

"We did neither right nor wrong. Our emigration was predestined. It was predestined that we should live here. It was our fate."

"Do you mean that? Predestined? Our fate?"

He in turn was surprised, even astonished.

"It was our lot, as it fell to us. We need not ask about right or wrong."

"I only wondered if you hold me responsible."

"No one is responsible for it. There's only one who rules."

And before he had time to say anything she went on. She still remembered very clearly the Bible text Pastor Törner had chosen when he gave them the Sacrament in their old log house: God had ordained how far and wide people must travel to find their homes on earth. He chose and decided the places for their settling. And they just happened to be of a family God had moved from one continent to another on his wide earth.

That was predestination.

But now Karl Oskar shook his head, firmly and definitively.

"I can never in life believe that we don't decide anything for ourselves."

In his wife's eyes he was not the instigator of their life's great undertaking; she relieved him so entirely from all part in it that she demoted him merely to a blind tool of the High One's will. But in his own eyes Karl Oskar did not even have a partner in the emigration. He only, he alone, was the originator and the one responsible for the decision which had given them and their family a new homeland and decided where their children, grandchildren, and grandchildren's children, and their descendants for all time would be born and live.

Karl Oskar had now reached the age of his full manhood, and everything he had tried and experienced and gone through strengthened him in the belief of his youth: it was given to man to decide for himself, to take care of his life and make of it what he could. Never must one give up in adversity and distress, always one must seek and try another way. If one wanted something done, one must do it oneself, never leave it to an inscrutable and unreliable Providence. In this faith he had lived his life; it had never failed him and he felt sure he would stay with it until the end of his days.

Since his wife's miscarriage, he had noticed a great change in her. She often appeared absentminded and preoccupied, she was more closed up within herself than before, yet at the same time she displayed a greater steadfastness of character, an even temper and inner

473

peace. It had seemed to him that her old longing for her homeland, her worries and doubts, had at long last disappeared. And he had felt greatly relieved that she was rid of this bitter suffering.

She had, however, never given him any clear indication that this was so. Now he asked, "If I'm right, Kristina, I believe you don't long for the old country any more?"

"No, I don't. It doesn't matter where a person lives in this life on earth. One corner of the world is as good as another. The only thing that counts for me is that longer life."

"Have you changed—because it can't be otherwise?"

"I haven't changed. On the contrary. I have only accepted this preordained, earthly life . . . that's how I've gotten over it."

Kristina's voice indicated the truth of her words: it was not a voice of surrender—it was calm, firm, full of conviction. Karl Oskar had a feeling he need not venture any further, need not ask any more.

To reconcile herself to the settler's lot, to fate, that had been Kristina's struggle. And when now at last she had reconciled herself to what Providence had ordained, it was not that she had given up. She had not lost her battle: to accept was to her to conquer.

2.

In the thickening dusk they could no longer discern the blossoming decorations or the festive arch which they had raised today outside their home. In America the night of St. John was not light. Over the young settlement fell the cloak of darkness and Ki-Chi-Saga's water turned black under the evening sky.

And so Karl Oskar and Kristina sat up late and talked of the land they never again would see.

XXXVI. The Letter to Sweden

New Duvemala at Center City Post
offis in Minnesota State North
America Christmas Day Anno 1860

Dearly Beloved Sister Lydia Karlsson,

Hope you are well is our wish to you, you must be waiting for a letter from Your Brother, I am slow in writing.

We are well in our family up to date and all is well with us. Our children have grown a lot and are well, Johan is our Hired Hand and Marta our Maid. All the boys are full of life and activity but that is their age. Christmas has come again, I bought a Sewingmachine for Kristina, she was glad for the Christmas Present. She didn't like it here so well the first years but now it is over. She planted a new flowerbed in front of our house with many Swedish blooms, Reginas, Pionees, Yellow Striped Lilies, Brushblooms and poppies. Kristina astrakhan tree has not yet had any fruit on it on account of because the blooms have frozen two springs in turn. But the tree will undoubtedly give us Fruit in the Future.

You asked in your last letter if I ever regretted my emigration—I cannot say that I have. I won't boast but my situation here is on a level with the best farmers at home. Last fall I harvested 125 Bushel Corn, 73 Bushel Wheat and 51 Bushel rye, all heaped measure. I have also bought a horse.

I am master on my claim and do not bow to anyone. But no lazy fool will have success in North America. It takes a man's whole life and daily toil.

All the Land here in our settlement around the big Lake is now taken. This Indian water is in daily talk called Swede Lake. One race leaves this world, another comes along.

I have this year served on the jury in our Swedish district. I have long been a member of our Parish Council. You may well tell people at home that your Brother in North America has become both Churchwarden and Sheriff.

Last November 6 I voted for the first time for Government of our new Country. I voted for Abe Lincoln for President of the United States. He was also chosen. Abe was born in a log house exactly like the one I built the first year I was here.

The Slavestates want another president and there are rumors of war to free the Slaves. We hope to be spared the destruction and devastation of the Country, I am sure Father Abe will find some way to escape war.

How is Our old Mother? Greet her from her Son who lives in a distant Land in the far West.

Anno 1860 is nearing its end and we have also come one year closer to Eternity. To my Dear Sister and all who still remember me in my old Village I send you Christmas Greetings and wish you Peace.

Written down by your devoted Brother
Karl Oskar Nilsson

Exciting Reading from WARNER BOOKS

Get the whole story of
THE RAKEHELL DYNASTY

The bold, sweeping, passionate story of a great New England shipping family caught up in the winds of change—and of the one man who would dare to sail his dream ship to the frightening, beautiful land of China. He was Jonathan Rakehell, and his destiny would change the course of history.

THE RAKEHELL DYNASTY—
THE GRAND SAGA OF THE GREAT CLIPPER SHIPS
AND OF THE MEN WHO BUILT THEM
TO CONQUER THE SEAS AND CHALLENGE THE WORLD!

Jonathan Rakehell—who staked his reputation and his place in the family on the clipper's amazing speed.

Lai-Tse Lu—the beautiful, independent daughter of a Chinese merchant. She could not know that Jonathan's proud clipper ship carried a cargo of love and pain, joy and tragedy for her.

Louise Graves—Jonathan's wife-to-be, who waits at home in New London keeping a secret of her own.

Bradford Walker—Jonathan's scheming brother-in-law who scoffs at the clipper and plots to replace Jonathan as heir to the Rakehell shipping line.

Excellent Fiction by *Joyce Carol Oates*

A BLOODSMOOR ROMANCE

(A30-825, $3.95, U.S.A.)
(A30-826, $4.95, Canada)

So it begins . . . one beauteous autumn day in 1879, a sinister black balloon swooped from the skies and abducted Miss Deirdre Zinn as her four sisters gaped, mute and terror-struck. For their family nothing was ever the same again . . .

ANGEL OF LIGHT

(A30-189, $3.95)

In this book, Joyce Carol Oates explores our political heritage and gives us a novel of mounting drama with all the import of Greek tragedy. It is a story of loyalty, betrayal, revenge, and finally, forgiveness. Oates weaves a strand of history throughout—the quest for justice against those in power begins with America's founding—but dominating the novel is the story of this highly placed family whose private lives are played out in a public arena.

BELLEFLEUR

(A30-732, $4.50)

Travel through a "dark, chaotic, unfathomable pool of time" with Joyce Carol Oates as she explores the Bellefleur curse. Your journey begins one dark and stormy night when Mahalaleel arrives at the 64-room castle and everything begins to happen. Back and forth you pass through six generations of the Bellefleur family, enchanted by a novel "rich, extravagant, varied" filled with "the magic of pure storytelling."
—*Chicago Sun Times*